AJ Wilton
Author

john@ajwilton.com
ajwilton.com
+61 400 794 097

@aj_wilton_author   AJ Wilton Author

19th July 2023

Claire Cobb

Dear Claire,

Book Read -A-Long – You Killed My Wife'

*Thanks for supporting my book and your involvement with the exciting **Read-A-Long** campaign.*

Attached is your copy of the book!

I look forward to seeing your review and answers to the questions as you go!

All reviews welcome 😊

*You will no sooner be finished **'You Killed My Wife'** when book 2 **'Mortice – Justice Mort Style'** will be available!*

Thanks again!

Regards

AJ Wilton
Author

Claire, enjoy the read!

YOU KILLED MY WIFE

You Killed My Wife © 2023 A J Wilton.

All Rights Reserved. No part of this book may be reproduced in any form or by any electronic or mechanical means including information storage and retrieval systems, without permission in writing from the author. The only exception is by a reviewer, who may quote short excerpts in a review.

This book is a work of fiction. Names, characters, places, and incidents either are products of the author's imagination or are used fictitiously. Any resemblance to actual persons, living or dead, events, or locales is entirely coincidental.

Printed in Australia
Cover design by Shawline Publishing Group Pty Ltd
First Printing: May 2023

Shawline Publishing Group Pty Ltd
www.shawlinepublishing.com.au

Paperback ISBN 978-1-9229-9304-5
eBook ISBN 978-1-9229-9309-0

Distributed by Shawline Distribution and Lightningsource Global

A catalogue record for this work is available from the National Library of Australia

More great Shawline titles can be found by scanning the QR code below.
New titles also available through Books@Home Pty Ltd.
Subscribe today at www.booksathome.com.au or scan the QR code below.

YOU KILLED MY WIFE

A J WILTON

FOREWORD

I used to work with a bloke named Mort.

A Vietnam Vet, he was a hardworking, no nonsense bloke. Sadly, even with a loving and supportive family, Mort struggled with day to day life after his years serving his country.

This story is dedicated to him and all who have served their countries.

Thank You.

This is an act of fiction, so please forgive me if my imagination doesn't fit with reality, my aim is to entertain not write history!

All characters and events are figments of my imagination, and the political environment is pure fantasy.

Or is it?

ACKNOWLEDGEMENTS

My thanks to the following for their guidance and support.
- The Shawline Publishing team!
- Editor Daniel Car – Thank you – I learnt a lot!
- Roger Marsh for guidance on Australian Army life and culture
- My two daughters Shannon and Courtney for their help and guidance
- My wife for her patience!

Those that know their Queensland political history will recognize the name Jack Herbert the notorious police 'Bagman' from the 1980's.
It seemed appropriate his name should have a role in this modern tale as well!

1

'You killed my wife.'

There, I had said it. Finally, after all these months of wondering how it would sound. It was out there. The reaction was about what I had expected.

Dillion Benson turned his focus to me and was about to tell me to 'F… off' no doubt, but seeing me, he stopped. It had certainly stilled the various conversations amongst his group (and some surrounding groups as well).

Benson wasn't the first to respond. Joe Lancaster, his boss and the detective inspector, responded, 'And who might you be?'

'He knows,' I said, nodding at Benson.

Benson looked at me and asked, 'Mort?' He offered his hand, and I nodded and shook hands with who I believed was my wife's killer. He continued, 'It was an accident – the coroner has signed off on it. But I must say I am truly sorry for your loss.'

I did not say anything, just stared at him, making him and some of his colleagues uncomfortable. I am a big man and admit I do know how to intimidate.

Another of his colleagues, whose name I wasn't sure of, piped up. 'What do you care? You didn't even make the funeral.'

I turned the stare onto him, causing an increase in the tension

Eventually, I replied, 'The army were unable to extract me, didn't even tell me she had been killed until our mission was complete.'

I continued to stare at him, gradually broadening my look to include the Detective Inspector and Benson, and said, 'I have read the coroner's report. I find it intriguing it is not mentioned anywhere that you are a serving policeman, or that a blood test was carried out. So that alone makes the report interesting reading.'

I let that hang, slowly placing my empty glass on their table without breaking eye contact with Benson.

As I left, I told him, 'You will be seeing me again.'

Upon this, I left the bar and the pub. There, I have set the ball rolling – let the dice fall where they will. If I had known then what those four words, 'You killed my wife,' would lead to, would I have uttered them?

You betcha!

2

SIX MONTHS PRIOR
Lavarack Army Barracks, Townsville

One last salute, and I am out of here.

Lavarack Barracks had been my home for the last eight years. Yet, for over five of those years, I was on deployment in Afghanistan, so not really home home if you know what I mean. Whilst I was away, my wife Liz had left Townsville and headed back to Brisbane to further her teaching career with Catholic education.

As I approach the gate, I snap a final salute to the guards, who naturally respond before giving me a ribbing about being unemployed. I sling my duffle up onto my shoulder and walk (not march!) down towards the main road to wait for my Uber. It was good of the Colonel to come out again this morning to say goodbye. He, like me, wouldn't have gotten much sleep last night after my farewell – which had surprised me – anyone would think I was famous or something! But it was a good night, as my head constantly reminded me. At least I had had the sense to book an afternoon flight so I could sleep in a little.

Still, I have a plan – the army had taught me some pretty unique and usable skills at which I had become pretty adept. But before I can think my plan through a little more, my Uber arrives and off to the airport I go.

Townsville Airport is nothing flashy. Hasn't changed too much in twenty-odd years, but it's still functional. It is also used by the Royal Australian Air Force (RAAF), and of course, with my luck, my Jetstar flight has to wait whilst a couple of fly boys roar off into the blue.

Now that I am unemployed (not for long, I hope!), I had to slum it and bought the cheapest ticket I could to Brisbane. Mind you, I did splash out the $25 to get an exit row with the extra leg room – I am a big boy, after all.

My plan – well, let's see – I need to:

- Get my business set up.
- Find a car (Liz was killed in ours, so it had been written off by the insurance company).
- Find somewhere to live and work – hopefully at the same address.
- Investigate Liz's 'accident' – I have a few questions I would like answered as the investigation doesn't smell right – a little too vague on some critical points, in my biased opinion.
- Check up on and catch up with Pig. He, of course, claims he's doing great, but Pig was/is always full of shit.

My business, well I have already registered the company, 'Digital Data Solutions' and website and through my former CO Colonel Richards, who has settled quickly and easily into some senior 'security' role on Civvy Street (even he admits it's cushy!). But when he heard I was cashing out, he sent me an email saying he had at least one client who would pay good money for my particular skill sets. So, I am keen!

Well, I think that's enough to focus of for now – let the future take care of itself.

Whilst I have a certain number of the specialised 'tools' I will need, I will have to spend a few bucks in the right place to get the rest. Don't have the army quartermaster to hand them over anymore.

But I need to find a decent joint to build my workshop/office in first. Of course, my priority is catching up with Pig, then the old man, now retired to his Bribie Island home. Mum passed away a few years ago, and Dad has gone to pot a bit. And sitting down with Liz's parents, or trying to at least. They were very unforgiving when I didn't get home for the funeral. And I couldn't blame them.

*

The flight down to Brisbane from Townsville takes a couple of hours – Queensland is a big state, after all – so I drift off after they come through with the service cart. $7.50 for a coffee and muffin – not too bad, I think. It isn't long before they are announcing our arrival. Brisbane, my home again after the eight years based in Townsville. Liz had moved back down about three years ago, once it became obvious I wouldn't be back for a while. She had rented a unit in Stafford, close to her job at Mt Maria College and also close enough to the nightlife precinct of the Valley.

The landing is nice and smooth, better than most air force transports I am used to arriving in. I head down the back stairs, so it's quite a quick exit from the plane, follow the crowd in, go down the escalator to the luggage carousel and wait for my duffel.

Out of the corner of my eye, I see a familiar shape approaching – Pig!

'You big ugly bastard, about time you got shot of that mob,' is Pig's welcome. Not as crude as I would have expected – maybe he was respecting the crowd around us.

We give each other a big 'man hug' and shake hands fiercely. Pig was invalided out, losing a leg when our Bushman was hit by an IED whilst on patrol. So, we were as close or even closer than brothers. There were many memories to hold us together, each having saved each other's lives more than once.

'C'mon, let's get out of here. We're headed to the pub, going to the Brekky Creek – you remember our sessions there way back?' says Pig as we walk from the terminal. 'Hasn't changed much, still best steaks in town and more beers on tap than you can handle!'

We join the taxi queue and wait our turn, and Pig continues, 'So what's the plan? Man, I've been looking forward to seeing you!'

'What about you, Pig?' I ask. 'I never hear too much about what you're up to. Where's George, by the way, not joining us?'

'Nah, he's got some big meeting going on, usual government bullshit – you know, talk, talk, talk, do nothing stuff,' is his reply.

Our turn comes so we jump into the taxi, a Camry (*at least it's not a Prius*, I think – I can at least get in), and Pig tells the driver to head to the Brekky Creek Hotel.

'So where are you living?' I ask Pig. Letter writing and emailing are not his strong points; besides, I generally had limited opportunities for emails, Facebook, even Wi-Fi, so our communication in recent years was irregular at best.

'George has a nice joint at West End, a three-bed apartment with all the amenities, so we are pretty cool there,' Pig replies.

'And how are things between you two?' I ask with some trepidation, as their relationship has been rather volatile at times.

'Pretty good lately,' Pig replies, watching the cabbie watching us. 'It was pretty rough when I first came home, you know, with only one leg and having to get around. George was super supportive though, took time off work – weeks, actually – so I wouldn't be alone, but I was a pretty shitty patient.'

'I can imagine that!' I slip in, getting a wry grin in reply.

'But George got right up to the Department of Defence to make sure they did the right thing by me, forced them to prioritise my prosthesis – and that's another story.' He laughs.

We pull into the car park at the Brekky Creek Hotel; I get out and look around as Pig pays the driver.

'It doesn't look any different, does it?' Pig comments as we head towards the bar.

We head to the Staghorn Bar, our favourite from years ago when based at Enoggera Barracks here in Brisbane. *I can just about feel the hangovers from those days*, I think.

'What you having?' asks Pig (Pig is not his real name, but that's all he has ever been known as since he joined the army, fifteen-odd years ago).

'I dunno, I'll have what you're having,' I say.

'Two off the wood,' orders Pig.

'Shit, they still do that after all these years?' I say.

'Yep, reckon they won't stop now; it's one of the things they're famous for, that and their steaks,' he replies.

'Cheers, man,' we say in unison, and chug half our beers at once.

'Man, that feels good, my first beer as a free man.' I laugh.

Pig, noticing the odd look the bloke next to us gave me, explains, 'He just joined Civvy Street after fifteen years in the army.'

The bloke nods and raises his glass to us.

'Cheers,' we chorus.

Pig leans in and whispers, 'I think he thought you had just got out of prison,' and laughs.

'Not quite,' I say.

We settle in for a couple more beers, knowing it's going to be a long night, and we plan on enjoying it too.

'So, where you staying? What's your plan?' Pig asks again.

I reply, 'Colonel Richo has a client lined up for me! have a meeting next week – at the Tatts Club, no less. I've set up a company, and I'm going to use the skills I've learnt to make a few bucks, and I want you to come and join me as I'll need a lackey.' I sway out of the way of his good-natured back hander as we both laugh.

'Well,' he replies, 'depending on what's involved, it would be good to have something more constructive and consistent to fill my days. Sometimes I think how easy it would be to start drinking again. Heavily, I mean. I went through quite a period during my rehabilitation when I sought solace in the bottle. Fortunately, George saw it happening and helped me through it, sort of strengthened us too at the same time.'

He continues, 'So, I am his maid, if you like, do all the housework, cooking, etc... Must say I don't really mind, but if you're offering a bit of excitement and drama, I am in,' he says with a big grin.

'I'll go and order a feed before the line gets too long,' I say. 'You stay here. Same as always?'

Pig nods, so I go off and join the queue to order our meals.

After ordering a rare eye filet for Pig and a medium T-bone for me, I head back to where Pig is in conversation with the bloke next to him.

I let them finish their conversation, taking some time just to look around, refresh my memories, watch people young and old everywhere, vibrant, cheerful, noisy—

Such a contrast from Afghanistan, I think, *the tough, bitter, vicious life they have to live over there. The typical Aussie doesn't know how lucky they are. True of most developed nations, of course.*

Pig finishes talking to his neighbour and asks, 'So where are you staying?'

'I've booked a room at some joint along Kingsford Smith Drive for a week whilst I get my bearings,' I tell him. 'I've started searching for something to buy, but I want something, ideally where I can make an office/workshop downstairs and live upstairs so I don't have to travel too far. And it would be easier to secure that way as well,' I add.

'I have seen a couple of places worth looking at around Morningside, some new developments going up around there. You want to come along and check them out with me, maybe next week?' I ask. 'Only if your housekeeping duties allow, of course,' I add, avoiding another back hander.

'Cheeky shit,' Pig responds.

I tell him my plans for the next few days, going up to Bribie to see the old man, then down the coast to see Liz's parents.

'Man, that's going to be tough,' chimes in Pig.

I nod in agreement. 'But first, I have to buy a car so I can get there – ours was totalled when Liz was killed, so I have the insurance pay out to spend.'

'So, what are you looking at buying?' he asks.

'Not anything much, needs to be nondescript for the sort of work we will be doing, so maybe a Camry or one of these Hyundai's you see running around everywhere. Man, haven't they taken hold since I was last roaming around,' I add.

Pig says, 'I like the way you say "we",' and I smile.

Will be good having the old bugger around – Pig's some eight years older than me, not as big physically, but strong, tough as nails, never takes a backwards step either. And we have always got on well, ever since our first meeting in specialist training. Shit, that was eight years ago. Bugger. Like me, he is dark featured – swarthy, even – and we both have dark hair and big bushy beards when needed. One of the reasons we were both so good at blending in over there – until we opened our mouths, at least.

We start another beer, just enjoying the noise and atmosphere around us, a large group on the other side of the bar whooping it up, all good natured. Then our number gets called, so I jump up and go over to the window and grab our meals; they haven't changed much either – still big steaks, crappy coleslaw, and a baked potato. Still bloody good, though.

Pig nudges me halfway through his steak, pointing his fork at a passing lady. 'Plenty of options for you here, mate,' he says, smirking.

'The last thing I need is *you* trying to matchmake,' I say. 'Besides, it's too soon; I still think of Liz a shitload.'

Pig turns to me, putting his hand on my shoulder, and says, 'Mate, that was two years ago; you are allowed to move on.'

I nod but don't say anything.

We enjoy a few more beers, and we agree to call it a night. As we wander back to grab an Uber, some twit knocks into me, can hardly stand, but wants to make something of it, snarling, 'You bloody moron, why don't you watch where you're going?'

I stop and look down at him, not saying a word. His mates get the hint, telling me, 'Sorry, mate, he's a bit pissed,' and they head off back to the bar.

Pig shakes his head and says, 'That's the trouble these days: young dickheads can't handle their booze, or they combine it with drugs and then want to beat everyone up – cops included. You wouldn't believe the number of one-punch deaths there have been these days. Sad, really, where society is heading.'

'Man,' I say, 'when did you get so philosophical?'

Our Uber has arrived, drops me off at my hotel and heads off, taking Pig home. We agreed I would call him later in the week to catch up again.

Now that I'm out, I am really looking forward to spending time with Pig; we have a really close bond, real life 'blood brothers'.

*

Next morning, I let myself sleep in – no alarm, no need – wander down the road to a café for a decent breakfast, read the paper – normal things – wondering, *Can I do normal?*

Once fed and caffeinated, I head back to my room and start looking for a car for real. Time for action. I track a couple of likely prospects down, two ex-company cars at the same dealer, couple of years old, not too high in mileage; mind you, with the Toyota badge, they will go for ever anyway. So I jump another Uber and head over to the Toyota dealership just up the road from the Brekky Creek and have a look at the two I had seen online.

A young keen salesman, Doug, soon approaches and we chat about the two cars – the differences and the benefits. I take them both for a test drive, not noticing too much difference between them. I ask what else he's got similar, so he shows me a little Corolla, and I look at him and say, 'Look at me – look at the size of me – and you want to try and sell me that little thing?'

Of course, once he sees my point, he's embarrassed, so I take the opportunity to squeeze him on price. The white Camry looks the better of the two to me, and they want $18,500, so I say, 'Cash deal right now, I'll pay $17,000 flat.'

He shakes his head, says, 'No, no, the boss won't do that deal.'

'Okay,' I say, 'I am out of here, plenty of other Camrys to buy,' and start walking away.

'Wait, wait,' he yells, 'can't you come up a little so I can show the boss I am working hard? Say, $17,500?'

'No,' I say, 'but let's meet at $17,250, including six months rego and on-road costs.'

'Okay, wait here. I'll see what he says. You want a coffee, tea, or something?' he asks before heading off.

'No, I'm good, want to get going if it's no deal,' I tell him.

I wander back outside into the sunlight, a lovely day, not a cloud in the sky – as always. After all, as the saying goes, 'Queensland, beautiful one day, perfect the next'.

The salesman comes back and says, 'He'll do $17,500 with six months registration, and include twenty-four months extra warranty – how's that sound?'

'Okay,' I say, 'deal,' and we shake on it. 'Now, I want the fastest ever transfer you've done, so I can get going. Get me an invoice so I can make payment while you get all the forms completed, please.'

I take a cup of coffee off them now that we have a deal, and watch whilst they rush around getting the paperwork sorted, and I notice a detailer giving the car a quick hose down. *Damn*, I think, *I must be getting soft, can't have screwed them enough!*

I get the invoice, access my account via my phone, make payment and send through a remittance, and an hour later, I am on the road. Another first – in a civilian car; my own, no less!

3

A few days later I wake up, nothing specific planned for the day (*How long can this last?* I wonder). But it's still early enough to go for a run, so on with the running gear and off I go.

I'm still at the same hotel, so after I cool down and shower, I wander down Racecourse Road to my favourite café for breakfast, stir shit with the waitress – a twenty-something from Ireland, no doubt passing through on her 'backpacking holiday'. Always smiling – *bubbly most probably suits her*, I think.

Time to start actioning my plan on investigating Liz's accident. I pull out the coroner's report I had accessed overnight and printed out, putting it in front of me to read whilst enjoying my breakfast.

'What's this,' the waitress asks, 'a working breakfast?'

'Yep,' I reply, 'time I earnt my keep.'

After serving my coffee, then breakfast, she leaves me alone to read it through.

From my other research, I had found the other driver was, in fact, a serving police officer, detective sergeant no less, so I found it intriguing this was not mentioned in the coroner's report. Nor was there any mention of a blood alcohol reading, or blood test result, which, by law, are mandatory.

Double interesting. So, what to do next? I ponder.

The coroner's report mentions an inspection by the forensic crash unit, without providing any details, so I note this to check when I can. This will have to wait until I have a secure computer, one where I can't be traced, so I will hold off until I find my new home. The registration number of the other car is also listed, a Ford Falcon sedan, so at least that will be easy to see who the owner is. I already suspect it will be a police car, but I will need to prove this. This I can do from my hotel room.

A little later, back in my hotel room, I log on to a special server with a unique code and then access the Department of Transport, type in the registration number and bleep – up pops Queensland Police Service as the owner. *Damn*, I think, *where is this going?*

I search for the police wreckers' yard, or vehicle holding yard, note the address, and with nothing else planned, head off to have a look and see if the car is still in the police compound at Enoggera.

Upon arriving at the compound, I drive past it, getting an idea of how it's run. Pretty securely, by the look of it. Six-foot high barbed wire fencing all round, with only one entrance manned by a uniformed police officer. So, pulling one of my fancy new business cards out, I approach the officer in his booth, with a few bits of paper on a clipboard to make me look official.

When I reach him, I hand my business card over and say, 'Hi, officer, I'm an insurance assessor sent to check on'—I glance at my clipboard and recite the registration number of the police car— 'I understand you have this here.'

Looking bored, he looks up his computer and checks that it is here, and then says, 'Yes, we have that here, but no unauthorised visitors are allowed.'

'Mate,' I say, 'I'm only trying to earn a quid. No one's around; I am certainly not going to steal the bloody thing – can't you look the other way for a few minutes? Please,' I add.

He ponders this, seemingly not bothered either way, so I add, 'You can always come with me, make sure I don't pinch anything out of it, if you want. I just need a few photos, make sure the damage is similar to that reported, you know, usual shit.'

He comes to a decision, slides off his stool, grabs his keys and leads the way. 'It's in row F, this way,' he says.

'I'm Mort,' I say, sticking out my hand.

'Rick,' he replies as we shake hands.

I walk alongside him chatting about the weather and when the Broncos – Brisbane Broncos, Brisbane's local Rugby League team – may finally find some form, until we arrive at the right car. It's showing serious damage in the front passenger side.

'Shit, he must have been moving,' I say.

'Yeah, that's what I thought when they brought it in,' Rick responds.

I walk around the car, taking plenty of photos with my little digital camera, 24MPS, so I can zoom in on the images if I need to. There is a little green circle sticker on the front number plate, take a photo, then go to the back, where there is an identical circle sticker.

'What do these mean?' I ask my new mate.

'I shouldn't tell you,' he says, 'but that means the vehicle is used by a special squad within the police service, means they don't ever get stopped for RBT, and of course, no tickets are ever issued against this registration number.'

'So, special privileges then, ah?'

'Yeah,' he replies, 'bunch of arseholes if you ask me.'

'How many police cars have these?' I ask.

'Not sure,' he says, 'but my mate is chief mechanic at the police workshop, and he reckons there's about ten odd cars and SUVs with them on.'

'So, who are they?' I ask.

'No idea – obviously, the bloke driving this in the accident must be one of them,' is the reply.

I take a chance and say, 'You know, the coroner's report doesn't even mention it's a police car, and no blood test was done on the driver.'

Rick ponders this for a minute, then says, 'Shit, I thought blood tests were mandatory.'

'They are,' I reply. 'I checked.'

On the way back to his booth, I push my luck. 'So, whose name do you have on file for this car?' I ask.

Silence for a minute – then he shrugs and says, 'I shouldn't tell you this either, but they really are a bunch of pricks.'

I wait in silence, not wanting to deter him from what he plans on doing – helping me out against one of his fellow officers.

Once he's seated back on his stool – he's a bit overweight, so this takes longer than usual – he logs back in (I note his login – you never know if it might come in handy), types in the registration number and comes up with the driver's name.

'Detective Sergeant Dillion Benson, OIC DI Joe Lancaster,' he recites as I write this down.

'Well,' I say, 'Dillion Benson is listed as the driver in my reports, so that's a match. So, you reckon it's a fair bet these two are part of this "special force" you mentioned?' I ask.

'I guess so,' he replies, as a tow truck pulls up at the boom gate. 'Gotta go,' he says as he grabs a clipboard and wanders over to the towie.

I walk back to my car, parked back up the road a little (no sense letting him or anyone else know too much about me), get inside, turn the car on but don't move as I digest everything I've just learnt. He may not have intended to help me too much, but he certainly had.

I take out my phone, pull up the Notes app and start writing:

Falcon XR6 Turbo white sedan Rego 345 SRV, owned by police, special sticker identifies it as a 'special group' exempt from fines and RBT, etc. Driver confirmed as D Benson.

OIC DI Joe Lancaster. Badly damaged front passenger side.

Need:

Access to car's IVMS system, as this will show minutes, seconds leading up to the crash – i.e., speed, any attempt to slow down, etc. – How?

Next steps:

- Identify Benson and Lancaster
  - How?
    - Get their photos and hang around police HQ until they come out, see who else is with them, a few photos won't be hard, start building a profile and check their hangouts.
- Who else is in this 'special force?'
  - What do they do?
  - Are they a legit force or just self-important – check media about any special forces, might be secret too, I guess?

4

A few days later, Monday morning, I pull up in front of Pig's apartment building in West End. Pig is standing there waiting for me, jumps in, pulling a face at the shiny 'new' car.

'Well, aren't you something? Tidy wheels and all.'

I smile and hand him a coffee, straight black, like we all take it.

'Ah,' he says, 'I've gone a bit soft these days and take sweetener in it.'

'Well, this time, you will just have to toughen up, soldier,' I tell him with a smile.

'Where are we going?' he asks.

'Going to wander around Morningside, Balmoral, Tingalpa area, see what we can find,' I say, passing him a few property flyers I have printed off the web. 'These are a few we will start with.'

'Have you made any appointments?'

'No, just going to drive around first, then suffer the agents once I have a feel for the area and what's available.'

'So, how did it go with Liz's parents?' he asks.

I take a few moments before answering, 'Not pretty. They are still desolate at having lost her. I spoke to them about my plan to investigate the accident, and surprisingly, Bill told me to leave it alone.'

'That will only prolong the pain,' he said, 'and certainly won't bring her back.'

I continue, 'They also sort of confirmed Liz was seeing someone else, and had been for a while, Sandy saying in the last few months she seemed happier than she had been for a while.'

'Shit,' mutters Pig. 'Did you know?'

'No, but I had been wondering. She had missed some of our routine calls, texting me saying she was "tied up" and things, which I thought was odd. Then when she had the accident, she was down on the southside, in Moorooka, a long way from Stafford, and had an overnight bag in the car, so I had sort of wondered. Sandy was a little smug when I asked why she had the clothes with her when I brought it up last time I was there – you know, a couple of weeks after the funeral.

'I mean, it must have been pretty lonely and tough on a woman – or partner,' I hastily add, 'when we were away for such long stints. We had a pretty big argument when I told her I was signing on for another five years too.'

'What about your old man?' Pig asks.

I smile. 'Well, I turned up there on Friday, and his boat wasn't there, so I went in and made myself at home. I took some lunch and coffee so I wouldn't starve, then he turned up about half an hour later, bringing in his morning catch.

'So we sort of chatted whilst he cleaned and gutted his catch – his dinner! He seems pretty comfortable with himself, certainly pretty scruffy and untidy since Mum passed, but he doesn't seem to care, hardly sees anyone else, and he's happy with that. Deaf as a door post too, not much better when he remembers to put his hearing aids in!

'He moors his boat over the road from his house; he says he goes down to the local bowls club two or three times a month "to get a decent feed of something other than fish", he told me. He said there were a couple of "old ducks" down there that fuss over him. So, seems quite content with life. After all, he always wanted to spend his time fishing. The house was quite tidy, so I didn't ask if one of the "old ducks" comes and cleans for him.

'He still drives the old bloody Patrol too – shit, he's had that a long time, reckons it will see him out. He can take his boat anywhere he wants, was even talking about going up to Fraser Island during the Tailor season – asked if I wanted to go. "No bloody way", I told him. Awesome spot that it is, the largest sand island in the world; I've had my share of sand, mozzies and horse flies.'

Pig replies, 'I'm surprised he didn't retire to Moreton Island; after all, he used to say it was his favourite fishing hole.' And he adds with a grin, 'He did name you after it.'

'Yes, my surname is Ireland, and the old man did name me Moreton "after Moreton Island!". His sense of humour, I guess, like the Johnny Cash song "A Boy Named Sue".'

After driving past the properties I had identified, and with none standing out, I pulled over at a café. 'Let's grab a coffee and reconsider,' I say.

Settled with our coffees, I pull my tablet out and use the free Wi-Fi to log in and resume my search for 'work and home combined'. Nothing new pops up, so I try a different real estate website, and a couple of new places pop up. One in Tingalpa looks promising, so we note the address and finish our coffee.

'So what do you think about coming and working with me?' I ask Pig.

'Sure, I mentioned it to George last night; of course, he wasn't enthusiastic – I think he likes the idea of me being home, but what have you got in mind?'

I pause to gather my thoughts, although I had run through what

I planned on saying numerous times in my head.

'My business is called "Digital Data Solutions", so I will be using the skills we learnt from the Yanks over there, you know, communication surveillance, monitoring. They left me a back door into their search engines, so won't be too much we can't track down. But even though there will be a fair bit of digital, computer work, there's also going to be the old-fashioned PI type of work – following suspects and, of course, the use of drones. So, you can reunite yourself with some of the fancy drones you used over there.'

'Cool,' Pig replies, 'I have bought a couple of play ones just to muck about with.'

'Do you still have the contact details of that bloke you met in the mess that time, who told you he could supply drones even the FBI don't have?' I ask.

'Yeah, I stayed in touch. He sure has some real cool stuff – you should see them, real beauties, can hover forever, silent motors, awesome camera, heat sensors, infra-red cameras all swivel mounted, so no angle you can't get.

'Could get some naughty photos with those babies,' he enthuses, continuing, 'You know, you can also get accessory kits for some of them; they can drill holes, screw in screws, like a flying robot!'

'Well, maybe you should talk turkey with him then, see what deal you can get. I reckon we need at least two, and maybe a couple of more basic ones,' I reply.

'Anyway, back to the job,' I say, 'It won't be full-time, more when I have a job, but I also have a couple of fillers I am going to use when time permits. And I could use some help checking out Liz's accident. I downloaded the coroner's report, and there are a couple of anomalies in it.'

Pig replies, 'You know Bill is right, don't you? Any digging – even if you find something – is not going to bring Liz back.'

'I know,' I reply, 'but it will make me feel better.'

'All right then, how much are you going to pay me?' Pig asks.

Again, I pause. 'Well,' I say, 'you are a cripple, receiving a full disability army pension, so I reckon about $5–$8 per hour – how's that sound?'

We both laugh, and I say, 'Seriously mate, what I owe you no amount of money can pay.'

We are both silent for a while, and I say, 'I was thinking about $50 per hour, plus a bonus when we succeed in a job where you have helped.'

'Deal,' he says, and we shake on it.

'Good, your shout for another coffee then!' I reply with a smile.

It will be good knowing Pig has my back. As well as being a great soldier, Pig also has superb computing skills and just a little expertise in hacking which, along with my own special skills, will come in handy.

We dawdle over the second coffee, just chatting, and Pig tells me he has taken up running, and is trying to get to the Invictus Games in Victoria, British Columbia, next year. I tell him I will be his coach and training partner if he likes, but he says we live (or will live) too far apart to run together. But I tell him I am on the plane with him if he does go to Invictus. He tells me he is entered in the upcoming 'Bridge to Brisbane' ten kilometre fun run, so I am thinking I might sign up too. I run early most mornings.

After a little while, we head off to check out the new property, which looks ideal with a large workshop, garage space, three-bed apartment upstairs – just what I am looking for. With the sort of technology I'll be installing, I'll need top-class security, so having everything under one roof will make that so much easier. And, knowing me, I will work long hours, so only having to climb up or down stairs to start work sounds ideal. So, we phone the agent, and as usual, it goes to message bank. Then the agent, 'Cherie' (do any of them ever have plain names?), rings back, and we make an appointment for tomorrow at 9:00 a.m.

On the drive back to West End to drop Pig off, I ask if he can drive. His left leg was amputated below the knee and he wears a prosthesis but only has a slight limp.

'Yeah, sure,' he says, 'I have a full license, so no worries there.'

So, I tell him my plan to buy a panel van, again something plain that will always blend in.

5

I am now settled in my new home/office in Hamilton Street Tingalpa, after negotiating a quick fourteen-day cash settlement. I had my office purposely built into the extensive downstairs area and have fast and secure internet access – it's time for the next step in investigating Liz's accident. I've dug up photos of DS Benson and DI Lancaster, so late in the afternoon I take off in the van to watch the entrance/exit of Police Headquarters to watch for them leaving. But there is little suitable parking, so I position myself in a little café with a good view of the entrance, hoping they will walk out, not drive out of the underground car park.

Alas, there is no sign of them; it's getting dark, and the café is closing, so looks like it's a wash for today. Maybe I'll try first up in the morning so I can see them arrive for work.

The next morning, by 7:30 a.m. I have the van parked diagonally across the road from police HQ car park Makerston Street in the city. I have set up a mini video camera on the dash, very similar to a dashcam from outside, so this captures not only pedestrians, but also all cars, utes [a ute is a popular vehicle type in Australia, a four door utility, typically a smaller version of the F-150, Dodge Ram], etc., going into the underground car park. By 9:30 a.m., I again haven't seen either of them, so I head back to the office, hoping the video might show them driving into the car park.

Back in the office, I upload the video along with the images I have of them and set the facial recognition program to do its thing. *Bing*! My lucky day, the system alert goes off telling me it has a match – two, in fact. The camera has captured them both driving into the car park in separate cars, Benson in a Kia Sportage and Lancaster in a Ford Falcon. I zoom in on the number plate of both cars, and yes, they both have the little green circle sticker on them. By loading an image of the sticker into the software program, I set it off again to see how many other cars it can find with the matching sticker. I wander over to the coffee machine for a caffeine boost.

Sure enough, half an hour later, the program has finished its run and has flagged up four more cars with the same sticker. I again zoom in and take a close-up of both the number plate and the driver's face for future reference. So, at least six of them are in this special clique. I record their photos, registration numbers and a question mark for their names for now and start a new file called 'police SC' (Special Clique).

Later in the afternoon, I am back outside police HQ on the lookout for any of the faces I've seen, but before sitting down in a different café, I rig a little video camera to a convenient lamppost so it will video all traffic coming and going from the police car park. You would think it would be obvious, but clothed in hi-vis, with a white van and a ladder, no one takes the slightest bit of notice. I even parked in a no parking zone, left a note on the dash saying I'm carrying out emergency repairs to street lighting. Easy as.

With the camera filming and streaming direct by Bluetooth to my phone, as long as I am within 200 metres, I will capture all footage, which is also uploading to our secure cloud-based database. This time, I'm in luck: Benson and three others come out as a group and wander up the road to the Grosvenor Hotel. I follow at a distance. They order a schooner each and then wander over to a large hi-top table tucked away in a corner away from other tables. Their level of familiarity makes me think it is a regular drinking spot. I then realise it is a Thursday, the same day that Liz was killed (yes, I think of her as being killed, not just dying).

I stay in the adjoining bar so I can see them in the mirror behind them without being visible. A little while later Lancaster joins them – in time to buy the others a second round. Again, there's that air of familiarity as they all settle comfortably into what seems their usual spots. I finish a second beer, contemplating how I can hear what is being said and what I want to do next. As much as I want to confront Benson, I also need to know as much as possible about him and his cohorts.

I leave after my second beer to ensure I am not noticed and also to ensure I am ready to follow Benson when he retrieves his police car from the car park. Sure enough, around 7:30 p.m., I see Benson and a couple of the others coming up the road and walking down the car park ramp; I am sitting in the van as anonymous as ever. The first two cars to come up are Hyundai Santa Fes, so I let them go; then up comes a Sportage – I check the registration number and, yep, this is him.

I let him head off up the road and around the corner before I follow, making sure no other vehicles are coming out to see me take off after Benson. The van is fitted with high-quality dash- and rear-mounted cameras so I can see and record action in front and behind me. Benson heads out of the city on the Captain Cook Bridge, heading south on the M1, which is a bit unexpected as he lives at Springfield Lakes and the best way there from the city would be the Centenary Highway – almost in the opposite direction.

He exits the M1 on the Marshall Road exit and continues along suburban streets until pulling up outside a unit complex in Regina

Street Stones Corner. He gets out of his car and heads up the stairs and knocks on the door of a unit up on the second level. From my viewpoint, I can't see who opens the door, but my suspicion is it is a woman. I turn the van around, find a vacant parking spot and settle down to wait. One thing my time in the forces taught me was patience. Plenty of waiting, waiting for duty or waiting whilst on duty on stakeouts – usually in far less comfort than my van, into which I had fitted a little fridge which I keep stocked with bottled water and snack bars.

I contemplate getting out and walking over and putting a tracker unit on his Sportage, so we will know where he is – well, where the car is – at all times, but decide against it, not knowing how many suburban eyes might be watching. A couple of hours later, I see Benson come back out (*double interesting timing*, I am thinking!) and jump in his car, looking at his watch as he does. He starts up, does a quick U-turn and heads back towards the freeway. He rejoins the freeway heading south, continues until the Loganlea Road and follows that over to the Logan Motorway and heads off west. Heading home, I assume.

Sure enough, he takes the Centenary Motorway exit and continues on to Springfield Lakes exit, and a few minutes later pulls into his home in Summit Drive. I drive straight past and pull 100 metres farther up the road, watching in my mirrors and using the rear mounted camera to zoom back onto his car and surroundings. After fifteen to twenty minutes, I assume he is home for the night and head home myself, contemplating if what I have found out today helps me.

What have I learnt, I ponder, making a list with my fingers:

1. He is clearly part of some clique within the police.
2. I will check next Thursday but am already assuming their drink session is a regular Thursday evening gathering,

meaning he was more than likely to have been affected by alcohol when he killed Liz.
3. Likely, he has a mistress or is at least having an affair – of course, he could have been visiting his mum, but I doubt that after spending a couple of hours at the pub!

So, what else do I want to know? I'm already thinking how I can learn more. But now I am home, and it's time to hit the sack.

With the camera mounted on the lamppost outside Police HQ, I don't have to run the risk of sitting around outside, but by running the sticker through the image recognition program all day, I have come up with two additional cars showing the sticker and one more driver. So now we have six cars and six officers apparently part of the SCs, as I have branded them. Having matched the names of all officers through their licenses and police IDs, I have a list to work off. DI Lancaster is the ranking officer, Benson and a Jack Fleming as detective sergeants, and two more detective constables.

- DI Joe Lancaster
- DS Dillion Benson
- DS Jack Fleming
- DC Josh Armitage
- DC Byron Bruce

Having decided it would be interesting to see what they talk about at the pub on their Thursday evening gatherings, I decide to put in a camera and microphone to capture their conversations, and I am keen to hear what they talk about next week.

Now that I have my secure server and hidden IP address, I have accessed the coroner's office's server and downloaded the full coroner's report on Liz's accident. To my surprise, this comes with his scribbled notes as well. In one scribble, he writes, 'Message from DI Lancaster—wanting to know what I am saying.' Then a few weeks later, another note: 'DI Lancaster again, this time trying to put words in my mouth, and making it clear it is in everyone's interest (including mine!) that there should be no mention of Benson being a serving officer'.

Hmmm, some pretty heavy pressure was being applied and was totally unethical, I would have thought. The coroner is supposed to be totally independent, so he must have felt the pressure to not only leave out that Benson was a serving police officer, but that no drug or alcohol testing was done. I'm certainly looking forward to making my appearance at their Thursday night gathering. When the time comes.

6

A couple of weeks later, I am sitting in the bar at the Grosvenor Arms myself, having just completed an 'install' in the ceiling above. Dressed in my hi-vis work gear, carrying a toolbox and ladder, I had wandered in earlier and told the receptionist I was with Telstra and needed to access their phone lines in the ceiling. She showed me where the manhole was, so I set up my ladder, place the usual danger warning signs around the ladder so some dumb arse doesn't knock into it, then work my way through the ceiling until I am above what I hope or expect is the SC's (as I've dubbed them) usual table in the bar below. I then proceed to drill two tiny pinprick holes through the ceiling, only around 1.5 millimetres, so hardly noticeable, and certainly not in the dark and discoloured ceiling below. One for the mic, the other for a 360 camera.

As the bar is nearly empty, I don a pair of high-quality headphones from my toolbox and try and listen to what is going on below. I also open the app on my phone and check that the vision from the little camera is okay. Yep, not too bad, easy to recognise the different patrons, but audio not working well enough, so I fiddle with the controls to enhance the mic, and then someone walks into the bar, and bang, I have sound. These little knickknacks aren't the sort you can buy at Bunnings or even online. I doubt our Australian Federal

Police even have them, but I saved a few (quite a few, actually!) from the army days once I knew what I was going to be doing on the outside. Now I have the benefit.

As I go back down the ladder, I hear a male voice saying, 'What's with the ladder?'

The receptionist says, 'Some bloke from Telstra needed to check the lines.'

'Hope they're not going to be sending us the bloody bill,' he replies.

With that, I shut the ladder with a bang and yell out, 'All finished, thanks,' and head out the door to my van parked up the road, affixing the ladder to the roof rack before driving off.

After driving the van around the corner and up the road, I park again and go back to the pub, order a beer, and sit, not near the SC's table but not too far away. I am not expecting them as they don't usually meet up on a Wednesday, but I want to keep an eye and ear on things so I can then compare to the vision and audio when I download it later. As I sit down, I notice a smartly dressed lady sitting at the bar, sipping her white wine, apparently deep in conversation with a suit. *Cool*, I think.

There is only a smattering of others in the bar, so it's quiet and pleasant. Then the suit starts raising his voice to the lady, getting in her face, and she is quite forceful back, telling him to back off, but he becomes more insistent. I look along the bar towards the barman, who is serving another patron, and appears not to want to get involved.

As the suit becomes more aggressive, demanding the woman leave with him, I decide enough is enough, put my beer down and walk up to them and say, 'Is this man bothering you, miss?'

She seems to be startled by my arrival, stumped as to what to say.

Not the suit, though – he turns and snarls, 'Fuck off, this is none of your business.'

'I'll make it my business if you don't leave quietly,' I tell him in a level firm voice.

Something in my tone must have struck a chord, as he pauses and takes a look at me, and I guess he does not like what he sees. As I've said, I am rather a big unit, and rather intimidating when I bother.

'So, what's it to be, quietly or a heave out the door?' I ask him.

'Fuck you,' he says to me, rolling his shoulders, and with one more snarl at the lady, he mutters, 'This is not the end of it' and storms off.

I watch him go, then turn to the lady, still sitting on her stool, and surprisingly composed for what she had just encountered.

'Everything all right here?' the barman asks now that the problem had gone away.

'A bit late, mate,' I tell him with a look; he shrugs and walks back down the bar.

I ask the lady, 'Are you okay now?'

She smiles and says, 'Thanks, I appreciate your help.'

I smile back and return to my seat across the bar. I must confess, I continue to watch her surreptitiously in the bar mirror; as I said, she is rather attractive.

The barman comes over with a fresh beer for me and says, 'On the house. I appreciate what you did before – we don't have any security this early, and I don't earn enough to get into that sort of shit.'

I nod and say, 'Thanks for the beer, appreciated.'

I notice the lady getting ready to leave. Instead of walking out, she comes directly over to me and says, 'Thanks, I really appreciate you stepping in. Hugh can be a real arse when he's had a few.'

'So you did know him?' I ask.

'Yes – may I?' She indicates a chair.

'Sure,' I say.

'I am Susie,' she says, putting out her hand.

We shake and I say, 'Mort.'

'Yes, a former boyfriend who can't take "no" for an answer. He's done this a few times lately, getting a little worse each time – he got dumped by his last girlfriend as well, I believe.'

I dig out a business card and hand it to her and say, 'Well, if he ever bothers you again, you give me a call, and I can assure you it will be the last time he does.' I deliver the last part with a smile.

She looks at me for a long time, then says, 'I think I believe you,' and smiles. She then digs out a card and hands it to me. It reads, 'Susie Dunn, Lawyer of Legal Minds' with the usual phone numbers and contact details. 'So, if you need good legal advice or just want to call me, make sure you do!' Again, it's delivered with a flirtatious smile. *Well, that's what I'm thinking – or is that hoping?*

'So, Managing Director, ah?' she says, looking at my card. 'You don't look like the usual MD, what with your hi-vis on.'

'Just want to blend in,' I say.

She looks around, seeing most patrons in suits and says, again with that smile, 'Not in here. Well, Mort, thanks again, and I hope I hear from you soon.' Another smile, and she's gone.

Wow, I think, *was she flirting with me?* I watch her walk away, long shoulder-length blonde hair, obviously fit, with a graceful and purposeful walk. *But shit, how would I know? Nearly eighteen years since I bothered with that shit.* Nice lady, though, Susie, good on the eyes too.

After I finish my beer, I walk to the van and head back to my new home and base. Cost more than I wanted to pay, but it will be fine. Fifteen years in the army, no living costs and no tax for the most part whilst on combat duty overseas, plus a rest of life pension – I wasn't rolling in it, but I didn't have to worry about next month's mortgage, either.

7

'Good afternoon, Sir, how can I help you?' asks the maître d' when I arrive early the following week all spick and span for my meeting with Colonel Richards and my potential client Bruce Campbell, CEO of Campbells, a large (by Brisbane standards) family-owned pharmaceutical company, at Tattersalls Club in Brisbane CBD. Tatts, as it is widely known, was one of the last vestiges of 'gentleman only' business clubs, only recently voting to allow female members. It's an exclusive old-school sort of establishment.

'My name is Ireland; I have a meeting with Colonel Richards,' I reply with a smile.

He gives me the once-over, no doubt noting the tight top button and sloppy tie knot. Getting the top button done up was a bitch – hadn't had to do it on Civvy Street for a long time; didn't even wear a tie when I got married.

After checking details on his little tablet 'Follow me, Sir,' he says, then escorts me over to a table where the Colonel is sitting with another man, medium height, a little overweight, chubby face – *too much of the good life*, I think.

The Colonel stands as I approach, and we shake hands – I was half tempted to throw up a salute but managed to avoid embarrassing myself.

'Ireland, good to see you,' he says with a smile as he gives me an inspection. 'You look like you're keeping yourself fit, Mort.'

I nod.

He introduces Bruce Campbell to me; we shake hands, and all sit down.

The Colonel asks what I've been doing, and I do likewise. He retired a couple of years ago, going out at the top of his game, a highly regarded and respected leader. Not one to focus on the fringe elements but always kept a strong interest in the wellbeing of the men he led.

He reached out to me when he heard I was cashing out, asked what my plans were, knowing full well what skills I had developed whilst in the army. In fact, it's fair to say, his support firmed up my interest in pursuing my little business. And here I was, meeting my first serious 'prospect' through the Colonel's efforts.

After a little more chatter around the table, and ordering drinks and lunch, Bruce settles down to business.

'I have read your proposal, Mort. You seem confident you can solve our little problem, but I would like to hear you elaborate on the proposal for me.'

'Fair enough,' I say. 'You are convinced someone is leaking your product plans to your competitors, as over the last two to three years, your competitors always seem to come out with a similar product to that you are about to launch. Is that a fair summary?' I ask.

'Pretty much,' he replies.

'Who in your organisation is privy to this sensitive data and product information?' I counter.

'That's the issue,' he replies. 'Only people, staff I trust implicitly – most have been with me for many years.'

'Okay then,' I reply. 'With your permission, I will access your server, tracing and logging all regular users, set up some tripwires and traps. We will also use some pretty hi-tech methods to monitor and track all staff and their associates who have access to this data. Do you have a new product coming on stream shortly that would be at risk?' I ask.

'Yes, that's what has brought this to a head; we do have a new product we are working on, and it is pretty damned exciting, so we certainly don't want it being shared.'

'What is the timing of this new product and who is already aware of it?' I ask.

'Right now, only me and Keith Drabinsky, our research and development chief – and there is no way he will share. He is very proud of this and most excited for the company. He's been with the company forty years – worked closely with my father when he ran the business,' he tells me. 'He's also not well liked by most of the staff, being a bit like the absent-minded professor type and rather rude and abrupt as well.'

'That's likely going to be a good thing,' I reply. 'So, Sir,' I continue, 'that's about all I can tell you – the ways and wherefores we will use will remain confidential.' I smile, then add, 'And let's be very clear: any information, data we bring to the table, cannot be used in a court of law, so if that's your intent, you need to look elsewhere.'

'Good gracious, no,' replies Bruce. 'That would be the last thing the company needs.' He then adds, 'So, Mort, tell me what your characteristics are and why I should trust you with this delicate but crucial issue.'

I nod. 'As I am sure the Colonel has told you, I and my colleague have some very advanced skills in the area of digital data, trained at the highest level in the US, and we worked very closely with them in Afghanistan and other countries. We have equipment superior to any currently used by any police service in the country; we are disciplined, resourceful, committed and never take a backwards step. The Special Forces team I led were not just back-room analysts, but hardened frontline soldiers; in fact, more time was spent behind enemy lines, so working in Civvy Street is a bit of a hoot in comparison.'

We pause whilst lunch is served, waiting for the wait staff to move away. We then spend a few minutes eating before Bruce continues, 'Well, your rate is pretty high, Mort, considering you are just getting started. Besides, we are only a modest, family-owned business – anything you can do about the rate?'

I smile, and reply, 'You will be getting some of the best digital data analysts around, and considering how much you have already lost by your competitors swiping your new products, I would think our rate very reasonable. Modest family-owned business: turnover $50 million last year with net profit likely around $4 million, and here we are in Tatts, so I don't think that line works too well.'

After a pause that lingers a little longer than is comfortable, he responds, 'Fair enough. So, what is the next step and how do we go about this?' He extends his hand, and we shake and nod to each other. Deal done.

'Okay,' I say, 'I have a copy of the proposal here and would like to sign it whilst we are here together; the Colonel can act as witness. The reason: I don't want anyone in your office, or anyone at all, knowing about us or what we are doing. I want you to buy yourself a prepaid phone and let me know the number, and this is NOT to be used in front of other staff, or even family. Sorry,' I say, seeing the look of displeasure on his face, 'but the stakes are that high, and you can't afford to take any risk.'

He nods, so I continue, 'I will need the names of your senior staff, those who have known about the previous products, and even any that may have left the company in the meantime.' I pause, thinking of a different angle. 'You know, there may be a way we can speed this up. Do you have another maybe older product you are refreshing, something that could be used as bait?' I ask.

After a pause, he replies, 'Well, actually, we do. Before Keith made the breakthrough on the new product, we had been planning on doing a refresh of our very successful and popular hand cream – Pleasure Plus Cream.'

'What I am thinking,' I reply, 'is I will give you and Keith secure – and I mean lock-tight – USB drives that this new product MUST be saved onto. I will have to configure his computer. Does he use a laptop or desktop?'

'Laptop.'

'Good. This little drive has a fingerprint sensor, it can't be opened without it, so it won't leave any data or material on your drive or his laptop. But I will have to meet you both to set it up, and this should not be at your offices. Maybe I can meet you both at a café somewhere? Do you trust him enough to let him know what's going on, or do we need a cover story?'

'No, I actually think he will be pleased at the precautions we are taking for this product. We call it "S Cream", by the way.'

'Bruce, it's imperative you don't email or discuss this anywhere around your office. You just don't know who might be listening. Also, ideally, my advance and progress payments need to come from your private account or an account not connected to the business, or that anyone else has access to, to prevent anyone knowing of the deal. Is that an issue?'

'No, I will pay your advance from my personal account – just have to tell the wife where the money's going.'

'Does she have any active involvement in the business? Is she someone we need to look into?'

'No, no,' he replies, 'she doesn't have any interest. We hardly even discuss the business, nor does she have access to the server or any data. My laptop is secure and she's not exactly tech savvy; she just pecks away on her iPad doing her shopping and travel bookings,' he says with a grin.

'Okay, then. When can you get me the staff details?'

He pulls a folder sheet of A4 paper out of his jacket pocket and hands it over, saying, 'I came prepared, and even typed this up myself without saving it, so there's no record of it.'

'Great, now all we need is to sign the agreement and settle the advance payment,' I say with a smile.

The Colonel, who had been quietly reading the agreement whilst this conversation was going on, takes off his reading glasses and says, 'Well, all in all, this seems fair, so if you're both happy, let's sign it and get started on sorting Bruce's problem.' He pulls out an old-fashioned fountain pen and hands it to Bruce, who hesitates a second and then signs. I do likewise.

Once we have both signed, the Colonel signals the waiter and asks for two copies of the agreement. 'One each,' he says with a smile.

Bruce then tells me he will make the payment tonight, so it should be in the account in the morning.

I nod. 'Great, I will get straight onto this.'

As we have all finished lunch, we shake hands all round and I head for the door. As I walk back to the car park, I text Pig, 'You're on the clock 8:00 a.m. Monday – sharp!'

The response is immediate: 'Bells on!'

I reply, 'Uber over as I have a van for you to drive.'

'Cool,' comes back the reply.

We're in business.

8

'You killed my wife.'

Finally, after all these months of wondering how it would sound, it was out there. The reaction was about what I expected. I am now securely ensconced in the van, listening and watching the 'SC's' of cops after making my accusation. There is a fair bit of silence; then DI Lancaster mutters, 'Maybe we went a little too far, leaning on the coroner.'

'And we would have been better fudging the blood test, rather than not doing one,' adds DS Fleming.

'Nah, he's only some army snot – what can he do?' asks DC Armitage.

'Well, I am glad it will be Benson meeting him one night in a dark alley and not me,' smiles DC Johnstone.

'Hold on,' adds Benson, 'if the coroner's report is confidential, how come he's been able to read it? It hasn't been published yet.'

'Shit,' responds Lancaster, 'I didn't think of that. How the hell has he managed that?'

It's silent around the group for a while, then DC Bruce says, 'Come on, my shout. Drink up, then it's time to hit the road.' He gathers their glasses and heads to the bar, where he chats to the barman, the same one who was on when I met Suzie.

The conversation drifts back to sport and politics, and it is obvious they are very pro-Labour – the current State Government – who have been in power for fifteen years now. There are comments like, 'He [referring to the long-standing Queensland State Premier Clyde Alfred] can't do without us now.'

'Yeah,' growls Lancaster, 'we have made sure of that!' Then, an obscure reference to the Brothers Mob bikie gang, which makes them all laugh.

They finish their beers and start wandering back to the car park to retrieve their cars and head home. I decide on the spur of the moment to tail Benson again, but this time, he heads straight home to Springfield.

*

It's the second Thursday after I installed the bug and camera, and a week after I made my pronouncement, and I am sitting in my office having a beer and watching the SC boys enjoy their beers at the Grosvenor Hotel. There is a bit of interplay between DI Lancaster and one of the others now identified as DS Fleming.

Fleming tells the group, 'Harry from fleet was on the phone again today asking when DI Lancaster was going to hand over the "old Falcon" and pick up his new Santa Fe. I told him that DI wasn't available –I should have told him he would tell you to fuck off, but I didn't.'

DI Lancaster replies, 'Fuck them. I am holding onto my Falcon as long as I can; I don't give a shit if it's contrary to the rules. Who's going to order me to change cars? Certainly not our commissioner.'

'Anyway,' DI Lancaster continues, 'you all better listen up.' When the group goes silent, he continues, 'It's going down tomorrow night. So make sure you are where you should be, as I want to make sure we are first on scene to ensure no other glory boys get a chance. So, Benson, make sure you're home in your own bed, ah?'

DC Armitage pipes up, 'Shit, you still screwing that bird, Benson?'

Lancaster silences him with a look and continues, 'We need to make sure it's ours, so no fuck ups, and don't be late. Be ready to leave when the call comes in – should be around seven or eight tomorrow night.'

Silence is the only answer, but I can see them all nodding their heads.

Lancaster finishes the conversation by saying, 'This will teach the bastards to keep their noses out of other people's business. AND a good lesson for everyone else too.'

Bloody hell, I think, *what's this about?*

So the next day, I keep an ear to the radio and an eye on the headlines, but it's not until after 9:00 the following evening when a news flash crosses the TV announcing a major bikie figure has been gunned down in Logan somewhere. Bevan 'The Knife' Hogan, former sergeant of arms of the Brothers Mob bikie gang, was shot down as he came out of a restaurant having eaten alone.

Shit, I think, *and the cops, or at least our Special Clique, knew about it beforehand. Clearly had no intention of trying to stop it, either.*

Next morning, I am keen to see what the papers have to say, which is that it's a suspected gang killing, one gang trying to break into the other's territory, and bugger me, there's DI Lancaster on the news, assuring everyone this is not the start of a bikie war. He should know – he knows more than everyone. I give Pig a call and we chew the fat, trying to make sense out of it all. But it's hard to know, we just don't have enough facts. We decide just listening to their pub talk is not enough; we need to find a way to hear more. Doubting they would talk this stuff over in police headquarters, we talk about how we can put bugs and trackers into the police cars. If we can access their phone numbers, we should be able to at least keep a record of their call logs. Then again, I bet they all have more than one each.

This started out as a way to see what they knew about Liz's death, but it was quickly turning into something bigger. Exactly how much bigger, I had no idea.

9

Early morning. Alarm going off.

Shit! I think, *Bridge to Brisbane, need to get up and get going.*

Bridge to Brisbane is an annual fun run, either five or ten kilometres, and Pig and I had both entered the ten kilometre run. So up I get, dressed for running – it's August, so it's cooler (for Brisbane, at least, with its sub-tropical climate) – and head down to the car with water bottle, towel and a quick change of clothes in a little backpack. I arrive at the bus stop to catch the shuttle to the start point; on I hop when the next bus arrives, and I am dropped at the start point.

Pig and I had agreed to do the ten kilometre run 'together', knowing we would both be trying to beat the other – nothing new there. Having not seen Pig run, I am surprised to see him rock up with one of those curved blades (aka The Blade Runner) on instead of his usual prosthesis.

'Man,' I say, 'you look the real shit!'

He smiles back and says that he's bloody lucky that George had helped him through the process of having his artificial leg fitted, and they actually got one supplied and fitted by some genius from Iran. 'Yeah, this fella was a refugee from Iran who worked over there helping amputees with their rehabilitation. He was lucky enough to get residency here in Australia and designed and developed this really cool prosthesis which has a carbon fibre rod up into my thigh, so I don't suffer any of the stump pain common with amputees. I can also change from my usual leg to my blade easily and without discomfort. So, good all round!' he says.

We wander off to the toilet so we don't have to wait too long and then head back to the starting point. He heads to the B section (runners under fifty minutes) and me to the C section (fifty to sixty minutes). We threaten each other with penalties for the loser – as I said, no pressure.

The crowd of some 25,000 runners is pulsing, excited and ready to go when the starting pistol goes off. Us slowbies walk towards the starting line and then break into a trot as the road clears in front, and we are away. Of course, there is a large number of runners and walkers behind me, but they are not my focus. My focus is a certain blade runner in front of me. I head off in search of him.

Some forty-five minutes later, I am catching my breath after finishing and just a little miffed that I had not seen or passed Pig along the way. *Shit*, I think, *how will I live this down, beaten by Pig?*

Then I recognise someone in front of me. 'Suzie?'

She looks around and smiles. 'Hi,' she says, 'did not expect to see you here!'

'Ah, just out for my morning stroll,' I say with a smile.

'Sure,' she says, smiling back.

Just then, Pig rolls up with his medal around his neck, and quite smug, really, slaps me on the shoulder and says, 'Well, what was your time?'

'44.55,' I tell him.

'Mmm, a bit slow, mate.'

'All right, what did you do it in?' I ask to get it over and done with.

'43.25!' he says with a smug smile.

'Shit,' I say, 'I'll have to up the training – can't take getting beaten by a cripple!' We both laugh, whilst Suzie seems taken aback by my comment.

Pig seems to notice Suzie watching us for the first time. 'Hi,' he says, 'I'm Pig.'

She pulls a face and says, 'That can't be your real name?'

'Nah,' he says, 'but it's the one I get called by – how do you know this slug?' He points at me.

Suzie and I smile at each other, and she replies, 'He saved me from a difficult situation a few weeks ago.'

'Okay,' he says, 'but what about today?'

'I recognised her... brightly coloured top,' I say, getting a smile from them both, but maybe Suzie's was just a little forced with a half frown.

I introduce them both and Suzie says, 'I am sorry, but I cannot call you Pig. What is your real name?'

I snigger and say, 'You don't really want to know – and he doesn't want you to know either.'

But Pig takes her hand and says, 'Suzie, I am Julien Winchester Le Tonge, and I am very pleased to meet you.'

I reply, 'See, it's hard to tell who is more embarrassed – you or Suzie.'

Suzie replies, 'I am pleased to meet you, Julien. I hope your manners rub off on your friend here,' pointing at me.

We all have a laugh as we head to the finishers' T-shirt collection area to collect our T-shirts.

As we go, I ask Suzie what her time was.

'Oh, I am a lot slower than you guys,' she says.

'Yes, but how did you go?' I persist.

'I did 49.55, so just squeezed under my goal of fifty minutes.'

I turn and give her a fist pump. 'See, there you go,' I say with a smile.

Afterwards, Pig turns to Suzie and says, 'I'm heading off now –

George will be waiting for me – but why don't you two go and have brunch or something?'

I give him a look that says, 'Matchmaking is not your thing'.

He adds pointedly to Suzie, 'Take it easy on him, but he's worth it!'

As Pig heads off, I smile and shrug to Suzie and say, 'Well, suits me, if you have nothing better to do.'

She smiles and says, 'Love to – I would only be washing my hair anyway.' As we walk off, she asks, 'So how did Julien lose his leg?'

I take my time responding. 'We were in a Bushman – you know, an armoured troop carrier – which ran over an IED – an improvised explosive device. We crashed. A couple of others got minor injuries, but Pig was the worst hit. We were in an isolated position, so it took the medics longer than it should to respond and extract him. Time he couldn't afford.'

Suzie pulls a face and says that she had not realised we were ex-army.

'Yes, we were both in for around fifteen years,' I reply.

'Why do you call him Pig then? She asks the obvious question.

I smile and say, 'Why do you think?'

She responds, 'Because he is messy, I guess.'

'In fact, he is very OCD – everything has to be just so. He used to take heaps of shit from others. His bed, shoes, everything was exactly in line, picture perfect. So of course his nickname implies the exact opposite.'

Suzie smiles and nods in reply.

After collecting our bags from the luggage tent, we decide we aren't too smelly so we can cope without showers for now, and head off to find a suitable café, as there are a few around Southbank where the race finished. Settling in at a café, we're a little nervous, neither quite knowing what to say.

After we've ordered, Suzie decides to take the lead and says, 'So,

Mort, let's hear your story.'

But I demur, smiling and saying, 'Ladies first.'

I get a look, and she then says, 'Okay. I am thirty-four years old, I grew up in Bundaberg, where my parents still live, and I still miss it, but I am here in Brisbane making my mark and now live in my own apartment in New Farm.'

'So what sort of law do you practice?' I ask.

'Well, Legal Minds covers the full gamut, but I prefer and focus on family law. There are a lot of broken families that need help.'

'Yes, but can they pay for it?' I ask, perhaps a little unkindly, as I get another look.

'True, that is an issue,' she replies, 'but we are doing okay. Trouble is, the boss is a real arsehole – an old-fashioned sexist pig! But his specialty is litigation, so he and I rarely cross paths.'

'So, do you enjoy your job and the law in general?' I ask.

She pauses before she answers, 'Yes and no, I guess. I haven't actually thought about it like that, but I love dealing with people and helping them find solutions, but the law can be so hard on people too, often those that are at their most vulnerable.'

'Family, brothers or sisters?' I ask.

'Yes, an older sister, Nat, who has two lovely little kids – Ollie, who is eight, and my goddaughter, Amelie, is six – and a husband, of course – Dave, who has his own accountancy practice.'

'So, does Nat work as well?'

'Yes, she is a nurse. Doesn't work full-time, but seems to end up doing a lot of odd shifts. Don't know how she does it with the two kids, and Dave doesn't seem to be much better.'

'So, anyone I need to be jealous of?' I ask, surprising myself, hoping I am not blushing.

She gives me a radiant smile and says, 'No, I was in a long-term relationship for four years, but it ended badly over twelve months ago, and I have been content enjoying my own company since.'

I nod in reply. 'You obviously keep fit – not many can run ten kilometres under fifty minutes, you know,' I tell her.

'I guess,' she says, adding, 'I have always liked running, getting out in the fresh air.' She also admits to being a regular at her gym (who isn't these days?) and still plays competition netball as well.

'What position?' I ask (as if I would know, but hey, it sounds good!).

'Centre,' she replies, commenting that not many guys know the different positions.

I reply, 'My only knowledge of the game is from TV. Whist on deployment, they used to show the Australia versus New Zealand netball tests, so we used to take sides and cheer them on.'

'Oh,' she says. 'How long were you in the army and where were you deployed?'

'Yes,' I reply, 'a fifteen-year vet. Did tours to Afghanistan – two tours, and the last one was an extended tour – also spent time in Iraq, Kuwait, Turkey, and a while ago East Timor.'

'When did you leave the army?'

'Only three months ago – it was time to get out and make a fresh start.'

'Okay, keep going – your turn now,' she says as our coffee and lunch is finally served.

'Okay, I'm thirty-seven, signed up in the army when I turned twenty-one, served a total of eight years on deployment overseas, in various theatres but mainly Afghanistan. Based mainly in Townsville. Grew up in Ipswich, was married to my high school sweetheart for twelve years, but she died in a car accident whilst I was on deployment the year before last. No kids.'

'Oh, I am sorry,' she gasps, reaching out and putting her hand on top of mine in an instinctive gesture.

I'm happy for it to stay there, but after a few moments, she pulls it back, and we eat our lunch in silence for a while.

After she finishes her meal, she wipes her mouth with the serviette, and then with that half smile, she says, 'So, you recognised my… top, ah?'

'Yes, I remember passing you in the race and thinking, *Gee that's bright*, then bugger me when I saw it again. I noticed it was you, so I had to say hello and hoped you would remember me.'

'So with literally hundreds of tops the same colour as mine, you recognised me?'

Hmm, I think, *getting backed into a corner here*, but I decide to go with the truth. 'Well, you do have a cute butt.' This gets a nice, pleased smile, as if she liked the answer and maybe that I had been honest.

She continues, 'Yes, I have been hoping you would call.'

I reply, 'I haven't plucked up the courage yet.'

'Tough army boy, ah?' she responds with that impish smile that I am beginning to like seeing, and we both smile.

'Well, you have to have a bit of sympathy for me – one thing we don't learn in the army is "social etiquette", so my social skills are a bit basic, and to make mine even worse, I was with Liz right from school, so never learnt the skills for dating either.'

She laughs at this, but with a questioning look in her eyes. 'So, how did the army set you up for Digital Data Solutions?' she asks, and I'm taken aback by the fact she remembers my company name. She seems to sense this and adds, 'Oh, I checked you out, don't worry.'

'Well, I was in 1st Battalion RAR, but in a special operations group where we were deployed to monitor the Taliban, Al Qaeda and other baddies, often in very hostile and difficult terrain, so I was well-trained in eavesdropping and capturing signals, and frankly, hacking their email servers. They might be portrayed as wild and nomadic, but the Taliban and Al Qaeda are actually very well organised and resourced. Supposedly backed by Pakistani intelligence. Their comms was particularly sophisticated. I was trained not only in the field but was sent stateside for high-level training as well, even did a couple of little clandestine "projects" for the Yanks as well – that worked out well.'

'So, a bit of a spy, ah?' she teases me.

'Nah, nothing like that, but I am glad those days are behind me. Happy to be free of the army and be my own man.'

'And you obviously enjoy running,' she continues.

'Yes, I do, have always ran. Like most kids, played footy all through school, made a few rep teams, so I was always training. Then, of course, in the army, running used to entail running with a forty kilogram pack, ammo pouches, etc., so I am really enjoying running these days. Sometimes I think I am flying, not being held back by the weight of the bloody backpack.'

'You move well for a big bloke,' she replies.

I smile and say, 'I used to know a bloke, a big bloke, a lot bigger than me, and he ran full marathons, was a member of a running group. They call themselves the "Galloping Clydesdales", but I like to think I am not in that class.'

Surprisingly, the day has flown, and when I look at my watch, I say, 'Wow, I've been enjoying sitting here talking to you. Look at the time – I need to get going.'

'Well, maybe we can do this again sometime?' she suggests with a smile.

'Okay, I'll have to find the courage to call you!' I say, getting a smile in return that I can't quite read.

I pay the lunch tab and we head outside.

'Can I drop you off on my way home?' I ask.

'No,' she replies, saying she will take the City Cat, a Catamaran

Ferry service on the Brisbane River, which will drop her off 200 metres from her apartment.

It's a bit awkward saying goodbye, neither of us seeming sure how or what to do. Again, in the end, Suzie takes the initiative and kisses me on the cheek. *Well*, I think, *that will do for a start.*

As we are separating, she says, 'And I meant what I said in the pub; it would be nice to hear from you.'

'Okay,' I reply, 'I've got a bit on over the next couple of weeks, but I'll give you a call.'

She smiles as she waves goodbye.

10

Next morning, Monday, just before 8:00 a.m., Pig is at the door. I let him in, and we shake hands as always. I tell him he has to fill out employment forms and shit and tease him about needing a medical to prove he is medically 'fit for work'. I get the expected response – two fingers.

As I haven't got around to preparing his employment forms, we will sort these later. We each grab a coffee from the fancy new Nespresso machine I bought and installed in the office (plus, an identical one upstairs in my apartment), and I run through the job with him.

'So, first task,' I tell him, 'is to identify each of the senior team, where they live, what cars they drive, their mobile phone numbers, whether they have more than one – makes them suspicious if they do – where they bank and, where possible, the balance of their bank accounts.' As I warned Bruce, he can't use anything I give him in court, but we do have ways to access all of this info through the 'backdoors' we have been given access to by our grateful American friends.

I also tell Pig I have already been into the Campbell intranet and give him the login details I had set up, and let him know of the couple of tripwires I installed so we will get an alarm if someone starts snooping around generally on their server – a long shot at this point, but hey, we could get lucky!

Pig sets himself down at the second computer station I've set up and goes to work.

'Hey,' he says, 'where's my van?'

'In the garage next door,' I tell him.

Downstairs, I've portioned off about a third of the ground floor area, making this the office, so plenty of room for four to five people – not that I envisage ever needing that many, but this still leaves plenty of room for three to four cars in the garage. I had 'Bob the Builder', a one-man builder, come in as soon as the house settled and made the changes. I paid him some folding stuff (i.e. cash) to have it happen straight away. Upstairs, I have a three-bedroom apartment with separate entrance, but with internal stairs up/down to the office. Nice and convenient. All locked and secure with state-of-the-art security.

Pig quickly gets traction on the staff, easily coming up with their names, cars, home addresses (some also have second and even third investment properties, so these are noted too), photos of driver's licenses, any company directorships they or their partners have, details of their partners' employment, if any, and names and addresses of any kids, if not still underage and at home. He compiles a comprehensive list, put together in a spreadsheet, showing their photos as well. I then realise I did not ask Bruce for their salaries. *No matter – I expect to see him when we chat to Ken the Research and Development man in the next day or so.*

As I'm thinking this, my phone rings with an unknown number, and when I answer, it's Bruce on his new prepaid phone to tell me we are going to meet Ken tomorrow morning at 8:00 a.m. (before work) at a café in Loganholme near his home, so I tell him I will bring the list of staff and will need their salaries and any significant bonuses they may have received in the last few years.

When he asks why, I explain, 'It is highly likely whoever is leaking your secrets is being paid well for them, so we are looking into what assets they may own and the value of these.'

By mid-afternoon, Pig has largely compiled a good history and background of each of the staff named by Bruce and laid it all out in a spreadsheet.

*

Next morning, a little after 7:30 a.m., I am at the Nikkalatte Café in Loganholme, having arrived early to suss out Bruce and Keith as they arrive. They both arrive almost simultaneously from different directions, and I let them get settled before joining them. Bruce introduces me to Keith, who is of medium height, lightly built, a greying beard and strong South African accent. He is a little nervous or apprehensive of me; knowing I can have this effect on some people, I let the conversation drift to give him time to settle down. For now, I am willing to trust Bruce's judgement on Keith, as, if he was the leak, it would have been far easier to jump ship and 'invent' the new product for his new employer. But we will still be digging into him the same as the others.

I then explain the purpose of the special USB drives, stress the importance of saving all information about S Cream on it – no emails either, just swapping USB sticks to share updates – and to meet off site for any discussions. I suggest to Keith he also buy a separate phone, but he's reluctant to do this, explaining he rarely uses his phone, and only for family purposes, anyway; he doubts anyone at Campbells would even have the number. So I let it go at that.

Once I've set up the new drives, I access Keith's files and copy all the data from his 'S Cream' folder onto the USB and remove all trace of the previous folders, so even if someone as sophisticated as me was looking, they wouldn't be found. Bruce does not yet have any S Cream data on his laptop, so I don't need to worry about his.

We discuss how we can subtly let it be known about the refresh of the hand cream and also exaggerate the importance of these changes so someone might start digging. We decide not to make a big deal about it. Ken would drop into Bruce's office early next week and tell him proudly about some improvements and how these will make it significantly better and much more marketable, then let the usual office rumour mill move the information along,

That night, I give Suzie a call and we have a nice light-hearted chat for – dare I say it – over half an hour. Where did I learn to chat for that long?

*

The following Thursday, I decide to pay the Grosvenor Hotel a visit to see how my presence affects our SC. So there I am, sitting at a bar table not too far from their usual corner in clear view, when they walk in, this time in dribs and drabs, and pleasingly, each group stops talking when they see me, just watching me as they go to the bar to order. I reciprocate, watching each of them in turn, but particularly Benson, who I can see is unsettled by my presence and staring. Lancaster is the last to arrive, and as Fleming has already bought his beer, he goes straight over and joins the crew, giving me only a cursory glance as he goes. Then when he's taken his first drink, he indicates towards me and says something along the lines of, 'What's he doing here?'. They all shrug, and then try to ignore me.

Likewise, I ignore them, mostly, just making sure I give any of them that look my way a good glare. I am beginning to think they are all powder puffs – none seem inclined to do anything on their own, just like good soldiers only do as their leader, in this case, that's clearly Lancaster, tells them.

I could tell them that's why I was an excellent soldier; I was able to think and act on my feet – essential when behind enemy lines and totally exposed if you fuck up.

When it's Benson's turn to go to the bar, I time it so I'm up there at the same time to get a refill. I lean down close to him and whisper, 'Remember me?'

I get a glare, and he quickly glances back to his colleagues to see if anyone is coming to his aid. I'm watching them in the mirror as well, a fact not noted by any of them.

Armitage gets off his stool and heads over and says to Benson, 'Need a hand here?'

'Sure,' says Benson, handing him three of the glasses.

Before he leaves, I say quietly to him, 'Can't handle a friendly chat on your own, ah? Wonder how you will go on a dark night in a dark alley, ah?', paraphrasing what I had heard them saying the previous week. Then, giving them both a friendly smile, I head back to my stool to watch the next episode. Sure enough, Lancaster is giving me a look as they relate the interaction with the group when they get back with the beers.

I decide to order some food so I can prolong my presence, so I order the house beer battered fish and chips and enjoy this with the rest of my beer. When I am nearly finished with my meal, I glance up and see Suzie walking into the bar. She sees me and comes straight over smiling, and says, 'Hi, did not expect to see you here!'

I smile back and say, 'Just been working around the corner so popped in for a quick feed.' I quickly finish eating and ask her, 'Why don't we go somewhere nicer for a quick drink before I need to get going?'

'Hi Suzie,' rings out across the bar, and I see it is DC Armitage smiling at Suzie, who gives him the barest of acknowledgement.

She then says, 'Good idea,' so we leave and head into the lounge bar, which is far nicer and away from the SC.

Bugger, I think, *I did not need them knowing a connection between Suzie and me.*

I have to ask, 'How do you know DC Armitage?'

She replies, 'We dated a couple of times a few years ago.'

I reply, 'Well, at least your taste in men has improved recently,' to which I get a lovely smile.

11

Whilst waiting for the Campbell enquiry to ramp up, Pig and I discuss how and where we can access the SC's cars so we can install trackers and mics. He suggests sending a mini drone into the police garage, maybe on a Thursday night whilst they're at the pub, to at least get a feel for the set up in there. We mull over the pros and cons of this and decide we'll look into this Thursday but try and see how busy it is that time of day generally. We pull up the video footage from the pole outside their garage and check how many cars are coming and going from around 7:00 p.m. each night, but particularly on Thursday nights. The cars leaving the garage start thinning around 6:00 p.m. each night – seems most senior coppers are nine to fivers too – and certainly after 6:30 p.m., there is very little traffic. Of course, we don't know if it is manned in the garage, which is an underground car park typical of most high-rise office buildings, but we are unsure if it has special security, which you would expect it to.

On Thursday, we don our hi-vis and jump in the van around 4:30 p.m. and head into the city, managing to get a park just along from police HQ. We pick a power pole further away from the HQ, and I place the ladder up against the pole, then the barrier around the base. Pig climbs up, and when at the height of the streetlight, he unzips his shoulder tool bag and extracts his new mini drone, matte black and battery powered with excellent camera clarity and makes no more noise than a hummingbird – or so the marketing blub claimed. We're about to find out.

Pig launches it from his hand and whilst secured to the pole by his harness, he is able to use both hands on this tablet to control and manoeuvre the little thing. I'm also watching on my phone, leaning against the van. He slips the drone inside the garage and has the camera do a full 360, which shows an empty control booth just inside the entrance, so he moves it farther inside along the left wall first, enabling us to get a feel for how the cars are parked inside. It looks like a fairly typical parking garage with clearly marked parking bays, some reserved, others not. He scans the reserved signs, looking for our little SC sticker to see if they have their own parking area, and sure enough, off in the back right corner, we find four of the cars known to belong to the clique.

There's an elevator entrance midway along the left wall, and Pig has to move the drone back at one stage when a couple of cops exit the elevator. We watch as they separate and drive out. The exit seems to be straightforward: they both lean out and scan their security passes, and the boom lifts.

He then brings the drone back over to the control booth and films the notices on the windows, hoping it might say what hours it is manned, but it only gives a phone number to use when not manned. Not much else to be gleaned for now, so he brings the drone home, packs it away in his shoulder bag and climbs back down the ladder.

I stow the ladder on the van roof, and we head back to the office. On the way, we decide Pig will access the garage next Thursday whilst I am down south chasing new clients. We decide he will dress in hi-vis, clipboard in hand, and pretend he is from the motor pool (he will dummy up an appropriate pass) doing random inspections.

We hope the cars are left unlocked as this will make it so much simpler; if not, his little ceramic tool works just as well as mine.

It's late now, so Pig jumps in the van and heads off home, commenting, 'George is getting a bit annoyed at the irregular hours I am keeping.'

So I say, 'And what about you – you okay with it?'

He smiles and says, 'Loving it!'

*

With digital tripwires set throughout Campbell's intranet, we can remotely monitor all accesses and identify who is making them. Pig has also accessed the office security system so we can tell who is in the office and who is not, in case this becomes important. We quickly see a pattern emerging, by monitoring our eight employees of interest – 'the 8', as we have started calling them:

- Donna McIntyre, Chief Legal Officer
- John Morse, Operations Manager
- Keith Drabinsky, Head of Research
- Pam Martin, Bruce's long-serving PA
- Ahmed Khan, 2IC of Research
- Paul Barton, CEO
- Clyde Donald, Head of Marketing
- Bruce Campbell himself

Whilst not seriously suspicious of Bruce, we would be remiss if we did not check him out as well.

None of their bank accounts have surplus money; a couple of them have second, and one even has a third investment property, but these all have mortgages on them. No one seems to be living above their means, so nothing stands out. Other than Clyde, who is single and does seem to enjoy an active social life, the others are what you might call boringly normal.

On the Tuesday of our second week, Pig notices a new, unknown device roaming around, randomly opening files, then closing them, looking for who knows what. We quickly start tracking them. It's mid-afternoon, and as they have accessed the intranet remotely, we know it's none of our eight, as they are all fully occupied in their offices. We track the IP address, then overlay this with Google Maps to find it is coming from Bruce's home. Strange – we understood Bruce lived alone with his wife, and if she doesn't have access, who can this be?

Pig and I discuss how quickly we can get across to Bruce's home at Fig Tree Pocket, an upmarket enclave on the banks of the Brisbane River, and too far for us to quickly get there. We even discuss launching a drone, which would be far quicker, but decide the distance would be too great, even for one of Pig's specials. So, we continue to monitor the user, who has accessed Bruce's emails and is reading through them. A pretty sophisticated operator, we decide, certainly not likely to be Bruce's wife Linda. From the emails he is sourcing, it looks like they have picked up on Pleasure Plus Cream, as they go from email to email mentioning Pleasure Plus. Then they move on, opening more folders, particularly any seeming to originate from Research.

After about an hour of searching, they seem to settle on a folder called 'Refresh of PP Cream'. So to ensure they don't get too much, we send a pulse through their computer, which causes it to lose connection. We wait to see if they reconnect, but no, they don't.

'Well, well,' we say, and Pig goes back over the last two weeks to see if there is any sign of this same user previously but can't find any. We set an alarm for when that IP address accesses the database again. We suspect it won't be long after the interest they took in our bait Pleasure Plus Cream. We discuss ways to be ready next time, but not knowing any pattern, and not wanting to ask Bruce in case he says something at home, after discussing basing a drone near his home that could be launched remotely, we decide our best option is to set up a CCTV camera outside his home, so we can track all comings and goings there.

Pig, in particular, is something of a drone expert, as we used some pretty hi-tech models on deployment in Afghanistan, so launching remotely even from up to twenty kilometres away is no longer an issue. We didn't buy these from Harvey Normans, after all.

Next morning sees us both in hi-vis in the van, once again with Telstra stickers (we have a selection of magnetic stickers to use, depending on the purpose – anything to do with ladders, it's normally Telstra or Optus; then we have Toll Courier logos, and a few other fictious electrician and plumbing brands as well), my turn to go up the ladder, so Pig sets up the barrier and warning signs, and whilst I'm climbing the ladder, I notice a lady watching me from the house opposite Bruce's. I warn Pig in case she comes out. We have a cover story sorted anyway just in case.

Sure enough, she comes out when I reach the height of the streetlight and approaches us. As I am pointing her way, I wave out and say, 'Hi.'

She half smiles and addresses Pig when she gets close enough. 'I'm just wondering what you're doing; the light works fine,' she states.

Pig turns and smiles and says, 'Hi, just routine maintenance, Ma'am, nothing to worry about.'

She continues, 'The brightness of this light has been dimmed as it was so bright my husband and I couldn't sleep well.'

'Well, that's fine, Ma'am, we won't be adjusting the brightness at all, just routine checking of the fuses and wiring.'

She replies, 'Oh, that's good, it was so good of the council to put up a lower wattage bulb.'

All the while, I have installed our little camera, so small it is not visible from the ground, and with Pig occupied below, I pull up the app on my phone to check the image clarity and it's fine.

With an 'All finished up here', I start climbing down to where Pig is still chatting away to the nosey neighbour. I pull the ladder down and attach it back onto the roof of the van, whilst Pig says goodbye to his new friend and gathers up the barrier and warning signs.

On the way out of the suburb, and as we pass by the world-renowned Lone Pine Koala Sanctuary, we discuss the fact there is only one way in and out until you reach the Centenary Motorway, then you can go either east or west. We decide to put another camera up so we will know which way our suspect heads if we need to follow them with either a drone or in person. This time, no nosey neighbour as it is a busy intersection.

Job done. Time for a coffee. Now we just have to wait – something else we are pretty good at. In the meantime, our website was starting to work with a couple more enquiries for checking the digital security of some businesses' websites and confidential information. Five separate enquiries now look promising but means one of us would need to be away for a few days heading to Sydney, Melbourne and even Adelaide to meet these prospective clients. I've drawn the short straw, so I start putting together a travel plan for a southern sales trip, whilst Pig digs into the companies looking to employ us. I comment that it looks like I might have to sign him on full-time.

With the ongoing nature of the Campbell enquiry, I am not keen to head away just yet, so I offer to meet them in a couple of weeks, 'once our current assignment is complete'. Nothing much happens for the rest of the week as we do research into our new prospective clients down south.

12

Early evening that Thursday, I'm sitting down after cleaning away my dinner dishes – I had actually cooked myself (well, microwaved a meal) – when the front gate chime goes off. I look at the monitor and see it is Suzie. Well, that's unexpected; whilst we have called and texted each other a couple times since the Bridge to Brisbane. A surprise visit, that's exciting.

I let her knock before opening the door, and there she is, looking lovely, if not a little nervous. As I open the door, she smiles and raises the bottle of wine she is carrying and says, 'I fancied a drink but did not want to drink on my own. Care for a glass?'

I'm delighted to see her and lean in for a quick kiss and tell her 'hi'. A lovely surprise.

She smiles and says, 'Well, I enjoyed your company the other week, so I thought I–'

I take the bottle from her, put it down on a table, take her in my arms and kiss her. After a moment, she pulls away and gives me one of her delightful smiles, so I lean back in and kiss her again. Things get a bit fuzzy and frantic after that; needless to say, the wine remains unopened.

A little while later as we lie in bed, she asks, 'Is the way you greet all your female guests?'

I reply, 'Only the good-looking ones, or ones with cute butts.'

She smiles again, curls her fingers through my bushy chest hair and says, 'Is it so good you would rate it a ten or what?'

'Well, to go that high, I would need a closer inspection.' I pull her close again.

*

'Shit, it's after 8:00!' Suzie exclaims the next morning. 'I'll be late. Can I use your shower?' she asks, making a beeline for the ensuite.

'Sure,' I say.

She yells out, 'Can you do me a favour? Grab my keys and go down to my car – the red mini – and grab the overnight bag on the front seat.'

'Oh, so you came prepared, ah?' I say as I quickly get dressed, heading to the door.

'You bet, it was a test, you know – you either liked me or you didn't, and I am guessing you do, so… here I am!'

I head down to her mini, grab the bag, and at the same time slip a tracker underneath it. I head back up and quickly strip off and slip into the shower with her.

She squeals, and says, 'I will be late!'

As I kiss her and pull her to me, I tell her, 'You already are.'

'Mmm,' she says into my neck.

Not too long later, I've made coffee and put it into a takeaway cup and hand it to her at the door, where she pauses, and we kiss again.

She says, 'I think you need to ask me out on a date now, but I have to warn you I don't do sex on a first date.'

This kiss lingers, and I reply, 'Well, no sense bothering with a date then. I'll just wait for you to get sick of waiting like last night.'

She replies, 'Don't push your luck, buddy, and don't wait too long.'

'Okay,' I reply, and then tell her to use Old Cleveland Road which will give her a better run into the city than the motorways. Then, with one last kiss, she leaves. I watch her go trotting down the stairs and up the road to her car. As I've said, nice lady!

I fire up the laptop and access Brisbane traffic control, and whilst watching her progress on one screen, as she approaches each intersection, I trigger the light changes, so she hits a green each time, so she makes real quick time. After she arrives only a few minutes after 9:00, I text her and say, 'Is this soon enough?' and get a smiley face reply.

Over the weekend, I pluck up courage and phone Suzie and get her voicemail. I leave a message saying, 'Hi, call me back when you can.'

A couple of hours later, she calls back, and after pleasantries, I ask her if she is playing hard to get.

She laughs and says, 'No, I was shopping with my sister and her kids, so I did not want to answer all *those* questions from her if I had taken the call.'

'You're chicken, ah? Anyway, I was wondering if you would like to catch a movie or something next weekend?'

She replies, 'Sorry would like to but I'm playing in a netball competition next weekend, if we make the finals, it will go both days.'

I reply, 'Oh, maybe another time then. Who do you play for?'

She laughs and says, 'Not sure what you're implying by something, but yes, let's take a rain check.'

'I play for Valley 3rds. The comp is on at the Stafford courts.'

We agree to chat through the week again, and I hang up a little disappointed. But hey, I had not been dumped, so there is hope!

13

The following Tuesday afternoon, 'bing' goes an alarm on the computer, and we find our friend with the foreign IP is once again snooping around in Campbell's server. Whilst Pig monitors his progress, I access the live feed from the camera outside Bruce's home, and sure enough, there is an older Toyota Hilux ute parked in the drive. Not one we have seen there before. I back the feed up and see where Linda, Bruce's wife, leaves the house with her golf clubs around 1:30 p.m., and then just before 2:00 p.m. the ute arrives. By accessing the camera by the motorway, I see that the ute came into the suburb around 1:15 p.m., I suspect in time to see Linda leave, then left in another thirty minutes to make sure she doesn't come back unexpectedly. If she is a regular for golf Tuesday afternoon, whoever is in the house can expect a decent four-hour opportunity.

I watch two men get out of the ute and head to the front door, where the younger of the two uses a key to open the door. His companion is carrying a shoulder bag, not uncommon these days. I zoom the camera in so I can note the ute registration and then zoom in on the front door, ready for when they come out, and try to get close-ups of their faces.

Pig yells out they have again accessed the same folder, where we gave them a jolt last time, so we decide to do it again and see what happens. This time, they wait about ten minutes and then re-access the same folder. We let them in a little longer before jolting them again. Third time, they seem to have put a patch in as the jolt doesn't drop them out. No dummies, these blokes, we muse.

I enter the ute registration into our special database and it comes back saying the ute is owned by Randall Smythe of an address in Jindalee, an outer-western suburb. The name 'Smythe' is vaguely familiar, so I ask Pig, who says, 'Isn't Linda Bruce's second wife, and wasn't her surname Smythe?'

We go back and check our files, and sure enough, he's right. A little further digging, and we verify Randall is Linda's second son with her first husband, who she divorced twelve years ago, before marrying Bruce ten years ago. With Randall now twenty-four, he would have been twelve at the time of the divorce and highly likely lived here with Mum and Bruce through his teenage years. A little further checking, and we see Randall has had a few run-ins with the law, having been charged with driving under the influence, and for drug possession twice as well. He has a few thousand in his bank account, which is a bit surprising as there is no record of him working, with his occupation stated as 'Student'.

Around 3:00 p.m., Pig lets me know it looks like they are shutting down, so I get ready with the camera, and a few minutes later, they walk out the front door together, and I zoom in, getting good face shots of them both as they get into the Ute. Once they leave the driveway, I switch to the motorway camera and see them turn left towards Jindalee.

Pig lets me know. 'They stayed long enough in the Pleasure Plus folder to have copied everything. If it has any value, they are now likely going to try to sell it.'

I reply, 'It'll likely take a few days to understand the chemistry and tidy it up as a form of presentation.'

Pig nods his agreement then adds, 'Let's head over to Jindalee and check out Randall's address, see who else may be there and, well, see what we can find out.'

We jump in the Camry this time, Pig grabbing a drone on the way out, as you never know if it may be useful. We cruise past Randall's house in Tyrrell Road, a typical Queenslander, high-set, of a certain vintage, and see the ute is parked in the driveway with a couple of other cars parked outside on the road. Our dash cam has picked up the registration numbers of the cars as we went past, so we can check these later. Suspecting he has visitors, with a high probability one is his stalking mate, we decide to stop at the park a block over. Pig gets his drone out of the boot and walks into the park to make it more difficult for anyone to watch what he's doing.

Whilst these drones are pretty powerful, they are quite small and very quiet, making it next to impossible to see or hear them. He launches it, lets it circle a few times above the park to ensure there are no malfunctions, then heads it over the rooftops, controlling it from his iPad. He identifies Randall's address and lets it drift down to just above the roof top, having carefully checked the neighbouring houses to ensure no one was out on a balcony to see it. Once in position hovering above the roof, he activates the boom microphone to see what he can hear from inside, but whilst he can hear voices, they are indistinct, so he drops the drone down in the back yard behind a large shrub, and whilst the vision is only passable, he can hear what they are saying. He turns to me and gives a thumbs up. The conversation is automatically being recorded to our cloud database, so we can download it and listen later, but Pig is getting the gist of it now anyway, and I gather from his smiling, he is happy with what he's hearing.

As the conversation he has been listening to starts to wind up, with the visitor showing signs of getting ready to leave, we are caught between wanting to keep monitoring Randall and our need to know who his visitor is. We decide I will follow the visitor, leaving Pig here to continue to listen and learn. If need be, he will take an Uber home as it's now getting into the evening, and we will reconvene in the morning. As it turns out, the visitor jumps into an old Jeep Wrangler soft top and heads off with a roar. I follow from around the corner, and in no time, he has pulled into a townhouse complex in Toowong, driving into a garage, apparently home. I note the address and contemplate slipping a tracker under the jeep but decide it is too open and too many people around. I hope with the good photos from the camera and the address we will be able to dig up his name.

I scoot back to pick Pig up; he is still recording, so I leave him in peace and wait for him to finish, pack the drone up and come back to the car. He's pretty excited at what he has heard, saying they were talking about contacting a Russ Watt to suss out what the new formula for Pleasure Plus might be worth, and it sounded as if they had dealt with this bloke previously. So I drop him off at his home in West End and decide to grab a Thai takeaway from his favourite Thai restaurant down the road before heading home to eat it, knowing full well I won't get around to cooking tonight.

Once home, and Thai takeout consumed, I log in and do a search of the address in Toowong to see who comes up as tenant or owner. The name 'Michael Sinclair' pops up as tenant. I then cross reference the registration number of the Jeep, and sure enough, it's Michael Sinclair. I then access his driver's licence details, check the photo – yep, same long bushy hair, quite the surfer look going on, and just a couple of years older than Randal.

Likely uni buddies, I muse.

Further digging shows he too has been charged with drug offences, in fact, once at the same time as Randall, a couple of years ago. This is all coming together pretty quickly and nicely, so even though it's getting late, I press on, now entering Russ Watt into our database to see what pops up. No drugs or anything like that, but we have an address for one Russ Watt in Castledine on the north side of Brisbane. He is listed as a company director, so I log onto ACIS, enter his name and a list of companies to which he is associated pops up. *He's a busy boy*, I think, going through them one by one, checking their websites out as I go. Most seem to be small businesses, but one piques my interest: Watts Consulting, with an office at nearby Aspley. The website blurb is more in line with sourcing information to enable you to 'better your competitors' than any of the usual management theories.

By now I am restless and wired, knowing that it's a good thing to keep momentum going, and also with the expectation that Randall and Michael are likely to contact Russ any day. I grab the keys to the van and head off to Aspley to check out the office there – yes, with an ulterior motive.

The office of Watts Consulting is in a side street just off Albany Creek Road, in a block of four shops and offices. A long way from salubrious, but not really dingy either. I circle the block, but nothing is moving, it being 11:30 at night now. I park in a nearby Macca's and walk back around the corner, checking for CCTV cameras as I go. I drift down the driveway at the side of the building; all the shops and offices are closed up and no lights on. I can always claim I need a piss if anyone should query what I am doing.

I count the back doors along to the third one, which whilst it has no name on it, is the back entrance to Watts Consulting. I check the door and back window, looking for any sign of an alarm system, seeing nothing. I check and see the lock is a straightforward Lockwood, and I pull out my special key, turn it a couple of times and the door pops open. Not wanting any light to show, I pull out my little penlight with the hooded cap which ensures the beam always goes downward, making it difficult to see from a distance. I check for an alarm pad, but there isn't one near either the front or back door.

There is only one office, with the rest of the space open plan, with a receptionist desk and a portioned back room used for storage and as a lunchroom. I don't have time or inclination to search the office, but I put a phone tap under the desk phone and also a combination bug of camera and microphone in one in the wall power points, so we will be able to see anyone who visits. I also check the receptionist desk phone for speed dials, and sure enough, there is one for Russ, so I take a quick photo of these numbers. Knowing his phone number will mean we can access his call log and even track him if need be.

Once done, I ease back out the back door, ensuring it is locked behind me, and stroll back to the road. In and out in three minutes. Job well done. I treat myself to a soft serve ice cream from Macca's for the drive home.

*

Next morning, Pig arrives early just after 7:00 a.m., and I am still recovering from my run, having slept a little late after my late-night prowl. So whilst I eat breakfast, with Pig helping himself as well, I recount my exploits of the night before, detailing Michael Sinclair and how that led me to Russ Watt. We are now confident we have the main players identified, just need them to all connect, and ideally find out who Russ Watt then approaches to sell the Campbell secrets.

Pig logs into Telstra's database and inputs Russ's mobile, but nothing comes up, so he tries Optus, the second largest network, and sure enough, he gets a hit. He then accesses the call log and prints these all out. We realise we don't have phone numbers for either Randall or Michael, which is a bit of an oops on our part, so we go back into both Telstra and Optus and find them both on the Telstra network.

Now we do have their phone numbers and cross reference them to see if either has contacted Russ yet. It doesn't look like it, so I access the bugs in Watt Consulting's office, but all is quiet there – obviously late starters. Back to waiting again, we spend the time discussing how to approach Bruce, considering it looks like his stepson is in the thick of things. Bruce had not mentioned any issues with his family, but then I had not specifically asked either. We decide to tell him someone has gone for the bait, without identifying who, so I send a text to Bruce on his throwaway phone asking for a meeting. A little while later he gives me a call, sounding both a little excited but also apprehensive, and I tell him we need a quick catch up. We agree to meet around 11:00 a.m. this morning at the Coffee Club at Forest Lake, not too far from his factory in Wacol.

This time, I take Pig with me to the meeting, and we arrive before Bruce so Pig can check to see if anyone follows Bruce into the car park. Eventually Pig joins us, giving me a small shake of the head. I introduce Pig to Bruce as they had not met, explaining that he's part of my team on his assignment.

Making it sound as though there are more on the team doesn't hurt, I think.

I explain to Bruce that we have a suspect we are following, waiting to be certain before we reveal who, as it would be wrong to tell him until we have solid proof. Grudgingly, he accepts this, and we explain we believe we have also identified the middleman and hope he may lead to one of their competitors who is interested in buying the formula for the enhanced Pleasure Plus Cream. Bruce wants to know how much longer we think it will be, as he says it is wearing him down, the uncertainty around his close colleagues. Of course we can't reassure him they are all likely to be in the clear as that would probably reveal where our investigation is headed. He is, of course, still apprehensive about the outcome, and once he leaves to head back to the factory, Pig and I decide to stay and have some lunch. We mull over what to do with the two boys, knowing no charges will be brought against them, and also how we might give Russ Watt a warning, maybe even a little scare.

Back at the office, we listen to the few conversations emanating from Watt Consulting, and it's obvious Russ hasn't been in the office today, so far at least. Of course, we have no idea if he works out of any of the other businesses he is associated with. Pulling up the phone logs for all three – Randall, Michael, and Russ – shows three calls between Randall and Michael, which is not unexpected, but no contact with Russ yet. We are confident this is going to happen sooner than later and debate how we can get bugs into their phones or cars. It's not easy to separate anyone from their phone these days. So we wait, and get on with preliminary work for our new prospects.

*

A couple of days pass, and we notice a call from Michael to Russ. Of course, we can't hear what has been said, but we can track their movements by the GPS in their phones – not as reliable as the trackers we put on cars (and people, when need be). Later that day, Russ actually visits his office, and as we hear him talking to his receptionist, he asks her to type up a report on a new formula for his client, so clearly he has already met with Michael or Randall, or both. Having missed this initial meeting, we have to ensure we are all over the follow-up meeting, at which it sounds like they will read through Russ's formula letter, so we decide we need to put trackers and bugs in all their cars.

Randall's should be easy – it's left in the driveway at his Jindalee address – but not so much for Michael's as his is locked away in this garage at night, and we have yet to find a vehicle Russ drives, as it must be registered in one of his many companies.

Pig has a thought. 'Well, the two of them are students, so surely they leave them at the campus car park when at university.'

We take one each with a plan to follow them and affix a bug and tracker to their cars tomorrow. I take Randall and am in the van parked around the corner from his home in Jindalee early the next morning. Of course, I need not have worried about getting there early as he did not head off until after 10:00 a.m. First stop is a café at the servo at Darra on his way to the Nathan campus of Griffith Uni, parking in the student's car park and wandering off to class, I assume.

Being a little old to blend in, I decide to don a hi-vis vest, grab a clipboard, and start walking through the car park. As I go, I bend down and check and record registration numbers of cars in the car park, thus, making me look like a car park inspector. A couple of guys watch me for a few minutes, then jump back in their cars and take off. Clearly, they weren't authorised to park here. I eventually get to Randall's ute and slip the tracker under the rear bumper. The bug is a little harder, but with no one around, I use my little ceramic window opener gadget to open the driver's door and slide the bug onto the topside of the sun visor – it's the same dullish grey so it would only be noticed by someone already suspicious, and even then, they wouldn't really know what it was.

I continue my circuit of the car park, not wanting to head straight off after fixing Randall's ute. Once I leave, I text Pig to let him know I'm done. I decide to check the bug at Watt Consulting's office to see if Russ is there, and – bonus – he is, so I head straight over to Aspley and slowly drive into the rear car park where I see a white Land Rover Discovery parked behind their office. With no one around and knowing there is no CCTV covering the car park, I quickly slip a tracker under the front bumper, and I then test the driver's door, finding it unlocked. Opening it, I slip a bug onto his sun visor, quickly shutting the door again. I slip back into the Camry just as another car comes up the driveway, the driver giving me a quizzical look as we pass each other. I head back to the office to await further developments.

Later that day, we get the call we have been waiting for. Russ is calling Michael from his office, and when Michael answers, they set up a meet for tomorrow at 10:00 a.m. at Alcove Cafe in Windsor, a small trendy suburb on the north side of Brisbane. Pig and I grab another coffee and sit down at our planning board to make plans to monitor the meet between Russ, Michael and, we assume, Randall. We quickly realise there is no sense planning anything without checking the place out, so off we go to do just that. We head over to Windsor, a twenty-minute drive at this time of day, and we arrive just as the lunch crowd is finishing up, so we easily get a table and decide on lunch, grabbing a wrap to go with our coffees.

We sit outside and look around, taking in the structure and surrounds, trying to decide how we could wire it so we hear the conversation no matter where they sit. We decide inside won't be a problem as the décor is a rustic style with old memorabilia lining the walls, so whilst waiting for our wraps, we both get up, going in different directions and inspecting the old photos, and placing a few mics strategically around the room. We finish just as they serve our wraps, so a good and easy job done; if we can park the van anywhere within 200 metres, we will hear them easily.

The outside is a different proposition, with constant traffic going past, making it pretty difficult to be able to hear much of what is said. Of course, they will have the same problem being heard, so hopefully they will decide to sit inside. If not, we are going to try our best using a boom mic camouflaged and hidden in one or two palms growing in oversized pots adorning the footpath. This will need to be set up after dark, and we decide Pig will set this up tonight. We enjoy our lunch and head back to the office.

*

Needing to ensure we can park the van close to the café, we arrive just after 9:30 a.m. the next morning. We position the van just around the corner and decide we could actually use a boom mic from the van if they sit outside on the side road. Pig is happy he has two other boom mics installed in the palm pots; he has actually attached them to the palms, making them almost invisible, so if he's happy they will do the job, that's good enough for me. I will sit in the café and Pig will stay out of sight in the back of the van to ensure we are getting the audio we need; I will have an earplug so he can keep me abreast as the meeting proceeds.

First to arrive is Russ, pulling up in his Discovery. This is the first time I've seen him in person; he's a middle-aged man, rather obese, with thinning hair, and frankly, rather scruffily dressed. Not my idea of a Management Consultant. Next, the two boys turn up together, getting out of Michael's Jeep, which had noisily arrived a few minutes ago, parking up the road. We are in luck, as Russ has taken a seat inside in the back corner, and one of our mics is directly above their table. I let Pig know to focus on mic 3, and I am a little bummed I won't be hearing what they talk about, but I stay, enjoying two cups of coffee and reading the *Courier Mail*, Brisbane's morning daily newspaper paper, whilst their meeting goes on.

So as to not draw attention by staying too long, I pay for my coffees and walk off down the road and sit down at a bus stop to await the all-clear from Pig. The meeting takes quite a while, and I am getting intrigued as to what they can be talking about, when finally Pig pulls up in the van and I jump in.

'Well,' I ask, as Pig grins and takes his time merging into the traffic.

'Well, we nailed it,' he says. 'It turns out Michael is a chemistry student, so he can decipher the formula, and Russ has contacts "always interested" in new formulas. They plan on asking $200k for this one, and it sounds like that's what they have got for the two previous formulas they have stolen. Russ hasn't come out and said who he will offer it to, but odds are it will be the same mob as last time – McAllister, I think Bruce said, who came out and pipped them. Of course, once they analyse the formula, they will realise they have been duped, but the money will have changed hands by then.'

On the drive back to the office, Pig offers to go back tonight to collect all the mics from the café. Knowing Bruce is going to be pretty upset with who is behind the scheme, we discuss ways to bring it to a head without destroying his family. We decide wiser heads are called for, and I call Colonel Richards and tell him Pig and I would like to catch up and have a conversation. He readily agrees to meet us the day after tomorrow, a Thursday at the Coffee Club next to Ikea on the southside. In preparation for our meeting with the Colonel, we compile a full report, documenting everything we have found out. This is a full and frank account, not hiding any facts, no feelings to be spared, and includes photos of the meetings and transcripts of the audio of the various phone calls and meetings we have recorded. It is a comprehensive and damning report.

The Colonel wouldn't expect anything less.

*

At the agreed time we arrive, this time choosing to sit outside, as it is a far quieter location and it's a pleasantly warm but not hot day. After the pleasantries are out of the way, which take a bit longer than expected as the Colonel was very keen to hear how Pig was getting on. Yes, he calls him Pig as well – Pig was, after all, a bit of a legend in our battalion. We get down to business, and I give the

Colonel the brief overview, i.e., we have identified Bruce's stepson and his friend as the source of the formula theft, and who they are selling through, so we want his input as to how we tell Bruce this. The Colonel listens intently, not interrupting, but then firing off the questions once we had completed our joint narrative; then he flicks through the report, commenting on the details.

He's quiet for a little while as he considers options; then he asks, 'How do you suggest you finalise this?'

This is something Pig and I have discussed at length but did not want to throw up without a wiser head.

I respond, 'Well, we can't see how we cannot tell Bruce it's his stepson; he may not like it, but he has to know he can trust his staff implicitly. We aren't aware how the stepson/father dynamic works here. I'm guessing Randall resents Bruce for some reason; maybe he doesn't get a big enough allowance or something, but Bruce has to know.

'As for the other two, well, we reckon we can easily scare Michael off, won't be too hard; actually, we think we should also give Randall a pretty big scare just to reinforce whatever Bruce does to him. Meet him one night and put the bejeebers up him. Michael gets to be hurt though; he has to learn a lesson. Russ is just a sleazy businessman, so we can get to him another way, and he will burn bridges when McAllister pays him good money for a dud formula anyway, but again, maybe a night visit for him as well. Might put something up on Facebook or LinkedIn about his dubious business practices, but I still like the idea of scaring the shit out of him.'

Pig and I were good soldiers – bloody good soldiers in fact – so we will quite enjoy putting the fear of god into these three. The Colonel agrees this is a good outcome and suggests we add it to the report as a recommended outcome, maybe not mentioning the scaring of Randall – we just do that after the dust settles. With that agreed, I text Bruce on his prepaid and let him know we have an outcome, so we need to meet so we can submit our report. He is pretty keen, so we agree on 10:30 a.m. the next morning, again at the Coffee Club at Forest Lake. I tell him I will be inviting the Colonel along, which seems to surprise him.

That night, I call Suzie to say hi, and as neither of us had got around to starting dinner, on the spur of the moment, we agree to meet at the Norman Hotel (an iconic Brisbane Pub renowned for its steaks) for a quick dinner. I quickly shower and change and am out the door. Can't believe how keen I am to see her!

I beat her, but only by five minutes, and she greets me with a lovely smile and quick kiss, dressed again in one of the light summery dresses she seems to favour (and which I am in favour of). We order our steaks, (you don't consider anything else at the Norman – they advertise themselves as 'The Worst Vegetarian Restaurant in Brisbane'), and she has a glass of chardonnay to my XXXX Gold, the local iconic beer. We just chat for a while, talking about our weeks, nothing too serious, but then, she asks the question.

'Exactly what did you do for the Army?'

I take my time preparing my reply, although I have thought a lot about how to answer this question, knowing it was going to be important to be honest, but I also limit what I say due to the Official Secrets Act.

'As you know, I was in for fifteen years, so naturally, I did a lot of different things. In the early days, I was taught a good deal about the basic trades – mechanics, welding, electrical, etc. – so I can turn my hand to most of these things. These actually came in handy in ways you wouldn't expect in the later years. Then I was sent on an electronic surveillance course with computer programming, and I found this almost second nature.

'Another thing that stood out early on was that I am an excellent marksman. Didn't know that going in – I had never fired a gun – but it's just natural to me. Eventually, I was invited to try out for a sniper course. That's where I first met Pig; he was on the same course. I excelled, one of the highest scores on record, so that got someone's attention as I now had two good skills the Army wanted me for: sniper and digital communication and hacking.

'I was transferred to a new group called Group111, and I went through some very difficult and severe training. But I survived and came out the other end a new man and was accepted into Group111. A couple of months later, Pig also earnt entry. So Group111 worked closely with LEWTs – the "Light Electronic Warfare Team". We were trained to infiltrate enemy lines, and one of the reasons why Pig and I both did well was our swarthy skin and dark hair, making it easier for us to blend in, as long as we kept our mouths shut.

'Group111 became life for the next eight years – the last five or so, I spent more time behind enemy lines than not. Pig and I teamed up early on and thereafter worked as a two-man team and had a lot of success, destroying targets and putting our sniping skills to good use.

'I can't say too much more about those days, as I am forbidden by the Official Secrets Act, but I will say I have a lot of medals in my drawer that I am proud of. In fact, I am not really meant to tell you this either, but you might find it in my drawer one day and wonder – but Pig and I were both awarded the Presidential Medal of Freedom – awarded by the US President in person, no less. Not many of these are awarded to foreigners, so pretty proud of this, but also it was awarded in secret, because what we did isn't recorded in history.'

Suzie has been taking this all in without a word, and then the next big question comes. 'Okay, so have you killed people?'

I take her hands in mine and look at her and say, 'Yes I have, but only in battle and only soldiers or militia, never any civilians. Suzie, in war, it's kill or be killed, it really is, so I am comfortable with what I achieved; in a very small way, I helped some very poor and hardworking people, which essentially includes all Afghanis, get a better life. So, I sleep at night, without nightmares about what I did. I don't brag, but I – we – were very good at doing what we did. I hope that makes sense to you. I have never had to explain it before, so keep asking questions – I will answer if I can.'

She leans in and kisses me, so I guess I have passed that test.

Our dinners arrive then, so no more questions, but after we finish and order another drink, she asks, 'So you and Julien clearly have very strong ties – how come?'

Of course, it is another question that had to come. Is it too early to tell her the full story, or just the short version? No, the full story, I decide. 'Us Army types are superstitious; once you have a seat in the Bushmaster or Troop Carrier, we always sit in the same seat. No question. Except this day, Pig was being a shit-stirrer and took my seat for our daily patrol. No amount of wrangling would get him to move, and finally I gave up and took his seat.

'Then about halfway through the patrol, when we were furthest from support, we hit an IED and the explosion tipped us over; then of course, we came under fire when we tried to escape out of the Bushie. We had a fire fight on our hands, and Pig with his leg trapped on the underside of the truck. Jordie – one of our platoon – and I managed to squeeze out by kicking out the rear window, and were able to take on the hostiles until they turned and hightailed it.

'Only then were we able to carefully get Pig out, and only by causing him extreme pain – even the morphine injection didn't help him much.

'We had radioed in for an evac chopper, but they wouldn't come in until we had cleared the ground, which meant we had to clear 500 metres in each direction. Then the medics flew in and took him away. He had lost a lot of blood, and they eventually decided to amputate his leg above the knee. One of the others in the platoon also was hit – not seriously – and evacuated with him. Of course, we were all evacuated a little later, after we had destroyed the Bushie – can't leave anything behind for those bastards.

'After they stabilised Pig, he was flown to the American Forces Hospital in Germany for quite a few weeks, until he flew home – to continue his treatment and get a medical discharge, of course.

'His partner, George, has never forgiven me, claiming it should have been me that was injured, which, of course, I understand, but he of all people knows how stubborn Pig can be.

'So, after all Pig and I went through together, this could have destroyed our friendship, but it only seemed to make it stronger. There's nothing in the world I won't do for Pig, not only because of this – I don't really feel guilty about it, he chose to sit there – but he has saved our hides so many times it's hard to remember them all. And, if I'm honest, vice versa, as he will say exactly the same. So our bond is far stronger than being kin; it is a true "blood" relationship,' I finish with a wry smile.

She takes all this in, nodding, and says, 'He is such a nice bloke as well. It is a little strange with you being straight and Julien gay, considering how close you are.'

I nod and say, 'He and George have been partners longer than I've known him. They are such totally different people; as they say, opposites attract, I guess. Pig took a lot of flak in his early years in the Army, when being gay was largely frowned upon and resented by many of our colleagues. Pig used to get in many a scrap, but he can take care of himself, so he usually came out better than his opponent, although he was ambushed in camp one night by four guys who gave him a right beating. They officially never found out who they were, but Pig knew and each of them suffered eventually; he has a long memory and is happy to play a long game. His early record was full of disciplinary notes, and this held him back from promotion, which personally, I am happy about, as we would never have been teamed up if he was higher than private in those early years.'

'So what rank were you then?' Suzie asks.

'Sergeant, we both did. Whilst I was invited on a few occasions to apply for officer school, I had no interest in going that route. I thoroughly enjoyed doing what we were doing, and if I became an officer, I would not have been able to continue doing those assignments. Besides, this suited my skill set better as well as my temperament.'

All of a sudden, they're giving us the hint – they want us to leave. The evening has flown, so we make our departure and I walk Suzie to her Mini, where we have a nice leisurely kiss before she hops in and drives away, and I wander back to the Camry.

14

Next morning, Pig and I arrive a little early as always, so Pig can ensure Bruce is free of a tail. He also sees the Colonel arrive, letting me know he's driving a Volvo.

'He just needs the hat now,' he tells me though the earpiece, having a laugh.

I've taken a corner table, and ask the waitress to put 'reserved' on a couple of adjoining tables so we aren't disturbed or so people aren't close enough to overhear; she's happy to do this when I say there will be a nice tip on the table when we are finished.

Once Bruce and the Colonel are seated and our coffees served, I get straight to the point. Having earmarked the necessary pages in the report to back up my various statements, I tell Bruce his problem is not with any of his staff. The relief is obvious, but it then hits him.

He says, 'Hold on, if not any of the staff, who is it?'

'Your stepson Randall, and a friend of his, Michael Sinclair.'

At this, his shoulders slump and he mutters, 'Shit.'

I let him digest this, and he soon comes back, looking straight at me, and says, 'How?'

I show him the photo of them both leaving his home – the photo is dated and time stamped – and then show him the photo we had taken of them opening the Pleasure Plus folder a short time earlier. I give him a summary of what he could read later in our report, and I ask him what sort of relationship he and his wife have with Randall.

He replies, 'Randy got in with the wrong crowd in his last year at Brisbane Boys'. They just weren't interested in their schoolwork, most from affluent families, so they didn't see the need to work, just play and party hard. I have always worked hard, and Linda respected that and expected her boys to be the same. Her eldest son is now a doctor, and she is rightfully very proud of him, so Randy had high expectations on him. But first year at university, and he's busted for drugs, coming home all hours high, strung out. We couldn't cope with it, so we ordered him out of the house. I still pay his rent, for Christ's sake, and this is the thanks I get for it.'

'Do you know Michael Sinclair?' I ask.

'Yes,' he replies, 'they have been thick as thieves since that first year at university.'

'What about a Russ Watt?' I ask, 'Or Watt Consulting?'

'No,' Bruce replies, 'never heard of them, who is he?'

'He's the middleman organising the sale of the formula.'

After a lengthy pause, as Bruce digested the news, he says, 'Shit, this is going to break Linda's heart. Whilst Randy has been difficult, she still loves him. I don't know how I am going to tell her.'

My turn to be silent, and I look to the Colonel, who gives me a slight nod, guessing what I am about to suggest. 'Well, Bruce, if you prefer us to handle it, I think you can get the same outcome without having to tell Linda.'

He looks my way, raising an eyebrow, so I continue, 'Pig and I are – were – very good soldiers. We know how to frighten people, and worse. If you would like, we will meet Randy somewhere he is not expecting anything and give him a little talking to. At the same time, you need to change the locks on your house and ensure he no longer has access. You'll have to tell Linda something so she doesn't turn around and give him another set. I would also have an alarm installed, with CCTV cameras so you can see if he is loitering around. Personally, I would stop paying his rent as well, make him grow up.'

Bruce takes his time digesting this, then asks, 'So what would you do to him? Would you hurt him?'

'Not physically,' I reply, 'but he will be looking over his shoulder for a while, maybe even staying awake at night for a while.'

'What about Mike then?'

'Don't you worry about Michael,' I say. 'We will give him a lesson he won't forget. Likewise, Russ Watt will learn the hard way he needs to keep his nose clean.'

Bruce is clearly distressed by the conversation and asks if he can have a few minutes alone, so we all get up to go for a walk, but he asks the Colonel to stay. Pig and I wander off into the shopping centre, find a quiet corner and discuss the meeting, although neither of us has much to say.

After fifteen to twenty minutes, I get a text asking if we can come back.

We walk back to the table, and it's clear Bruce has been crying although he is trying hard not to show it. We sit back down, and the Colonel tells us, 'Bruce would like you to carry out your recommendations and stresses he doesn't want Randy hurt physically. The other two, he doesn't care less about.'

I nod and look to Bruce for confirmation. He looks me in the eye and nods.

'Good, that's all good, Bruce. You won't hear from me again, except for my final invoice,' I add with a slight smile, 'but I would also suggest your IT setup could do with a good security improvement. In fact, I also think you should come clean with all your team – tell them you have solved the leak problem, and set up a more rigorous security process to stop any third parties or hackers gaining access in the future.' I smile and say, 'This is one of our specialties – accessing IT systems and identifying weaknesses – happy to give you a quote.'

The Colonel grumbles, 'Geez, he's only been on Civvy Street five minutes and he's already a spiff.'

We shake hands all round, and Pig and I take our leave. As we head back to the office, we discuss how best to approach the next stage, meting out the punishment.

*

To try and work out how to give Michael Sinclair his 'warning', I've taken to monitoring his movements, normally checking on him randomly from early morning and late at night. After a few early mornings, I find he is a bike rider, heading out around 6:00 a.m. and getting back around 7:00 a.m. Monday, Wednesday, and Friday, and this gets me thinking.

I suggest to Pig, 'Bike riders are always riding into car doors, so we could stage it so it looks like an accident, maybe just around the corner from his home. We could then tell him why he ran into the door, whilst he is lying on the ground in pain – that's if he is not dead, of course.'

Pig likes this course of action and volunteers to be the driver, so we set about tracking his bike route and where we can plan his ambush. At the same time, we're still monitoring Russ Watt's office phone and his car, but it's clear we need access to his mobile, as he must have more than one car because we aren't getting anything from either the office or his car. Well, we are getting plenty of other shady type deals he seems to be into, but not anything to do with Campbells. But what we are hearing sets up our next plan for him.

In one conversation we hear from his car, he is helping a major concrete company to manipulate the market to bring down a long-standing, small, privately owned concrete company 'HardAs Crete'.

He has his staff ringing and booking dummy orders with HardAs, so when they come to deliver, there is no order, at the same time pushing down the prices and giving away cartons of beer with each order of concrete.

With what we have recorded, we decide to approach the owner of HardAs, knowing we can't take what we have to the authorities. Peter Wilson, the owner, is not surprised with our little story, saying the major companies seem to take it in turn to try and squeeze him out and have been for years. His loyal customer base has seen them off so far. We play part of the audio and ask if he recognises the other voice.

'Yeah, that's Martin Bateman from QuarryMix.'

Pig and I exchange a glance, and I say to Peter, 'What is the best thing that could come to you from this – you looking to sell?'

'Why?' he asks.

'Well, you can get your own back with this. You send a formal letter, maybe even a lawyer's letter, to QuarryMix and Bateman with a copy of this audio and tell them a copy of it plus transcripts will be posted to the Australian Competition and Consumer Commission along with a complete record of every other tactic they have employed over the years unless you have a signed and watertight sale contract within fourteen days. They will shit themselves, and likely, you will get a fair price; they clearly want your business, but just don't want to pay.'

He asks if we can leave a copy of the transcripts and audio, which we do – there's nothing tying these back to us – and he says he will talk it over with his wife and take it from here. Fine by us.

Pig and I decide on next Wednesday morning to do the hit on Michael, just after he leaves home as it will be quieter on the roads than an hour later. We have planned it for one of the back streets he rides down as he leaves his townhouse. Pig parks the van, with me set up in the Camry back on the previous intersection, so I can see him as he comes down the road before turning and passing Pig. We have timed this for a couple of mornings, hiring different cars, so as not to stand out, and it works out that 90 seconds after he turns the corner, will see him at the contact point.

'You're on,' I say into the phone so Pig can start the stopwatch.

I watch it and Michael approaching in his rear vision mirror. *BANG!* It works – Pig opens the door a fraction before Michael rides into it – timing couldn't be better. He's sprawled on the ground, writhing in pain. Pig jumps out and asks if he's okay.

Pig takes his helmet off, makes sure Michael is conscious and then tells him very clearly, 'We know what you and Randy did, and if you ever do it again, this will seem like a pinprick. Understand?'

With no one else around and with Pig holding his Lycra top pulled extra tight, and the fierce look Pig is giving him, he lets out a moan and nods his head, acknowledging message received.

We can't just leave him there – it is our van, after all – and by now, I have joined them, asking as I arrive if I need to stamp on his hand as a reminder. Sinclair whimpers at my suggestion.

Pig says, 'No, message received,' so we call an ambulance as others come out of their homes to see what has happened.

They take him off to the hospital with a suspected broken arm, and maybe shoulder blade, but he will live.

Of course, Pig has to give a statement when the police finally arrive, but he was just a delivery driver going about his morning deliveries. We had a docket for a delivery to the house he was parked outside as proof – made up in the office but looks legit.

One down, two to go.

The punishment for Randy is going to be a little tougher. But having spoken to Bruce a few days after our meeting, he tells me he has told Linda the full story – didn't want to keep such a secret from her. She has readily agreed to change the locks and Randy has been told he is no longer welcome there. He admits he still is paying the rent, not wanting to make the situation worse. So, Pig and I decide to tone down what we do to Randy. Late the next Saturday night finds us in some noisy Fortitude Valley bar, and when Randy heads to the bathroom we follow him. Whilst he is relieving himself at the urinal, we come up behind him, grab his head and force it down into the urinal for a moment, until he is choking and gagging. We pull his head up and tell him we will be back if he tries anything against Bruce or Campbells again in the future. Message delivered – and we disappear into the night.

15

Having decided to have Friday off, I head up to see the old man, stay overnight and come home Saturday before flying to Sydney Sunday afternoon. Another enquiry has come in over the weekend from another company in Sydney, so I decide I will go see them whilst I am down there, likely making the trip the full week.

Once I get settled at the airport (no lounge for me now – I am no longer Department of Defence), I decide to give Suzie a call. Since our impromptu dinner, we have texted each other a couple of times.

She answers, 'Hello, stranger,' which is a relief and makes the conversation a lot easier. I soon relax as we chat.

I let her know I'm heading interstate for the week, and she seems quite interested in the sorts of clients we are attracting. Then, as they call my flight, I suggest getting together again and she seems keen – she even suggests a movie she wants to see – so we lock in a weeknight the following week as she has the netball competition this coming weekend.

I can't believe how excited I feel. Damn, it feels nice.

*

Monday morning sees me dressed to impress in Sydney where our first prospect is a small biomedical company, Ryde Biomedical, who, like Campbells, suspects someone is stealing their work. The meeting is with their CEO and founder Ivan Petroski in their small office/laboratory in Ryde.

It soon becomes clear they already suspect their senior lab technician who seems to be living above her means. Lydia Small has been with them for five years, during which time she has had an ugly divorce and now seems to be content to float along, taking her pay slip each week without really earning it, but seemingly spending quite freely.

I offer to do a quick audit of her logins, bank account, etc. for a set fee, taking pity on Ivan, who is clearly committed to inventing some new gadget which sounds too technical for me, but which he assures me will be a 'game changer' for everyone with heart disease if he ever gets it to work properly. We sign an agreement, I take all the relevant details down on my tablet, and I tell Ivan we will have an answer for him within two weeks. Out of the meeting, I email Pig with Lydia's details and login details for their intranet and let him do his thing.

My second appointment in Sydney is with Paramount Wireless, one of the smaller phone companies, rather aggressive in the market. *They have to be,* I ponder, *considering their size compared to the two or three majors.* I google their CEO with whom I am meeting, who seems to be pretty well connected.

At 2:00 p.m. sharp, I am sitting waiting in their reception, fancy offices in North Sydney, directly across the harbour from the CBD. The receptionist, who introduces herself as Christina, a South American beauty, escorts me into the boardroom to meet Cameron Carmichael, CEO, and also their CFO Margaret Wyatt – both forty-ish, smartly dressed in suits, making my best rather shabby in comparison.

Cameron gets right to the point and states they suspect someone is selling secrets, as their competitors always seem to know what they are going to do before they do.

I ask a few questions, seeking more details, like 'How do you know?' and 'Who do you suspect?' and it's clear he has little idea, using the tone, 'Well, that's why we are talking to you.'

'Okay,' I say, 'who is privy to your plans?'

He details himself, Margaret, the board, and senior management, and concedes some of their assistants may also be aware, after I push him on the point.

Not taking to Cameron and his arrogant attitude, I add fifty per cent onto the price I had in mind before discussing likely fees. Naturally, our fee gets the expected reaction, to which I reply, 'Well, you are welcome to use anyone you choose, but the old maxim certainly applies here: you get what you pay for.'

He reluctantly agrees to the fee. I agree to a split fee of fifty per cent up front, balance on success, and we shake on the deal. He immediately ups and leaves, telling me Margaret will provide all the details I will need.

Margaret, who has been taking notes the whole time, comes out of her shell somewhat once Cameron has left, asking what information I will need. I tell her I need the names and addresses for all suspects – yes, including her and the board – along with their respective positions and salaries, including any bonuses, and tell her we will take it from there.

As we are saying goodbye, I comment, 'He must be a pleasure to work for.'

She smiles and says, 'Yes, he has his moments.'

Once back at the hotel, I do up the invoice and send it to them both, confirming we will start once it has been paid. Marg (as she asked me to call her) replies a short while later with a copy of the remittance and the listing of staff as requested.

More digging for Pig, and I tell him he should be as happy as a pig in shit.

He also thanks me for the bonus I had paid him from the successful conclusion of the Campbell assignment – 'much more than I was expecting' he says.

Well, two out of two, hitting above my average at the moment!

Of course, this is the wrong thing to be thinking as my average crashes immediately at the third prospect, there being no way they would be willing to pay our fee. Whilst they were only looking for an audit of the security of their website and intranet, the price they wanted to pay did not warrant the effort we would go to.

Strike one.

Next morning, off to Adelaide, for a meeting in the afternoon. The prospect is SA Tech Inc., a technology supplier to the oil and gas majors. It had been recently hacked, so they want to prove their new security measures will stand up. It is soon apparent at the meeting with their CEO, Fergus Monahan, and IT manager, Sunil Patel, whilst the CEO wants the audit, the IT manager is quite smug and confident it isn't needed, so I give them a ball park cost and leave them to it. Being a bit of a shit stirrer, that night I hack, sorry – access – their server and change the IT manager's password.

At 9:30 a.m. the next morning, I send a text from a prepaid phone I keep for just such occasions (so the text can't be proven to have come from me) to the CEO, reading, 'Sunil's new password is letap$120320. I fly out at midday if you want to reconvene.'

Sure enough, I get a call within ten minutes asking if I can go back to their office. It is obvious Sunil is very upset and embarrassed by my little prank, but even more so, horrified that I so easily was able to access their server. We agree on terms, and I head home with three agreements. *Not a bad week's work,* I think.

16

The Thursday I'm interstate, and Pig is gearing up for his intrusion into the police garage. Once again, he parks down the road, accesses his pole, and launches the little drone. This time, the booth is manned, so he hovers the drone over in the far corner, watching, and sure enough, around 6:15 p.m., the guard is closing up for the night. Pig lands the drone inside the garage in the back corner, as it will be easier for him to pick it up and not have to wait for it to come back to him on the pole. Whilst he is up there, he installs a little receiver module, so that all the mics he installs will automatically download their recordings each time they are within 500 metres of the pole. Then we can access each recording at our leisure from our cloud-based server.

Once he has the ladder back on the van, he jumps in and takes it around the corner, out of sight, and changes to a green hi-vis vest so no one will make the connection between the lineman up the pole in a yellow vest and the bloke wandering into the garage, clipboard in hand. Making sure he's alone, he scoops up the drone, putting it into his shoulder bag, then heads over to the SC cars. The first one he tries is the old Falcon we know DI Lancaster drives. He has left it unlocked, so Pig quickly pops the air conditioner vent out and places a mic inside the vent, pops it back into place and then slips a tracker under the front bumper. One down.

The Santa Fe driven by DS Fleming is parked next to the falcon, and as this is locked, it takes a couple of minutes longer; and so it goes on, until he has covered all five cars he can find. The trackers we are using are 5G enabled so we can track these in real time. He has already paired the mics to the trackers, enabling us to have live coverage of any conversations any of them have in their cars, including phone calls. These are all recorded and stored in our cloud-based databank as well.

Job done, Pig exits the garage, whistling away like the happy chappie he can be. Once in the van, he texts me to tell me we are live. He then sits back and waits for Lancaster to leave so he can check that both the tracker and mic are working. He learns quickly they are, as he listens to Lancaster call his wife to say he's on his way home. All five cars show up as different colours on our GPS tracking app.

17

It's Saturday morning after my trip down south, and I am moping around, not too inclined to do anything, when I notice the box full of Liz's belongings, so I dig through this until I find her last phone account and start studying regularly called numbers. One stands out more than the rest for both texts and calls, some lengthy calls in the evening, so I access the Telstra database (don't mean to, but hey!), type in the phone number, and I come up with a Kevin Clark of an address in Moorooka, a suburb on Brisbane's southside. I google Kevin Clark to see what comes up – not much, but he seems to be a teacher.

With nothing specific in mind, I grab a coffee, write down the address, and head to Moorooka, pulling up outside a nicely restored old Queenslander in a street full of nice homes. I go up to the front door, knock, and a few moments later a man opens the door, forty-ish, thinning hair but lean build and a pleasant smile.

Before he says anything, I say, 'Hi, I'm Mort.'

He steps back, a little uncertain, with a look of concern on his face, so I hold my hands up and say, 'I come in peace.'

With a relieved look, he invites me in and we head back to the kitchen and he offers me a coffee.

'Sure,' I say, 'straight black, thanks.'

'Kevin,' I say, 'I'm only guessing, but were you and Liz…' I can't quite say it out loud.

He doesn't reply, but his reaction is all the confirmation I need, as he looks embarrassed, nervous, and apprehensive all at once. I take a moment to compose myself, as I have no choice but to accept my wife and I had truly grown apart.

'I don't wish you any harm, Kevin,' I again assure him, as he gets up to finish making the coffee, 'but on a whim, I thought I would come down and meet you, just so maybe I can put Liz's death behind me. I don't know if you knew this, but I didn't find out about the accident until after the funeral – I was on a mission, and the powers that be deemed it too important to jeopardise by letting me know, and certainly not to extract me. So once the mission was completed, I caught the first plane home, not that turning up until over a week after the funeral helped much.'

Kevin slowly starts to open up, telling how they had met at Mt Maria College where Liz was working, but it was only after Kevin left there to accept a deputy principal position at a South Side College that they started to see each other.

We end up having a lengthy chat, and I learn they had plans to move in together, but Liz was adamant she would not do that without telling me in person we were over. They lived apart through the week, and she usually spent the weekend here at his house. He has three kids who he says all adored Liz, and they were all truly devastated by her death.

Towards the end of our chat, the doorbell chimes, and he says, 'That will be the kids now,' and sure enough, three kids aged (I am guessing) seven to twelve come bounding in, coming to a rapid stop when they see me. Kevin tells them I was Liz's former husband calling just to say hi. They all seem nicely adjusted kids. They say hi and head off to who knows where. I take my leave and leave him with his kids and apologise if I have opened raw wounds and memories for him.

As I drive away, I have a feeling of tremendous sadness. Liz had developed a whole new life, and from all accounts was very happy; for that, I am truly glad, which, of course, makes me feel worse. Almost subconsciously, I end up in Stafford, and here in front of me are the netball courts, full of flying bodies.

I find a park (no easy feat with so many players and spectators around) and ask where I might find Valley 3rds. I'm told they are playing right now over on court six, I head over and see Suzie out on court, but before she sees me, a couple of her teammates obviously see me, saying loud enough for me to hear: 'Wow, look at handsome over there!'

Being honest, maybe I always knew I was going to end up here, as I had put on a bright yellow polo with tan shorts – and it does not hurt that the polo happens to show off my physique.

I see Suzie's mouth drop when she sees me, and so does one of her teammates as she immediately shouts, 'Suzie's blushing!'

Fortunately, it's near the end of the game, and Suzie comes trotting over after they complete their end-of-game routine.

As she approaches, she smiles and says, 'Hi, this is a nice surprise.'

I smile back and say, 'Ah, just passing through'—*yeah right*—'so thought I would pop in. How are you doing? I'm guessing you won that last game?'

She nods.

'You know they're having bets to see if you will kiss me here in front of them, don't you?' I tease her.

She smiles and says, 'So what's your money on?'

'I know what I want to happen,' I say with a semi-serious look on my face (well, I do not want to look too hopeful).

'Ha,' she says. By now, some of her teammates have come over, so she says, 'Girls, this is Mort.'

They all chorus, 'Hi, Mort.'

I smile and give a small wave.

They are then called back by Shan, their captain apparently, who seems like an Energizer Bunny type, buzzing around everyone. Suzie steps up on her tip toes and gives me a quick peck, then a wave as she trots off.

I say to her, 'That doesn't count,' and get another wave.

Then one of her teammates, a big Māori girl with a full sleeve of tattoos and tattoos all over her back, leans close and says, 'Suzie is a real good friend of mine, so you hurt her, you deal with me.'

We stand there looking at each other, and I smile and say, 'If I hurt Suzie, I would deserve to answer to you.' This takes the sting out of her attitude.

She introduces herself as Maria Scia Scia and waves a hand at four young kids playing around on the adjoining court. 'And they are my brood.'

We shake hands, and I notice a tat signifying '1st NZR' on her shoulder, so I say, 'Army?'

'Yeah,' she says, 'until I got a DD.'

I raise an eyebrow.

'Yeah, we had a bloody captain who couldn't keep his hands to himself, so I slugged him – 'course they stood firmly behind him and ran me out.' Sadly, not an unfamiliar story in the armed forces around the world.

'So how did you end up here?' I ask.

'Well, one good thing came of my time: I met Ronnie, my husband. He was in your mob, 2nd RAR, so when it turned to shit, he invited me over here, and we have been breeding like bloody rabbits since,' she says with a laugh.

'Is Ronnie still in?'

'Nah, he works up the mines now, so I only see him a week a month; just as well. Otherwise, we might have ten kids,' she says with another laugh. 'You in too?' she asks.

'Was, yeah,' I reply. '1st RAR.'

'Old big blue,' she says with a smile. 'So, what was your specialty?' she asks, as we both watch the start of the team's next game.

'How come you're not playing?' I ask.

'Oh, they're resting me for tomorrow. Seem to think cos I'm a bit older I can't handle the pace!' she exclaims. When I don't answer her question, she says, 'Well?'

'I was in a special operations unit, Group111, a special comms unit.'

'I think I've heard of that – you used to do some dirty shit if the stories are true.'

I smile and say, 'Well, you can't believe all the stories, Maria, can you?'

It's nearing half time, the girls are leading comfortably so I take my exit, waiting for a chance to wave when Suzie is facing my way. I think I get a smile but I'm a little too far away to be sure, but I'll take it. As I'm leaving, I text Pig to see if he wants to grab a beer, but he's out somewhere with George, so back home for me. I ring Suzie through the evening to see how they got on, and yes, they are into the finals tomorrow, so depending how they go will determine how many games they play.

I confess to her I am not likely to be on the north side tomorrow and I wish her luck.

She replies, 'It was really nice of you to come out today, Mort, even if the girls gave me plenty of stick! By the way, they agree with you: it did not count as a kiss,' she adds.

'Well,' I say, 'that's one you owe me!' and we say goodnight.

18

It's the Monday after my southern sales trip, and Pig and I are reviewing our new projects. The first one, Ryde Biomedical, was easy, Pig advises. Lydia is certainly up to something: $50k in the bank, spending far more a month than she earns. Leading quite a social life – clubs and casinos three or four nights a week, with $10,000 coming into her account at the beginning of each month. Pig is just waiting to confirm where this comes from so we can file our report and close the file.

Paramount Wireless hasn't progressed as far, as everyone on the list seems to be in the clear. I tell Pig to focus on Cameron and his close associates and family, as he is such an obnoxious bloke that he must have pissed someone off. Pig goes digging again, deeper this time.

A little while later, he yells out, 'Looks like you're right. His wife, Sofia, has separate bank accounts with NAB in her own name – shit, $240,000 in it too. We'll see where this is coming from.'

'Do they still live together?' I ask him.

'Yeah, according to all the records. Some stylish joint in Vaucluse.'

'Okay, see if she has a credit card on the NAB account and let's see where she spends this money.'

Pig replies, 'On it.'

Sometime later, he lets me know that Sofia is receiving regular

$50k payments from Absolute Management Consultants.

'Well, Russ Watt taught us not all management consultants are above board; let's see what we can find on this mob. You keep digging on Sofia; I'll take Absolute,' I tell him.

Pig also comes back and tells me there are a few hotel nights on Cameron's company Amex for the Four Seasons Hotel in Sydney. 'So I wonder who he's shagging?' he says. 'Looks like every second Wednesday night he spends there.'

'Well, at some point we're going to have to go to Sydney to wrap this up, so we'll check that out, even if just for the hell of it,' I say.

I check Absolute Management Consultants out, starting with their website. The CEO is a Claudia Petrov, forty-something with the Russian beauty looks that go with the Russian name. A few other suits are mentioned, but Claudia seems to be the main player. Paramount Wireless is not listed as a client, but Optus – one of their major competitors – is. I check her out on LinkedIn and other less popular websites; she clearly is active on the social scene and seemingly well connected in the business end of town. A bit more checking, and I come up with her mobile number. This then enables us to access her call log, so once this comes in, I input the known phone numbers of all our suspects into our number matching software, press go and let it do its thing. She's a busy girl, so I expect this to take some time.

Meanwhile, Pig is still waiting on Sofia's hidden credit card details, so we can have a look see. Nor has he come up with who is paying Lydia the $10k per month, so we decide to go out for a late lunch at our favourite local café. Tough life, ah?

Whilst eating, I let Pig know Peter from HardAs Concrete left me a message saying QuarryMix had signed a contract for his business at a 'fair price', so he wouldn't be pursuing any other action. We then set our minds to making a plan to give Russ Watt a lesson.

On our return from lunch, I find we have a match from Claudia's phone log – a match with Sofia, Cameron's wife! Interesting. In fact, there are a few calls and texts both ways over the last few weeks. This does need some focus. We download photos of them again and compare what we know of them. We have no record of Sofia ever working, whereas Claudia, as CEO of Absolute, appears well respected around town. We sit and ponder how they could be connected, and if they could, in fact, be the leak we are hunting. Cameron had stressed his wife wasn't involved in the business and had little interest in it, commenting rather harshly, 'She is only interested in spending the money I earn, not how I earn it.'

Pig and I agree we need to head to Sydney to continue the assignment. I will drive the van down early next week, and he will fly down early the following morning. Pig then makes a list of what we need in the van, including ladders, a couple of drones, back-up disc drives, bugs, and trackers, whilst I check out accommodation options and decide on a two-bedroom apartment at the Quest Potts Point, being close to both Sydney CBD and Vaucluse where Cameron and Sofia live. We haven't tracked down Claudia's home address, but this is easily found on her phone bill we have already. She lives in Bondi just off the beach, so also not too far away.

Pig also gets a message saying that Lydia's monthly $10k is coming from a law firm in England, and from what he can ascertain, she's the beneficiary of an old aunt who died a year or so ago, and the monthly payment will continue until all the aunt's assets are sold off, at which time she will get quite a windfall. She is clearly not selling secrets to fund her lifestyle, and I am sure Ivan will be pleased. He will just have to improve his management of her.

A bit early, but we decide to call it a day – but we have a plan for later in the evening.

*

I pick Pig up around 5:00 p.m. that afternoon and head over to Watt Consulting's office in Aspley, knowing Russ is there and has a meeting. We plan on being there when it finishes. I park out in the back next to his Discovery, and we decide to sit in his Discovery so, when he exits the back door, he will see us clearly.

Sure enough, a little while later, he comes out the back door, not noticing us sitting in his car until he turns around, having locked the door behind him. He comes towards the car with a look of anger mixed with uncertainty. I let him approach the driver's door, which I have deliberately left open.

He says, 'What are you doing in my car?'

I don't answer for a couple of minutes, letting the tension build; then I say, 'We need to talk to you, Russ. It might be better if we go back in your office.'

'Why?' he asks.

I reply, 'You don't want what we are going to say to be heard in public, now do you?'

Looking rather apprehensive, he turns back to open the door, and Pig and I quickly exit the car and crowd him at the back door, further intimidating him. He opens the door and proceeds through to his office, turning lights on as he goes, and takes his seat.

Without any further discussion, I tell him, 'Listen to this,' and start playing the tape of him and Martin Bateman from QuarryMix discussing tactics.

I don't play too much of it as he quickly gets the gist of it. So I say, 'What do you think the ACCC will say when they hear this, along with a formal complaint from HardAs?'

He doesn't reply, so I continue, 'Russ, we have you by the balls. QuarryMix are shitting themselves over this, so you can be sure they won't be doing any more business with you. But this isn't what we are unhappy about.'

Again, I let a little silence add to the tension before continuing, 'You were involved in selling secrets from Campbell Pharmaceutical. That has now stopped, and I am pretty sure McAllister won't want to do anymore business with you either. You don't have a good track record, do you?

'Russ, look at us. It wouldn't take us two minutes to give you a thorough beating, leave you with severe injuries, maybe injured for life. You need to understand the sleazy way you do business has to stop. You have damaged good, honest, and trustworthy businesses, putting thousands of staff's jobs at risk. All for your own personal gain. We don't think that's fair. Do you?'

By now, he is pretty scared, not exactly shaking, but getting close.

I lean in closer, saying louder and firmly, 'Well?'

'No,' he mutters.

I wait a couple of minutes, allowing the tension to build. 'Okay, here is what we are going to do. Type this name and number into your phone'—I give him the name 'Elizabeth Willis' and her phone number, then continue—'Elizabeth runs Meals on Wheels here on Brisbane's northside. She's expecting your call. You will do 100 hours of community service, unpaid, of course, for them. Elizabeth will let me know if you don't call her, or if you miss any of your shifts. If that happens, we will be back. You won't know when. You won't know where. We don't do second chances. You will be hurt. You will spend time in hospital. We may even send the tape to the ACCC just for the hell of it. So, Russ, you do not want to miss *any* of your shifts. One hundred hours, and you have three months to complete them. Are we clear?'

He has now moved over to lean on his desk. I suspect he's not sure his legs will hold him up much longer. He nods.

I say again, 'Are we clear?'

'Yes,' he replies.

'Okay then, we are out of here. You can wait five minutes before leaving. Clear?'

He nods.

We move to the back door, exit into the van and drive away. Once clear and back on Aspley Road, we fist bump and nod to each other. Time for a coffee!

19

It's 6:30 a.m. the next Sunday, and I'm knocking on Suzie's door. Eventually, she comes to the door, opens it and says, 'Hi – do you know what time it is?'

I smile and say, 'Now that I've seen you, the best time of the day!'

She pulls a face but opens the door to let me in.

Once inside, we have a kiss and I say, 'Hi.'

Eventually, we pull apart and I say, 'Come on now, into your gear, we're running back to my place so you can sample the famed Ireland Eggs Bennie.'

She again pulls a face and says, 'We could drive like normal people.'

I reply, 'But then you won't have earnt the right to sample my Eggs Benedict.'

'Well, it better be good,' she grouses, but it's only half-hearted. I pull my day pack off my back and toss it to her, telling her to put some clothes and things in, and I carry them for her.

As she walks away, I say, 'By the way, your nightie is rather becoming.' I get an arse wiggle in response.

I wander around her unit, being nosey basically. It is, as expected, pretty clean and tidy, so I'm looking at photos, one being of a wedding with Suzie as bridesmaid for, I'm guessing, her sister. It looks a few years old, so I presume her older sister; her parents are also in it. Plenty of other family photos, but none showing Suzie with a male – which I take as a promising sign.

A surprisingly short time later, she comes out in her running gear: three-quarter-length tights and a nice pink top – and hands me my backpack, which isn't too heavy.

'So,' she says with that half smile – impish, I call it. 'What would you have done if I had company?'

I hold her head in my palms and say, 'Well, I would have made a bloody big fool of myself' and plant a quick kiss.

'How far is it anyway?' she asks.

'Only eight kilometres,' I reply.

'And you ran here already?' she queries.

'Yep.'

'Well, come on, then; lead the way,' she says.

After we've done a few routine stretches, we head off towards Fortitude Valley and across the Story Bridge – a Brisbane icon and still a critical traffic artery into the CBD. Running over the bridge at this time of day – and of course, it is a lovely clear morning – gives us awesome views of the river reflecting in the many office towers along the riverfront. Naturally, I keep my pace down to match Suzie's, but I am not one for talking whilst running; I need to focus and need my breath to keep going, so not much is said on the way back to my joint.

On arrival, we are both puffing a little, and I put my right index finger to the sensor to open the front gate.

Suzie comments, 'Fancy!'

We climb the stairs to my front door, and this time, I use my left index finger to open the door.

This time, she says, 'What's wrong with normal keys?'

I reply, 'I have some pretty sophisticated technology down there'—pointing down to my office—'so don't want to make it easy for anyone to access it.'

We step inside and do a few stretching exercises and drink plenty of water whilst regaining our breath.

'Well, mister, you better not have got me here on false pretences. I am getting hungry, so let's see you with the apron on!'

I tell her, 'I'm going to have a quick shower first. Care to join me?'

That impish smile plays at her lips as we step in close, and she says, 'I was hoping you would ask!'

It's a bit later before I get my shower. A little later again, I'm in the kitchen and have put on an apron (don't worry, also have a T-shirt and shorts on), firing up the hotplate whilst mixing the eggs with my secret ingredients. With the eggs simmering, coffee brewing and toast cooking, I set the table, and almost as if on cue, Suzie comes out, still with her hair in a towel and dressed in a colourful summer dress, which shows her tan (and long legs) off nicely.

I point to her seat with the spatula and serve up the famed Ireland Eggs Benedict, and after placing the toast and coffee and vegemite, jam, etc., on the table, I too sit down to enjoy my well-earned breakfast.

Suzie takes her time, eating not one mouthful, but three, before putting me out of my misery, and then, only after she breaks out laughing, watching me waiting on her opinion. 'Well, I must say, Mr Ireland, not half bad – and I am talking about the eggs, not the first course.'

We smile at each other and touch coffee cups and continue to eat in comfortable silence.

We're just finishing the last of the coffee and toast when a small alarm beeps from my phone. I glance down and say, 'That's Pig,' and a minute or so later, he walks up the internal stairs.

To my surprise, he doesn't do a double take on seeing Suzie there. Wet hair and all, she gets up and gives him a quick kiss and hug.

Pig nods to me and says, 'Hi, Suzie, good to see you again. Any leftovers?' This later question is directed to me.

'Yeah, a little in the pan still, might need to microwave it.'

'Nah, this will be okay,' he says as he grabs a plate and knife and fork and sits down at the table whilst I brew him a coffee.

'So, what is going on?' he says, looking at Suzie.

'Well,' she says, 'this friend of yours is banging on my door at 6:30 this morning, and so as not to wake all the neighbours, I had to let him in. Then he tells me I had to run over here just to try his – wait for it – his "famed eggs bennie", and you know me – anything not to disappoint. So we ran over here, and I must say, his eggs leave mine for dead!'

'And what's with the wet hair then?' he asks.

She smiles and says, 'Well, we did have a first course.'

Pig puts his hands over his ears and says, 'No, no – I don't want to know!' and we all have a laugh.

We continue to chat whilst he finishes his eggs and coffee, and I ask him what he is doing here.

He replies, 'Well, George had to go into the office again today, so I thought I would come over and do some more work on SA Tech as we are a little behind after being so focused on Campbells these last few weeks.'

Suzie pipes up, asking, 'Who's Campbells?'

I reply, 'Just a client; we finalised their assignment on Friday.'

But of course, being a little nosey, she persists, 'What was the assignment about?'

I smile and say, 'You're not the only one who has client confidentiality agreements! Anyway, when you two greeted each other earlier, it did not look like only the second time you have met.'

Pig and Suzie look at each other and laugh, Pig commenting, 'Well, he was going to figure it out sometime.'

'Figure out what?' I ask.

Pig and Suzie share another look, and Suzie says, 'Well, Julien has sort of been guiding me, pushing me, knowing you would probably leave it too late.'

'Leave what too late?' I ask, a little perplexed.

Pig joins in and says, 'After I met Suzie with you at the Bridge to Brisbane, I thought she would be really good for you, and knowing you'll dither around, I texted her and asked how the lunch went, and well, we sort of stayed in touch, with me telling her if she did like you even a bit, she would have to be the one to take the first steps.'

I stay quiet for a couple minutes and then respond, 'So you two have been conspiring against me, ah?'

Smiling, they both say, 'Yep' in unison.

Suzie then says, 'If it wasn't for Julien, I wouldn't be here now. So, thank you, Julien,' she adds with a smile to Pig.

I look at Pig for a few minutes, then say, 'Man, as if I don't owe you enough now, I've got to thank you for her too!' I point a thumb at Suzie, who gives me a dig in the ribs.

We all laugh.

Pig helps himself to another coffee and then heads off down the stairs whilst I tidy up the breakfast dishes.

By the time I'm finished, Suzie has finished her hair and is sitting on the couch with her legs tucked under her, checking her phone. I sit down next to her and say, 'What's happened in the world since you last looked?'

Suzie looks up and smiles and says, 'Not a lot, but I am addicted to it the same as the rest of the world.' She pauses and then says, 'Except for you, maybe' with a raised eyebrow.

I respond, 'Never bothered with Facebook or whatever, did a little FaceTime-ing with Liz back in the day, and of course, she, like the rest of the world, was addicted to it, although being a teacher, she was very careful not to say too much in case pupils found out.'

As I say it, I think, *Ah, maybe bringing Liz up is not the smartest move, buddy boy.*

But Suzie seems to want to address it because she comes back asking, at the same time gently putting her hand on mine on the couch. 'So how did Liz die – you said it was an accident?'

'Yes,' I reply. 'She was killed in a car accident on a Thursday night. She was T-boned – car went through a red light and slammed right into her. She apparently died at the scene.

'I was on a mission behind enemy lines at the time, and the hierarchy chose not to tell me until we had been extracted days later. By then, they had already had the funeral, so I was pretty shattered. Of course, all my family and Liz's couldn't understand how come I hadn't replied to all the messages and emails they had sent.

'By the time I did get home, it was a week after the funeral, and her parents still haven't forgiven me – nor I the army, for that matter.'

'Shit,' she says, 'that's terrible; you must have been devastated.' She leans her head in against mine, sensing my mood.

We stay quiet for a little while before I say, 'Righty-o, that's enough of the dreary stuff. What are we getting up to today?' I stand and pull her to her feet, bringing her close enough to have a lingering kiss.

When she pulls away, I say in a husky voice, 'Just as well, or we wouldn't be going anywhere soon.'

She laughs and takes my hand and says, 'Come on, show me around downstairs.'

We descend the interior stairs and enter the office, having to again use my left index finger on the sensor, Suzie rolling her eyes at this. Pig is sitting at his desk positioned along the left wall. He looks up from his screens as we come in and smiles but goes back immediately to his task.

I point to his desk, where everything is pinpoint straight, everything lined up and square, and say to Suzie, 'See what I mean?'

Suzie smiles, first at me, then at Pig, who knows damn well what has been discussed.

I then point out my desk at the far end, facing the front entrance. Both are big desks – four screens each – and in between us is a large, air-conditioned cabinet housing our main computer hardware, and I explain all this to Suzie as we stroll around the room.

'All our data storage is cloud-based and very secure,' I add.

I point out off to the right where there is a small meeting room and kitchen, and also a door out to the garage and storage area. The gym equipment in the back corner immediately takes her eye, and we wander over to have a look.

'Who uses this?' she asks.

'Mainly me, but sometimes Pig if he gets bored, frustrated, or is not in a hurry to go home.'

She looks at the weights sitting on the rack and says, 'Wow, they look heavy.'

I tell her, 'Currently 125 kilograms.'

She asks a little incredulously, 'And you can lift that?'

I smile and nod.

We head into the garage proper which only has the Camry in it, with Pig having parked the van in the drive when he arrived. In the storage area on racks are our selection of drones.

Suzie picks one of the smaller drones up and says, 'Gee, these are tiny; what do you use these for?'

'Well, they have multiple uses, but primarily to photograph things or people we are monitoring.'

This gets a frown from her, and I can see she is puzzling over what to say next, so I wait, deciding it will be better to let her ask her questions, as I have no plans to hide what I do. Our friendship is developing nicely, so no time for secrets.

Eventually, she says, 'Well, what exactly does Digital Data Solutions do?'

I guide her back into the office, getting another eye roll as I use the sensor to open the door. She immediately goes over and sits in my chair, saying, 'I always like to sit in the boss's chair,' which gets Pig to raise his head with a wry smile.

'Well,' I start as I take one of the visitors' chairs, thinking maybe I am the first person to actually sit in it, as we rarely have visitors. 'Pig and I are rather highly skilled computer programmers, both having a natural ability in that field, but more so from the training we received in the Army and from US forces and agencies as well. We can track or trace most anybody or anything digitally, but sometimes you can't avoid good old-fashioned boots on the ground, so we also are skilled at following people and have some pretty fancy kit to help us – some even the police don't have access to. We can give people who have been hacked or who suspect industrial espionage guidance, and also often find the culprits and therefore solve their problems for them.'

Pig pipes up, 'What he means is we are hackers – but hackers for the good guys.'

I quickly add, 'He means "ethical hackers", but we are much more than that, with our skills and also the sophisticated equipment we have. They give us the ability to solve a lot of digital crime, but never so the evidence can be used in a court of law.'

'Why?' Suzie askes, still swinging idly in my chair.

'Because we don't always get the evidence legally. We might have accessed someone's computer records to obtain evidence; also, we have access to some pretty high-level and secure US search engines that have been left open to us after some of the work we did for the

Yanks overseas,' I add.

'It's also highly unlikely anyone would ever know we have been into their files – we are that good. In fact, the assignment Pig is working on now for SA Tech Inc. – they were hacked a couple of months ago and approached us to do a digital audit of their new security platform. I accessed their files from my hotel room down in Adelaide and changed their IT manager's password, as he was pretty cocky they did not need us. I was quickly asked back in the next morning, so now Pig is walking them through the levels of security they need and testing them as they go. So, a nice cushy job,' I finish.

'Most of our work so far has been for industrial espionage – one company stealing the secrets of another. But,' I stress, 'we only ever work for the ones who have had their secrets stolen. And, touch wood, we so far have a 100 per cent record in finding the culprit and providing the client with a solution.'

'How much does this pay? How do you set your fees?' she asks, coming to grips with the business concept.

'Well, we don't really work off an hourly fee, and having no real competition at the level of sophistication we are, I really pluck a number and double it,' I say with a smile.

'Or triple it as you did for Paramount,' adds Pig with a smirk.

I smile with him whilst Suzie looks from one of us to the other.

'Well, being a lawyer, I am not sure I like the idea of you doing things illegally,' she starts.

I butt in, saying, 'We might not use technically legal means to achieve our goals, but the authorities would be hard pressed to ever find evidence to convict us of any crime. And show me a lawyer who hasn't bent the rules at least once a day,' I finish.

This does get a smile from her, and she says, 'I would love to know about some of your cases and how you solved them.'

'Maybe one day when we are old and grey,' I tell her with another smile, getting one of her impish grins as a reply.

We decide to head out for a late lunch, leaving Pig to his work. We jump in the Camry and head down the road to Bulimba, an old but newly-fashionable suburb on the river. After finally finding a car park, we wander down the road. Suddenly, Suzie's hand is in mine. I'm not even sure how that happened, but I like the feel of it, and I carry on nonchalantly, big macho me making out it's of little consequence.

She chooses a café with a good selection of light and cooked lunches, and we settle in. Before she can bring up our work again, I pick her hand up and say, 'Suzie, I want to circle back to Liz.'

I note a look of alarm on her face and quickly say, 'I just want to say that in the last few weeks, I have managed to put Liz behind me, and I have to admit, largely because of you.' This brings out another fresh and delighted smile. 'But I want to explain what I have found since coming home.'

I pause as our coffee is delivered, mine a long black, and a vanilla latte for Suzie, then continue. 'I had suspicions about the accident, having read the reports. Something did not sit right. I mean, the other driver went through a red light but was never charged with anything, so I started digging and have found the driver was a serving policeman – a detective sergeant no less – and he wasn't even breathalysed. The coroner's report doesn't mention this either. So I'm continuing to dig into him, and he seems to be a member of a special clique within the police service.'

This gets a snort from her, but no comment.

I continue, 'My mother-in-law had intimated Liz was seeing someone else and had been for a while before the accident. I also couldn't understand what she was doing in Moorooka on a Thursday night when she lived in Stafford. So the other weekend, I dug out her old phone records and traced a frequently called number to a

Kevin Clark, a teacher who lives in Moorooka, so I paid him a visit.'

This brings a sharp intake of breath from Suzie, so I smile and give her a calming motion, 'It's all right, I went in peace, and after the initial fright and being a little wary of me, we had a good honest chat, and it appears to me I had lost my wife some years ago and had not even noticed it. It made me very sad, in fact. That was the day I came past your netball comp – just wanted to see a friendly face.'

Suzie doesn't say a word but takes my hand and squeezes it, then reaches over and gives me a lingering kiss. Bugger, our lunch did have to arrive right then!

20

The next morning is Monday, and whilst preparing for the trip to Sydney, we decide to check the audio from both the SC's recent Thursday sessions and also from their cars. We listen to the audio from the pub together on speaker whilst enjoying a coffee, both taking notes at different points.

Lancaster says quietly, 'Well boys, our retirement fund is growing nicely, so here is your quarterly bonus,' and he pushes brown envelopes around the table, each one having one of their names on it. 'As always, you all get equal amounts – except Flem here; he gets a bit more for helping me out more.' The envelopes are quickly tucked away in jacket pockets, away from prying eyes – but not ours.

Pig and I look at each other round-eyed.

Pig pauses the audio and says, 'Shit, I wonder how much they get each?'

I nod, so he restarts the tape. Of course, we have it all on video as well, so quite incriminating when the time comes, I think. Nothing else of consequence comes out, although Lancaster also suggests 'royal battalion' would be worth a few bob in the fifth race at Eagle Farm this Saturday, so Pig and I decide to split $20 to back it as well.

Once finished with the pub coverage, we split the cars, Pig taking Lancaster and I taking Fleming as the two main players. Whilst there are a few interesting conversations (and we are grateful they use Bluetooth so we can hear both sides of the conversations), not knowing who they are talking to is quite frustrating.

What can we do about this? I ponder.

After listening to this, we discuss the need to expand our access to Lancaster's and Fleming's calls. Police headquarters is clearly not an option, so we decide we need to bug their home offices. We agree, nothing like the present, so we grab a coffee and head off first to check Lancaster's home in Chelmer – a lovely tree-lined street with well-established and maintained homes. In the van, we pull up outside his home, adjacent to a power pole, and immediately two large Alsatian dogs are growling and barking at the fence. We disregard them as we are simply servicing the streetlight atop the power pole, with it being my turn to climb up and fit the camera, whilst Pig manages the protective barrier at the base. Up and down in under five minutes – we're getting expert at this! To ensure it doesn't look suspicious to anyone watching, we stop at another pole further down the road and fit another camera up there. No reason other than it would look better 'maintaining' two lights in the street rather than only one.

As we depart Chelmer, heading for Fleming's home in Carindale, we discuss Lancaster's guard dogs and how to get around them. As we enter Broderick Street, we see Fleming's house up ahead as a woman and two school-age children get out of a white Pajero, a common family sized SUV, and go into the house. This solves a problem for us. Now we know who lives there. We quickly repeat the process to the nearest streetlight, this time 50 metres down the road, affix the camera, do a second pole near the corner, and exit the area.

We review the footage every morning, trying to get a feel for movement, and it looks like Fleming will be easy. After he leaves every morning around 7:00, his wife packs the kids into the Pajero.

Its fair to assume she drops the kids at school then heads on to work, as the car doesn't come back until around 4:00 pm normally. Lancaster too should be easy – his wife leaves early, at a similar time as he, and doesn't return until after 6:00 p.m. most evenings. We decide Thursday morning we will slip inside and put in a mic and camera into both homes in the study or home office.

Thursday morning, we head first to Lancaster's as, they both leave earlier – having first checked to ensure today is no different. Our plan is for Pig to park the van the same as last time, adjacent to the power pole outside their front fence, and then access the pole. This will act as a distraction, keeping the dogs occupied whilst I slip through their back neighbour's property and access the back door.

Everything goes smoothly, my key opens the back door, but I am met with a sophisticated alarm system with a fingerprint sensor – similar to my own, in fact. I let Pig know it's a no-go, and exit as I arrived. Pig dismounts the pole, packs up, and picks me up around the corner in Jarratt Street. As we head to Carindale, we work out a plan B.

Fleming's home is as easy as we expected, this time the frontal assault. We pull up in the driveway with our ABC Plumbing sticker on the van, and wander round the back, out of sight. We enter through the back door, quickly access the upstairs study – clearly a male domain – install a mic and camera into the desk lamp, retreat, and, back outside, away we go. Job done.

We go back to the office, grab what we need for plan B for Lancaster's place and head back over there. This time, we park in Halsbury Street across from the park, and get out. Pig grabs a drone from the back of the van and we head over to a nearby picnic table, taking coffees and muffins bought at a little café along Oxley Road on our way into the suburb.

Pig had bragged that drones can now be used as 'flying robots', so now is his chance to prove it. He launches the drone and directs it to Lancaster's address, and once there lowers it, doing a 360 of the house. We are both a little relieved the dogs aren't alerted to the drone, thus making our job a little easier.

It isn't hard to recognise Lancaster's study, with file cabinets stored along one wall, a large desk with a PC sitting on it against the other wall. Pig then sets to work, commenting that the windows have full security screens over them as well, making his drone's job of drilling through the window just a little more difficult, having to position it just so, so that its arms extend between the mesh to access straight onto the glass. With no time pressure, he does this, and the drill does its job. He then brings it back and fits the small, combined mic and camera into the drone's claw and sends it back to insert it. This, of course, is also a delicate process as we are talking a very small mic into a very small hole and controlling it by remote control from approximately 600 metres away. No pressure!

Pig finally gets it secure, and we turn it on and have clear vision of the room, and although we had positioned the camera at the best possible angle, we can't get vision of the PC screen, and unlike most people these days, he only has one. Never mind, we will have audio, so we will hear his side of any conversation he has in there. Pig brings the drone back. We fist bump and head on home. Job done.

Being a Thursday, we have to wait until quite late in the evening before we hear any audio. But I have nothing better to do, so I check it regularly, and sure enough, I hear Lancaster talking to 'Mike', but nothing of interest to us. I listen over the next few nights, but he doesn't seem to make any important calls from here. So it looks like his car is still going to be our best option. Maybe Mrs Lancaster doesn't know what her husband is up to.

21

Early evening, I'm upstairs putting the finishing touches to a lamb casserole for my dinner, when the gate chime sounds. I look at the monitor and see Suzie standing there, looking very upset. I buzz her in and go and open the door for her, waiting as she climbs the stairs, clearly not herself.

She comes in and starts crying, saying, 'Hold me, just hold me please.' I pull her into a gentle hug, just holding her as she is sobbing uncontrollably, her body being wracked by her sobs.

I manage to get her to the couch in the lounge, half carrying her as she is beside herself. I sit there stroking her hair, letting her cry herself out. Clearly, something heart breaking has happened. I'm thinking maybe her mum or dad has died, and I'm also pleased I am the one she has turned to. Eventually, the tears slow, and I hand her a box of tissues I had managed to find in the bathroom, for which I receive a wan smile.

When she feels ready, she explains that her client Emma Johnson had been beaten by her ex-partner Rhys O'Connor and is now in ICU. Suzie explains that she had been hounding the Family Court judge to issue an arrest warrant as he had breached numerous DVOs, and his behaviour was becoming increasingly threatening. She finally got the warrant signed on the Tuesday night, but the police had not actioned it as urgently as they should have, and then it was too late. Emma, with two young children, had escaped from the family home after one beating too many and had been living in a women's shelter. Now, with their mum in ICU, the kids had to become wards of the state until Emma's sister, Heather, arrived from New Zealand in the next two days.

Telling me the details brings another flood of tears and sobbing, so I'm getting pretty good at stroking her hair. Not really being the sympathetic type, I don't have a clue what else I should do. I encourage Suzie to go and have a shower and find a T-shirt of mine to put on while I finalise tea – hoping it hasn't burnt, as I am not keen to leave Suzie even long enough to go turn the casserole down.

Once I hear the shower running, I go into the kitchen, and to my relief, it isn't burnt, so I put the potatoes on to boil. You can't have a casserole without mashed spuds, after all. Suzie comes out just as I am serving up dinner and pouring a glass of New Zealand Wither Hills Sav Blanc. She is dressed in one my tourist T-shirts – I have a habit of buying T-shirts when I travel. This one is a nice red one from Glacier National Park in Montana. I give her a big hug, holding her tight.

She breathes, 'Thank you,' as I guide her to the table and serve her dinner. She again mumbles, 'Thank you,' taking a couple of mouthfuls and a sip of wine, then saying, 'And he can cook!' There is no smile, but it was meant.

After she has eaten some and pushed the rest around her plate, without prompting, she starts in on the full story. 'I have been representing Emma since she moved to the shelter and picked up one of my cards. She had been married to Rhys for six years, with two lovely little girls – five and three, but it had been a violent relationship since the birth of the eldest daughter, Rhys not liking the loss of attention, or having to share Emma's affection. About the same time, he had been promoted within the Jackals bikie gang, and this had gone to his head, thinking he was bulletproof, and no one would argue with him.

'Emma had tried to leave once before, but with help from a few of his bikie mates, they had surrounded the women's shelter and whilst they hadn't done anything, Emma felt she had no choice but to go back. Boy, did he beat her up good that time. Emma secretly took photos of the injuries and could not go out for a couple of weeks so no one would ask questions. Rhys liked this as it made him feel more dominant. Her daughters, April and Eveleigh, were petrified of their father, and traumatised having witnessed their mother being beaten and belittled frequently.

'Then Rhys was arrested a couple of weeks ago, which was a bit odd,' Suzie adds, 'as the cops generally seem to turn a blind eye to the Jackals' activities, sort of like they have an agreement or something.'

I filed this for later thought.

'With Rhys locked up, Emma took the chance to grab the girls and not much else and fled to a different shelter, which welcomed her and immediately organised a full medical for her and both daughters. The doctor was shocked at the number of different injuries she found on Emma, but fortunately, no physical harm to the girls.

'I got involved a couple of days after she arrived at the shelter,' Suzie continues. 'I had done work for a few of the girls moving through there and have a good rapport with the staff there, and I guess they recommended me to Emma. By now, Rhys was out on bail and creating mayhem trying to find Emma, so we had to find a private flat she could hide out at. The women's shelters all have access to a few apartments they can slip these types of victims into, never for more than a month, which should be time to get DVOs in place and enforced before enabling the family to again move, hopefully discreetly.

'We managed to get Emma and the girls moved, and I know I am not supposed to get personally involved, but I often can't stop myself, and with Emma, she seems such a lovely girl – she's still only twenty-five; so, so young to have been through so much.'

More tears as she remonstrates how the system has let Emma down. I reassure her *she* didn't let Emma down, but she counters this by saying, 'But I am part of the system – in her eyes a big part – and look at her, half dead up in ICU.'

'Anyway, she must have agreed to meet Rhys on Tuesday – God knows why, but they all seem to – and he got her into his car and took her somewhere. Last I heard, the police still didn't know where, and then dumped her at a servo near the PA hospital. Fortunately, there was an ambulance pulling in to refill just when she was discovered, so they tended her and took her straight to the PA, and she was then transferred to Queensland Women's Hospital, as her injuries were so severe.'

Of course, there had been more tears through the telling, and we were sitting side by side on the couch again, with her head comfortably leaning on my shoulder.

'I tried to go and see her when I heard, but of course, ICU is immediate family only, so she had no one.' More tears at the thought of no one being there for her.

'One of the women from the shelter was babysitting the girls at the apartment, so when she heard what had happened, she had grabbed the girls and took them back to the shelter. But rules and procedure must be followed, and so they had to be handed over to Child Safety. Hopefully, there won't be an issue when her sister, Heather, arrives.

'Of course,' she continues, 'the arsehole denies touching her, claims to have an alibi, so the cops haven't even arrested him. Bloody cops, anyone else would have been locked up, but not any

Jackals bikie, it seems.'

I try and settle her down, grab a tablet (and not one you can get from your local chemist) from the bathroom and give it to her and tell her it's time for bed. When she says she needs to get home, I tell her she's not going anywhere tonight. She's going to take this pill and get into bed. Next thing she will know, it will be morning, and a whole new day. She doesn't resist, and I tell her there is a new toothbrush in the cabinet (I don't tell her I bought it after her last visit, hoping she would be the one to use it) and then tuck her into bed with a good night kiss.

'Aren't you joining me?' she asks, trying for a playful tone.

'No, you need sleep, but I will be close by.'

She puts her arms around my neck and says again, 'Thank you for being there for me tonight. I don't know what I would have done if I hadn't come to see you.'

I reply, 'You're a tough cookie; you would have got through.' I pause and say, 'A tough cookie with a great arse – now get some sleep!'

Another kiss, and I retreat out of the bedroom, seeing a slight smile on her face as I turn the light out.

Next morning, Suzie is a lot better – still very upset, of course – and she leaves early to get back to her apartment to change, determined to find out how Emma is doing. I tell her to keep me posted; I am invested now too.

When Pig arrives, I lay out the full story for him, at the end of which, neither of us says a word, but we nod to each other – we know what we are going to do.

'So what's this arsehole's name?' Pig asks.

I tell him, 'Rhys O'Connor, no idea of date of birth or anything, but he's a nob in the Jackals, so I'm sure you'll find his details easy enough.'

I log onto the Courier Mail website to see if the story has broken yet, but no, nothing. I tag it so I will get an alert when a story does show.

'Looks like he lives down at Eagleby; a small apartment complex. Security gates and all,' he adds, looking at it on Google.

We decide we need to have a better idea of his apartment complex setup, so we grab a drone and head out in the van, taking coffees with us, of course. On the way, I text Suzie to check on her and Emma, and good news on both fronts: Emma has awoken from a coma and seems to be making good progress, and Suzie seems so much stronger now, clearly with a new focus as well.

Rhys's unit complex is typical of the area, except for the security gates – that is not normal in Eagleby! We cruise past, having a good first look, and then find a nearby park where we stop. We grab our coffees and Pig's shoulder bag containing the drone, and wander off to an isolated picnic table from where Pig launches the drone. He quickly brings it over to the complex and we identify his apartment – number three in the back-left corner. The whole complex is surrounded by a six-foot brick perimeter fence, no barbed wire on the top, so no biggie for us. After checking and finding there are no dogs or anyone sitting around outside any of the units, he brings it down over the top of number three to get a closer look at windows, doors, etc., so we can get an idea of the best access points. We also note there is no evidence of other bikies at other units, as one of our concerns was maybe the complex was full of Jackals bikies, but this doesn't seem to be the case. He then lowers it down into the backyard of number three, which is poorly maintained with long grass and kids' toys strewn around – a trap for young players. He brings it close to the back door and hovers there whilst we have a good close-up to see what sort of locks are installed. Satisfied, he brings the drone home, and we sit at the picnic table to discuss best options.

Clearly, entry via the back door will be our preference, pending any issues on the night, with easy access over the wall at the back of the complex which backs onto a rural property with a few head of cattle. They won't be easily spooked, but we send the drone up again to see if the house on this property has dogs – highly likely, but more importantly, are they restrained or left loose?

A quick sortie with the drone confirms the three dogs evident on the property are within a chain link fence, so whilst they may bark if they sense us, they shouldn't be an issue. With the drone still up, we have it follow a path from a nearby isolated road where we can park and move through the paddocks to the back wall, some 500 metres. Bringing the drone home again, we look at each other and nod; we agree on our route and insertion plan.

Back in the van, we agree on the 'spleen' plan and that we will leave the office at 2:00 a.m. the next morning. Pig decides it will be easier if he stays the night with me, so he heads home to grab his duffel.

At 2:00 the next morning, it's a little overcast – a good thing if clouds are covering the moon, as there will be less chance of anyone seeing us. We're back in the van, both dressed in black, rubber soled boots, well equipped with small tools and accessories we might need, and balaclavas to use once inside, but not armed. We cruise down the highway to Eagleby, past the Macca's on this hill, into Eagleby proper, turn right onto River Hills Road, then eventually take a left onto Schmidt Road. We then take a right onto an unnamed road – well, track mainly, moving slowly and with lights out. We turn the van around, ready for a quick exit should this be necessary.

Getting out, I don the night vision goggles whilst Pig will depend on normal eyesight – he has excellent vision, and this gives us the best of both worlds, as night vision is great in a fully darkened environment, but you can't beat good old-fashioned eyeballs. Again, the nod –we have set off on so many night-time sorties that we don't need to speak, having complete faith in each other's abilities. We trot along the fence line until we get to where we need to cut across the paddock, having worked out a track we hope is far enough away from the farmhouse so as not to waken the dogs. A few minutes later, we're at the back fence of the complex. I pull a telescopic periscope from my pocket and raise it over the top of the wall, doing a slow 180 degree to see if there is any movement; this is a night vision periscope, so I get clear vision, and not a thing moving. Good to go.

I jump up and grab the top of the wall, and when my chin clears the top, I hold myself there, once again checking for any movement. Nothing, not a peep. Over I go, shortly joined by Pig, and we move silently towards the back door of number three. I try the door handle, and bugger me, it's unlocked, maybe showing the arrogance of the man, believing he is untouchable. He's about to find out how wrong he is.

We soundlessly enter the house and quickly identify the bedroom from the snoring. We check the rest of the apartment before entering the bedroom. Pig pulls the pre-cut piece of duct tape out of his pouch as we approach the slumbering body, on either side of the bed. At a nod, I grab Rhys's head in both hands and Pig places the duct tape over his mouth, sealed tight. He then moves down the bed, pulling two pre-linked cable ties from another pocket, grabs both legs that are kicking frenziedly, pulls them together and zip ties them tight. All the while, I've been holding his head, squeezing all pressure points, and none too gently. Of course, he is trying to break my grip with his hands and arms. I continue to squeeze his skull, making him moan with pain, and his arms stop trying to rip my arms off. Pig now grabs both his arms and wrestles him onto his side and zip ties his arms behind him whilst I still hold his head facing me. Neither of us has said a word. Yet.

Pig nods, confirming he is secure, so with one last squeeze of his skull, I let him go and wait a few moments for him to come to terms with his predicament – being trussed up in his own bed. Big tough guy now.

Once I have his attention again, I explain, 'I am going to hit you, one punch, but in a very delicate spot. This punch will rupture your spleen, and you will be in agony like you have never known. You will need surgery, and it will be at least three months before you can do any sort of exercise. This will only be the start. Your life is going to be hell. And we are not scared of your bikie mates, so don't think they can protect you. That is your future.'

I pause for a few moments to let this sink in before continuing. 'If you want a better, safer future, you need to make a full confession to beating up Emma, and you need to do it before surgery; otherwise, I will be waiting for you when you wake up, and that won't be pretty – just think of the pain I caused just holding your head; I can crush your skull with my bare hands. Clear?'

He nods.

I grab his head again, holding him exactly the same as last time so I am squeezing all the pressure points at once.

'Clear?' I ask again.

This time, there are tears in his eyes as he nods.

I keep the pressure on as he starts to moan, and I continue, 'You will also sign over custody of your two girls to Emma – no ifs, no buts. Clear?'

He nods his head again as the tears of pain start rolling down his face again.

'Close your eyes,' I tell him.

Pig unleashes a powerful punch, hitting just above the left ribs but angling down as we had been taught many years ago. Rhys immediately screams behind the duct tape, squirming in pain. We watch him for a few minutes, and while I watch him, Pig finds his phone and gives it a blast from our electronic gun – sort of like a taser but much more effective, both on humans and electronic devices, which it scrambles.

I grab his head again and start squeezing a little harder until he drops into unconsciousness; we then remove the zip ties from his legs and arms, leaving the duct tape in place. He's going to be in pain for some time, and not being able to use his phone will hopefully prolong anyone finding him. Then we'll have to wait and see if our scaring him is enough for him to give up his confession.

Pig has grabbed all the zip ties. We didn't bring anything else except the duct tape, and we only handled that with our gloves on. Likewise, we have worn gloves the whole time here, so no chance of having left fingerprints if he doesn't play ball and calls the cops in.

Quietly back outside, standing silently next to the back door to ensure there is still no movement, we're about to jog across to the wall when a movement catches Pig's eye, and he raises a finger to his lips and points. Sure enough, there is someone on the back deck of an adjoining unit—looks like they are having a smoke. Fortunately, they don't have direct line of sight, so we slide along the unit wall, farther away from them, check the other corner which is all clear, go up over the wall – a nod – and we trot back across the paddock, over the fence, but stop 200 metres from the van, again, purely precautionary in case someone is waiting around to see what the van is doing there. Taking an angled approach, I can see with the night vision goggles that it's clear, so we jump in and quietly drive off, waiting until we're back on Schmidt Road before turning the lights on. Just after 3:00 a.m., job done, we turn and nod and grin to each other with a gentle fist pump. Good job.

22

A couple of nights later, I am once again cooking my dinner, this time a chicken curry, when the gate chimes, and there is Suzie looking much happier and carrying both a bottle of wine and a large pizza. I buzz her in and go to the door to let her in. She has a big smile on her face as she climbs the stairs and comes close and nuzzles me as she walks past and into the kitchen.

She looks around, sees I am preparing dinner, raises the pizza and says, 'I thought I would cook tonight.' With a bright smile, she puts it down, along with the bottle.

I take her into my arms and we kiss; I tell her, 'It's great to see you back to yourself.'

The kiss lingers; then she pulls away and says, 'You wouldn't believe it. Rhys, Emma's former partner, was admitted to the hospital yesterday and made a full confession to beating up Emma, so he'll be going down for a long time!'

I smile and say, 'Well, that's karma for you! Why was he admitted to the hospital?'

'Apparently he was found in his unit with a ruptured spleen. A mate hadn't been able to get hold of him, so went and knocked the door down and found him writhing in pain half passed out on the floor of his bedroom. He had been like that since early Thursday morning. Yes, isn't karma wonderful?' she says happily.

'So how's Emma?' I ask as I open the wine bottle and grab a couple of plates for the pizza. We sit down at the kitchen table to eat.

'She is making a slow recovery, and the doctors are confident she will recover fully. Her face is still a mess from the beating, but hopefully when the bruises go, she will look a lot better. You can't believe how the news that Rhys had made a full confession and would be going to prison for a long time lifted her spirits. Amazing really, how that arsehole has ruined her life.'

'What about custody?' I ask.

Suzie pauses, looks at me and says, 'Custody, what about it?'

'Well,' I say, 'whilst he is feeling remorseful'—she gives a snort at this—'maybe… there's a chance he will relinquish custody as well.'

Suzie again looks at me appraisingly and says, 'Shit, no harm in giving it a go. I'll talk to Emma tomorrow and lodge the paperwork.' She raises her glass to me.

We clink glasses, and I say, 'Good luck!'

'Okay,' I say, 'time to clean up the dinner dishes.'

She replies, 'I cooked dinner, so that's your job.'

I grab the pizza box and the two plates and move them to the bin and sink respectively. Suzie moves into the kitchen to see what I had been cooking when she arrived.

'What did I interrupt?' she asks.

'A chicken curry,' I reply.

'Mmm, maybe next time I won't bring pizza,' she says as I put my arms around her. She turns, and I get one of those lovely smiles from her as our lips meet.

A little later, she snuggles in and says, 'I can't stay tonight.'

I reply, 'Why? You know you can get to work quickly from here.'

'Yes,' she replies, 'I want to talk to you about that. It was somewhat freaky – I got every green light all the way. Never had that happen before.'

'Just goes to show it must have been meant to be,' I reply.

'Hmm, I am not sure about that; don't know how, but I think maybe you might have had something to do with it.'

'What? I've got magical powers now, do I?' I ask. 'Maybe my lips do too,' and I gently pull her lips to mine.

*

The next Sunday, I hit the road for Sydney early at 3:00 a.m. with a plan to stop in two or three hours, maybe around Ballina or Woodstock for a break and breakfast, but I hadn't taken into account that these sleepy towns don't wake up until a little later on a Sunday, so I am well past both before anything is open. I decide to keep going to Coffs Harbour, have a good breakfast there, and a bit of a longer break.

Coffs is a pretty seaside regional town, so plenty of good-looking cafes. I choose one at random – busy but not too crowded – and sit down and enjoy both the coffee and a full breakfast. I then take a bit of a wander down along the foreshore, getting hit by the sea breeze but enjoying the freshness of it. Pig has texted to check on my progress, so I reply, 'I am in Coffs, Mother!' and get a smiley face as a reply.

I head on south, passing through Port Macquarie, Foster, before the outskirts of Newcastle and then onto the M1 and into Sydney. Of course, the traffic jams up around Hornsby, slowing my momentum, and I eventually arrive at the Quest and check in. After parking the van in the car park, I go up to the room, dump my duffel and shoulder bag with my laptop, and then head out again to the Woolworths around the corner to buy the basic needs for the coming stay. I have booked for a week, with a warning we might be longer. 'Depending on our assignment,' I had told the young receptionist.

In the unit, I check out the view, then decide on a refreshing shower. The drive has taken all day, covering 900+ kilometres, so I am a little weary and decide to order in pizza; good on you Uber Eats! After devouring this, I text Suzie to say hi, and she replies asking how the drive went, as I had told her I was going to be away for a couple of weeks on an assignment. After checking emails, I have an early night, with Pig due in around 7:30 in the morning, depending on Sydney's notorious air traffic delays.

Next morning, on Monday, Pig texts me around 8:00 a.m. to say they have landed and he is heading to the taxi stand, so I should see him in 30 to 45 minutes, and sure enough, just as I return from the café across the road with two coffees and muffins, he pulls up in the cab, so we head upstairs to the unit, and I give him his key pass so he can access not only the room but the lifts. We sit down at the little table with our notes to plan how we are going to do this. We agree we have to tag both Claudia and Sofia and try and put a bug and tracker on them both, so we have some chance of knowing where they are and can monitor them when they get together.

We have all day, so we take the van and do a recon of their addresses. We head over to Bondi first to see where Claudia lives. We find her address in Hastings Parade North Bondi, a short walk off the beach, and find it is a smart, stylish apartment, one of two in a street, perhaps not as upmarket as I was expecting. Pig notes there is a convenient streetlight almost directly opposite, so setting up a camera won't be an issue, and no obvious CCTV camera – always a bonus!

We head on to Vaucluse and find Cameron and Sofia's home in Olola Avenue, a delightful, treed street with luxurious homes, and theirs is certainly no exception. Again, we're lucky with both power poles and streetlights adjacent to their driveway, and no obvious CCTV camera that we could see on a drive pass – and we know where to look. No cars are visible in the driveway, but with a big double garage door, it's likely they both drive into the garage to access the home.

Then it's off to North Sydney to suss out the Paramount offices as, whilst I've been there, Pig hasn't, so we check out convenient car parks and coffee shops. Absolute has a small office also in North Sydney, but not in one of the big high-rise offices, rather a stylish older building, where it appears they share with three other small businesses.

I get out of the van and walk down the street, pausing outside the door to the building, checking to see if there is any CCTV, but I can't see any. I noted there was CCTV set up in the ground floor foyer of the Paramount offices when I went to visit initially. Back to the Quest, and luckily we beat the traffic and take the tunnel under Sydney Harbour. Now to make a plan.

We agree we need to be able to monitor Sofia, Claudia, and even Cameron if possible, so we decide we need to put cameras up outside their homes, and even Claudia's office, Cameron's being out of the question. We also need to put mics in their homes, if possible, but need to check this out first. First up Tuesday morning we will split up and I will go monitor Cameron and Sofia's home to check what time they depart in the morning, whilst Pig will do likewise with Claudia. We can then decide when to install the cameras and monitor their homes.

We have brought with us magnetic door signs for the van saying, 'Contractor for Waverley Council'. Luckily, both areas are covered by the same local council, and of course we always have our standard Telstra and Optus contractor signs. And to avoid anyone noticing our Queensland plates, we bought a set of New South Wales plates from an iLoad Hyundai van from a wrecker, so we won't stand out.

As always, we have wiped these plates with a special coating so they will be blurry on any camera footage, but clear to the naked eye – handy when you are trying to avoid being detected. Another toy from our American mates. Plan sorted, I decide to head off over to Vaucluse for a run. I do a cooldown walk past their home as a sort of early recce. Later we wander down to Woolloomooloo Wharf for dinner.

*

Tuesday there's a little drizzle around, so not the perfect weather we are used to in Queensland, but as always, we are prepared with waterproof hi-vis jackets, and we head off in our different directions. I take the van, and I drop Pig off at a little café on the corner just up the road from Claudia's apartment. Once in Olola Avenue in Vaucluse, nice and early just after 6:30 a.m., I find a convenient parking spot half a block from Cameron's home, and as we had not been able to find a car registered to him or Paramount, I have to keep an eye out for any car coming from their drive.

I am a patient man, so waiting until I see an XF Jaguar backing out of their drive just after 7:30 a.m. doesn't faze me, and somehow the Jag seems to fit Cameron. I let it go, as we need to know what Sofia's routine is as well, having not found anything about her on LinkedIn, or any business type of platform. Society pages, well, that's a different story. Maybe she doesn't have time to work, but to be fair, she is mother to two twenty-something kids, both now off doing their own thing.

It's not until after 10:30 a.m. that Sofia backs out in a Honda CRV and heads off. This time, I do follow her, as we know nothing much about her. She heads down to Double Bay, parks in a small shopping centre, and goes into a hair salon.

Well, I think, *she's taken care of for a couple of hours.*

I text Pig to see how he's going, and he texts back saying he's on the train with Claudia, having caught the 333 bus to North Bondi Junction Station and then onto the train for North Sydney, so I ask him to call me when he is clear.

In the meantime, I decide to head straight back to Olola Avenue to install the camera on the lamppost. I park adjacent to the pole, pull down the ladder off the roof and put all the usual barriers down to protect the base, put on my tool belt, and up the ladder. For the sake of anyone watching, I remove the bulb, fiddle with it before replacing it, at the same time attaching our little camera to the top of the light protector. Then I pull out my phone and pull up the vision to check that it is centred and clear, adjust it a little, and we are good to go. I make a pretence of recording details, looking at my watch as if recording the time, then down the ladder, remove and stack the safety gear, and drive off, thinking I will head over towards Bondi. If Pig gives me the all-clear, I will do the same again.

Once in the area, I pull into the McCafe at Bondi to pick up a coffee (and yes, a muffin as well). I sit down to wait on Pig's update, and he calls about five minutes later to tell me Claudia took the bus and train to work, and it seemed pretty routine for her, as if it's a regular thing. We had not been able to find a car in her name either, so now we wonder if she doesn't have one, as it would be a lot quicker to drive to North Sydney than bus and train each day. Then, of course, we don't know where else she is going to end up through the day, not being too familiar with media consultants and how they go about the business. Pig confirms she is a good-looking woman, and stylish – as suggested by her public profile.

He is going to get an Uber back to the Bondi McCafe and wait for me as I am going to go and install a camera outside Claudia's. This was just as quick and easy as Olola Ave, and I head back for another coffee. Yes, I am addicted.

Now we have the car registration numbers of both Cameron's Jag and Sofia's Honda (recorded by the dashcam in the van, so I don't have to even try and remember them), Pig does a search whilst waiting for me, and we find they are both registered to a company we had not heard of, which had not come up when I searched the ASIC database checking on Cameron. A recheck shows that Sofia is the sole director, which we think is odd. We agree again that we need to try and get a mic and trackers onto both ladies, but, how? As we discuss, even if we can get one into their handbag, what odds these ladies use various handbags, likewise coats, etc.. Pig then suggests he can most probably manage to get one into Claudia's bag, as she sat with it open on the train whilst reading her phone, but then it was decided I should do it, as he had been on both the bus and train this morning, just in case she was more observant than she looked. So, that's my plan for the next morning.

We head back to Double Bay to see if Sofia has finished at the hairdressers only to find she has already left, so we cruise back down Olola Avenue to see if there is any sign, but no, and nothing showing on the CCTV that she has returned, so we head back out of the area. We need a second vehicle, ideally another van, so we don't become too obvious around our target homes. Pig finds a good deal with the local Hertz franchise, so we book it and roll around there to collect it.

The next morning, we swap targets as agreed, so I get to follow Claudia as she walks briskly through the morning drizzle (again!) to her bus stop. Knowing where we expect her to go, I have headed direct to the bus stop, so I'm there when she arrives. I let her and a few other commuters board the bus before getting on myself. Pig had bought a pass, so I use this to get on so I don't draw attention to myself by not having the pass.

Once at Bondi Junction, we all dismount as it's the end of the line and disperse through the station to the platforms to wait the arrival of our trains. I wander along behind Claudia, at no stage getting too close to her, but when the train arrives, I slip in close to ensure I get in the same carriage as she does. The train is a little crowded, so we both end up standing, but after passing through the CBD there are quite a few empty seats, and Claudia takes the closest one and immediately pulls her handbag up onto her lap with the top splayed open. I squeeze past and slip the tracker/mic into her bag, and as I do, a quick glance around confirms no one is taking any interest, all too wrapped up in their phones or tablets, one older bloke actually reading a paperback!

I ease away from her now, finding a seat farther down the carriage, and stay on the train as she disembarks at North Sydney. I then log into the Tracked app on my phone and can see her walking up Blue Street towards Miller Street, clearly on her way to her office in Mount Street. I follow her progress until she stops moving, when I am guessing she has reached the office. I plug an earpiece in hoping to get some audio, and yes, this is working – perhaps not as clearly as we would like, but I can hear her saying 'good morning' two or three times as I surmise she moves through the office. That's as good as we can expect from her handbag, as I am sure it will be left on the floor near her desk.

The audio is automatically recorded to our secure cloud database, so we can review it whenever we wish. I think, *What we really need is a bug in her phone, but this would be pretty difficult to do. No one leaves their phones lying around these days, do they?*

Pig texts to see what's going on, so I call him back to tell him bug one is in place. He's had no luck with Sofia. She could have left early before he got there, which is unlikely as he was there to see Cameron leave in his Jag around 7:30 – same as yesterday – and he is not close enough to see movement at the windows, so he is sitting tight. He is in the rental van, a Toyota HiAce, so it is at least new to the street.

We agree that I will hang around North Sydney to see if Claudia heads out anywhere, so I find a coffee shop near to Cameron's office, which is only a five-minute brisk walk from Claudia's. If she is headed to the station, I can cut through and be there before her. Then again, if she jumps a cab, I will be challenged. Around 11:00 a.m., Pig texts me to say Sofia has just driven out and he is following, and a few minutes later, he calls to say she has pulled up at Your Gym on Old South Road, and he has wandered past and sees an 11:30 a.m. yoga class advertised, and a number of ladies arriving, so we guess it is a regular session for her. Whilst he hangs around the vicinity of the gym, and with Sofia's car in a relatively private car park, he quickly slips a tracker under the rear bumper before he too finds a convenient café to re-coffee. Back to waiting.

*

Back at the Quest and with nothing else to do whilst we wait for a break, I decide to check on the tapes of the SC's latest Thursday night drinking session. I grab a coffee, feet up on the desk, headphones on, and flick the video up onto the 24" computer monitor.

Not much is said for a while, other than usual pub talk and a couple of references to me 'having not shown myself again'.

I make a mental note to go sit in the bar one night again, close, but not too close, to see if it unsettles any of them.

Then Lancaster tells them all, 'This new opposition leader, Dyson, is starting to look like he might become a nuisance, gaining popularity and even overtaking Sir Premier as preferred premier in the last couple of polls. We might have to keep an eye on him. We don't want him to come along and upset our little apple cart; we haven't had anything to worry about since the Brothers Mob ran off.' This last comment met with a few sniggers around the group.

Note to self: check out what happened to the bikie they had killed – had not read anything in about an arrest or leads.

DS Fleming adds, 'We've checked him out and he and his wife are both squeaky clean; he's had a couple of speeding fines, she hasn't even had a parking ticket. Silver spooners both of them, too, so not short of a quid. I've even checked into his days as a topflight lawyer, and not too many disgruntled clients; it seems he was a pretty good lawyer, did a couple of high profile cases and won, so no friend of the police.'

DC Bruce asks Lancaster, 'So what have you got in mind?'

'Nothing yet,' replies Lancaster, 'but thought I would ask you lot for some suggestions, you know, like a democracy.' He lets out a harsh laugh, which gains a few half-smiles around the group, looking like most weren't too sure how to take his comment.

Lancaster continues, addressing DC Armitage. 'What happened to those two hookers, sorry, escorts you looked after – what were their names?'

Armitage quickly comes back, 'I did not look after them.'

'But you were screwing them,' claims Benson, and is met with a group snigger.

Armitage looks indignant. 'Their names are Christi and Stacey; they are still around, just not as high profile as they used to be, why?'

'Oh, nothing,' replies Lancaster before changing the subject. 'Whose shout?'

Fleming does the honours, collecting their glasses and wandering off to the bar. By the time he returns, they're back talking about football and how the Broncos might go this week against the Rabbitohs. After this bit of footy chat, DI Fleming expands on their plans for a bit of character assassination by using Christi – one of these 'escorts' – to claim she had a fling one night with the new state opposition leader, Noel Dyson, who is presently running rings around the Premier, who these blokes seem keen to protect.

He spells out their plan to put her in front of an orchestrated press conference with a prepared statement, claiming she met him at a function on a certain date and went up to his hotel suite at the Sofitel (where he's known to stay if attending functions in the city) and spent the night with him there.

Hmm, I think, and flick it to Pig to listen to, with a suggestion he dig into Dyson as well. I then look up our records to see what car Fleming is driving so I can access the tapes of conversations from the car over the last few weeks. After about 40 minutes of skimming through the various calls (he does actually do some police work, I realise), I hear him talking to Joe Lancaster about the 'hookers' as Lancaster calls them. They agree they'll round both girls up, as they work and live together, and give them a 'deal they can't refuse', which seems to include sending them both off on a holiday to a secret destination for a month straight after the press conference, to let the dust settle.

During the conversation, Fleming mentions he has the draft allegations on his laptop, which gets me thinking. We decide we need to listen to all the audio we have saved from the SCs. Not a small task, considering the hours of recordings we have now. This time, I take Lancaster, and Pig takes Fleming i.e. leader and 2IC as we see it.

Listening to Lancaster, I realise he spends an awful lot of time on the phone, and more than one phone at that. He talks to a lot of people, and only occasionally about police work. He has fingers in many pies and speaks with authority across all of them, so he is clearly high up in whatever 'gang' they are involved with. Of course, rarely are names used, and I don't recognise any voices, but some of the conversations are interesting to say the least.

After listening to the various conversations for an hour or so, Pig and I take a break and compare notes, and I express my frustration at not knowing who Lancaster is talking to.

We then run through their plan for Dyson and agree this needs to be stopped, but then, I think, if we let it happen, but on a day where Dyson has a rock-solid alibi, that would be a better outcome.

'We need to access Dyson's passport so we can then change the date in Fleming's little claim to be a date where Dyson and better still, his wife as well, are clearly out of the country.'

We look at each other and say, 'Midge!' and then laugh.

After a moment, I say, 'Hold on, wasn't it Midge that claimed they had literally thousands of Aussies in their voice recognition system? I wonder if we could ask him to run some of this audio with Lancaster as well!' Now we have a plan.

Midge is a bloke we met whilst working for the Americans. We were never quite sure if he was with the National Security Agency, another clandestine department, or a contractor they used when needed, but he and Pig have stayed in touch, and he has intimated he is open to helping us if the need arises. There did not seem to be too much he couldn't access and he was treated with high regard by all the Yanks.

Pig immediately starts the process of contacting Midge, as he is not the sort of bloke you can simply pick the phone up to. You send a coded email to one of these dark web addresses, and your message will eventually bounce into his inbox, wherever he may be. Message sent, we wait. In the meantime, we discuss the easiest way to access DS Fleming's laptop, as he always has it with him. We decide we need to wait until we know he is at home, then Pig should be able to pick up his IP address, and once he has that, he can access it (yes, we don't use the term 'hack' – that's for the baddies).

'Even better,' I say, 'would be access to Lancaster's, but we have never seen him with one, so he must only use his home PC.'

Later that evening, we track both Lancaster and Fleming until they arrive at their homes. Pig leaves it a little while, assuming Fleming will have dinner before maybe logging on again, as we know he has a wife, and two kids in their early teens.

Around 8:00 p.m., Pig says, 'Gottem,' using the phrase and tone made famous by an Australian cricket commentator. Sure enough, Pig has accessed Fleming's laptop and already copied all his files to our data storage files. Being just a little nosey, he watches to see what else Fleming is doing, but he seems to be doing legitimate police work, writing files.

I'm keen to read Fleming's 'Escorts escapade', as the file is headed, and it looks to me to be well written and certainly plausible, so we'll have to get our ducks in a row to combat it.

As we're winding up for the day, I say to Pig, 'We're going to have to move these two girls once we expose it as a fraud.'

He replies, 'Well, why don't we arrange a second interview with our own favoured journo, so the girls can say they were coerced by crooked coppers to make the claim? That should make them keep their heads down for a while.'

I nod. 'Now that's a plan!'

We decide we need to ramp up our coverage of the SCs and review their action most nights from here on.

23

We're nearly two weeks into our surveillance of Cameron, Sofia and Claudia, and whilst we have all the hardware in place, with trackers and mics now in both Cameron's Jag and Sofia's Honda, along with the bug in Claudia's handbag, we haven't heard anything suspicious, nor have there been any phone calls between the two ladies.

Cameron spent a night at the Four Seasons, as he seems to do once a fortnight on average, but this caught us off guard and we weren't able to see who (if anyone) he was with. Being the prick he is, we want to find something damning on him. So, Pig decides to head home to spend the weekend with George, which is fine with me; I'm only monitoring, and can jump on anything that comes up.

Fortunately, we've also won two more assignments. Nothing exciting – simple intranet audits to confirm they are relatively secure. One is very good. Pig struggled to get in, so we actually congratulated them and only charged a nominal fee. We certainly took note of their IT consultant, a Bruce Pollock, and made contact. We caught up with him over coffee, as he is a freelance contractor, moving from project to project. We have his details should we need him in the future.

The other assignment, well, their firewall is not so flash, so I spend the weekend opening all the holes in their security platform, sending them their report and invoice on Monday morning. Exciting life. I then access the most recent SC audio files to see what mischief these boys have been up to, but not much has happened in the last few days, and we still haven't heard back from Midge. I give Suzie a call Saturday night, but I only get her voicemail, so I assume at least someone is out enjoying themselves.

Pig flies back down early Monday morning, but nothing much is happening. Cameron had his usual golf game Saturday morning, both ladies went to their respective gyms, and all went out to dinner Saturday, again separately. Sunday, Cameron and Sofia did not venture out, whilst Claudia met a lady friend at a high-end café for Sunday brunch. Being a bit bored, I went along and enjoyed the meal as well. I haven't shaved whilst being in Sydney, so after two weeks, I have a fine full black beard, so Claudia is not likely to remember me from the bus or train journey.

Then, all of a sudden, there's some action early Tuesday morning, as Claudia leaves the house a little early, and immediately steps into a waiting Uber, catching me on the hop. As we had become so accustomed to their routines, we had become a little blasé – worthy of a slap! I trot down the road after the Uber – with peak hour traffic, it isn't moving too quickly – and then after a couple of blocks, I spy a Lime scooter, so I quickly swipe my credit card, slip the helmet on and scoot off down the road after the Uber. It's heading away from the city, and I suspect towards the airport, so after a few kilometres and near a train station, I get off the scooter, pick up a cab and ask to go to the airport.

'Which terminal?' the cabbie asks.

Good question, so I punt it and say, 'Qantas.' It is, after all, the preferred airline of the business classes – or so I've heard.

As we travel, I check on the bug in Claudia's handbag, but that hasn't moved; she has clearly changed bags this morning. Bugger, but it was going to happen.

We arrive at the Qantas terminal, and I head inside, checking the check in area first, but no sign of Claudia, so I move through security and head towards the lounges thinking someone of Claudia's standing is bound to be a Qantas Club member. Not seeing her, I take a seat at a café at the bottom of the escalator she will have to come down to get to her flight – unless she's at the Virgin terminal, in which case I am screwed.

I wait an hour and a half, but no sign of her, so I guess she must be flying Virgin. Ah well, we'll have to wait until she returns home.

Pig, at the same time, has had a routine morning. Cameron left as usual, and Sofia attended her Tuesday morning yoga class. So again, nothing changes.

Late Tuesday afternoon, we notice on the phone log of both Sofia and Claudia a five-minute phone call, instigated by Claudia. Boy, wouldn't we like to know what they spoke about.

Later that evening, around 9:30, I note Cameron logging off for the night from their home, and comment to Pig, 'I have to give him his due; he might be a prick, but he does put in the hours.'

As there are no other active users on their system, I close my own laptop for the night as well. But fifteen minutes later, Pig says, 'Hang on, did you say Cameron was working from home?'

I reply, 'Yes, he logged off just after 9:30.'

Pig replies, 'Bingo! He has just been dropped off by a cab, so he hasn't been home tonight!'

Shit. Sofia.

Well, no chance of us hitting the sack anytime soon now. We immediately backtrack both the video of Cameron's comings and goings and comparing to his online access, and it appears that every Tuesday and some Thursday nights, he heads out somewhere. We hadn't tracked to where, as he usually goes by cab, but his login is used whilst he's away. No one else at home but Sofia, who is not supposed to know anything about Paramount business, or IT, so someone must have been teaching her some tricks.

Coincidence or not, with Claudia calling Sofia today as well, we decide we need to be right on top of both these ladies, in case they are planning to meet. Action time – much better than waiting!

*

Next morning, Wednesday, as we don't know where Claudia is, or when she will be back, I head to her office to basically hang around, hoping to see if she returns. With the camera in place, we'll know if she goes straight home, but she's pretty diligent and spends most days at the office. Thank goodness for all the coffee shops and cafes around North Sydney!

Pig, on the other hand, is hanging around Vaucluse with the camera in place. He doesn't need to be on Olola Avenue, just nearby; to head anywhere, Claudia has little option but to turn left onto Vaucluse Road. So far, nothing out of the ordinary with her routine either. Big expectations for the day, but it's heading for a bust.

Later in the afternoon, just before 4:30 p.m., my phone pings an alert, and there is Claudia entering her apartment, having just been dropped off by a departing Uber.

So we can only hope tomorrow brings us more action. Marg at Paramount has been calling and emailing me for an update, and all I can say is that these things take time. I'm sure Cameron will be on the phone next, and he won't be as pleasant as Marg. To cap off a disappointing day, Pig and I decide to head down to the wharf at Woolloomooloo for a good feed and a couple of beers.

Later that evening, Pig notes, 'That's interesting, Cameron hasn't come home tonight. I just double-checked as I did not notice him.'

He logs into Cameron's Amex account and sees a charge for

tonight at the Four Seasons in Sydney and repeats his comment from earlier: 'I wonder who he's shagging!'

Around 5:00 a.m. Thursday, I head into the city and manage to get a park near the entrance to the Four Seasons in a loading zone and have to use the barriers to be allowed to stay there, pretending to be working on a manhole. Naturally, I leave the camera running, both on the dash and the one mounted in the rear window. Sure enough, around 8:00 a.m., I recognise Cameron coming out in his Jag. He's alone, but I then watch the footpath closely to see if I recognise anyone I know. I wonder if I'll see Marg (I was hoping she had better taste than that!) or Claudia, but who I see is neither of them. Who came striding out of the main entrance was Christina, the South American beauty, the Paramount receptionist. She was a stunner, as I first thought when arriving at their offices.

I freeze frame a photo off the surveillance tape and send it to Pig, saying, 'That's who!'

He replies 'Mmm, can't doubt his good taste! Who is she?'

'Christina, the Paramount receptionist.'

'Interesting,' he replies.

Then back to work. I note Claudia has not left at her usual time, so I double check the tape to make sure, and then let Pig know.

Around 10:30 a.m., we get double action. Sofia and Claudia both leave almost simultaneously, with Sofia heading towards the city, but she stops at Rose Bay, parking in the shopping centre car park. This is a little odd as it's not one of her usual haunts. Then Pig gets a look at her. As we know, she's a petite lady, and today she is very smartly dressed, heading somewhere important. She has a small overnight bag with her, and she hails a cab, jumps in, and they continue on towards the city.

At the same time, Claudia has climbed into an Uber waiting outside, and also has a small overnight bag, but the good news is it looks like she has her regular handbag today, so let's hope we can hear her talking shortly. Sure enough, I hear her confirm with the driver they are headed to the Shangri-La Hotel, another fancy hotel in the CBD. I give a fist pump, A) because we have audio, and B) because something is finally coming together. I let Pig know and voice my suspicion that he is going to end up there as well.

As I am already in the CBD and only five minutes away, I quickly park in a nearby car park, head over to the Shangri-La, and take up a seat in the café in the foyer. Claudia is the first to arrive, and it's obvious she too has spent a bit of time in front of the mirror, looking most becoming, and with her usual dominant presence she is quite a force. She proceeds to check in, not once glancing in my direction, and as I have trimmed my beard back to the fashionable two-day shadow look, again I am confident she would not recognise me; I'm wearing tinted glasses as well, as a further safeguard.

Just as she finishes checking in, Sofia arrives and they greet each other – a little reservedly, I think – kissing each other on the cheek, but with a little finger squeeze from Claudia, they head to the elevators together. *Interesting,* I think, *Sofia isn't checking in.* Of course, it would be a bit too obvious to try and get onto the same elevator as they did, so I watch to see what floor they get off, noting it is level twelve. So, not the cheap rooms.

I head outside and wait for Pig at an adjoining café, where we put our heads together. We head straight back to the Quest so Pig has a more stable IT platform to try and access the Shangri-La system and see what room they are in, and also to see if Claudia or Sofia have had previous bookings here. I get the short straw to stay here and see if either of them leave, whenever that may be.

The audio from her handbag isn't very good, and Pig will see if he can enhance this once back at our room. This is not too far, either – only fifteen minutes. In the meantime, I've found a quiet spot and can hear some of the audio, which is nearly making me blush, as these two ladies are clearly lovers. Hadn't seen that coming!

I warn Pig to cover his ears when he does improve the audio, and this doesn't take him long once back with the power of our own system. After the appropriate comments back and forth, he lets me know they're in room 1515, and both have previous bookings – it seems they take turns booking a room every second Thursday. A very interesting development. One that means we have to go back through the nights Cameron has left his laptop at home whilst he goes out, and we need to know where he goes each Tuesday and occasionally Thursday (wouldn't mind knowing what excuse he uses for his night at the Four Seasons either, but this doesn't look to be relevant to our investigation).

We need to put mics into both their homes, so we have a better knowledge of what is coming up. Pig decides no better time than now to go and do the deed. I suggest he should wait so I can act as lookout, whilst as easy as it is to break into someone's home, even if they have an alarm system, we always do it reluctantly, as it does cross a line, even if only an imaginary one for us.

There's no deterring him, so off he goes to Claudia's first. Of course, we've done a full reconnaissance of both homes, and know in Claudia's case that the best access is through the rear neighbour's yard, which is narrow with high fences on either side, but only a hedge between their place and Claudia's. So in he goes, surprisingly no alarm, but he was prepared for one just in case, with our little alarm tapper, which has a Bluetooth reader to identify the code and show it on the screen. A great little gimmick we obtained whilst working with the Yanks a couple of years ago (one of many handy toys they gave us).

So he's in. We know she lives alone, but not taking any chances, he moves silently through the ground floor, identifying the rooms to me over the phone (we are both wearing earpieces, so both hands-free, and we talk in our own shorthand, often no more than grunts – after years of working silently as a team, we know what each other is thinking almost intuitively). Upstairs, there are three bedrooms – hers, a spare, and her office, which is well set up with a 21" monitor, printer, etc. We agree a bug in here is essential, and he can also fit a camera to a light fitting which will enable us to read her computer monitor. When she connects her laptop, we should have clear vision of the screen. Bonus! We decide not to bug her bedroom but do put one under the landline phone in the kitchen. This will record any conversations on the phone, but also act as a mic here in the kitchen.

Done and dusted. Pig's out of there and off over to Olola Avenue. There, he decides on the frontal approach, parking his van in the driveway, and going around the back after grabbing his toolbox and strapping on his tool belt. He looks every bit the Telstra man, or electrician – take your pick. Again, he quickly picks the lock, and as they do have an alarm, he uses the alarm tapper, which quickly gives up the code, and he's in the clear. Again, he talks me through the house, all one level, and in what is clearly Cameron's study, he basically replicates what he did at Claudia's with a mic and a light mounted camera to record vision of the computer screen. A smaller sewing room appears to be Sofia's sanctuary, so another mic goes in here – no sign of her having a laptop, so we guess she has her iPad with her. He resets the alarm, out the door and home free. Easy peasy.

Pig heads back to base, whilst I am still hanging around the Shangri-La entrance. Then around 3:00 p.m., Sofia walks out. The doorman flags a waiting cab, and in she gets. I don't bother trying to follow her as I'm pretty certain she'll be heading home so she is there before Cameron, not wanting him to know what she has been up to. From the audio coming from Claudia's handbag, it sounds like she's talking to someone, and mentions a USB she needs to deliver, so whilst listening in, I text Pig to make sure he's getting this.

'Yes,' he says, 'loud and clear.'

Once she finishes the call, Pig lets me know that she and her caller, Rowan, had agreed to meet tomorrow morning around 9:00 a.m. here at the Shangri-La Café. So it seems pretty clear she is going to stay for the night – she has paid for it, after all.

Pig and I have fiddled around in the past, trying to determine if there is a particular sound for each phone key with the iPhone, and reckon we have it sussed, so he listens to the replay of Claudia's dialling Rowan with the high-definition headphones, and reckons he has the right number. He then calls it and asks to speak to John; when told he must have the wrong number, he chats to Rowan who identifies himself as Rowan.

When Pig asks, 'So, what do you do, Rowan?' the bloke hangs up.

Boom, we now have Claudia's contact or maybe partner in crime, and he puts the phone number into our Telstra portal and up comes the owner as Rowan Smith with an address in Cremorne, a leafy inner suburb on the North Shore. A search of LinkedIn and other business-related websites doesn't tell us much, nor does a search of ASIC, where he is only listed as a former director and no current directorships, which is a little interesting.

Now with it relatively certain Claudia is staying put for the night, I head back to the car park, retrieve the van, head back out through Rose Bay, note Sofia's car has gone, cruise past their home, and note a couple of lights on, so I guess she's home safe and sound. Back to base for me too, and we have to devise a plan to cover the meeting tomorrow between Claudia and Rowan. This time, it needs to be Pig roaming around, as we don't want the hotel staff to become suspicious of me loitering for two days straight.

Fortunately, I have spent a bit of time in the café today, so I can describe it to Pig. I suggest if he can get a seat against the front wall, facing the entrance, he will have a good view of the room, as we want to try and get a photo of them together. If he's really lucky, a photo of the USB changing hands. Even better would be if he can video either of them talking – we might be able to lip read what they are saying. And of course, we need a photo of Rowan, as it is highly likely Rowan is not his real name. That way, we can run his photo through our facial recognition software. I'll go with Pig into the city; I'll stay well out of sight, but within easy reach with a van in case we have to move quickly.

All of that's for tomorrow, so now for a run and a feed. Feels good now that we are making progress.

I get another phone call from Marg at Paramount asking for an update, and I tell her I'm a little busy at present but will send through another email update later in the evening. She asks if I would like to catch up for a quick drink maybe Friday after work. This takes me a little by surprise and I thank her, but explain I'm already committed, but thanks anyway.

I then think, *Okay, Marg is a nice lady, so maybe you're more committed to Suzie than you have admitted to yourself!*

With that thought in my head I decide to give Suzie a call after dinner, not just a text as we have been doing.

*

Next morning, we head in early, arriving just before 8:30 a.m. Pig wanders in and orders the big breakfast with coffee, so he has plenty of time. Claudia comes in around 8:45 a.m., taking a seat with her back to Pig (good, means Rowan will be facing him!), and she too orders breakfast, but looks like an egg white omelette for her (why, doesn't that surprise us?) with a pot of tea. Like yesterday, we are both plugged in with earpieces, but not saying too much.

At 9:10 a.m., a small dapper man comes in, looks around and

then slips into the chair opposite Claudia at her table for two. Pig, who has surreptitiously taken a couple of photos of Claudia's back, continues to fiddle with his phone and manages to get a good close-up of him. He only orders coffee, and once served they chat for a while. Pig notices the USB being slid across the table. Rowan slips his hand over it and it disappears into his pocket. Neatly done, but Pig did manage a couple of photos showing it on the table, then disappearing under his fingers.

They stay chatting whilst Claudia finishes her breakfast, and as Pig senses they are getting ready to leave, he beats them to it, settles his account, and leaves, then pretending to be on his phone in the lobby, whilst waiting to see who goes where. We have agreed I will tail Rowan, if possible, not wanting me too close to Claudia again.

Rowan walks out of the lobby and heads off down Cumberland Street before hailing a cab.

Crap, I think, but fortunately there's another cab idling behind the first, so I jump in and say, 'Follow that cab' (always did want to say that).

The cabbie gives me funny look, and away we go. Rowan's cab heads across town past Wynyard train station and then onto Market Place, coming to a stop outside 1 Market Place, so I tell my cabbie to stop a little behind, quickly pay him and follow Rowan into the lobby. He presses the lift. To be on the safe side, I choose not to join him in the lift, but watch it go right to the top – level thirty-two, a serviced office joint, so full of small businesses not needing a full office of their own. Bugger, won't be easy to track down who or what he is operating under.

Through this journey, Pig texts me to say he has heard from Midge and we are set up to talk to him later this evening. Cool – I am looking forward to that!

Claudia, with Pig trailing behind, has taken the train across to

North Sydney and is presently walking to her office. So I head back to the Quest and get started on trying to identify Rowan by putting his image into our face recognition system. I do this and leave it to do its thing. Pig meanwhile has taken up station adjacent to Claudia's office in yet another café. I'm thinking I need to put coffee down as an 'extras' cost on our invoices.

Whilst he is sitting there idly, we run through what we know:
- Sofia and Claudia are lovers.
- Sofia appears (no proof of this yet, but…) to be stealing Paramount secrets by accessing Cameron's email and the Paramount system whenever he is out in the evenings.
- She is then sharing this with Claudia.
- Who, in turn, is sharing the data with Rowan – is she being paid? If so, how/where?
- Who is Rowan sharing it with?

We need an action plan. We need to know where Cameron goes on Tuesday evenings – and the occasional Thursdays as well. Even if it's not relevant to the investigation. We need proof of Sofia accessing Cameron's laptop – we have this covered with the bugs and cameras now set up in their home. We need to find how and where Claudia is being paid. Hopefully by watching her when she is online in her home office, we might catch a break and see where she may have these extra accounts.

A reminder we need to monitor our new cameras and mics in both homes.

Then we need proof of Sofia and Claudia's relationship, so we need to make some plans for Thursday fortnight on the basis they will meet again at the Shangri-La. Pig will book a room there for next Thursday, and then early in the day access their system (see how we don't lower ourselves to call it hacking?) to ensure Pig and Claudia get rooms that are adjacent, or at least on the same floor.

This will provide a base to work from.

I have an idea: we could use Maria, Suzie's netball teammate – put her into a maid's uniform so she can access their room as housekeeping. Pig agrees this has promise, although he has never met Maria, and I explain her background with 1st NZR and my belief she would be a good soldier and handle this assignment with aplomb. After all, neither Pig or I will look too flash in a maid's uniform, and a male housekeeper would certainly raise more suspicions. We agree on this plan of action as neither of us could think of a better candidate for the role. Knowing Maria is not working and has her mother in the background to look after the kids, I am sure she will jump at a little excitement! She would be ideal.

However, we will wait until the room booking has been made before pursuing it.

*

We're back in our room at the Quest when Pig's phone starts ringing a different ringtone from normal. We both look at each other, raising our eyebrows as if saying, 'that's weird'. Pig answers and puts it on speaker, and there, as clear as anything, is Midge asking, 'Hey, do you like your new ringtone?' and having a good laugh. Clearly just showing off.

We reminisce about days gone by and our lucky escapades. Pig and I (well, mainly Pig) had saved Midge's life in one such action, for which he is truly appreciative, and we all know that's why he is happy to help us. We lay out what we want from him, but only giving him the barest of details as to why, even though we know he has encrypted Pig's phone just by calling it.

'So,' he says in his Southern drawl, 'all you want is copies of this dude and his wife's passport, showing when he's been out of the country. I'll need to access your Department of Immigration – or is that Border Force now? Should be a cinch.'

Then we ask about the Australian recognised voices they have on file, and he says, 'Sure, load up the files,' giving us a link to use, and warns us to ensure we have each file logged and dated, as any response will come back showing the date and time with the name of the recognised voice. He confirms they have thousands of Australians on file, so here's hoping for a double breakthrough!

We don't insult Midge by asking where he is; if he answered, we wouldn't believe him anyway, but we do tell him to make the trip down here sometime so we can look after him. After we hang up, Pig and I are a little wired; we had a pretty successful day, and then chatting to Midge with an even bigger outcome now likely, we decided it was off to the pub for a decent feed and a couple of beers.

24

It's mid-afternoon on Friday, and as we aren't expecting anything further to develop today, we agree Pig should join me back at the Quest, so he can finalise the SA Tech Inc. digital security audit. We now have two more to prepare; I'm thinking I might have to charge a bit more – they're coming in thick and fast, these new jobs. The scourge of the global hacking making headlines was good for business!

Before Pig gets back, I get a little *ping* from the facial recognition software: we have a match. Rowan is, in fact, one Dermott Ross. Now that we have a true identity, we can start digging and see what we can find. We're keen to wrap the whole process up. We know it starts with Sofia, through Claudia, and on to Rowan/Dermott, but who is the end buyer? That's the question!

Dermott is registered as a director of DAR and Associates, another management and marketing consultant (I didn't know there were so many of these types out there making a living!), with their registered office listed as 1 Market Place Sydney, which matches were he headed after the meeting at the hotel. He has a pretty bland website, not saying anything about who his clients might be – no help there – so I decide to ask a few discrete questions about our Dermott. I'll have to wait and see what answers come back. These won't be today; most city types have an early mark on Fridays and either hit the pubs or make tracks home early.

His address is listed as a unit in Belgrave Street, Cremorne, another treed inner suburb, and I google the address to see it is a modern and stylish multilevel apartment complex – so a few bob's worth, I think. Pig arrives and I update him with this news, and we agree I'm it for an early morning trip to Cremorne Monday morning to keep tabs on Mr Ross. We too decide to have an early mark ourselves and sit down to a couple of beers, before heading to the Potts Point Hotel, which has become our local whilst staying at the Quest.

Saturday morning, we both take off for our usual runs, never together as that will only end up in a race, so we have developed our own circuits of eight to ten kilometres each. After a cool down and a breakfast of Weetbix (yes, I am still a Weetbix kid), we review the video and audio from the night before; I take Claudia, and Pig takes Cameron and Sofia.

Pig comes up blank, and the CCTV confirms they spent the evening out. I meanwhile had a bit better luck with Claudia, as she chatted with Rowan/Dermott on Microsoft Teams, and I was able to view the text of their conversation. It appeared they were old friends and clearly had done business together previously. But nothing about what might be happening right now.

After that, she actually accessed a bank account at Scotiabank, Cayman Islands, and I took a screen shot of the account details, showing a tidy balance of US$732,000.

Some business deal she has going, I think.

Talk about luck! I share this with Pig.

We discuss whether it's worth reaching out to Midge to see if he could log in and get a copy of the transactions of this account, knowing it's beyond our capabilities. We decide we don't want to push our luck with Midge, considering what we had already asked him for, and we let this slide. We do have an image of her bank account, after all.

25

Monday morning comes around, like every other day, and it finds me sitting in our van up the road from Rowan's apartment (we've decided to continue calling him Rowan), from where I will see him when he leaves. We found out he owns a white Lexus IS300 Hybrid, so I'm also on the lookout for this. But like most in Sydney's inner suburbs, he comes out onto the footpath, heading for the bus stop just up the road, so I sit tight until he boards his bus, and then I follow slowly – not that that's too hard, considering the peak hour traffic.

Whilst sitting at the lights, I check the timetable for the #430 bus he's on, and see it's actually heading to the city, so I take the next left and, using the GPS, work my way up the side streets a few blocks, park, and get back out onto Military Road in time to squeeze onto the same bus as Rowan. I start way at the back, whereas he's standing towards the front. As opportunities arise, I manage to move until I'm standing slightly behind him. He's standing holding a handle, and I notice he has an old-fashioned leather-zipped briefcase next to his feet, and the zipper is open. Bonus! I slip a little mic and tracker device out of my pocket, and while bending down and pretending to do up a shoelace, I slip the mic into his briefcase, and then ease further away from him, even managing to score a seat, but then, being the gentleman I am, I quickly give this up for an elderly woman getting on at the next stop.

We're in the city now, so I watch to see where we are going, getting more and more confident he's heading for his office in Market Street. Sure enough, he gets off at Wynyard Station and heads off towards Market Street. With the tracker now in play, I can dawdle along watching his progress on my tracking app on my phone. I text Pig to let him know as well so he can monitor progress.

He heads into the lobby and I head to an adjacent café to take up post. I have my laptop with me, so I log on using my phone's secure access and also plug my earplugs in so I can hear any conversation. Sure enough, a few minutes later, I hear Rowan saying, 'Good morning' a few times as, I assume, he walks to his office. However, as the morning progresses, it becomes quite obvious Rowan is the silent type. Although I can hear his keyboard tapping, I haven't heard one conversation. By now I'm on my third coffee, and with the lunch hour approaching, the staff are giving me the hurry up. After discussing it with Pig, we agree and I head back to retrieve the van and give Rowan's apartment block the once over, not being overly confident we would gain much by trying to tap it, as he is more than likely using his office for any critical meetings or data storage. We don't even know if he lives alone.

Twenty minutes later, I'm in the van pulling up in the visitor's park at his apartment block with my Telstra hi-vis jacket on, grab my tool bag and wander around the front of the complex as if I am looking for something, when what I'm really doing is sussing the joint out to see how easy it would be to get in. I decide not hard at all, but it's quite a busy complex, and everyone nods or chats to each other, so I suspect I would get questioned if I tried to get in. I decide to leave it for now. Pig reckons I'm a wuss. I head back to home base and monitor Rowan's movements, which is easy, as he doesn't leave the office all day, not even for lunch. Maybe he does have a good wife who makes his lunch for him!

He only has two phone conversations – nether of much interest to us. Then, around 4:45 p.m., he packs up, exits the building, and seems to retrace his route from this morning. Until he gets off the bus back in Cremorne where, instead of going home, he heads into what we later discover is the Barrel Bar. We can hear a lot of background noise, but as I said earlier, Rowan seems to be the silent type. He stays here for a little over an hour and a half (two schooners, we reckon), and then he heads home and doesn't budge for the night. No phone calls either, and only background noise from the TV all evening, so we suspect he lives alone.

Some of my inquiries had come back. He has a police record, having been charged with fraud some eight years ago, and even spent eight months inside at Emu Plains Prison. Looks like no family; his wife divorced him whilst he was in prison, and the apartment he's living in is owned by a company he is the sole director and shareholder of, valued at $1 million plus. No record of a mortgage, either, tidy bank balance as well, so he's doing okay.

We decide any dealings he's handling are likely being done by email, so Pig accesses DAR's website to then access their email server. Dermot (Rowan) and 'accounts' are the only email addresses, so Pig accesses both and trolls through the emails since he met with Claudia the previous week. And yes, we get lucky: there is an email exchange between him and a Gmail account called 'phoneking1', discussing the next instalment of data and confirmation of the fee of $250,000, so woohoo, we are making good progress now!

Surprisingly, it's not too hard to access Gmail account data (If you know what you are doing!), and Pig quickly comes up with the IP address and holder of the phoneking1 account as one Matt Hoskins, who we soon find out is president of another small telephone and internet provider, Futurcomm. We find Matt seems to be a clean skin, with no police record or anything adverse circulating in the business world – just looks like he's cutting corners to grow his business. Not a bad day's work, we reckon.

The next day, Tuesday, we monitor all five players: Sofia, Claudia, Cameron, Rowan, and now Matt, and it's a routine morning, but being Tuesday, we need to follow Cameron on his weekly night out to see where he goes. I've again caught the short straw, with Pig staying put to trace Sofia as she logs in through Cameron's laptop whilst he is out. None of our mics have picked up anything much out of the ordinary other than Claudia had a male friend over for dinner, who did not leave until the next morning, so we're wondering if she bats for both teams.

26

I've hired a car – another bland Camry – to avoid using either van again in this area, so it won't stand out. There I am, sitting down the road near the junction of Olola Avenue and Vaucluse Road, and when Cameron's Jaguar comes along, he indicates turning right onto Wentworth Road, not left towards the city. I follow at a discrete distance, and he then turns right into Chapel Road and pulls up outside a comfortable, well-maintained home. There's another car pulling up at the same time, so I drive past and watch as Cameron and the other man shake hands and head towards the front door. There's already another car parked on the road, likely making it three visitors. I'm already thinking a mate's poker night, but that's simply a guess.

I pull up outside a block of flats, where I think there's likely to be different cars parked there regularly, only half a block from the poker lair. I've already disengaged the courtesy light in the Camry, so when I get out, it doesn't light up, and I head off round the side of the unit complex as if I know where I am going, and with it being another nice tree-lined street (like all of Vaucluse) it is easy to keep to the shadows as I backtrack and take a quick photo of the three cars parked in the street, plus one in the driveway so we can identify who Cameron is meeting with. I also take the opportunity to slip a tracker under the rear bumper of Cameron's Jag; hadn't planned on it, more a spur of the moment decision. You just never know.

With the front windows open, I can hear male laughter coming from the house, so using the hedge and its shadow I quietly get close enough to hear parts of the conversation, and yes, I was right, they are playing poker. And drinking, as I heard one of them ask, 'Who wants another beer?'

I ease back from the house and continue walking up the street away from my car, as I won't be going anywhere anytime soon, so really just out for a stroll. At the end of the street, I turn crossing over to the other side and wander back to the Camry.

When comfortably back in the Camry, I text the number plate photos to Pig to trace the owners whilst I relax and wait. Pig tells me Sofia has been busy, and as he can now see the screen of the laptop from the camera he installed, he tells me she seems to be copying all his emails for the week, plus any files he has accessed through the week, so a comprehensive package of data we now know is worth $250k – not that Sofia will be getting it all, maybe only a small portion considering how many others are getting a feed from her treachery.

Pig texts me again around 9:30 p.m. to say she has downloaded it onto a USB and closed the laptop down, and he had a couple of photos showing the data on the USB as she checked to ensure it had all saved properly. He also confirms this included the little tracking program he had created and stored in one of Cameron's regularly used folders. This little program would enable Pig to track it and open up access for Pig to identify the IP address and identity of where the data is stored. A Trojan horse virus, in other words, but only for the good guys – us! Sophia had then sent a text to Claudia to say, 'All good tonight. Can't wait for next Thursday!' Claudia's reply was a heart emoji.

Around 9:45 p.m. Cameron and the other two drivers parked on the road come out a little noisily, saying, 'Goodbye, see you next week,' with one of them crowing about being happy to take their money again next week. As I follow Cameron home, I think it's just as well he isn't driving too far, as he is weaving a little.

Now that we had nailed down Cameron's Tuesday night movements, and confirmed Sofia was in fact the guilty party, we start making plans for the following week, when we expect Sofia and Claudia to again have their little rendezvous at the Shangri-La (and maybe Cameron and Christina at the Four Seasons), and need to be ready to get proof of these plus be in a position to capture the flow of data from Claudia onwards. With Pig's Trojan horse, we are confident we can trace the data all the way now.

*

When I get back to the Quest, Pig says, 'Look at this,' pointing to his laptop screen.

I go over for a look, and there is Noel Dyson and his wife Samantha's passport images showing their travel dates.

'Boom,' I say, and we fist bump.

Then he says, 'That's not all. Look at all these names of known contacts Lancaster has been talking to.'

Sure enough, there are pages of identified names we have recorded talking to Lancaster, all logged with date and time of the recording (as we had supplied to them). There's also a note from Midge saying they had Lancaster down as an unknown talking to some 'seriously bad dudes', so it's good to have his voice identified now too; a favour returned. Some pretty heavy work to start in the morning – sifting through all these names, identifying who they are, etc. – but hey, better than not having the information. Besides, we have coffee, right?

*

Wednesday morning and we make an early start, keen to see who is on the list of Lancaster's phone calls. We split the list, agreeing to identify any names that appear three or more times, and deem these regular contacts; others less than three times will get looked at later. We start by adding each 'regular' contact into a spreadsheet, noting the date and time of the logged call along with their phone number. Then, through Google and other less known sources, we identify who these people are and record this as well.

Whilst we are working separately, we are working in a live Excel spreadsheet, so we can each see what the other is doing. I'm the first to say 'shit' as I see a well-known union heavy hitter's name come up – so well-known I don't have to look him up. Then I've got a minister in the state government, supposedly a junior minister, but reputedly big behind the scenes, often called 'a numbers man'.

Then an 'aw, shit' from Pig as he points to the name Jack Herbert who is the Queensland Premier's assistant chief of staff. Pig says, 'George and Jack are good mates, have worked together for years.'

This causes us to pause and look at each other whilst we digest the implications that George is likely to be involved, even if only on the edges, of the SC's carrying on.

I get up and make us both a fresh coffee, giving Pig space whilst he mulls this over. When I come back with the coffee, he looks at me and shrugs and says, 'What we're seeing is not right; let the pieces fall where they do.'

I look at him and nod: agreed.

After a few hours, we've got a long list of contacts from politics but only from the Labour Party, union heavies from three different large unions here in Queensland, three or four senior Jackals outlaw bikie members including Rhys O'Connor, and two brothel 'madams'. We take a break for lunch, and I wander over the road to bring back a couple of fresh chicken sandwiches, and whilst we eat these, we discuss the next step.

Whilst I am out, Pig has accessed DS Fleming's data and reads the escort's planned statement, and checked the date against Dyson's passport, but no luck – he wasn't out of the country. No matter. By checking both his and his wife's passports, he has gone in and changed the date from August to April, when it looks like the Dyson family were in Hawaii for a family holiday.

'That will be hard to refute,' he tells me when I get back.

He also tells me Fleming had a note saying a Derrick Byrnes from the United Workers Union had confirmed they had their member Sonia Parsons, a receptionist at the Sofitel, add the fake booking into the hotel's system.

Back to Lancaster's contacts, and now that we have identified some of the names, we need to go back and listen to their specific calls to see if this will help give us some relevance. I take the politicians and unions, whilst Pig focuses on the bikies and madams, but I remind him we need to stop by 3:00 p.m. to ensure we aren't late for our rendezvous at the Four Seasons tonight.

As my first focus, I decide to go back over the audio for the calls with Jack Herbert, seemingly a direct link between Lancaster and the state premier. Considering what they are planning to do to her main opponent makes this more critical. We have five separate conversations on file between them, so I listen to them sequentially and find in the first call where Herbert and Lancaster agree to a meet at the Frisky Goat Café in the city. I take a note of the date and add a footnote to check phone calls after this date between Lancaster and Fleming to see if the meeting is discussed between them. It seems imperative we understand this political angle. In the second phone call, Herbert points out to Lancaster that 'this Dyson looks like he's becoming a nuisance. Anything you can do about him?'

Lancaster replies, 'Leave it with me; I'll check him out.'

The third call was again Herbert, asking for an update, and Lancaster replies, 'We can't find anything on him at all.'

Herbert replies, 'Well, I'm sure you have a good imagination then!' and hangs up.

Well, I think, *no doubt he wants something by fair means or foul!*

The fourth call is Lancaster advising Herbert they have a hooker – sorry, 'escort' – willing to go public on a night of frolics with Dyson. 'So watch this space,' Lancaster tells him.

The fifth call is just updating Herbert that they are planning a press conference with Christi in the next week or so, and Lancaster will let him know where and when.

Hmm, no doubt these blokes are doing the heavy lifting for the Labour Party, and I am now keen to switch focus to the union heavies, but time to prepare for our evening escapade. Also, the timing of the planned press conference means we need to get ahead of this, identify Christi, and where the SCs are planning on stashing Christi after the press conference. We can then retrieve them when the timing is right.

Whilst driving into the city, Pig tells me it looks like Lancaster actually is running the bikies' illicit businesses; if not in charge, certainly he has major input. So far, he has discussed with the Jackals hierarchy drugs, coming in from both Mexico and Columbia, loan sharks, and of course, the brothels. We need to find a way to access Lancaster's PC and his files to see what he actually owns and earns. So far, we haven't been able to trace it, in spite of where it is located physically.

But now it's time for our evening entertainment!

27

In the evening, we're both sitting in the foyer of the Four Seasons, waiting on Cameron and Christina's arrival. Pig had logged into the hotel's system earlier to confirm their booking so we knew which room they will be in.

Sure enough, they actually come up from the car park together, with Christina hanging back a little whilst Cameron checks in. Then up they go in the elevator. We finish our coffees and go back outside where Pig sits down on a bench seat along the street, donning his headphones and pulling his iPad out of his satchel. He gives me a nod, so I wander around the side of the hotel where it is quiet with very few people passing, as it's not a thoroughfare. Positioning myself behind a couple of trees, I pull a drone out of my satchel, turn it on, then hold it in my palm, and seconds later, it takes off as Pig takes it airborne. I move back and sit next to Pig, donning my headphones and iPad as well so I can see what he is seeing.

We had worked out which windows were Cameron's, both knowing, of course, that if they bothered to pull the curtains, we wouldn't be seeing much, but with the view they had and no overlooking buildings, we hoped they wouldn't. Sure enough, once the drone is hovering outside their window, it is obvious they had not had time to think about pulling curtains as they are already entwined on the bed, so a couple of photos showing both their faces (and lots more!), and we are done for the night, and now reverse the process with me going back around the side to take possession of the drone as Pig brings it back down.

Since we're in the city and quite presentable, we head off to Kingsley's for a decent steak. In fact, Pig is booked into the Shangri-La for the next two nights – just to ensure we have access whilst the girls are in the house.

Thursday, we hope it's a big day. I had spoken to Maria (Suzie's netball mate) late last week, once we knew the girls had made their hotel reservation (Claudia's turn, this time), and she had quickly agreed to fly down to Sydney for the day. I even had to ask her size so we could get her a maid's uniform that would fit – that was an interesting conversation to start with.

She is due to arrive in Sydney around 8:15 a.m., so we are hoping she will arrive at the Shangri-La by 9:00 a.m. as she won't have luggage. We will meet her in the coffee lounge in the foyer first and then go up to their room so we can run through our plan in detail with her – and hope she doesn't pike out on us!

I get into town early and join Pig for breakfast whilst we wait for Maria. I see her getting out of the Uber, so I get up and go out and meet her, so she doesn't feel lost and stand out in the foyer. I hope she has her tats covered; otherwise, she'll be noticed. Fortunately, she does have on a long-sleeved blouse and is rather smartly dressed – looks the goods, in fact – a tall and stylish lady, but one look at her face tells you, 'don't mess with me'.

As Pig has gone back up to the room, I grab Maria a tea (she tells me she doesn't drink coffee) and we too take the elevator up to level fifteen. When we get to the room, I introduce Pig and Maria, and she reacts with 'Ooh, aren't you the looker? I thought this one here'—pointing a thumb at me—'was a bit tidy, but if I wasn't happy with my Ronnie, I reckon I could get you to swap teams!'

Pig doesn't know what to say whilst I have a good laugh – doubt anyone has ever told Pig they could get him to swap teams.

We settle down so we can go through the plan, and we explain to Maria what we need, that the two 'marks', as she has started calling them, have a room booked for their romantic interlude, and her job is to knock and enter quickly, pushing her housekeeping cart, which Pig snaffled through the night, and it was sitting there in the room. We would have her wired with a chest-mounted camera and mic, with a second camera on the front of the cart for a different angle.

We will already have sound – Claudia has her favourite handbag with her. We checked the camera when she left her house this morning, as she has gone into the office first, unlike their last rendezvous when she came straight to the hotel. Pig had also logged into the hotel system and changed Claudia's room to 1511, so just down the hall from his room, and further away from the lifts.

Maria has a few questions, then goes into the bathroom to change into the maid's uniform, coming out giggling as it is too tight in the bust and way too loose around the hips. We suggest holding her chest in, getting more giggles in reply. After a bit of fiddling, I leave Pig to help her, and as she had cleverly brought her sewing kit with her (we certainly didn't think of that!), she ticks and tucks here and there and goes back into the bathroom for another fit up, telling us she will tighten her bra, and the outcome of this plus her fiddling around the skirt makes her quite presentable. It isn't as if she'll be on the fashion walkway, after all; it's more a case that she won't stand out if anyone sees her in the hallways – well, more than a six-foot-tall housekeeper would ordinarily stand out, that is.

Now it's time to wait. Maria asks a couple of questions about the marks, coming to terms it is two ladies she is going to barge in on. As well as the uniform and housekeeping cart, Pig has also snaffled a housekeeping card through the night. I didn't ask how or where from. It's certainly simpler, but our lock kits would have worked just as quickly.

Maria has been doing a few practice entries coming in from the bathroom, practicing positioning the cart, so she gets a different angle, but also not making it too difficult to back out of the room. We only need a few seconds of video, after all.

As 11:30 a.m. approaches, we hear Claudia tell someone (Uber or taxi driver, we guessed), 'The Shangri-La, please,' so I nod and head out of the room back down to the lobby and, you guessed it, have another coffee whilst I wait for the girls to arrive.

I notice Sofia has already arrived and is sitting in the lobby waiting, again dressed smartly. About fifteen minutes later, Claudia arrives and there are little waves and smiles to each other whilst Claudia waits to check in. As she walks to the elevator, Sofia joins her and, again, the little hand squeeze.

I let them go, texting Pig to say they are on their way up. I wait a few minutes – have to finish my coffee, after all – before venturing back up to our room. When I enter, I can sense Maria is getting a little nervous. To calm her down, I talk to her about her kids, and that takes her mind off what she is about to do, even with the sound of their voices coming from Pig's iPad set up on the desk. Still only idle chatter, and as none of us three have any clue how long they might take to get lovey-dovey, we settle down to wait.

It's not too long until we hear the sound of kissing then a bit of moaning, then what sounds like clothes being removed and the squeak of a bed. We all look at each other, trying to decide how quick or how long this might take, and after seven or eight minutes of much moaning and sounds of movement, we all nod in unison. Pig and Maria head to the door – Pig first, to ensure the coast is clear. He walks towards the elevator to check to see if there is likely anyone about to arrive, and of course, checks that there are no housekeeping carts floating around. The coast is clear, so he gives the word. I give Maria a silent thumbs up and she is out the door and off on her mission.

As Pig is a guest in the hotel, and therefore has a right to be out there, I am designated to stay and monitor what happens. Shortly, I hear a muffled knock and, 'housekeeping', then the door opening, followed by silence, then the camera vision comes in, showing our ladies right into it, Sofia lifting her head off the pillow at the intrusion and Claudia likewise lifting her head and turning to see what the noise is. Fortunately, neither of them scream.

Within a few seconds, thought it seems longer, Maria backs out of the room and they both come scurrying back into our room with big grins on their faces. A round of high fives follows.

Maria breaks the silence, saying, 'Boy, were they into it, made me horny as – my Ronnie might get lucky tonight!'

We all laugh.

Back to business, Maria quickly goes into the bathroom and changes into her own clothes, whilst Pig and I pack up our laptops – but not before a second review of the photos. There is no doubt both the chest-mounted and cart-mounted cameras got the shots we needed. The girls had gone quiet for a few minutes, not really saying anything, but they were right back into it now by the sound of things, so hopefully they will hardly remember it, or think it was a hallucination.

I slip on a pair of work overalls, sling a lanyard around my neck so I will look like a hotel maintenance man, and head off with the cart whilst Pig and Maria leave together. I have time to abandon the cart somewhere and meet up with them in the car park where Pig has parked the Camry.

We promised Maria her choice for lunch before she heads back to the airport and home. She chooses BLACK Bar and Grill at the Star Casino, as it had featured on TV on some show. Good enough for us; Paramount would be paying anyway! So off we go and have a thoroughly enjoyable lunch, and of course recapping our little episode to regular chuckles throughout. As it approaches time to leave, I ask Maria not to mention our little adventure to Suzie as I had not told her I was reaching out to her.

'Hold on,' she comes back, 'if Suzie doesn't know about it, how did you get my phone number?'

I smile and say, 'What else would you like to know about Maria Anahera Scia Scia? Date of birth, date of discharge?'

Pig jumps in, 'What sort of name is Anahere, anyway?'

Maria laughs and says, 'It's Anahera – it's Māori for *angel*.'

'Ha, they got that wrong,' he rejoins, getting out of the way of a swat from Maria.

She goes on, 'So how do you know this stuff?'

'That's our business, knowing and finding stuff; that's what we have been doing down here for the last nearly five weeks,' I add.

After a pause, she comes back, saying, 'Suzie hasn't seen you for over five weeks?'

'No,' I say, 'I hope she remembers what I look like and how cute my smile is. But we have talked a few times, so she does recognise my voice.'

'Well, I reckon you better hot foot it home – that girl doesn't have to wait for anyone. It'll be your loss if she gets sick of waiting for you!' she finishes.

Great, I think, *I do not want that happening.*

As we are finishing up, I ask Maria, 'Would you be available for a "babysitting" job? Might go for a couple of weeks, but you will be at a nice resort tucked away somewhere.'

She looks at me. 'Babysitting? I've got four kids, don't need anymore!'

I smile and say, 'No, this will be two ladies we will want kept out of sight. It's likely people – including the police – will be looking for them.'

'Well, shit, sounds like fun; what do I do if they don't behave?'

'Your job is to make sure they do,' I say with a smile.

'Well, I reckon I can handle two girls, no worries' she replies. 'How much are you paying?'

'Yes,' Pig adds, 'how much are you paying? I might take the job!'

This gets him a dig in the ribs from Maria, who retorts, 'Piss off – he's asking me.'

I tell her she will be suitably recompensed once we sort out if or when it becomes necessary.

'Okay, book me in!' she replies with a grin.

We drop Maria at the airport ourselves, getting out for hugs all round, and as she leaves, she turns and says, 'Thanks, fellas, I'm really glad you rang me. It was a hoot, and my Ronnie might think so too by the time I'm finished with him.' She smiles and waves and is off through the doors to the departure area.

As we head back to the Quest for Pig to drop me off, we chat about plans for the next morning and how it would be really helpful if we could overhear the conversation between Claudia and Rowan. Pig says to leave it with him, that he'll do a late-night prowl around the lobby café, leaving mics in the sugar or salt holders. He drops me off and waits whilst I go up to our room and grab half a dozen more mics, just to ensure he has enough. Each of these has a radius in normal conditions of hearing voices from up to two metres away, so with a few strategically placed around the café, we should have them covered, no matter where they sit.

Then Pig heads back to Shangri-La for another night of luxury. He's been bragging about the 5,000 thread count sheets – sorry, I mean the 5,000 thread count Egyptian cotton sheets, or some such

– and of course, the fancy brand of toiletries, none of which mean anything to me. Shampoo is shampoo, right?

Later after a local pizza, I give Suzie a call with Maria's warning ringing in my ears, and after a bit of chat and banter, I say, 'Anyway, things are slowing down a bit here, so I was wondering if you would like to come down for the weekend?'

This is met with silence for a few seconds, and then she replies, 'Are you asking me to come for the weekend?'

'Yes,' I reply, 'I'll send you the tickets if you like. You'll be impressed where we'll be staying. And I thought if you wanted to bring something fancy to wear, we could hit the town on Saturday night, some classy restaurant.'

'Shit, Mort, you do know how to get a girl's attention, don't you? You know how awesome the shopping is in Sydney? No, I guess you wouldn't. Yes, I would love to come. You don't have to pay for my flights – I am happy to spend the money; not to see you, mind, but for the shopping.'

'Great,' I reply, 'but I hadn't planned on doing any shopping.'

'What did you have in mind?' she asks, and I can sense her smile.

'Well, I was hoping it would rain all weekend,' I reply, which gets a loud burst of laughter which settles down into a giggle, even sounding sexy to me. I've been deprived of her company for too long, obviously.

She tells me to 'piss off,' she has to book her flight and pack her bag, and, 'Shit, I'll need to wash my hair; I gotta go and THANK YOU!' and hangs up.

I text her and ask her to text me her flight details so I can pick her up. I then ring the Four Seasons and ask for a high level harbourside room from Friday to Sunday. Ouch, not cheap – but then, I don't want to be.

28

I am back outside the Shangri-La Hotel again next morning before 9:00 a.m., sitting in the van, as Pig is a guest and therefore fits in better than me as a visitor. From where I'm positioned, I can see the entrance, so I'm keeping an eye out for Rowan. Pig lets me know Claudia has taken a seat in the café and looks like she is ordering breakfast. We take a guess that it will be another egg white omelette with tea, and yes, we are right.

Pig's mic is picking her voice up nicely and we can both hear through our earpieces. But then I notice a traffic warden taking too much notice in me parked where I am, so I must take off before getting a ticket. I warn Pig I'll be off station for a bit and why.

There's a public parking building in the next street over so I head in there, winding my way up to the top, and then I realise it has a clear view of the hotel entrance, so duh, I could have been up here all along. Audio is also clear up here, and from the sound of it, Rowan has arrived as I hear a male voice asking for coffee with a croissant.

Pig has turned the other mics off, so we don't get any sound contamination. Claudia and Rowan chat for a few minutes about the weather and the upcoming spring carnival horse racing. Once breakfasts have been served, Claudia once again slides the USB across the table, and Pig just as diligently and surreptitiously takes a video of the exchange.

We hear Claudia say, 'I haven't had a chance to read through it all; as usual, I will this afternoon so we can chat about it on Monday. When are you meeting Mr X?' she asks Rowan.

He replies, 'I haven't set it up yet. I want to see what we have to offer; makes bargaining easier if you know what you're selling, so I'll have a good go through over the weekend. Usually contact him on the Monday and we meet within a couple of days.'

Claudia then comes back with, 'Okay, but my payment will be made today?'

'Yes,' replies Rowan, 'I'll transfer it this afternoon.' He then raises his coffee cup in a toast and says, 'Here's to good business,' and Claudia raises her teacup, and they clink cups.

A short time later, they split up. Claudia goes to check out and Rowan heads outside. I don't need to tail either of them as we still have the trackers active in his briefcase and her handbag, so I wander down to an adjoining café and Pig comes out a short time later to join me.

Once our coffee has been served, I say to him, 'Mate, we are all but wound up down here. Why don't you head home this afternoon, surprise George and have a few days off? If I need you down here again next week – you can always jump on a plane – but you can then make a start on some of these other assignments. Plus, we need to put some more attention onto our copper mates the SC!'

'Yeah, I think I will. Thanks, mate,' he says, before pausing. 'So you're not just wanting to get rid of me over the weekend then?'

I think I colour a little and say, 'Well, Suzie is coming down for the weekend.'

'You dirty bugger,' he says with a big smile. 'Good on you!'

'Yeah, I rang her last night, Maria's words ringing in my ears, and she seemed keen – especially about the shopping, which, of course,

I had not considered.'

Pig laughs at that and says, 'What were you planning?'

I reply, 'Well, I told her I hoped it rained all weekend,' which makes Pig laugh out loud enough for others in the café to turn and look at us. I tell him Suzie had laughed just as much as he had.

With this change of plan, we up stakes, me back to the van and Pig to grab the Camry from the hotel car park. We both head back to the Quest – Pig to pack up and head to the airport, me to make myself presentable before heading to the Four Seasons to check in for what I hope to be a very enjoyable weekend. We say goodbye with our usual man-hug and shake, and he's off to the airport in the Hertz HiAce rental where he'll off-hire it, leaving me with the Camry for the weekend. We also agree we need to fast track our plans for Christi's Press Conference, which is planned for this coming week, but we do not yet know where or when. And we need to put in place our strategy to ensure their plan blows up in their faces!

Suzie has texted through her flights, and she isn't arriving until 7:30 p.m., so after I arrive and check into our 16th floor harbour view room and admire the view. I have time to write a few notes on the day's events, and I make plans for early next week, which will be critical. I wonder if I should get Pig back for a few days, just to make sure we can cover everything and don't miss a point in the final run home. Something to mull over.

Time to make myself presentable and get to the airport as I do not want to be late. Before leaving the room, I call down and make a 9:00 p.m. reservation for a late supper at the Mode Kitchen and Bar.

*

Fortunately, I had a good run to the airport, so I'm parked and at the gate with ten minutes to spare before her flight arrives. Once they announce the flight arrival, I join others waiting for the passengers to disgorge, holding up my little card for Ms Suzie Dunn, making sure I am not too close to the exit. Eventually she comes out of the tunnel, sees me, and bursts out laughing.

She comes over to me, gets up on her tip toes to kiss me, saying, 'What, did you think I wouldn't recognise you?'

I grab her and pull her off her feet in a real body hug (but a gentle one), and we kiss for a few moments, totally oblivious to those around us. Only when someone starts to clap do I put her down. She keeps her arm around me, which makes me feel even better. With a few comments of 'young love' and various comments from others around us, we head towards the exit.

After a few minutes, she stops and reaches up to give me another kiss and then says, 'That's the last one until this comes off.'

'This' being my thick bushy beard I had grown again. You see, I had taken advantage of my beard, put on a turban, dark glasses and had slouched so as not to appear as tall, and with my hair a little overgrown as well, I was planning on teasing her, but of course she had seen right through it. Which of course, was a good thing. We chat all the way to the hotel, her eyes going as large as plates when I tell her we're staying at the Four Seasons.

'Ooh, I will have to be on my best behaviour.'

'Yes,' I say, 'especially in the bedroom,' which gets me a poke in the ribs.

'Careful, I'm driving,' I remind her.

On arrival, I valet the car and we head up to the room. I open the door and watch as she takes in the room and the view, which has the lights of the Opera House front and centre.

'Wow,' she exclaims, 'this is beautiful!'

'Yes,' I reply, 'and so are you.'

Somehow, she has forgotten about no more kissing with a beard, and I am not going to remind her, but I do stop long enough to pull the curtains. You never know who or what might be lurking out there.

We never do make it to the dinner reservation.

*

Next morning, I sneak out of bed early, hoping to have a shave and slide back into bed fresh shaven so there won't be any rejection, but alas, when I come out of the bathroom, Suzie is propped up on one elbow, waiting for my return.

She smiles when she sees I've had a shave and says, 'That looks better.' She points out the window at the blue sky and adds with a lovely smile, 'Hard luck – doesn't look like rain today.'

I shrug nonchalantly and say, 'Ah, well, can't have everything, I guess,' as I jump onto the bed (literally, making her squeal, then giggle) as I run my fingers around her ear until I find her lips, then kiss my finger and put to her lips, which somehow is followed by my lips meeting hers.

A little later, Suzie asks, 'So what are we doing for breakfast?' looking at her watch and saying, 'It's nearly nine o'clock already.'

'Well, one of us better hit the shower as breakfast finishes at ten,' I tell her.

Suzie jumps out of bed and says, 'Ah, well, might as well be me,' and heads to the bathroom.

Of course, I have no intention of letting her shower alone, so after a little squeal and a couple of giggles, we have a quick shower and get dressed to meet the day ahead.

Over breakfast, she asks, 'How is Paramount'—giving it air quote marks—'going?'

Without giving too much away I tell her we are on the home straight and tell her about Maria's involvement dressed as a maid.

Suzie's a little indignant about involving her friend without her knowledge. 'Hold on,' she says, 'how did you get her number?' A pause, and then she smiles and says, 'That's what you do – I remember.'

I tell her about the salacious goings on we've been filming, and how the whole process is coming together.

'Sounds like something out of *Days of Our Lives*,' she replies.

She has a good laugh when I relate how Maria suggested she could make Pig 'change teams'.

The day goes quickly with a cruise on the harbour after breakfast. Whilst on the cruise, I take a photo of us together with the Opera House in the background and send it to Maria, adding, 'I took your advice!' explaining to Suzie that Maria told me I better hurry up or someone else would get her.

A reply comes back: 'You dirty shits – have fun!'

A quick lunch and then, surprise, surprise, I find myself shopping, or more accurately, carrying Suzie's bags for her. But she's enjoying herself, and it's her money, after all, and the day is capped off by a lovely meal at Bennelong Restaurant at the Opera House. Suzie had brought a lovely slinky number, and I had brought a good jacket, so I don't look too out of place, and as we sit their enjoying the vibe of the place, she points out this is our first real date. I think it better not to ask what all the other events we had shared were if not dates, choosing instead to just enjoy the evening and her company.

Next morning, we decide not to waste the view from our room and order room service for breakfast, and really just lounged around, wasting the morning, having fun together.

We're all packed and ready to leave the room, Suzie sitting on the bed, playing with her phone (of course!). I sit down beside her, take her hands in mine, and say, 'Suz, I just want to say what a great time I have when I am with you. You bring out the best in me, and this weekend has been so enjoyable and relaxing – and I am not just talking about the sex.' This last comment, I make with a smile.

She gives me a lovely smile and says, 'But?'

I reply, 'No, no "but", that's just the way it is and I hope we can see a lot more of each other – if you feel the same way,' I add, looking expectantly.

As a reply, she leans in and kisses me.

After a few moments, I manage to get out in a hoarse voice, 'If you don't stop, we'll be late leaving!'

She laughs and pushes me away.

The moment seems to have passed, and I am a little disappointed I didn't get a more positive response. Maybe she's only after my body, after all. We check out and wander down the road to a nearby café and settle in for lunch. After we've ordered, she takes my hands in hers (well, my fingers fit, anyway) and says, 'Remember the Sunday you came over early and we ran back to your place for your "renowned" eggs benedict?'

I nod, wondering where this is going.

'Well,' she continues, 'the next day, my PA and best friend I guess, Jenny, comes into my office, closes the door and tells me, "We have a problem". I turn and give her my full attention, wondering what has happened, and she goes on, "You're a lawyer. Lawyers are meant to be serious, yet all morning, you have been walking around with a smile on your face and being nice to everyone – you have everyone talking! So, stop it. Now, I want the details, all the juicy bits, who is he, where you met, have you slept together yet – I want it all!".'

Suzie pauses as our coffees are delivered, then continues. 'So I told her how we met, how you sorted Hugh out, then ran into each other at the B2B run, and well, everything! She teased me about "throwing myself at you" that Thursday I came over, too, but I told her it was fine – I got what I wanted.

'You should have heard what Jenny had to say when I turned up at work on Friday and told her I was coming to Sydney to be with you – something about a "good old-fashioned dirty weekend" and "vaguely remembering such times". Jenny is a bit older and has three teenage kids.

'So in answer to your unasked question earlier, I, too, love being with you, Mort – I have from our first meeting. You make me feel wanted and alive, and safe. And yes, the sex is good,' she adds with another of her impish smiles.

I can't resist and lean in and give her a quick kiss and say, 'Just as well you didn't say this while we were still in the hotel room – we would still be up there.' I squeeze her hand, and we keep holding hands, but not saying too much until our lunch is served.

After finishing our lunch, we head back to the hotel to collect the car and head to the airport. She suggests I just drop her off, but I insist on parking and going in with her and waiting whilst she checks in. Of course, her flight is delayed 30 minutes, so we wander through the departure area and sit down at a café and order coffee and banana bread. We seem to be like gooey teenagers, smiling at each other, holding hands – it feels nice. Of course, this doesn't last long, or doesn't seem to, as all of a sudden they're boarding her flight, so after all that, only a quick peck, and she's gone.

I text her later on once I am in bed, saying, 'I am lonely!' The reply is a smiley face.

29

Monday morning, back to work. First up, I review the video from Claudia's study, and sure enough I can see where she checks her account at the Scotiabank in the Caymans on Friday night, and that a $150,000 payment has been received today. She seems pleased.

Pig is now online back in Brisbane, and we chat about our respective weekends. I tell him Suzie and I had a really fun time staying at the Four Seasons, and he comments, 'You know, I can tell when you have seen her, even sometimes just after you've talked to her – you light up'!

I tell him Suzie's PA had said something similar about her.

Unfortunately, Pig's weekend did not seem to go as well, with George heading off to work on Sunday morning, which seemed to be getting under Pig's skin.

For a public servant, even a high level one, George certainly puts in the hours, I think. *Or something else is going on,* I suddenly wonder.

Next, I need to wait until Rowan arrives at his office as he doesn't seem to do any business from anywhere else, and whilst we have access to his emails, our phone coverage is dependent on the bug in his briefcase. Being the silent type, hopefully he will communicate with Matt Hoskins the 'phone king' by email. Sure enough, after arriving at the office a little later than normal, just after 9:00 a.m., I see an email go out to phoneking1 stating he has another instalment to discuss, and suggesting they meet either Tuesday or Wednesday at the 'usual place'.

Pig, of course, has seen the email as well, and we agree he needs to fly back down to Sydney later today to ensure we can cover their meeting either Tuesday or Wednesday and split up to follow them afterwards if we need to. An email reply pings into Rowan's inbox a short time later, confirming a 10:00 a.m. meeting Wednesday 'at the same place'. Bingo!

The bugger is we don't know where the meeting will be, so we'll have to follow Rowan to find out. We agree we can't just depend on the tracker, so Pig will go to Cremorne in case he heads directly from home, whilst I'll head to Rowan's office so I can track him from there. Bases covered, we hope.

Now we know the meeting will be Wednesday, Pig decides he'll come down tomorrow late morning, as we do not need him tomorrow specifically. With nothing much else urgent to be done, I start on the full report to Cameron at Paramount, being very careful to ensure the report is not in any way personal, simply factual, knowing it will cause him considerable angst and embarrassment. But the pictures tell a thousand words. And I am not only meaning the sex photos (we don't plan on including the photos of Cameron and Christina, as these, in our view, have no connection to the assignment), but also the photos showing the handing over of the pen drive and photos of secret bank accounts, so all of our assertions are supported.

It will be an impressive report of a job well done, I think. I'm impressed by what we have achieved, and I start thinking about offering them a resolution, but of course, that's a separate proposal at an additional fee. In the meantime, Pig has listened to more audio from both Fleming and Lancaster and learnt that Christi will be fronting the media next Monday afternoon, and it looks like it is going to be an exclusive interview on *A Current Affair*, a popular program on Channel Nine. No doubt it will go to air that night. It will be an interesting few days!

Pig has managed to get phone numbers for both Christi and Stacey, but we are going to have to get a tracker onto one of them before they disappear, so we know where to pick them up from when it all turns to shit a few days later. Suddenly, we have two plays in action.

We discuss our options and plans for the Dyson play. Pig has found out the interview will be done at Southbank, a public park on the banks of the Brisbane River, and a Brisbane icon – an appropriate backdrop – and we agree Pig needs to be there and hopefully tag either of the girls with a tracker.

Now that we've changed the date in their script, we know Dyson can produce his and his wife's passports to refute the claim, which will be nice and embarrassing all around. I plan on texting Dyson the night it goes to air, telling him to check his passport, and to wait a few days to let the storm brew before he blows it away. We'll pick the two girls up before Dyson holds his press conference, so they are safe, and then invite a respected journalist from the *Courier Mail* to meet them and hear how they were 'bullied into making the claim by crooked cops (but too scared to name these cops)'. We will then send them on a different holiday, likely with Maria as their escort (pardon the pun!). Certainly is going to create a stir about town. Sounds like fun.

With a few hours to spare, I decide to track back through the audio between Lancaster and Fleming shortly after the meeting Lancaster had with Jack Herbert, the Queensland Premier's deputy chief of staff. We had heard Lancaster and Herbert making the meeting appointment, so now want to glean what we can, as this political connection seems highly relevant to what is going on with

Dyson. Now that we know the date of the meeting, I quickly pull up the relevant audio tape of Lancaster's car for that day. Sure enough, he and Fleming do discuss it, and now that we know what the meeting was about, it certainly puts their conversation into context and perspective.

Lancaster starts the conversation, saying, 'I met with that twerp Herbert earlier. He is quite open to the softening of the gang laws, so that's a good start; he even went on to say the Attorney General has already flagged this need. I gave him a few suggestions on how these can be eased without too much public outcry, which he said they would take on board.'

Lancaster continues, 'With the Attorney General already pushing for these reforms, that means Dave Levers of the CMFEU [Construction, Forestry, Maritime, Mining and Energy Union, a heavyweight and militant trade union] has been putting the pressure on her as we suggested. So, I'll let Dave know he has to keep the pressure on, as it's working.'

Fleming then asks, 'What do they want in exchange?'

'Well, nothing specific as yet; it seems they want to build some credit in the short term, implying we would be able to assist them somehow down the track,' Lancaster replies.

Lancaster and Fleming then go on to discuss real police work, so that is the end of the audio of relevance to me. I flick this recording to Pig, along with my notes, adding them to the data cloud.

Next, I listen to another Lancaster conversation with Anton Kovac, the president of the Jackals Bikies' Gang in Queensland, where Lancaster updates him on the progress of their efforts of watering down the gang laws. It's clear from this conversation there is a close tie between Lancaster and Kovac, and even Dave Levers of the CMFEU gets a couple of mentions, so these three appear to be close.

Now we have union heavies and the current state government

both working to lower the legal standards where gangs and bikies are concerned and clearly in cahoots with the bikies themselves, simply meaning it will be harder and more difficult to prosecute any bikie or gang behaviour. Isn't Democracy great!

I then swiftly check the audio tapes after each of Lancaster and Herbert's phone conversations, and note after the second one where Herbert brought up 'Dyson becoming a nuisance', and Fleming's response when updated by Lancaster was, 'Well, didn't take them long to find their quid pro quo, for easing the bikie laws did it!'

30

It's Wednesday morning now, Pig finally getting in late afternoon after flight cancellations and delays – just as well we weren't on a tight timetable! Pig told me he heard Lancaster ask Fleming to go to his house for a meeting the previous night, and had been able to finally track Lancaster's IP address by matching it to Flemings when they were together. He had now downloaded Lancaster's hard drive, but as yet could not find anything at all incriminating. Everything was above board; as Pig said, 'He has to have another laptop or tablet he uses for all this other shit he has going on, because it simply isn't on his PC.' Bugger.

I had rung Suzie the previous night to say hi. We chatted for ages, and I must admit, I really enjoyed just talking to her. Of course, I asked what Jenny had to say on Monday.

Suzie giggled and said, 'Well, she really teased me, asking how the dirty weekend went and was I okay to work a full day, etc., so was fun, and she also told me three or four times to stop smiling. She wants to meet you, by the way, suggested we go out to dinner with her and her husband Morrie when you're back.'

'Sounds fine to me,' I said. 'I'm keen to get a bit of dirt on you, so that should be fun!'

'Ha ha,' was her response.

She asked how we were going, and I told her Pig was back down and we expected the final piece to fall into place tomorrow.

'So, you might be home by the weekend?' she asked hopefully (well, at least, I thought she sounded hopeful).

'No,' I told her. I had a few days to write the final report and had a meeting set up with their CEO for Monday, and it was also possible there would be another shorter assignment to come from the report.

'Oh,' she said, this time the disappointment obvious.

I suggested she might like to fly down for another weekend, and she laughingly said no, that she had plenty of memories, so she could wait a few weeks.

She also said, 'Mort, it's great talking to you – not as good as seeing you – but don't think you have to call me every day or anything. I am a big girl. I can cope.'

It seemed a strange thing for her to say, but I guess she was trying to let me know she is quite independent and not needy. So I let it go, and we chatted on for a few minutes until Pig banged on the wall, saying, 'Come on, you two, you only saw each other two days ago!' which got us both laughing, and we said goodbye.

Next morning and we are all set to go, Pig in the van at Cremorne, and I am heading into the city to babysit Rowan's office. Pig tells me Rowan has left home at his usual time and is walking towards the bus stop. Rowan gets on his usual bus, with Pig squeezing on as well. The bus seems particularly full this morning; I have also confirmed the tracker is still working. Rowan carries on reading his phone the whole way into the city, so it looks like he is coming to his office first anyway, which makes us think the likely rendezvous will also be in the city.

Sure enough, he treads the same path and heads up to his office. Pig arrives a few minutes later and we adjourn to a little café in Kent Street, adjacent to the office building. We agree I will wait on the other side of the building and Pig will stay where he is, so whoever has him as he exits will tail him, whilst the other will follow discreetly on the other side, and then we will play it by ear, with likely swaps as necessary. We also discussed that the 'usual place' could be Rowan or Matt's office; we would be buggered, except we still had Pig's Trojan horse software bug, which we have not activated yet, as we know where it is. We also have the bug in Rowan's briefcase – if he takes it with him.

At 9:45 a.m., we have split up as planned, and then Pig grunts, indicating action, and I see him move out and head down the road, then notice Rowan up ahead of him. I check the phone tracking app, but nothing is moving: Rowan has left his briefcase behind, so we better be on our mettle.

I quickly move up towards Pig before crossing the road and wandering along a bit slower than Rowan is moving, so I am not staying equidistant, just in case Matt is a suspicious sort and is watching Rowan's approach. He strolls along, eventually heading into Maximus Café at the Sydney GPO, a popular city haunt. Bugger, this might be tricky. I slip in a side entrance, watching for Rowan and Matt, having checked out what he looks like on LinkedIn and other websites, including their own website. Not afraid of the camera is our Matt!

I see Matt, sitting quietly at a back table, and Rowan is heading his way. I manage to get a table facing away from theirs only a couple of metres away, so I prop my old-fashioned umbrella with its wooden head on the edge of my table. This, of course, is not a normal umbrella as it has high-tech mics built into its handle (I can't tell you what is hidden in the tip of the umbrella). I turn it on. Hopefully I will hear their conversation through this. Pig heads across and gets a table on the other side behind their table, so we have them between us. He also has a similar umbrella mic, and he has done exactly as I have, with his umbrella on the edge of his table closest to theirs. My phone has a mirrored surface on the back, so I prop it up against the salt and pepper shakers backwards so I can see their reflection, and I see the waitress is taking their order and then heads straight to Pig to get his. Suddenly, I have a different waiter at my elbow asking what I would like, so I order a coffee and a muffin. Plain and simple – that's me!

Not much has been said between Rowan and Matt so far, and my audio is okay – I'm able to hear their conversation, and knowing this, I know we can enhance it later if we miss anything. I text Pig a thumbs up so he knows I have sound, and he does likewise – seems we both have them covered.

They chat about the weather and the cricket until their coffee is served, and then Matt gets down to business, saying, 'Okay, what have you got for me?'

Rowan, as seems to be his way, responds slowly, saying, 'More of the same, really, a continuation of his market development plan, who he has been in contact with, a couple of major players or prospects this time, which will interest you, I am sure. The fee is the usual $300,000, and if you take the USB, it's payable today.'

Matt nods his agreement, so Rowan slides the USB over, and Matt pockets it. Pig, I hope, is getting a video of it, as I can't.

Their chatter returns to mundane matters like politics and business, so clearly, the meeting is over. As agreed earlier, I get up, leaving cash plus tip a on the table, to get outside so I can follow Matt when he leaves. We know his office is just up Martin Place from the GPO, so I'm standing on that side of the entrance when Matt comes out. I watch him from across the street, as he walks straight up Martin Place, head down, tapping away on his phone, and I mentally note we need to access his phone records, so we can see who else, if anyone, is involved in this. He heads straight to the Futurcomm office in Martin Place and into the elevator, and I watch to ensure he goes to the tenth floor where it says their office is.

I wait for about ten minutes, then I head up to their office as well, just to get a feel for the sort of company they are. I get off the elevator and wander around, looking a little lost, eventually approaching their receptionist.

Not a scratch on Christina over at Paramount, I think, *but still pleasant enough*.

I tell her I'm looking for Baker and Company (a name I grabbed off the tenant's board in the lobby), knowing they are on the eleventh floor, and she tells me I have the wrong floor, but she is not sure where they are.

I say, 'Okay, I better go back down again.'

I go down in the elevator and head back to catch up with Pig, who has settled himself at an outdoor café back up the road a little. He has already ordered me a coffee, so once we've been served, we recap and we confirm we both got good audio and he got good video of the USB exchange.

I tell him the Futurcomm office is a typical office setup, receptionist with what looks like secure access to the rest of the offices. He reminds me we don't have to worry about that as once he opens his Trojan horse malware, this will show us all we need to know. I tell him it would be good to know if Matt shares his news with anyone, and he agrees he will access their phone system so we can check his phone log, believing Matt, like ninety per cent of others, will use his mobile to make any important calls. He also confirms he tracked Rowan back to his office.

We agree we will head back to the Quest, so we have our more stable platform, but only after we have finished our coffees!

Back at the Quest, Pig tracks and opens his Trojan horse and, from the IP address, confirms it's on the Futurcomm server. He opens it and, all of a sudden, we have access to Matt's computer – in fact, the whole company's server. Pig skims through it before telling me he has a folder called Paramount, so he opens this and looks like six sub folders all labelled with dates, so we assume this is the complete list of data he has bought, six transactions in all. Pig copies this complete folder and uploads to our cloud-based server, so we can review at our leisure. This will look good in our final report, I tell him, when we give them back everything his competitor has learnt about him.

Whilst monitoring Matt's transactions, Pig sees him access his bank account and transfers $300,000 to DAR & Associates (Rowan/Dermott's company).

'Wow, that's more than is trickling down the line,' I say.

Pig gives me a shrug and smile, saying, 'Not surprising, really. I wonder if Claudia knows how much he is getting?'

We check Rowan's email through his server, and sure enough, he has received the remittance advice and actually has his bank account open on his screen when we are looking. We note he then authorises a payment to Claudia for $150,000. We know from our early searches that Sofia is only getting $50,000 a pop, so her partners in crime are diddling her, no doubt about it. Maybe what they say about 'honour amongst thieves' is not true anymore.

'Well, looks like a wrap,' I say to Pig, and we high five.

He replies, 'Yes, maybe we deserve a couple of beers and a decent feed. I was reading about this fancy steak joint on the flight down, Bistecca. That's all they have on the menu – T-bone steaks – so maybe we can go there and try it.'

'Sure,' I say, 'I'll book a table and let's get the good gear on!'

A bit later, we grab an Uber and head off for what turns out to be a very good steak. We can't decide which is better, Bistecca or Kingsley's, both very good. Through the meal, I tell Pig my plan for Paramount, that as well as submitting the full report, I am also going to offer them a chance of retribution, or payback. Naturally, Pig is all for that!

I spend the next couple of days writing and fine tuning my report. I set up a meeting with Cameron, having told him we have completed our assignment and would be tabling our report in full.

'Good,' he says, 'who do I need to fire?'

I tell him, not over the phone, and that it won't be that easy.

Whilst I am typing away, Pig is collating the data so we can give them a complete digital copy of the report and all supporting documentation, although we agree to leave out the photos of Claudia and Sofia. A couple of these will be in Cameron's report, but no one else's. Pig gets this done early Friday morning and then heads off back to Brisbane again. I'm starting to be a little concerned as he doesn't show much enthusiasm about getting home again. I ask him if everything is good, and he assures me it couldn't be better, but I have my doubts.

I then spend the weekend researching and preparing my retribution proposal, and Pig and I finetune our plans for the girls' appearance on *A Current Affair* on Monday.

31

Monday 10:00 a.m. finds me once again sitting in the lobby of Paramount, where Christina is keeping a wary eye on me. It's Margaret who comes to get me, saying Cameron will be a couple of minutes finishing up a phone call, and escorts me through to their boardroom, and yes, I say I would like a coffee, straight black.

I take a seat with two copies of my report on the table in front of me, one clearly marked for Cameron, the other unnamed. Both have executive summaries and start with a flowchart showing the movement of the data, from Cameron (well, it's been accessed from his laptop, so he is guilty of lax security if nothing else), through Sofia, Claudia, Rowan/Dermott, and ending up with Matt at Futurcomm. The flowchart also shows the amounts of money flowing back as payment for each transaction. I'm impressed as I think the flowchart shows the process rather succinctly.

Cameron comes buzzing in, and we shake hands and nod. As he left the boardroom door open, I nod at it and suggest it might be appropriate to close it. Marg quickly gets up and closes it, and I'm thinking maybe it's beneath Cameron to do such mundane tasks (I cannot help disliking him!)

Once we are all settled, I start by saying, 'Cameron, there is no easy way to say this, but the loss of data – and we can confirm a significant amount of data has been stolen – has been taken via your laptop from your home whilst you are out playing poker on a Tuesday night.'

He starts to interrupt, but I raise my hand, and I pass the blank copy of the report to Marg and open Cameron's to the photo of Sofia and Claudia in bed.

I can see him deflate as I continue, 'Sofia accesses your laptop every Tuesday night whilst you are out, then once a fortnight meets her lover, Claudia, and hands her the USB. As you can see from the photos, we have followed the USB through each step of the process, and in the last image on this section, you can see it being handed to Matt Hoskins of Futurcomm.'

'That arsehole,' Cameron responds.

Ignoring his comment, I continue, 'As you can also see from the flowchart, each party in the process has been paid in diminishing value, till Sofia only gets $50,000 per transaction. We have confirmed there have been six transactions in total, the first one back in March this year, and these have recently become a lot more frequent. We have managed to get a copy of everything they have taken for your review.'

I then remain silent, enjoying my coffee, letting them both read through our report which, with the supporting photos, etc., is quite a lengthy document. Marg, being the diligent 2IC, is choosing not to say anything until Cameron has stopped flicking through the report. When he has, he flips back to the first photo before closing the folder with a bang and puts his head in his hands, clearly very upset. I sit quietly, patience being one of my virtues.

He eventually looks me in the eye, and I can see tears there. He says, 'So there is no doubt about any of this?'

I soften my voice and say, 'Sorry, none at all. The photos you have are taken off videos, and all the videos, well, most of the videos are on the digital copies I have included in the report.'

He nods, acknowledging he understands which videos we have excluded. 'Fuck!' he exclaims loudly, continuing to look down at the folder.

After another lengthy silence, I slip out my retribution proposal, holding two copies under my palm and say, 'Whilst I understand you have a helluva lot to digest, I have taken the liberty of preparing a retribution proposal.' I slide one across to both of them, whilst continuing, 'You can read the proposal later, but I stress we have a very tight timeline if you decide you want to get some payback on Futurcomm, and I can sort the middlemen out.'

I can see I have got their interest, as I am guessing there is no love lost between Paramount and Futurcomm, and Cameron nods for me to continue.

'I have done a little research into your industry and your competitors, and other than the likes of Telstra and Optus, there are a few other smaller competitors eating up your market space. One in question, Mypone, seems to be in financial trouble.'

'Almost dead in the water, more like,' mutters Cameron.

I nod and continue, 'So my suggestion would be for you to write a dummy business plan showing how you have taken, say, a twenty per cent equity stake in Mypone—'

'Not bloody likely,' he interrupts again.

I give him a look and he shrugs, so I continue, 'The business plan would need to show significant benefits in merging the two entities, and their major clients, a couple of whom do not have to be real, i.e., we inflate the size of some of their major accounts to make them more attractive. Remember, the purpose of this dummy business plan is to get Futurcomm to react to it, and hopefully invest in Mypone to their detriment. If our plan works out, you may even be able to buy Futurcomm for a song.'

'So how do you propose to do this?' Marg asks.

I nod, indicating good question. 'First step, Cameron is going to have to take Sofia away somewhere isolated – Fiji, or Bora Bora – somewhere where we can cut off her contact. I will then turn Claudia, giving her the fake data again on a similar USB, and then follow the same process. We have eyes and ears on all participants now and have something Claudia I am sure would not like to see out there on the internet.'

I can see Marg is dying to ask what that is, but glances at Cameron and chooses not to ask.

'We are confident we can swing this; after all, if Sofia is out of the way, and in a way that doesn't raise Claudia's suspicions, none of the other players will be aware anything is different. I would be suggesting'—said with air quote marks—'to Claudia it might be a good time to take an extended holiday; she has, after all, built a tidy nest egg.

'As you will see, I have already put the backbone of your business plan strategy together as a template for you to build on or not, no skin off my nose. And, as you will see at the back here, our quote for this little payback will be $150,000.'

'So, this is on top of what we have to pay you for this report?' asks Cameron.

'It does, yes,' I state clearly, 'and if you chose to move forward with this, it is an entirely separate transaction.'

After another few minutes of silence, I continue, 'I understand I've given you a lot to digest and to come to terms with, Cameron, but if you want to proceed, you will need to commit to it in the next day or so. You will need to book a trip away for you and Sofia – I suggest giving her as little notice as possible – and tell her it's a surprise holiday, so you don't have to tell her where you are going. Also, as a first priority, you need to upgrade your server security to stop anyone else from doing what Sofia has done to you. You of all people should know the risk of data access without passwords! Don't forget she has seen all of your emails too, so keep that in mind.' I look him in the eye when I say this so he knows what I am talking about: his email exchanges with Christina, which are often not work related and would be considered 'hot', if you know what I mean.

'Shit,' he says again. His arrogance has clearly left him in deep shit. Cameron stirs himself and says, 'Okay, I'll have to think this through, and we'll get back to you.'

'That's fine, but unless I hear from you, I will be heading home Wednesday,' I reply, and he nods.

We shake hands and he leaves the conference room. Marg starts getting ready to leave as well, but can't resist asking, 'What was the photo I didn't get to see?'

I smile and say, 'It was rather private.'

She nods and says, 'I thought so.'

As we are leaving, she adds, 'If you change your mind about that drink, I'll be glad to hear from you.'

I smile and say, 'Okay, thanks, but I'm committed,' thinking, *wow, maybe I should let Suzie know I'm telling women – good-looking women at that – that I'm committed!*

I head back to the Quest feeling a little flat; the assignment has been our focus for over five weeks, and now it's settled, I am feeling a little lost. I stop and buy a light lunch at a café I'm passing, sitting there in the sunshine, just enjoying it, then grab a cab back to the Quest, deciding I'll head off on a good long run through Centennial Park with its duck ponds and numerous trails just to freshen up.

Once back at the Quest, I give Pig a call to give him a run through of how it went. When he asks if I think they will go for the revenge play, I say that I'm not sure. I suspect he will, but he has a lot to digest. In fact, our report will no doubt be life changing for him; it's possible he won't even survive with his position and reputation intact. Then, taking that aspect one step further, it will be a helluva lot easier to gloss over this aspect if he purchases Futurcomm for a bargain – that would look like a good play in the city, no doubt.

A little later, Pig tells me the TV interview is scheduled for 2:30 p.m., and from what he has heard being discussed, Fleming and Armitage have booked the girls into the Rydges Hotel at Southbank so they can get themselves ready, and they will then collect them to get to the interview point on time. They are booked into the hotel for the night; then they are booked into the Sheraton Mirage on the Gold Coast for the next two weeks.

Once Fleming, Armitage and the girls leave Rydges, Pig quickly accesses their room and slips a couple of trackers into their suitcases, knowing they'll be travelling with them. Surprisingly, both their iPhones have been left on the bedside tables, so he is able to access these and add a hidden app, enabling us to track them and listen to both sides of any conversation as well. Bonus! He then heads over to Southbank to watch the recording of the TV interview, and texts me, 'Shit, Jack Herbert is here watching too, so I am keeping out of sight!'

I reply, 'Get a photo of him there, might come in handy!'

'Righto,' he replies, and a short time later I receive a photo of Jack, (not that I knew what he looks like) showing the interview set and Jack in the background.

'Great; worthy of blackmail, that,' I reply to Pig!

Later he texts to say, 'It's a wrap!' (he is watching far too much TV, that boy!) and tells me Stacey had been in the interview as well, but mainly as support. We're both keen to watch the program tonight, although I am unsure if it will be shown here in Sydney.

32

It is mid-afternoon when Cameron calls, asking if I could come to their office around 5:30 p.m. that night. I'm intrigued as to why after hours, but of course don't say anything, other than, 'See you then.'

I turn up on time, and Marg seems to have been waiting for me and whisks me straight into the boardroom and goes to get Cameron. They come back together, and I almost feel sorry for him, as he looks gaunt and withdrawn, clearly struggling to cope with what we had presented to them and how it had turned his life upside down.

He gets straight to the point and says he had spoken to the chairman and discussed what had been going on, and the possibility of a retribution play on Futurcomm, and whilst the chairman wasn't too excited, citing the risks as he saw it, had approved the plan.

So he asks, 'When can you start?'

I reply, 'Well, as you know, I already have. But how about you? Have you started the business strategy for the purchase of a stake in Mypone?'

Marg replies with a nod, saying, 'Yes. This is not the finished product, but we thought you might like to look through it and make any comments.'

I reply, 'I'm no financial guru, so I'll leave that with you, but I'm happy to look through for logistical and operational aspects. I'll come back to you tomorrow. We know Sofia and Claudia'—*no harm twisting the knife*—'get together every second Thursday, so working back from then, Cameron, you need to have Sofia uncontactable no later than next Monday – earlier if possible.'

He nods and says, 'She has always wanted to hike in the Himalayas, and I was lucky enough to get a cancellation, so we are off this Saturday. The board has given me a month of stress leave to get my house in order. There is very limited phone connection over there, so this should be good. I haven't told her yet – I will do that Thursday evening – and tonight I'm working late, so I had to cancel the poker night.' As he says this, he gives me a look as if to say, *how did you know I played poker every Tuesday?*

I ignore it and continue. 'Okay, so who is running the ship in your absence?'

Marg smiles at the same time as Cameron nods in her direction.

'Great,' I say, 'I don't need to bring anyone else up to speed.'

They both nod, and Cameron notes, 'The chairman, Sir Anthony Harrison, will likely want to sit in on your final report with Margaret.'

'Fine by me' I say. 'Okay, back to business, with you two out of the picture from the weekend'—I nod at Cameron—'we need to have the USB ready by Tuesday, so I can pick my time to have a discussion with Claudia to ensure she sees the way her future is headed. I will also need to know how Sofia explains her absence to Claudia, hopefully excited if she has wanted to do that for a while. So, Marg, I need you to have the business plan ready by Friday, as I will also have to copy Cameron's emails in the same format. Make sure there are no emails in there you don't want seen. You also must put in a couple of dummy ones about this plan. In fact, I will set up a dummy email for Jess@Mypone.com so it looks like you are emailing her direct.'

'How can you do that?' they both ask in unison.

I just look at them and say as I spread my hands, 'What, you think all this just fell into my hands? We even got a copy of all the data they had stolen.'

'Actually, that was very handy, too – thanks,' says Cameron.

Marg comes back saying, 'Yes, that won't be a problem. Do you want me to email it to you?'

'Yes, as soon as it's ready, please,' I reply.

'Great. We all good, then?' Cameron asks.

I reply, 'Yes, I'll get straight onto this once my last invoice is settled and this agreement signed. I will forgo the upfront payment in this instance, so full payment once we confirm Matt has acted upon your dummy business plan. Agreed?'

Marg pipes up, saying, 'I paid the invoice this afternoon,' and Cameron pushes the new agreement across to Marg to read before signing.

Once she is happy (it's the same wording as the last one, so simple, really), Cameron signs, I sign, and we shake all round. I wish Cameron safe travels and good luck with rebuilding his relationship with his wife. I would love to have asked if he had ditched Christina yet!

Marg, as usual, shows me out, and I smile and say, 'Good luck in the big chair.'

She smiles and nods and tells me quietly, 'The whole thing has knocked Cameron for six, and he got a real bollocking from the chairman. He'll be on thin ice for a few months. In fact, he really needs our subterfuge to work so it glosses over the reason for it.'

I nod in reply as we shake hands in farewell.

I'm out of there, and whilst waiting for a cab, I text Pig and tell him we're back on the clock. Not much we need him to do on this – it's really just a matter of picking the right time and approach to Claudia to ensure she handles her role and then disappears. The others don't matter – they might have an accident one night, just so they know someone knows what they have been up to. Pig will continue to help with the monitoring, etc. from Brisbane; he doesn't need to be in Sydney for that.

Later that evening, I give Suzie a call, letting her know I won't be back before next week now, as they have given us another assignment as we suspected they would.

'More sex and scandal?' she asks, with a smile in her voice.

I rejoin by saying, 'You know what's scary? I have now said "no" to a nice lady inviting me out for a drink; even went so far to say, "I'm committed". So, madam, what do you think of that?'

Suzie is quiet for a few moments, then replies, 'It's scary and exciting, but has she got a good arse?' and I can hear the smile in her voice.

'Don't sell yourself short, madam, you have a *great* arse, and I must say, I am quite fond of a couple of other attributes you have,' I add with a big smile.

'And what would they be?' she asks.

'You won't know until I see you next,' I reply.

After a bit more chit chat and giggling, we say goodbye. Then just before she hangs up, I say, 'For the record, I am talking about your smile and your personality – not what you were thinking!' I hang up before she has a chance to reply. I do get two smiley faces, though.

*

I'm right, and the Dyson scandal doesn't make it onto *A Current Affair* in Sydney, so I watch it on Pig's TV. Not the best vision, but audio is clear enough, and as soon as it's finished, Pig sends me a copy to watch before we discuss the next steps. I dial up a pizza and watch it through again before giving Pig a call.

Then, suddenly realising if George is home, we can't talk about it. I hang up and text Pig and say, 'Ring me if George not home.

Otherwise, we can discuss in the morning.'

I don't hear from him, so I assume George is home and I continue with the plan.

At around 8:00 p.m., I text Noel Dyson from my prepaid, saying, 'Check your passports. Stay quiet and let this build for a few days. Let me know prior to you going public. Also suggest you quietly have a word with Sofitel manager as one of their staff added a fictitious booking in your name in the last few weeks – part of the stitch up.'

Don't know what sort of response I would get, and then about half an hour later, I get a text showing the relevant page of his passport and the words 'THANK YOU!' – yes in capitals. So, nice to be appreciated!

Next morning, Pig gives me a call once in the office and tells me George had come home on a bit of a high, saying it looks like Dyson has 'hung himself'. So clearly, the premier's office was well informed. I bring him up to date on how Dyson had sent a copy of his passport and thanked us. We discuss plans for the week, and how Pig will need to be ready to go as soon as I hear from Dyson about the timing of his interview. We agree I need to ring Maria and get her sorted as it's likely we will need her in a day or so. We book them adjoining rooms at the Pacific Bay Resort at Coffs Harbour, four to five hours south of Brisbane, and most importantly in NSW, so out of the domain of our crooked coppers. We also book a car for the trip in Maria's name, a little ASX SUV, so plenty of room. Pig will go with Maria when they go to collect the girls and move them on.

I give Maria a call and we agree on her payment.

She asks, 'So who am I babysitting?'

I reply, 'Oh, just a couple of ladies that have to keep out of sight for a while.'

She pauses and then says, 'Shit, Mort, you're talking about those two girls on TV claiming to have been shagging that politician bloke, aren't you!'

I am a bit surprised at this astute guess and reply, 'Yep, any issue with that?'

'Shit no, they might be able to give me some hints, you know?' she adds with a giggle.

I tell her we don't yet know when they'll need to be collected, as a shitstorm is going to hit the news in the next few days, and we need them safe and sound for their sakes before that happens. I put on my best deep growl and say, 'And don't you say boo to anyone!'

She replies, 'Okay, okay!' So we are a go!

A little later, I get a text from Dyson saying, 'This is all getting pretty hard to handle, can we come clean soon?'

I decide to give him a call and introduce myself as 'Mort.'

Of course, he asks, 'Who are you and how did you know in advance?'

I reply, 'None of that is important,' but I'm as keen as he is to damage his opponents from this.

We agree he and his wife will call a press conference tomorrow, Wednesday, around 10:30 a.m. to show their passports. He even confirms the manager of the Sofitel had checked, and sure enough, a dummy booking had been retrospectively entered into their system to make it look like he had been staying there. The manager had agreed not to say anything until after the Dyson press conference and also confirmed they had let one of their staff go over this.

I tell him there will also be a follow-up interview from the girls in a day or so refuting their story.

He replies dryly, 'That will be interesting to see!'

He once again thanks me, and I wish him good luck, telling him that I am certainly looking forward to seeing his press conference. Pig and I agree he and Maria should check into the Sheraton Mirage on the Gold Coast this afternoon; that way, they can hopefully become chatty with the girls, and also just in case one of the SCs is keeping an eye on them.

Pig growls, 'I hope they have twin beds.'

'Oh, I dunno, Maria might take that as a challenge,' I tell him.

'Ha bloody ha,' is the reply I get.

He gives Maria a call, and they get themselves organised. Pig picks her up, and they go and get her rental and drive that down to the Sheraton.

Pig has our comms on, so through his phone I am able to hear their interaction.

Of course, on the way down, she says to Pig, and I can image the big grin, 'So, what are the sleeping arrangements here – are we sharing?' the grin again sounding in her voice.

Pig says, 'No, I ordered a twin room, and I hope you don't snore!'

Maria laughs and says, 'Not that I've ever heard, and Ronnie has never complained.' She then continues, 'Maybe the girls can give me some tips how to keep Ronnie happier too!'

Pig snorts (as pigs do!). I hear him give Maria a prepaid Visa – no records, no trace – and he tells her, 'It has $5,000 on it, so should be heaps. Let me or Mort know if you need more, but be warned, Mort's bookkeeper is a dragon, so make sure you keep all the receipts.'

Once checked in, from the background noise I can hear I assume they are wandering around, finally finding the girls at the pool bar, having a few drinks, so they wander in and take the table next to them. Not sure if it's Pig's good looks or Maria's tatts, that take Stacey's eye, but they are soon swapping banter.

Then Pig says, 'Hey, aren't you the two from TV the other night?'

They both giggle and say, 'Yes, that's us.'

That remains the topic of conversation for a while; then Pig turns to Maria and says, 'Well, we better be off, need to tidy up for dinner.'

They say goodbye and suggest meeting up for breakfast at 8:00 a.m., and the girls readily agree.

33

Next morning, I'm again listening in through Pigs phone, and hear Pig and Maria sit down to breakfast when Stacey and Christi come waltzing in, seemingly the free spirits.

'That might change shortly,' Pig mutters to Maria, who he briefed last night about the plan to lay out the options for the girls over breakfast, planning on scaring them and using Maria as their saviour and protector.

The room sharing had had its funny moments, (as I had nothing better to do, I had left the mic on! Enjoying the entertainment) neither are used to sharing with a stranger, so they had to swap bathroom visits, and of course, Pig got growled at for leaving the toilet seat up and had responded, 'Haven't you got a husband and two boys?'

'Yes,' came back the reply, 'but they know better than to leave the seat up!'

Over breakfast, I hear the girls sit down, and a few moments later I have visual as Pig positions his phone on the table, giving me vision of both Christi and Stacey. After a few minutes of pleasantries, Pig says to them, 'Christi and Stacey, today at 10:30 a.m., Noel Dyson is holding a press conference where he is going to present irrefutable proof your story the other day is a complete fabrication.'

Their faces drop and they look at each other, the fear obvious in their eyes. Stacey puts her hand onto Christi's and squeezes, then looks at Pig (or Julien, as they know him) and says, 'And how do you know this?'

'Believe me – I know. I also know who put you up to this and why.'

The look of horror on their faces shows they are really scared of the consequences of their story unravelling, so Pig continues, 'But Maria and I are here to help. If you want, we will take you interstate, right now, straight after breakfast, and tuck you away for a few weeks whilst this all blows over. Believe me, Lancaster and Fleming are going to have bigger problems than you two over the coming weeks.'

A look of consternation shows on Christi's face when Pig mentions the cops by name.

Pig continues, 'Maria will be staying with you as your protector. She is army trained and loves a bit of action.'

Maria smiles at this and nods.

A look of relief comes to their faces, and it is Christi who comes back with, 'But who are you and what is the catch?'

Pig replies, 'Who we are is not relevant. We are no one official, so we have no axe to grind with you, but we will want you to sit down with a journalist before the end of the week and explain the true story – how you were bullied and threatened to tell the story by a bunch of crooked cops, but you are too scared of them to reveal their identities.'

Maria speaks for the first time, saying, 'Girls, I don't know the full story here, but I know Pig, sorry, Julien, and his boss from his army days, and I can assure you they are the good guys. I also know you don't want to cross them, or me.'

Stacey nods and then asks, 'Why did you call him Pig?'

'Long story, but that has been my nickname for a long time,' replies Pig.

Stacey asks if they can have a few minutes to discuss it, and Pig says, 'I'll leave you for a few minutes, but Maria stays. You see, her role is not only to protect you, but also to make sure you don't break any rules we will agree to.'

I hear him get up and move away, leaving his phone where it is, so I continue to have both vision and audio.

The girls look at Maria, a girl-to-girl sort of thing, Stacey says, 'Will we be safe with you?'

Maria replies, 'Only if you do as you're told! Certainly, you'll be safe from anyone else, but there will be rules, like no phones, no internet, no contact. From what Pig told me, neither of you have close relatives, so this shouldn't be a problem, but you don't want to know what I am capable of if I get angry.' Not being able to see Maria, I can only imagine the smile accompanying this.

Having only heard how Maria has handled the situation, I'm quite impressed by her performance.

The girls look at each other and shrug and look out for Pig. He must have seen them looking as, a few moments later, I hear his voice saying, 'So what is it to be?'

Stacey nods and says, 'Okay, let's do it. Where are we going anyway?'

'South over the border is all you need to know for now. Right, both phones please, girls. Maria will be holding these for you; she will come back to your room now with you and help you pack. She's all ready to go, so in fifteen to twenty minutes tops, we need to be well clear when the shit hits the fan at 10:30 a.m.,' he finishes.

I watch as the girls hand their phones over to Maria, we had told her to turn them off and remove the batteries, so I can only surmise she has done this, as Pig has not reminded her.

The three girls all head off, and Pig picks up the phone and we confirm all good to go. He will see them off and is then going to hang around to see who comes rushing down to grab the girls after

Dyson crashes their party.

Once they were all packed, we had instructed Maria to take them directly down to the car park. With continuing audio and vision through Pig's phone I watch as Pig joins them in the car park to say goodbye and assures them saying, 'I will be in touch.' He has left his phone on and I hear him say, 'If you need anything, Maria will sort it or she will call me when needed. Make sure you listen to the news at 10:30.' Just as they are about to drive off, I hear Pig say to the girls, 'By the way, Maria is keen to learn some tricks so she can keep her husband happy.'

The last thing we hear is Stacey saying, 'That will be fun! What is his preference—' as Pig heads back upstairs, giving me a brief update as he goes.

34

It's not until 12:30 p.m. that Pig sees Armitage and DC Bruce bustling into the hotel, straight to the elevator and up to the fifth floor where the girls' room was. He quietly relays what is transpiring over the phone. Five minutes later, they are back down looking all around, splitting up, searching all the bars and pools, before he watches Armitage pull his police ID out as he approaches the receptionist, and whilst Pig can't hear what Armitage is saying, it is pretty obvious he is asking if they know where the girls are. He sees the young receptionist shake her head and then accept Armitage's card, no doubt to ask the girls to call him when they come back.

As he walks away from the reception, he pulls his phone out to make a call – one I am sure he doesn't want to make – to let Lancaster know the girls looked like they had done a runner, no clothes left in the room; it was a good pointer after all. It isn't hard to work out the reaction either, as he pulls the phone away from his ear while Lancaster vents, no doubt.

The press conference at 10:30 a.m. had gone really well. Dyson appeared holding hands with his wife, waited whilst the assembled media went quiet, and announced, 'As you are all well aware, the other day, a young lady claimed to have joined me in my room at the Sofitel Hotel on the fourth of April this year.' He waited a beat, and then continued, 'I am here to tell you this is absolutely untrue, and I have been talking to my lawyers about suing Channel Nine and the ladies for libel.'

A TV reporter in the front row yelled out, 'How can you prove it's not true?'

Dyson again waited a second, removed his hand from his wife's and pulled his passport out, opened it to the correct page and said to the crowd, 'This is my passport, and it clearly shows I left Australia on the thirtieth of March this year, entered Hawaii the same day, and did not return to Australia until the tenth of April. This was a family holiday, and my wife and two children were with me. My wife's passport is also here showing the same dates.

'As I am sure you would all agree, it would be rather difficult to get both Australian Border Force and US Border Control to make these entries if not true.' He finished the statement with a smile.

He then handed both passports down to different reporters in the front row and suggested they pass them around. The media throng had gone quiet as they absorbed this news, certainly not what they were anticipating when they arrived, I am sure.

Then, of course, the questions started coming: 'Who do you think is behind this hoax?' was the first question raised.

'Good question, Russell,' replied Dyson, 'I can only guess someone with something to gain from seeing me politically damaged.'

This, of course, created pandemonium, with everyone asking questions over the top of each other.

Dyson let the noise settle before asking for his passports back, and then added, 'I have also been advised by the manager of the Sofitel that they have found a falsified booking in their system for the night I supposedly stayed there, and they have let a member of their team go as a consequence.' Dyson declined to take any further questions, taking his wife's hand and exiting with much dignity and to much animation from the media throng.

Slam dunk! I thought, having watched the whole thing live.

Pig, of course, was sitting at the Sheraton down the Gold Coast and rang me, and we were both pretty happy with the outcome.

A bit later, and I access the audio from Lancaster's car, starting the tape a little before 10:30 a.m. There was no engine noise, so I wonder if he was sitting quietly waiting to hear the press conference. Then I hear Fleming say, 'Shouldn't be long now,' and Lancaster grunts.

During the press conference, not much was said by these two, other than the odd 'Fuck' or 'Bloody hell, I'll kill them'.

At the end, they turn the radio off and there is more silence. Then Lancaster says, 'How the fuck did we get this wrong?'

Fleming quietly points out they didn't have access to his passport to check, and Lancaster says, 'Yeah, but pretty bloody easy to check when Parliament is sitting.'

Then his phone starts ringing, and the first caller is Jack Herbert, demanding, 'What the fuck?'

Lancaster tries to appease him, but it's not working as Jack seems to be pretty fired up, saying, 'Well, you made the mess, so you bloody need to fix it quick smart, and make sure the Premier's name *does not* come up.'

Lancaster assures him he will take over the investigation, and he's sure they will find a patsy amongst Dyson's previous legal clients and point the media in that direction.

'You better,' is all Jack had to say before hanging up.

'Little fucking twerp, I'd like to ring his neck,' Lancaster muttered afterward.

35

Now that we have the girls safely ensconced in Coffs Harbour, I need to arrange the second part of the plan – that is, organising an exclusive interview with a reputable local journalist. Pig and I have agreed on Colleen Hill, a veteran political journalist for the *Courier Mail*.

The morning after the Dyson Press Conference, I call Colleen from my prepaid phone. First time, no answer and I don't leave a message. An hour or so later, I call again and after she confirms who she is, I ask, 'Would you like to interview Christi and Stacey?'

This is met by silence for a beat, and then she asks, 'Who am I speaking to?'

I reply, 'A friend of the girls. It's a simple question – a yes or no would be good.'

'How do I know you're legit?' is the next question.

'You don't. I'm asking you first, but there are heaps of others I can call if you don't want to.'

'Yes, yes, of course I do,' she hurriedly replies.

'Okay, these are the conditions.' I continue, 'One: no one else is to come with you. Two: you are *not* to tell anyone about the meeting – not your partner, Fred, or your editor. For clarity, the girls are very scared, and don't really know who to trust, and we know the people who set this up have a long reach, if you get my meaning.'

'Okay, I can handle that,' she replies. 'When and where?'

'Be in your car heading south on the M1 by 8:30 a.m. Friday morning. I will text you the contact point once you're on the road. Don't be late; if we get suspicious, the girls will disappear again and you'll see the story in *The Australian* or on Channel 7.'

'Okay, but what if I need to contact you if something comes up?'

'You can't. If you aren't there on Friday, we will move to the next.'

'Why me?' she asks with a hint of a smile.

I reply, 'You answered your phone,' and hang up.

Of course, that wasn't the reason we chose her. She has been a respected journalist for the *Courier Mail* for a long time, ideal for such a bombshell which we hope will make the front page of the paper on Saturday, once again putting Lancaster and company off balance. Pig put both a mic and tracker in her RAV4 the other night whilst everyone was asleep, so that's why we're sending her the location once she is in transit, as we will hear if she lets anyone know the where and when.

I let Pig know this is sorted, and we confirm the contact point will be Hungry Jack's at South Tweed Heads, an hour and half south of Brisbane and a three-hour drive back up for Maria and the girls. So, close enough, but far enough away from their hidey hole.

*

Friday morning comes, and Maria confirms she and the girls are headed north with an ETA of 10:00 a.m. in Tweed Heads. I've been speaking to Maria regularly, as has Pig, and all seems to be going okay. The girls are pretty easy-going (not surprising, considering their occupation, I guess!), seem to be simple, hard-working girls – not much thinking or planning goes into anything.

At 9:05 a.m. I text Colleen and tell her to be at Hungry Jack's Tweed Heads South by 10:00 a.m.

She replies quickly. 'On my way. ETA 10:10.'

I listen to the audio from her car and hear her send the text reply and then just the sound of the radio playing, and occasionally her singing along to the radio – not pleasant; almost as bad as my singing – and I cringe.

Pig calls me when he gets to Hungry Jack's at 9:40, earlier than everyone else as planned, with me on the phone, both with earpieces and throat mics in place, so he isn't walking around with his phone out. He wanders around the car park. Comfortable there are no suspicious looking people around, he grabs an outdoor table where he will see everyone arriving. He texts Maria for an updated ETA and suggests she park down the back corner and wait for him to tell her the next step, telling me as he does this. Maria knows the plan is to move to a nearby picnic area, so the meet will be on open ground and any photos will have an innocuous backdrop.

Maria replies, 'New ETA 9:55 a.m.'

Pig relays this, and I comment, 'They've made good time.'

Sure enough, just after 9:55 a.m., the ASX drives in; Pig turns on the camera so I can see them arrive. All three see Pig sitting there, and he gets three smiles and waves. Maria texts through their orders, so Pig goes in and orders three Angus burgers with the works, plus four coffees. The order is ready before Colleen arrives, so he takes it over to the girls, getting a chorus of thanks for his trouble. They then head off to the rendezvous spot to get themselves ready.

We chat idly as he takes his seat again. When he sees the RAV4, with Colleen driving it, pull in and park, he lets me know, describing her getting out of the car and heading toward him and the entrance. He goes silent as she approaches before I hear her say, 'Hi, I'm looking for a couple of nervous girls.'

Pig replies, 'You've found them.'

'Hi, I'm Colleen,' she says.

Pig smiles and says, 'I know.'

'You aren't the gentleman I have been speaking to?'

'No, I'm not; he's on another assignment, so you have me instead.'

'Okay, what is the plan then?' she asks.

'Well, first, I need your phone, please, and can you take your handbag and lock it in your car? You will be travelling with me from here on.'

'But I use the tape recorder and camera on my phone, so I need to have it with me.'

'Not going to happen,' Pig replies. He then pulls out a small handheld tape recorder and small Nikon camera, saying, 'You can borrow these instead.'

She is a little nonplussed by this but nods okay. 'Can I visit the toilet before we go?' she asks.

'Sure but leave your bag and phone here. Can I get you a coffee?' he adds.

'Sure. A skinny flat white, no sugar would be good.'

Pig lugs her handbag inside and orders the coffees, which are quickly dispensed, and he is back outside waiting before Colleen comes out. He hands her the handbag, and she goes over and locks it in her car, Pig briefing me on this whilst she is doing it, commenting when she re-joins Pig, 'I hope the crime is not as bad down here as the statistics suggest.'

Pig smiles and tells her to jump in the van; he is driving the iLoad. He exits the car park and heads south before taking a side exit, and quickly comes to a little lakeside park, where he stops. The girls and Maria are sitting at a picnic table finishing off their burgers as they approach. Pig introduces Colleen to Christi and Stacey (but not Maria) and explains the rules so everyone understands.

'One: the girls will not name the people that set up the whole episode – they are simply too scared of the consequences. Two: a few photos will be allowed, but only of the two girls, no one else. Three: Other than that, ask away.'

Colleen nods and says, 'I haven't used one of these little things for a while,' referring to the tape recorder, but now has it turned on, and introduces herself, then asks the girls to identify themselves. The next question is the obvious one: 'You, Christi, are the one who claimed Noel Dyson had a one-night stand with you back in April.'

At the end of the interview, when she has exhausted her questions, she nods and says, 'No wonder you're scared, you're saying there is a section of Queensland Police that are crooked and playing dirty, but you don't know why.' She takes a photo of the two sitting quietly at the table; then Pig takes one with Colleen in the middle of them.

Pig then hands her his phone, through which I have been listening.

I say to her, 'Are you happy with that?'

'Yes, very, I'm glad I answered the phone the other day!'

I say, 'you'll work this out for yourself, but as soon as your story hits, you can expect to be harassed by the police. Both the good ones and the bad ones. You won't know the difference, so I suggest as soon as you get back you need to sit down with your editor, and likely legal counsel, to make sure they protect you and the girls. It might even be a good time for you and Fred to have a vacation.'

'I'll think all this through on my way back to the office, but you're scaring me a bit.'

'Being scared is good; it will make you more alert. Make sure you are never alone. You and we do not know to what lengths they will go to protect their little patch – and their freedom, in fact. I'll send you a text in a minute. If you need help at any time, text your name to that number. Good luck, and for the record, we chose you – you have a fine reputation, not afraid to make the big plays, and as far as we can see, don't take a backwards step.'

Colleen is clearly chuffed with this compliment. I say goodbye, telling her I might buy her a coffee one day. She hands Pig his phone and he asks her to go wait in the van whilst he says goodbye to the girls, who are sitting in the ASX ready to go. He goes over, giving Maria an envelope, and says to open it later. He tells the girls they did well, and to be good. They giggle, and Stacey says, 'Would be more fun if you came too, Julien!'

I can only imagine Pig smiling at this.

Pig relays to me they are off as he heads back to the iLoad. Pig jumps in the van (I hear the door slam) and heads back to HJ's with Colleen quizzing him as to who we are and why we're doing this. He just stays silent.

I hear the van turn off and Pig says, 'Here is your phone.'

Again, I only have audio, but I can hear him fiddling with both the camera and little tape recorder; knowing what we planned, I surmise he is removing the tape from the tape recorder and the SD card from the camera.

They say goodbye, with Pig saying, 'We look forward to seeing tomorrow's paper!'

Later in the day, once they're back in the resort, I give Maria a call – just a catch-up, really, and to get a feel for how the girls felt about the interview. She replies they were fine, that it hadn't caused any concerns. She adds that they both take life pretty casually. She also mentions that Stacey kept talking about Pig.

I tell her there were two prepaid visa cards in the envelope, and she is to give them one each when it is time for Maria to come home. I tell her they have $2,500 paid up on each.

'Wow, who's paying for those?'

'Me, I guess – we don't have a client for this gig,' I tell her.

I suggest she organise for Ronnie and her mum to bring the kids down next weekend, book the unit next door, so Ronnie can give her a bit of a break, and they can catch up too.

'Mort, that's very generous,' she says, obviously excited at seeing her family again.

I say, 'You deserve it, so get it sorted.'

I get 'Yes, Boss,' as a reply.

36

I'm up early and go for a good run, then pull up the audio from our two favourite coppers. Just after seven, Fleming has rung Lancaster, asking, 'Have you seen this morning's paper?'

'No,' is the reply.

'You aren't going to like it. There's a full front page spread about Christi and Stacey and how they were duped by – get this – "crooked cops" to make their claim.'

'Fuck!' is Lancaster's reply.

'It gets better,' Fleming continues. 'It goes on to say they are scared for their lives and in hiding, hoping to stay safe.'

Silence for a couple of minutes, then Lancaster says, 'Meet me in half an hour at the McCafé at Annerley.'

Bugger, I think, *they'll meet inside and we won't hear their discussion.* However, an hour and a half later, Fleming comes back on the audio, calling the 'team' one by one to ensure they have seen the story and that they are to keep 'bloody silent' about it all. He also tells them Lancaster is getting push back from the commissioner when he tried to take over this segment of the investigation, and saying that that 'dickhead Wellington' was heading it up.

Then a little later, Fleming reports back to Lancaster to confirm everyone is on the same page.

Lancaster then says, 'You know, your suggestion of another Brothers Mob attack's not a bad idea. We can start pushing the bikies as a probable cause of the failed blackmail attempt; it's easy to imply one of his previous legal clients has bikie connections, and then if we eliminate Dyson, it will fall back in our hands as another bikie hit. Gets rid of the bugger totally then, too, and those politicians will truly be indebted to us. We'll get our softer gang laws. The unions will owe us big time as well, as it puts them in an even stronger position with their pull over the government. But we will need to control the investigation, make sure that idiot Wellington doesn't get it. Might have to remind the commissioner what we have in our back pocket, make sure we do keep the investigation.'

Lancaster finishes the conversation by saying he will think it through, and they will discuss Monday and tells Fleming to 'stay tight'.

Holy cow, I think, *what are these pricks capable of?* I flick it to Pig in case he hasn't logged on. Mind you, knowing he is now in an awkward situation with George being on the other side, so to speak, I no longer contact him on this matter of an evening or weekend.

*

I'm still in Sydney, of course, and on Monday morning I decide today is D-Day, and I need to confront Claudia. The weekend was too early, giving her time to take off and disappear, but we needed until Thursday to make sure we had the groundwork covered.

At 5:00 p.m., I'm outside her office, knowing she often works back alone after the other staff leave, and sure enough, bang on 5:00 p.m., I watch the three known staff exit and head their separate ways. I enter their office and ring the little reception bell, drawing Claudia out of her office. I introduce myself and say, 'Claudia, we need to talk. Is there somewhere private we can sit down?'

Naturally, she's hesitant, asking, 'What's this about?'

I reply, 'It's very private, and once you see what we'll be discussing, you'll be pleased for the privacy.'

'Very well,' she says, looking a little apprehensive, like all guilty people should.

She leads me into a meeting room, turning the lights on and then closing the door behind us. She heads to the head of the table. That suits me as I intend to sit between her and the door anyway, in case she wants to make a run for it.

Once we're seated, I look at her calmly and say, 'Claudia, you have been a naughty girl – very naughty, in fact.' I push a folder across the table to her, which after a moment's hesitation, she opens.

I have placed a selection of photos in the folder, showing her sliding the USB, not once, but twice, across the table in the Shangri-La Café to Rowan, a dummied up statement from Scotiabank Cayman Islands showing her current balance (I did this so she wasn't aware I had a bug and camera in her study), another photo of Rowan sliding the USB across to Matt, but I had blanked out Matt's face, so she would not know who Rowan's client was. And, lastly, the photo of her and Sofia in bed. Always leave the best until last!

When she sees this, she bows her head, tears running down her cheeks.

I sit there silently, quite content to wait to see how she responds. I even look around to see if there are any tissues I could get for her, but none in view. So I wait. Patience is a virtue.

After around ten minutes, she finally composes herself and says, 'Who are you, the police, or...?'

'No, I'm not the police or anyone in authority, but you have damaged my client's business, and they are not happy about that.'

I pause again to let this sink in, wanting to build the pressure, getting her apprehensive about what might be coming. I'm a big bloke and happy to intimidate when needed, but in this case, I make sure I do nothing threatening, as I don't want her trying to make a run for it.

Once this has sunk in, she sits up straighter, looks at me and asks, 'What happens next?'

I reply, 'One of two things. First option is this photo,' and I raise one of the two of them in bed, 'or this one, or even this one, or maybe all six of these,' fanning the photos out on my side of the table, 'appear with suitable captions on the internet, maybe even get one onto your LinkedIn profile – it may not stay there long, but it will get a reaction. Don't you think?'

She bows her head again, so after a moment, I continue, 'Or, option two, you assist us in sending one final data feed to Rowan – which isn't his real name, you know.

Clearly, she knows this by the look on her face. 'How?' she asks.

'Well, as you know, Sofia has gone off hiking in the Himalayas for a month, so I'll provide you with a USB similar to those you have passed on previously. You'll take up your booking in the Shangri-La on Thursday as usual, then meet Rowan on Friday morning and do the hand over. You can even tell him it's worth double the usual fee, and once he's seen what is on it, he will agree with you. Consider that a little bonus from us to you. By the way – how much do you think Rowan is getting each time?' I ask.

She pauses; after all, answering will confirm her guilt – not that there is any doubt, of course. 'He told me $200k, so I get $100k, and Sofia only ever wanted $50k.'

'Well, you can take it from me he is diddling you; he's getting more than that.'

'Prick,' she mutters.

I continue, 'Claudia, let's be very clear. We have been watching you and your cohorts very closely, so please don't be silly and think you can get away or escape – you're only likely to get hurt trying to do that. Assist us, and you not only keep your nest egg plus this last bonus; you can then quietly disappear and reinvent yourself somewhere else. Try and disrupt the plan, and your nest egg will likely disappear or be impounded by authorities as proceeds of crime; these photos will haunt you, and Sofia, so it's not just your future you have to decide on.'

I again go quiet and let her take her time.

It doesn't take long, and it's easy to see she has made a decision. She straightens her shoulders, looks at me, nods her head and says, 'Okay, I'll go with option two. No real choice is there?' This is said with a sad half-smile.

I nod, saying, 'Good choice. I'll be in touch with you before Thursday to give you the USB, and I stress, *do not* talk to anyone about this or any aspect of our plan. You have too much to lose. And remember, we are monitoring you every step of the way, not just on Thursday and Friday but tonight and the rest of the week.'

She looks a little bewildered and says, 'Have you been following me and everything?'

'Yes,' I reply, 'and everything.' Clearly, she's a little shaken that she has had no idea we have been tailing her and monitoring her.

I offer my hand and we shake. I say, 'I have your phone number, so I'll give you a call, likely Wednesday.'

She nods.

I let myself out and walk up the road.

Pig, who has been listening in through my phone, says, 'Good job, you happy she bought it?'

'Yes, I think so,' I reply, no doubt seeming strange to other pedestrians, seemingly talking to myself. 'But watch her – make sure she goes straight home. If not, I'll visit her again there tonight just to reinforce our vigilance.'

'Will do. What are you going to do?' Pig askes.

'Go and have a feed, I reckon; there is a place up here in Miller Street I like the look of, seem to have spent half my life here in North Sydney these last few weeks,' I finish.

'Enjoy,' Pig confirms.

37

It's Friday morning and I am once again sitting in the lobby café at the Shangri-La; we know Claudia had checked into her room the previous afternoon, and if she has done a runner she has left her handbag up in her room, so we are reasonably confident she will be down around 9:00 a.m. for breakfast and to meet Rowan, who yesterday she confirmed the meet with, as usual.

I don't try to hide, as I want Claudia to see me when she comes in. When she does show up, she sees me and heads to the other end of the café, which is fine by me, as I had done what Pig did last time and slipped a couple of mics around the sugar bowl and salt and pepper shakers on a few tables and, luckily, she's sitting at one with a mic on it. So, Pig and I both have clear audio when she orders breakfast – yes, the egg white omelette and green tea.

Shortly after 9:00 a.m., Rowan comes in glances around, taking no notice of me or anyone else, sees Claudia, and takes a seat. I'm too far away to see the USB transaction, but I hear her say that she's had a quick look and wants to double the usual payment, as it is pretty important data this time. She also tells him, as per script, that her contact has taken a month's leave, so this will be the last instalment for at least a month.

Rowan nods along, as always, saying very little, but does

acknowledge her request for extra, saying he will have a look and will up the ante if he agrees it's worth it. He agrees to pay her deposit this afternoon as usual and leaves once he has finished his coffee and croissant.

When he is gone, with Pig tracking him, Claudia surprises me by paying, then comes straight back to my table, sitting down and saying, 'There, that is done. Are we finished?'

'No,' I reply, 'not until we can confirm receipt of the data by the end client, and they have acted upon it. Would you like a coffee?' I ask.

She nods a reply, so I ask a passing waitress for a long black, and a half-strength skinny cappuccino for her. She merely looks at me, open mouthed that I know what coffee she drinks. I don't say anything, just keep looking at her and nod, silently reinforcing how much we know about her. I also ask if she demanded a doubling of her payment, and she nods and says, 'He'll read through everything over the weekend and will then make contact with his client, so I should know mid next week as usual.'

Out of curiosity, I ask, 'How did this all come about?'

She smiles wistfully and says, 'I've known Rowan for years, and yes, I know it's not his real name. I knew him in his past life, and we ran into each other nine-odd months ago and got chatting. He told me he had a client trying to make it in the small end of the telecommunications industry looking for "shortcuts", as he called it. I had just met Sofia, who was rather dirty on her husband, who she had found out was once again cheating on her. I asked how she found out, and she told me he leaves his laptop at home sometimes when he goes out, so she checks through his emails, claiming he thought she was too dumb to know how, so he never takes any precautions. Anyway, our friendship blossomed, and I suggested a way to get her own back, well, two ways, actually: to take copies of his emails and give them to me. Then, of course, we started our relationship, a first for her, so she started planning her own independent future, not necessarily with me, but I must say I have become quite fond of her and will miss her.'

'So where will you head after this?' I ask.

She just smiles and shakes her head.

We have both finished our coffees, so I tell her I'll take care of the bill and remind her, 'Big Brother is watching,' as she departs.

38

On Monday morning, Pig and I are discussing the week ahead, and firstly, we chat about the girls, still safely tucked away in Coffs Harbour. From Maria's account, the three of them are having a good, fun time. I agree with him – we need to switch focus to these bent coppers full-time as soon as we can. But back to the here and now, we know Rowan has emailed Matt, telling him he had a significant bonus this week and is seeking a double payment. We're waiting so Pig can book a flight down for the day of their meeting, as we have agreed the meeting between these two is too critical for me on my own. We plan the same double team with our special umbrellas with high-quality secret mics in the wooden handles, or better still, if at the same place again, we can set up mics amongst the tables, which will be far easier and less obvious. We can only hope.

In the meantime, Pig is working a couple of other digital data access audits, ensuring the individual companies' websites and servers are as secure as possible. We rate our clients' needs on a scale of one to five, depending on what their need for security is, with, say, a bank or major organisation dealing with confidential personal data (credit card numbers, address, date of birth, etc.) as a five; a small manufacturing business or trader with no secrets worth stealing would be a one. Most of our clients are, of course, somewhere in the middle, so helping them navigate through these waters can be rewarding. We have the fun part of trying to access their systems, usually after they have gone through an upgrade. We usually can, and then recommend what fixes they need. We're not code writers and don't write the software. The new term for what we do is 'ethical hacking', or as we say, 'hacking for the good guys'. No doubt, the recent increase in global hacking of both government and commercial businesses has made companies more aware of how vulnerable they are to such attacks. We don't mind!

It's not until mid-afternoon that Matt replies, saying the doubling of the cost is pretty steep, but he will consider it if it's worth it. He says he'll bring his laptop with him, so he can review the data whilst they meet. He suggests they meet for lunch at Crystal Bar Burgers, again at the GPO tomorrow, Tuesday at 12:30 p.m. This will give them more time and more privacy, he says.

Rowan quickly agrees, saying he will reserve a table, so they are all set, and it's time for us to get busy. Pig books a flight down, catching the first flight out of Brisbane at 6:15 a.m., the next morning arriving in Sydney around 8:30 a.m., and will jump a cab straight to the GPO to meet me. The Crystal doesn't open until 10:00 a.m., so we have plenty of time to plan our strategy. We expect they'll mark the reserved tables early to avoid any issue with the bookings come lunch time, so this should make it easier to identify where they will be sitting and mic these tables up.

Sure enough, I'm sitting at Maximus next morning when Pig arrives, so I order him a coffee and another for me, and a couple of muffins – these are a bit yummy, I've decided. We need to sustain ourselves, after all! We sit and chat for a while, Pig plying me with questions about my meeting with Claudia, and then, of course, he wants to know about Suzie, so I tell him, yes, we had a chatted a couple of times over the weekend, and he smiles and nods, like he approves.

We wander off around the block simply so we are not sitting still for too long and grabbing someone's attention. Around 11:30 a.m., we head into the Crystal and once again order coffee, looking through the menu whilst surveying the layout. We note a couple of reserved tables, one at each end away from other tables, so we decide to target these. Once we have ordered coffees, Pig goes in one direction, I in the other wandering around the restaurant, which is all but empty at this time, looking at the artwork and memorabilia on the walls, and using this time to secret a few mics, one each on the targeted tables plus a couple of floaters in case we get the tables wrong. Around 12:15 p.m., Pig ups and leaves to find somewhere out of sight to manage the volume of the mics and tweak the audio if need be, whilst I stay and order one of the fancy Black Angus burgers. I'm sitting midway between the two target tables with my back to the entrance, and it's not long before Matt strolls in and is shown to the reserved table on my left. He's talking on his phone the whole time (rather rude, isn't he!), and Pig gives me a grunt to know we're fine on audio. We don't need video, so I'm just sitting here listening on my earpiece, and shortly enjoying a very tasty burger, when Rowan comes in and we hear him say he is sorry he is late. He quickly orders a coffee and the chicken burger, to go with Matt's Black Angus.

Quickly down to business, and it's obvious Rowan is a little excited about what he has brought to the table, telling Matt it includes a strategy paper, including all financing options to buy Mypone. This is also confirmed by an email trail between Cameron and Jess Fergusson (Mypone CEO). In reality, this is between Cameron and me, as I had dummied up the email address for Jess.

Matt puts his hand out for the USB and Rowan hands this over, so he slips it into the port and fires up his laptop. His fingers fly across the keyboard, checking everything, and then suddenly stops and says, 'This data is incomplete.'

Rowan smiles and says, 'Of course it is, this is just a teaser. We need to agree to terms before you see the full proposal. I wasn't going to give you all the data and hope you would honour our agreement.'

Matt looks disappointed, but not surprised, and says, 'Well, if this is the real deal, yes, I will pay double for it.'

They shake hands and swap USBs whilst Matt shuts down the laptop just as their meals are served.

As I'm finished, I get up to pay and exit, knowing we have them on the hook. I wander outside without acknowledging Pig and go around the corner near the entrance to Futurcomm's office and wait patiently, whilst still listening to the two of them chatting.

I hear them settle the bill, and a few minutes later Matt strolls past me and into the entrance of their building. I head back and join Pig and head off up the road for somewhere quiet so Pig can have a feed. After an hour's wait, he logs into his Trojan horse to see if Matt has the full file of documents open, and as he does, he then opens the Trojan horse spyware and establishes this on his hard drive. Once done, Pig has full access to everything Matt can see and do.

We watch him going through the documents, pretty quickly; he is either a fast reader or he is simply skimming and coming back for another look later. He seems to read the 'Business Strategy' fairly thoroughly, and he is also writing notes for himself on a separate Word document he has opened. Pig and I do a fist bump, knowing we are in, and a short time later, he heads off back to the airport and home. It's also finally looking like I will be able to head home shortly too.

39

Wednesday morning, and I'm back in Paramount's reception and note no Christina, with another older lady tending the desk. Marg comes out and escorts me through to the boardroom, and as we are walking, I say, 'New receptionist?'

She turns to me and smiles and says, 'Yes, Christina up and left suddenly a couple of days ago,' seemingly watching for my reaction, but I just nod.

Their chairman, Sir Anthony Harrison, is already seated at the head of the table, and Marg introduces us. He nods and asks, 'You have an update for us?'

All business.

'Yes,' I reply, 'Matt appears to have accepted the data as the real deal, has paid double the usual fee, and modified the Business Strategy document, and this morning, he is meeting with a Shane Knight of Sentinel Finance, a second- or third-tier financier who specialises in short-term loans – at eye watering rates, I might add.'

Sir Anthony nods at this.

I continue, 'The proposal Matt is putting forward is seeking the full funding for a takeover of Mypone, exactly as scripted. Whilst he is also offering Sentinel equity to take some of the risk out of the deal, we will have to wait and see what the final deal will look like.'

'And how will you know that?' Sir Anthony asks.

'We are monitoring all documents and emails on or emanating from Matt's laptop, plus full access to their server, so we will know.'

Sir Anthony studies me for a long while, finally nodding and says, 'General Rutherford says you are competent; he says to say hello to you, by the way.'

I reply, 'That was nice of him, please tell him both Mort and Pig say hi back. You know the General, obviously?'

He smiles and nods. 'Yes, Charles and I go way back. So, what is your best guess on the timing of the next stage?'

I pause for a moment before replying. 'Judging by the speed Matt is working at present, and assuming he ties up his finances this week, I would expect he will start acquiring shares as soon as next week. Then once he approaches twenty per cent, he will have to stop or make a full offer, so no doubt he will seek to do some due diligence at that time. They will then see that there is no substance behind the business strategy, and he will be ripe for the plucking. So, my best guess is three to four weeks, and you should be able to wrap this up.'

He and Marg nod to each other, and I gather that is similar to their own timeline estimate.

Sir Anthony nods, picks up all his papers and glasses, leans over shaking my hand and says, 'You have done an excellent job on the first issue and also suggesting an excellent way to turn a negative into a positive, so thank you and well done.'

I nod and say, 'Thank you, Sir,' and he departs, leaving Marg and me sitting at the table.

She smiles and says, 'Well, you certainly have done well.'

As we are done and it's nearly lunch time, I ask, 'What's the food like at the café in the lobby?'

She replies, 'I've never eaten a proper meal there, but the coffee and snacks are great.'

So I say, 'I'm hitting the road home this afternoon, so why don't we pop down for a quick bite?'

She smiles, looks at her watch and then says, 'That's great, let me drop these back to my office and I'll see you out in reception shortly.'

Marg comes out quickly and we head down in the elevator, not saying too much with other passengers coming and going.

We get to the café where I order a BLT and coffee, and she a chicken salad and coffee – surprisingly no vanilla or caramel, just a long black, so I have to comment and say, 'Good to see a lady that doesn't have one of these fancy coffees.'

She laughs and says, 'No, always just taken it straight black; it's kept me going many an hour!'

Once we have ordered and settled at a table, she asks, 'Are you flying home?'

'No,' I say, 'driving.'

'Hope you have some fancy car.'

I laugh and say, 'Yeah, a Hyundai iLoad van! We brought a fair amount of equipment down that we needed, so it's all packed up and I'm out of here after lunch.'

'Which way will you go?' she asks.

'I came down the Pacific Highway along the coast, so I'm heading home inland along the New England Highway, hoping to make Tamworth tonight and then home early afternoon tomorrow. Lovely part of the world, with the rolling pastures and pleasant scenery and, without the stop-start of the coast road, more open highway to just cruise along.'

'Have you done all this yourself?' she asks.

I say, 'No, my off-sider has been here most of the time working with me – too much for one man.'

She smiles again and says, 'You know, I am intrigued how you've managed to get all this information and tracked the leak and everything down; it really is Impressive.'

I smile and shrug, not much to say. Fortunately, our lunch is served, so I'm saved from any more awkward questions. We continue to chatter over lunch, not about too much, and I try and quiz her on their plans for Futurcomm, but she doesn't bite.

After a pleasant lunch, we say goodbye. She heads back to the lift and I out to the street to grab a cab and return to the Quest one last time to grab the van. Once on the road, I ring Pig to let him know, give him an update on the meeting and tell him Sir Anthony 'goes back a long way with Major General Charlie Rutherford – even passed on his regards and told Sir Anthony I was competent!'

Pig lets out a snort and says, 'Well, your Sir Anthony must be all right if he's a friend of MGC's.'

'I passed our regards back to him, by the way,' I add.

Pig tells me nothing new to report on the Futurcomm front but he will let me know if anything changes.

I make Tamworth around 8:00 p.m. that night, just in time to get a feed before the kitchen closes – T-bone steak off the plate – you can't beat these regional pub meals, I think! Once settled in my room, I give Suzie a call to tell her I'm on my way home, and will be home tomorrow, and would she like to have dinner, and she tells me she has an in-house conference starting Thursday at lunch time through dinner Saturday night.

'Bugger,' I say, and she also sounds disappointed, so I tell her my room in Tamworth isn't a patch on the Four Seasons.

40

It's 8:30 a.m. Sunday morning as I pull up outside Suzie's apartment, and lo and behold, she must have been keeping a look out, as she is out the door and coming out the gate almost before I come to a stop. She jumps in after first putting a shopping bag on the floor in the back, leans over and gives me a big kiss and smile, so I pull her back for another one, and she is happy to oblige.

After we have settled down, I hand her a vanilla latte, saying, 'Your vanilla latte, madam – I trust you will enjoy it.'

'Thank you, kind sir,' she replies, taking a sip.

'So where are we off to?' she asks.

I smile and I say, 'Well, it wouldn't be a "mystery day out" if I told you, would it!'

Yesterday afternoon, knowing she was tied up in the conference, I had sent her a text reading, 'Booking confirmation. Please reply Y to confirm you are booked on a "mystery day outing" tomorrow Sunday at 8:30 a.m. sharp. The driver is instructed not to wait for late arrivals. Dress: casual outdoorsy.'

And she had replied with a 'Y' and lots of question marks, but I did not respond.

'And when did you get this?' she asks, pointing at the Toyota Prado I was driving.

'I picked it up yesterday,' I reply.

She comes back, saying, 'But you only got home Thursday afternoon?'

'Yes, but I asked Doug at Sci Fleet to keep an eye out for a good Prado a few weeks ago, and he's been holding this one for me for nearly two weeks. I would have had to fly up to inspect and pay for it shortly if I hadn't finished the assignment down there. He's the one I bought the Camry from as well.'

She looks around the vehicle, inspecting different things, saying, 'GXL model, too, so not the base model, ah?'

'Well, nearly!' I reply.

She lifts the centre console lid and says, 'Even got a little fridge in here.'

'Yep,' I reply.

'So why another Toyota?' she asks. 'There are plenty of other nice SUVs you could have bought, and cheaper too.'

I look at her in surprise and say, 'Such as?'

'Well, Ford Everest, Isuzu MU-X, Audi Q range, VW range – plenty to choose from.'

I again look at her, surprised.

She adds, 'What? Didn't you think I knew anything about cars? Just because I'm blonde doesn't mean I know nothing about cars, you know. Take this Prado 2.8l turbo diesel, 420 Nm of torque, largest selling SUV in its class!' she says with her impish smile. 'I learnt to drive in an old MQ Patrol short wheelbase, you know.'

'Well, Toyotas have got me out of a few pickles over the years. Over in Afghanistan, they're the only reliable transport.'

Suzie says, 'But I thought you all travelled in Bushmasters and things, you know – troop carrier thingies.'

And I reply, 'A bit hard to do that behind enemy lines, though.'

The look she gives me is tinged with uncertainty.

'Besides,' I say, 'the resale value on these means the "cost of life" ownership cost of the car is far less than any of those others you mentioned.'

'True, I guess,' she replies. Then, seeing me smiling at her, she pokes her tongue out at me, and we both have a good laugh.

'So, how did you end up in Sydney?' she then asks.

'Pretty good, it's still in play. We've set a trap now, having fed them false information, so we're waiting for them to act on it – then my client can pounce.'

'How will that work?'

'They think one of their smaller competitors will be good buying, and they're going to over stretch themselves financially. When they get access to the target company's books for due diligence, they will realise it's not worth buying, and that's when Paramount will pounce, buying up the target, and unless I am mistaken, also buying the third competitor, making it a rather unique triple play. That's the plan, anyway, and I'm banking on it as I invested a few bucks in both the target companies, so I'm hoping it comes off!'

She digests this and comes back with, 'What's your part on this second stage?'

'Apart from suggesting the concept and the plan, and then implementing it – nothing!'

'Now you're a businessman as well as a soldier!?'

I smile and say, 'Just because I was a soldier doesn't mean I don't have other skills or know stuff!' I then explain in a little more detail and how I left the triple play for them to work out, likening it to leading a horse to water, and then letting it decide to have a drink.

'So, they will think they are pretty clever, where, in fact, you set it all up,' she says a little admiringly (I think, anyway), adding a smile.

By now, we're a fair way down the Pacific Highway, and she seems to suddenly realise this, once again asking, 'Where are we headed?'

This time, I say, 'First stop is a coffee stop in Murwillumbah – then onward and upward.'

She turns to look at me, raising her eyebrows. After a little silence, she starts chatting away, talking about this and that, which suits me. I just have to add the occasional nod or grunt, and she doesn't seem to notice. I'm happy just letting her chatter, telling me she's planning on running the Gold Coast half marathon next year, and I agree to train with her, if not enter myself, but knowing Pig has the same plan, I'm pretty sure I will end up entering as well. At one point, she mentions her older sister Nat's fortieth birthday is in a couple of weeks, and she says pointedly, 'And you, mister, have nearly won yourself an invite.'

I raise my eyebrows in question.

She continues, 'You see, I haven't told Nat or any of my family about you, so if I tell Nat I'm bringing someone, I will get a very big "please explain", and then of course, it will flow to Mum and Dad as well. So, it is a very big decision I need to make.'

I turn and smile and say, 'But of course, you want me to come. How could they not like me?'

She just pulls a face.

'Besides, you'll need to get in quick; otherwise, my social calendar might be full, and you'll miss out on my company.'

This time, I get a snort, but she does say, 'Well, maybe you better keep Sunday the fifteenth – that's two weeks from today – free, just in case.'

I change the subject by asking, 'How is Nat coping with turning forty?'

I get a laugh in return. 'Not well; like for most of us, it seems so old!'

She goes on to tell me they are having the party at their home in Samford Valley, where they live on acreage. 'It's idyllic out there,' she finishes. Most of her extended family will be there, and she is having it catered, so it should be a fun afternoon.

'Well, you'll need to take me, so you can relax and enjoy yourself knowing I can drive you home; I can even wear my driver's uniform if you like!'

I get another face pull! She also mentions Jenny is wanting to meet me, and they're working out an evening that suits everyone. Although I don't get asked when would suit me, so I guess I will just be expected to be available. Suits me!

After a lull in the conversation, I ask, 'So, you learnt to drive in an old MQ Patrol, ah – what's with that?'

She smiles and says, 'Well, you know, Dad is a mechanic, and has always had his own small mechanical repair business. His hobby was stock car racing. He had this old MQ short wheelbase we used to pull the race car and all its bits around to the different race meetings.' She is smiling while recounting this story, obviously a fond memory.

She continues, 'Mum and Nat had no interest, but I loved it; I was the tomboy of the family, so I went to all the race meetings with Dad, and by the time I was twelve or thirteen, I was driving the race car onto the trailer, backing the trailer around the pits, and then when I think I was fourteen, Dad got pretty banged up in a race, so I offered to drive home, and did. I'll always remember as we got close to home, he said to me, "Maybe we won't mention this to your Mum, ah?". I thought I was so cool driving all the way home from Gympie that night – and sharing a secret with my dad! It became a bit of a habit after that. When I turned fifteen, I started racing in the junior category, using Dad's car! Again, I thought I was pretty cool – the only girl in Queensland registered as a stock car driver. Of course, all the boys tried to knock me out, but they soon learnt to leave me alone – I could be lethal if they pissed me off! Dad was always fiddling around dropping big-arse motors in the MQ; had a Chevy 454 Big

Block engine in it for a while. Boy, you could get the old MQ up on its rear wheels with that thing. We did, too – Dad used to show off a bit around the tracks! I must admit I did too. It was so much fun!'

The smile is still in place, so clearly a fun part of her life.

I tell her my dad is also a Patrol 'freak', still running his old GQ wagon we used to have when I was a kid. I take the turnoff off the Pacific Highway into Murwillumbah, a small town just over the border in NSW, and pull up at the little café and rest area on the outskirts of town, commenting, 'We always used to stop here when we came down here when I was a kid for picnics and camping, so I wonder if it's changed much.'

When going inside, I decide it hasn't changed much, but the coffee and cakes look good.

Leaving Murwillumbah, we head up the Tweed Valley, heading into the hills and into Nightcap National Park, where the road reverts to a track, with first stop the outlook over Protesters Falls, which, as usual, only has a trickle. Then onward along the track, fording creeks, and a bit of reminiscing on my part as we pass a nice little camping and picnic area I stopped at a few times as a kid.

'Why aren't we stopping here?' I get asked.

'Because I've got a nicer spot lined up for you, my lady,' I tell her.

The track becomes quite wet and mushy deeper into the forest, and then after crescenting the top of the range, we head down through open farmland before turning into the Rocky Creek Dam, with its lovely picnic areas and lush grass embankment, and I pull up under a shady tree. We get out and stretch, which also somehow includes an embrace and a kiss. I'm liking this more and more!

'Just as well you bought the Prado,' Suzie says, looking at all the mud all over the vehicle.

I reply, 'Yes, it's the passenger's responsibility to clean the car at the end of the trip.'

'Ah,' she replies, 'that wasn't in the terms and conditions I signed up for.'

'Blooming lawyers,' I grumble with a smile, whilst laying out the rug and pulling out an Esky with our lunch.

After a pleasant lunch of roast chicken rolls and muffins as a dessert, Suzie stretches out on the rug, enjoying the sunshine, whilst I go for a wander down to the water's edge.

When I come back, she sits up, smiles, and says, 'This is lovely, Mort.'

I can't resist, so I kneel down, kiss her and say, 'So are you.'

Then it's time to pack up and head home, and we head out from the dam through the delightful macadamia plantations and countryside, re-joining the Pacific Highway south of Bungalow and Byron Bay.

'You can see why the ferals like it around here, can't you?' I say, referring to the alternative types that live through this area.

She replies, 'Don't forget, the Hemsworth clan also lives around here.'

I amend my statement to, 'You can see why ferals and film stars like it around here!'

The road back to Brisbane is mostly motorway, and we travel mostly in contented silence.

As we approach my place, I say, 'The day ends with dinner for two, by the way.'

I pull into the garage, and we go upstairs, Suzie grabbing the bag she put in the back when I picked her up. Once inside the door, she pulls me into a full embrace and kiss. Then she pulls away before taking my hand and saying, 'Mister, you planned the day, but I've planned the evening,' and she leads me by the hand towards the bedroom.

I follow as meek as a lamb.

41

Monday morning, it's good to be back in the office after so many weeks away. Pig and I recap over coffee as a starter (our version of a 'toolbox meeting') and set priorities; he is to keep looking into Lancaster and Fleming, while I come back up to speed on the Paramount assignment.

He teases me early on by saying, 'You've obviously spent time with Suzie – you're smiling too much!'

So I say, 'Yes, we had a lovely day yesterday. Went on a picnic.'

He evades answering my question about how his weekend went, so I don't push it. We are blokes, after all; we don't talk about these things.

I start by logging into Matt at Futurcomm to see how he went with his financing meeting with Sentinel Finance. It appears they have come to an agreement, as I can see a terms sheet (a summary of critical facts that parties agree to) having been going to and fro, and I see Matt has signed the last one he sent. This shows the loan to be $2.5 million, in two tranches of $1.25 million each with the interest rate of eighteen per cent p.a., and Sentinel having the option to swap debt for equity up to a maximum of ten per cent in Futurcomm upon settlement of the merger. I quickly do the maths and work out Matt has to cover $37,500 per month in interest, so he'll have to make it a quick deal! The first tranche of $1.25 million is sufficient to get him to a shareholding of twenty per cent, a trigger point that he has to stay below. Otherwise, he will have to make a full takeover offer, which he won't want to do until he has completed due diligence, where his accountants will go in and basically audit the books of the target company. They will also verify the accuracy of the data they already have. This, of course, will create a problem, as the data we have given him is greatly exaggerated.

Then in theory, once he has completed his due diligence, he will draw down the second tranche so he can buy further shares and move to fifty-one per cent and effective control of the company. His further plan once due diligence confirms the values is to seek $5 million through a rights issue at fifty cents per share (currently trading at sixty-five cents) and an additional private equity issue. This will effectively double the value of the business, so, a big play, and a risky one, knowing what we know.

The next day, the first tranche of $1.25 million hits the Futurcomm bank account, so I trace it back to Sentinel and then access their account to see where the funds have come from. I see five investors have stumped up $250,000 each; none of the names mean anything, so I'm trolling through the Sentinel emails, being nosey, basically, and I see an email address I recognise: joedl@gmail.com and say out loud, 'Hold on, what have we got here?'

This is the private email of Joe Lancaster, but this one is signed Joe Lowry. Further digging, and I see Joe Lowry is a regular contributor to Sentinel's funding as there are frequent emails between Joe Lowry and Shane at Sentinel. This sends me back to Joe Lancaster's PC, and I check his email and no sign of these emails, so further digging, and I stumble upon a separate email hidden away in a folder on his desktop. I open this, and a whole new world opens up. He has a split hard drive; one is the 'front', if you like, where he does all his mundane Joe Lancaster business; slip through this folder, and it all relates to a Joe Lowry.

'Gottcha!'

Apparently, I said this out loud, accompanied by a fist pump, as Pig looks up and says, 'Got what?'

'Joe D Lancaster, meet Joe D Lowry – who has millions in his bank accounts.'

I scroll through his Xero accounting software which shows eight different entities, all with good bank balances. I go to the one that paid Sentinel the $250,000 and see it has a balance of $1.4 million after this withdrawal. He doesn't seem to spend much from this account, but there are funds coming in constantly from various other companies. Then I notice another large payment of $307k – roughly US$200k – going to an overseas bank account just last week. I wonder who he is paying US$200k to.

By now, Pig is watching over my shoulder, and on a sudden impulse, I start scrolling back through the account, asking Pig, 'What was the date the Brothers Mob bikie got hit?'

'Shit, about three months ago, I reckon.'

So I scroll back, and bugger me, there are two payments of around $230k each, equivalent to US$150k, both going to the same overseas bank account about a month apart. Pig quickly checks the date of the killing online, and we confirm one payment was made three weeks prior to the killing – likely the down payment, the other only five days after the killing.

'Shit,' says Pig, 'what have we got here?'

'A treasure trove, that's what,' I reply. 'Trouble is, neither of us are forensic accountants to try and work this maze out.' And we don't know one either.

Pig adds, 'Why don't we ask Midge if he can give us an identity connected to this bank account? Might be a coincidence and maybe related to drugs or something, although I agree it is probable it's a foreign hit man. And if it is, why has he just paid him another US$200k?'

'That is the sixty-four-dollar question, is it not? But I would put my dollar on a certain Noel Dyson. So yes, let's ask Midge and also tell him we have a new identity for Joe Lancaster – Joe Lowry – and see if this triggers anything in his databases.'

We high five and Pig sits down and sends Midge an encrypted message, asking the questions. I make us both a coffee as our brains spin.

Late morning, and Springsteen start's beating out 'Born in the USA' from Pig's phone as a ringtone. We look at each other and say, 'Midge!'

I move over and sit on the corner of Pig's desk as he answers, with Midge immediately saying, 'Hope you like Springsteen!'

'Yeah love 'im,' Pig answers with a smile.

Midge gets right to business. 'Boys, you have moved up to the big time with that bank account – what are you up to?'

'Why – who does it belong to?'

'One Carlos Santana. He's a well-known but shadowy hit man for the Columbians, but also takes on freelance jobs; he's good. Never been charged, or even arrested. He's a white American, so don't be fooled by the name. But authorities reckon he's good for at least a dozen hits they know of.'

'Well, make that thirteen by the look of it, as we have two payments of US$150k each being paid to him before and after a local bikie was taken out,' Pig explains.

'Okay, so how did you come across his bank account details and the name Joe Lowry?'

'Well, Joe Lowry and Joe Lancaster are one and the same,' Pig explains, 'and we have the money coming from his account, and, get this, he just paid him another US$200k last week.'

'Shit, so another hit coming up?' asks Midge as this sinks in.

'Yeah, looks like it. What can you tell us about this Carlos?' Pig replies.

'Just sent you his file, and Joe Lowry is another name on our files, but we couldn't figure out where he fits in,' is Midge's reply.

'Well now you do, it's a false name Joe Lancaster is using. And Lancaster is a detective inspector in the Queensland Police Service. Clearly bent. He has a wide range of contacts, some we suspect forced. We also have conversations of him dealing with our Queensland Premier's Office – like your US governors,' he explains. 'If there is going to be another shooting, we suspect it's going to be political, as we stopped a play by them to discredit the new opposition leader who is running rings around the premier.'

'So, who are you boys working for – which department?' Midge asks.

We laugh and Pig replies, 'We're on our own, really just stumbled across all this; one of the other bent coppers killed Mort's wife in a car accident whilst he was deployed and he started digging into him, and now here we are.'

'Shit, boys, good luck. Know I can bring some heavy resources to help if you need it.'

'Great, thanks Midge,' we both say.

Then I continue, 'Midge, can you go back into our Border Control and see if you can see where Carlos came into Australia, before and after then giving him the date of the bikie killing?'

'Sure can, will flick what I find through to you boys,' is the reply.

We say our goodbyes and Midge comes back, saying, 'You boys need to be very careful; Carlos is a true pro and knows his stuff.'

I reply, 'Thanks, Midge, will do, but we too have a bit of experience in this field.'

He laughs and says, 'Yes, I still have nightmares about what would have happened to me if you two weren't around back then.'

We hang up.

We look at each other, and I say, 'Shit, this is getting pretty bloody serious and bigger than Ben-Hur. The trouble is, who can we take this to?'

Pig just nods and gets up to make us both a coffee. When in doubt, make a coffee. Once we sit down again, he opens the encrypted email from Midge which shows photos of Carlos, in various disguises, and lists the hits he has been credited with. We look at his favoured modus operandi and we see he favours long distance shots, i.e., a sniper.

'Well, that fits, the bikie was taken down from 450 metres, they claim.'

Pig snorts, and says, 'That's not long, what have you been credited with?'

And I reply rather immodestly, 'A confirmed 865 metre kill, but I reckon I got duded on that 1005 metre shot – the bloke bled out later!' A couple of soldiers bragging.

There is no way we are going to stop now; some serious wrongs are going on in our community and we are the only ones even aware of it, so we need to sort it. Right.

I comment, 'I only started this thing to see if Liz's accident was legit, to see if Benson had killed my wife, and now look at us!'

Pig nods and agrees he will keep digging into Lancaster/Lowry and his various businesses, and I decide I need to refocus, even if only for a short while, on wrapping up Paramount. They are a paying client, after all.

Later that afternoon, Pig gets an email from Midge with a scan attached showing Australian Border Force entry point with a US passport photo of a Gerard Wall, but the photo matches the previous images of Carlos, and a second scan showing the same passport leaving Australia. Shit, so solid proof Carlos had been here when the hit went down. Damn.

Now we have accessed Lancaster's 'Lowry' file, Pig needs to do a thorough investigation of what he can find on that. As a first step, he copies the whole hidden drive onto our cloud-based database, so he isn't playing around on LL's (Lancaster/Lowry) PC, and maybe being noticed. He also sets up a backup, so every night at midnight, a secret backup will be done from LL's computer to our database of any data changes in the previous twenty-four hours. Just a simple and routine back up, but we get the update. Not a bad plan, ah!

Pig quickly identifies why Lancaster seems to work with impunity within the Queensland Police Service, as hidden in a folder simply labelled 'Police', he finds a couple of sub folders, one with photos of a thirty-something male paedophile in sex acts with a young boy. The caption reads 'Comm Tyler's son Adrian, Manilla 2018'. Then another folder labelled 'AC Dixon', and in here he finds photos of two men, let's say, busy. This time, the label reads 'AC Dixon and DI Gillies'.

Pig googles Adrian Tyler and, sure enough, a close likeness to the photos, and likewise with the two policemen – their official ID and the faces in the photos, and it is clearly the same men. Lancaster has them where it hurts. Impunity reigns!

42

With the money in the Futurcomm account, the next morning I check again and see Cameron has contracted Morgan's, a long-established stockbroker, to handle the Mypone share purchases. I email off a report to Marg confirming the basis of the funding, the receipt of the first tranche and how Morgan's are handling the buying of the shares.

A short time later, Marg gives me a call to ask if I would be available for a Zoom meeting with her and Sir Anthony later today, so we can again compare notes. Fine by me, so she sends me the Zoom link and we confirm an 11:30 a.m. appointment. We chat a little and I can sense that this action is exciting her – I'm sure more 'action' than she normally encounters.

Then 11:30 a.m. comes, and I sit down with a fresh coffee, adjust the camera so they can see my pretty mug (my face, not my coffee mug!), and Sir Anthony takes the floor, asking me if I still think a month is the likely timeline.

I must confess, since working out his interest cost I was thinking he would have to bring that in, so I respond by saying, 'Well, he has an interest cost of $37.5k per month, so he certainly doesn't want to be wasting any time. On the other hand, if he tries to buy twenty million Mypone shares on market in one hit, it certainly won't go unnoticed. There aren't really any major shareholders worth approaching either, so in reality, there's no choice but to hit the market quickly and get out.

'A long-winded way of saying I think he is likely to try and acquire up to 19.8 per cent shareholding this week, seek a meeting with Jess and let her know his plan to acquire Mypone, and seek the due diligence documents.'

Sir Anthony again nods whilst looking at Marg, and says, 'Yes, we agree. I am debating when is the best time to front Cameron at Futurcomm.'

I say, 'With respect, instead of taking the direct route, why don't you meet with Shane at Sentinel Finance and buy the Futurcomm debt, and if you time it right, i.e. wait until they have had a few days to go through the due diligence files and realise they've been had, you should get the debt for maybe seventy to eighty cents in the dollar, as Shane will know there is little prospect of Futurcomm being able to pay the interest cost, let alone the capital repayment. You then have Futurcomm by the balls – excuse my French, Marg,' I add.

She smiles whilst watching Sir Anthony for his response.

I can see him turning this concept over in his mind, taking his time to do so. Then he looks at me and says, 'I see why Charlie calls you competent; that is an outstanding play. However, I would like you to come along to that meeting with Margaret and me.'

I shrug, saying, 'Not sure what I can contribute, but happy to fly down for the day once the meeting is set up.'

We say our goodbyes and hang up.

Pig has been listening and says to me, 'When the hell did you think that shit up?'

'Mind's always churning,' I reply with a smile. 'I'm in business now – got to take every opportunity, you know!'

And I have to confess, I'm pretty impressed with myself too. Being new to all this high finance and business stuff and being able to teach an old dog like Sir Anthony a new trick did make me feel good.

I get a text from Marg saying, 'Wow, Sir A was really impressed with your suggestion, even said he may have to use you as a consultant!' with a smiley face.

I reply with a smiley face and add that I'll let her know some research we should do before that meeting.

*

I check in on the girls by calling Maria, and she, as usual, is happy and chirpy, saying the girls are all good, making plans to move to Melbourne and a fresh start, so I suggest midweek next week should be right for them to head off. But they are not to fly; I suggest that they rent a car to drive down one way. I remind her about the envelope Pig gave her, with two Visa cards in it, prepaid to $2,500 each – one each for the girls. We cleaned their bank accounts out before they disappeared and cut up their credit cards, so the cops couldn't trace them through accidental use.

Maria says, 'Mort, I am so looking forward to seeing my family. They're coming down Friday, so thank you! The kids are excited about staying at a resort with a swimming pool and playground and being able to just walk to the beach.'

I tell her to enjoy it, and everything being equal, she should be home by the end of next week herself. We discuss the ongoing headlines about the whole episode and how Colleen is certainly milking the story, keeping it in the headlines even though there is little new information. It sounds like the official police investigation isn't going anywhere. No surprise there.

43

Next morning, Pig, who has been beavering away (a pig beavering – get it?), says, 'Okay, time for a recap on LL – Lancaster/Lowry.'

I reply, 'Good idea, but first, coffee.'

I make two fresh mugs and sit down, and he shows me his spreadsheet, listing eight different businesses LL owns, with Pig commenting that Allegro Accounting is a service that handles all the bookkeeping for these businesses, but also seems to handle a number of others, doing minimal work for pretty good fees.

He adds, 'they only have two local staff and use a labour contracting business in the Philippines to do all the grunt work.'

He has listed all the different companies that pay Allegro Accounting fees every month along with the amount, so we Google them to see where they're based, finding many are based in the nightlife precincts of Fortitude Valley and West End.

I ask, 'Protection?'

Pig looks at me and says, 'Shit, what a good idea, can't really use the old brown paper bag anymore. No one pays by cash, and paying for bookkeeping is a legit business expense! This bloke is good!'

We fist bump.

We go on through the rest of LL's owned businesses and see most are doing pretty well, and Pig points out a travel agency is amongst them. He explains, 'I have checked their records and can identify where they actually booked Carlos's flights, etc. when he came over for the Bikie hit.'

'Are there any recent bookings pending?' I ask.

'No,' he replies, 'not in the name Gerard Wall.'

'Okay, dig up the booking – I want to see where he stayed and everything.'

'No, they didn't book him any accommodation, only the flights, and the booking confirmation was sent to LL, so I backtracked through his emails and found where he sent them on to another email, which was just a jumble of letters and numbers, but I assume it was Carlos. I sent the email address to Midge, but he came back saying it's a commonly used one-off type email service were you can set up to use the email address for either so many days or a number of emails received. These types often only use them for one email, then it closes, and they allocate a new one for their next client. No chance to trace – and for Midge to say that, it must be pretty solid. I also asked Midge to send through any other known alias Carlos uses so we can keep an eye out.'

I tell Pig, 'You've done a pretty thorough job,' and we fist bump again.

He brings us back to reality by saying, 'That's all good, of course, but we now strongly suspect LL has initiated a hit on Dyson, and for all we know, Carlos could already be in the country.'

'Mmm,' I reply, 'maybe it's time to check on Dyson's itinerary over the next few weeks, see anywhere that might suit a sniper takedown.'

Pig nods and says, 'On it.'

I go on. 'You know, Sir Anthony mentioning MGC yesterday got me thinking he might be our best shot to reach out to. From what I've heard, he still keeps his hand in in some semi-official capacity high up in the government, so if we lay out everything we have got, and though we can't take it to the police, even the Federal Police – we know Lancaster has an association with one of their Assistant Commissioners – he might be able to guide us.'

Pig replies, 'Good idea. Just as well you're good at writing reports, because he will want it thoroughly documented!'

'Something else to add to the list,' I reply. 'But the more I think about it, yes, this would be our best way to handle it.'

After checking on Futurcomm, where I see Morgan's have already bought the required sixteen million shares at an average price of 6c each – just shy of $1 million. Things are moving along on schedule. I need to start working on a couple of the other routine data audits we've been contracted to perform. These are rather rudimentary and easy to do sitting here in the office. So, I get into the first one – after making a coffee, of course!

*

It's now Friday at lunchtime, and Pig and I are headed to our local pub for lunch – what we call our 'Friday Recap', just an excuse to relax and catch up, really. We run through each of our cases, with most time spent on LL, of course, but also I tell Pig I've sent a list of suggested research Marg should do before our meeting (maybe confrontation might be a better word, as it will be clear we have set Futurcomm up, so Shane at Sentinel may be a little shirty), as this is likely to take place late next week or early the following.

We aren't too sure what else we can glean from LL's accounting records. Pig has done a drive-by of all the businesses we suspect are paying him protection, taken photos of them, and in most cases, been in to buy something, just to get a feel for them – he drew the line at the massage parlour. He has also identified a withdrawal of $60k from the main bank account a couple of days before we saw

Lancaster distribute envelopes across the bar table at one of their Thursday sessions – what he called 'their quarterly bonus', with the words, 'Don't spend it rashly; we don't want anyone thinking you're spending above your paygrade. Our retirement fund is growing nicely, so none of us want to jeopardise that, do we?' accompanied by a glare around the table.

44

It's Sunday and I'm off to meet Suzie's family at her sister Nat's 40th. Suzie seems a little nervous, so on the way out there I tease her about how I'll act the fool and embarrass her, but I don't get much reaction.

She has told me she got a big 'please explain' when she told Nat she would be bringing someone, getting the full inquisition and 'Why haven't you told me?' Typical sister chatter, I gather. Of course, it quickly spread to her mum and dad, who then wanted to know all about me, and she had told them they would meet me on Sunday, so I'm guessing there are a few questions headed my way.

It had been something of a watershed weekend for us, as we also had Pig and George over for a BBQ last night. I had suggested Suzie come over after work Friday and stay for the weekend. Which she happily agreed to. Mind you, after she arrived, I checked the bathroom cabinets, and when she asked what I was doing, I explained that, according to *Seinfeld* (*Seinfeld* episodes were almost on loop in the mess in Baghdad), if I had female sanitary products in my bathroom, I was officially in a relationship.

She replied, 'I've put some in the drawer. What are you going to say now, mister?'

I smiled and said, 'Good,' which got me another kiss.

Our BBQ with Pig and George hadn't gone too bad; George stayed civil, so I didn't antagonise him. Suzie had even helped in the kitchen, preparing the salad and the obligatory pavlova for dessert, so, another tick!

I follow her directions towards Samford Valley and pull into the driveway. Judging by the cars already here, we aren't early. A lady and two children aged, I'm guessing, nine and six start heading our way, and there's no doubt it's Suzie's sister – similar build with shorter blonde hair – which Suzie confirms along with telling me, 'That's Ollie and Amelie with her.'

We get out, and Suzie hugs her sister and the kids before turning to introduce me. Whilst she was doing that, I had grabbed a bunch of flowers I had in the back of the Prado and I hand these to Nat, wishing her a happy birthday. These seem to surprise both of them, and certainly Nat seemed to appreciate the gesture.

After I had been introduced, Ollie says, 'Will you play footy with me?'

'Sure,' I say.

Amelie says, 'I'm playing too!' Amelie then says to me, 'Mort is a funny name.'

I reply, 'I think it is a cool name; I'm named after Moreton Island.'

She replies, 'My name is French.'

'Well, that's cool too, isn't it?' I reply, and she nods enthusiastically.

Nat and Suzie head off, oblivious to the footy game about to start behind them.

'Who's your favourite player'? I ask Ollie as we start passing the football around between the three of us.

'Cadyn Ponga,' Ollie replies.

I ask, 'You don't like any Bronco players?'

'Nah, Cadyn is so cool and clever; I want to be able to play like him when I grow up!'

We start trotting across the lawn passing the ball to each other, and I become aware of everyone seemingly watching us. Here I am meeting the family for the first time, and I'm off playing footy with the kids – suits me!

Chester, the family border collie, tail wagging furiously, trots along behind us. Of course, Ollie wants to play 'proper footy', so we agree Amelie and I will play him, but I can only use one hand. For the next half an hour or so, we have our little play, and I go sprawling a couple of times much to their amusement (along with everyone else watching as well). I notice Suzie watching me and smiling too, so of course I ham it up a bit more. Then I see Suzie and I'm guessing her father heading our way. Sure enough, Pops tells the kids he wants his turn talking to Mort now, so they are a little downcast until their mum calls out to come and get some ice cream.

Suzie introduces me to her dad.

He smiles and says, 'Hi, Mort, I'm Henry; we've been hearing a bit about you.'

With a smile I reply, 'Should I run now?'

He laughs and the three of us head over to the group. I'm clearly being guided towards Suzie's mum, Caroline, who stands up as we approach and reaches out to give me a kiss on the cheek.

Caroline says, 'Come sit down; I have to meet the man who has put the smile back in my daughter's voice.'

I hear a little gasp from Suzie behind me, and her mother smiles at her and says, 'Yes dear, I knew you had a new man in your life; I even said to Henry, "I hope we meet him soon, as Suzie has got her old spark back again"!'

I'm not sure how to respond to that, but as Suzie reaches over and gives her mum a hug, I decided I didn't need to. I'm introduced to Dave, Nat's husband, also forty-odd, medium build, maybe a little overweight, and a bunch of other guests. We all sit there chatting.

Mostly quizzing me, to be honest, but that's what I was expecting.

The day passes quickly, and it doesn't seem long before we have cake, and then it's time to head home. We say our goodbyes, and I had to promise to play footy again next time I come, which I think is cool.

As we leave, Suzie seems very quiet, and then I see she's crying, so I put my hand over hers and ask in a concerned voice, 'What's wrong? I thought it went well! I don't think I upset anyone.'

This just makes the tears flow more, so as sympathy is not one of my virtues, I leave her alone for a while.

Once she settles down, she says, 'I'm sorry, Mort; I've been so apprehensive about today, worried something would go wrong, and Mum and Dad wouldn't like you or something.'

I spread my arms (yes, I know I am driving), and say, 'What? What's not to like?' As planned, this at least makes her smile and seems to break the mood.

She continues, 'I've been so happy since we met, well, at least since we became friends,' she adds with a smile, 'that I think I was scared something would go wrong today. Then Mum comes out and says I have to meet the man who's put the smile in my voice. It was all I could do to not cry then!'

I reach out and take her hand in mine, and say, 'Maybe you shouldn't be alone tonight.'

She looks at me and says, 'I don't want to be alone tonight.'

45

Back downstairs next morning, Monday, Suzie headed home earlier, so I make coffee before Pig arrives and we have a quick chat, agreeing Saturday's BBQ hadn't been too bad. He asks about the birthday party yesterday, which I tell him had been fun and I had played footy with Ollie and Amelie.

Down to business. As Pig sets up to see what our police cadre have been up to, I'm back into Paramount, hoping we might finally get this completed this week. I access Matt's emails and see where there was a bit of back-and-forth last week between he and Jess, the Mypone CEO, letting her know he was now a twenty per cent shareholder, and was interested in doing due diligence prior to potentially making a formal offer.

Of course, there was push back from her, wanting proof he had control of the shares; this necessitated him having Morgan's send a formal letter to her confirming they had purchased sixteen million Mypone shares on the market on Futurcomm's behalf. Jess then relented late Friday and confirmed she would make a data room available to his nominated analysts from Monday, so today. Matt advised he had contracted Bentley's, a second-tier national accounting firm, to carry out the due diligence, and that he would be there himself on Monday to start the ball rolling. Jess didn't seem impressed.

So, sometime today, or maybe not until tomorrow, they are going to get suspicious about the numbers when they compare them to those they obtained from Rowan. I look forward to seeing those emails!

I email a brief update through to Marg at Paramount, letting her know Bentley's are doing the due diligence and getting underway this morning. She comes back, asking when I think the penny might drop. I reply Wednesday or maybe Thursday, so a meeting with Shane at Sentinel on Monday sounds like a plan. She asks if we can meet a little earlier so we can discuss her research prior to meeting the chairman. A little later, another email from Marg comes in saying Sir A can't make Monday so it will be late morning on Tuesday with Sentinel, and asking if I can make a flight booking to meet them at their office around 10:00 a.m. Tuesday.

'Sure,' I reply, 'I'll get it booked.'

Before booking the flight, I turn to face Pig and say to him, 'I need to go to Sydney for this Paramount meeting Tuesday. I'm thinking I may as well go on to Canberra from there and hunt up MGC. What do you think?'

He nods before saying, 'Well, we do have most of the facts, and it's worrying they have paid that deposit, so we have to expect we don't have a lot of time. You'll have to get your arse into gear and write up the full report.'

I nod, thinking the same thing.

I book the flight to Sydney for first up Tuesday, with an ongoing flight to Canberra late afternoon. I decide not to book a flight home, being unsure how long I might be in Canberra, as I am not sure how long it will take to find the General, and then see if he can help.

Maria and the girls are all set to leave Coffs Harbour on Wednesday, Maria heading home and the girls setting out on a road trip to Melbourne. The whole issue of their story and the rebuttal has died now, and from what we have gleaned, the police aren't looking too hard for them, so unless they get up to their old tricks (pardon the pun) in Melbourne, there should be no reason the cops will track them. They are adamant those days are behind them, that they've been talking about doing TAFE courses, with Christi keen to do a bookkeeping course and Stacey a youth counselling one. They are close, like sisters, so we hope they'll always be there for each other.

I start in on the full report I will need to convince the General, and goodness knows who else. Where to start? The beginning, of course, with my desire to say, 'You killed my wife!'. But first, a coffee. Whilst I am working away on this, I decide I have to come clean with Suzie and tell her what we have discovered, as scary as that might be. Might have to pay her one dollar as a retainer so she is technically my lawyer before I start, too!

46

It's Friday night and I've invited Suzie over for dinner; we haven't discussed whether she will be staying. I am, of course, hoping she's taken that for granted, but I'm not. When she arrives, it's clear she has been home and changed before coming over, and she does bring an overnight bag in so, yes! We chat about the week, and she tells me about a couple of new clients and their troubles.

As we sit down for dinner – a simple chicken salad – I say to Suzie, 'I have something I have to tell you.'

A look of concern comes across her face, and she says, 'Is this my "but" moment?'

I laugh, reach out and gently hold her face in my hands and say, 'No, I am not married with six kids!'

She smiles at that, but also looks relieved.

I continue, 'This is work-related. As you know, I'm heading to Sydney on Tuesday, but from there I'm going on to Canberra, and I want to tell you the whole story of why. But first, here is one dollar, so does that mean you are now my lawyer, and our discussion is confidential?'

'Why Mort, what have you done?' That look of concern again.

I place our dinner on the table, take the chance to give her a quick kiss and sit down and start at the beginning. 'You know where we first met, the Grosvenor?'

She nods.

'Well, I had just set up a surveillance camera and mic there over the table where your favourite coppers sit every Thursday. I was sitting there checking to make sure it was working properly. As you know, one of them, Dillion Benson, is the driver who killed Liz.'

The telling takes some time – long after we finished eating – and I answer her questions as she asks them. When I tell her Maria has been nurse-maiding Christi and Stacey, she pipes up, saying, 'She put up photos on Facebook of her family in the pool at the resort, and I thought they were just having a family holiday.'

I finish by telling her, 'I'm flying on to Canberra after the Paramount meeting to talk to our old General and lay it all out, because the trouble is, who can we turn to? And we are hoping he can help. Clearly, the Queensland police are corrupt at the top, we can't trust the Federal or Victorian police with Lancaster's known connections, and it's highly likely he has a similar connection within NSW police. So, who is going to intervene?'

Suzie remains quietly composed throughout, and surely horrified at the prospect of a political assassination here in little old Brisbane. At the end, she asks, 'How can I help?'

This is a better outcome than I was expecting – whilst not expecting her to become a blubbering mess, how composed and analytical she is, is very comforting. For now, at least, I can't see how she can help, and frankly, I don't want her anywhere near the action if and when it starts.

Monday comes, and Pig and I have invited Maria to lunch now that she is back from her babysitting duties. She brings her husband, Ronnie, along. Ronnie is also a big bloke, maybe not in as trim condition as Maria – working in the mines clearly does not aid that, sitting driving a big seventy-five tonne dump truck all day. But he's a nice bloke and clearly in awe of Pig and me, having heard a few tales about us and our exploits whist serving himself. When introduced, he says it is a privilege to meet us.

Maria gives us a full rundown on their stay at Pacific Bay Resort, saying all three of them had a good time, that the two girls were fun to be with, and adding, 'I reckon Stacey has the hots for you, Pig; she talked about you all the time!'

Of course, Pig comes straight back with, 'And did they teach you some new tricks to keep Ronnie happy?'

Maria laughs and gives Ronnie a dig in the ribs and says, 'Well, Ronnie, any complaints?'

Ronnie is somewhat embarrassed by this turn in the conversation and is blushing a little, and as we all join in the laughter, this makes him blush even more. Then our meals arrive, prompting a change in topic.

After Maria has finished her meal, she looks at me and says, 'This thing with the girls backfired, so what's this mob's next step?'

Again, Maria's perception impresses me, but I dodge the question with a shrug of the shoulders and a smile, but she holds my eye, letting me know she knows I know more.

'Make sure you call me if you need back up,' she says. 'I can still crack heads, and I kept my guns when I cashed out – fully licensed now, of course.'

As we say our goodbyes, both Pig and I get a full hug from Maria, saying, 'Thank you, boys, first for involving me in your business, but especially the weekend at the resort you sprung for us; the kids haven't had a holiday like that so we all had a great time. THANK YOU!'

After we say our goodbyes, Pig and I head back to the office so I can finalise my report for the General.

Pig, who is driving, says, 'I forgot to tell you, Claudia has popped up in Bali; not sure if it's just a holiday or what, of course.'

I reply, 'I'll send her a text asking, "How is Bali?" just to unsettle her,' and promptly do that from the pre-paid phone I had used to contact her previously. 'The reminds me too, we haven't decided on Rowan's punishment either, or the timing of it.'

'Yeah, I keep meaning to bring that up too, but I think we can leave that until we get LL and Santana sorted away,' Pig replies.

'Agreed,' I say.

47

Tuesday morning, and I arrive in Sydney without the flight being delayed (wonders will never cease!), so I'm actually early getting to the Paramount offices, so I settle into the café in the lobby for a quick breakfast, where Marg sees me and comes over, ordering a long black on her way. She seems pleased to see me, giving me the once over. I'm dressed smartly in jacket and slacks, no tie though – I do draw the line at that.

We chat about the emails I had forwarded to her on Friday, showing the rising level of tension between Matt at Futurcomm and Shane at Sentinel over the large discrepancies in the due diligence to what they were expecting. Just what we wanted! She confirms she has all the data I had suggested she gather, so we take our coffees on up to their offices and she sets me up in the boardroom, joining me a short time later with her reports.

We analyse and discuss Sentinel's financials, some of which I had dug up from their server, and Marg, to her credit, doesn't ask! These, of course, show the real picture of their finances, not what is reported each year to the authorities. Whilst they are pretty secure financially, clearly a loss of the $1.25 million loan to Futurcomm would put a hole in their resources, and perhaps even more importantly, put a big hole in their reputation. Their funding model is that they have a network of high-net-worth individuals (like our Joe Lowry), who are invited to subscribe to any given investment opportunity. If a full loan goes bad, the reputational damage to them would be huge. Should be plenty of leverage in that!

We then move on to the Futurcomm accounts, and again, we use the data I have supplied to Marg, which gives the full view of their situation. And this is the crux of the plan—they simply don't have the resources to absorb the $37k a month interest cost on the Sentinel loan. So, what exit strategy options do they have? We debate this and can only see two really. First option is they need to convert the Sentinel loan into equity, but that will entail issuing a minimum of a further twenty per cent more shares, and none of the existing major shareholders will be happy with that, let alone the complications entailed by having to issue a prospectus, etc., which comes with its own set of costs and strict rules.

The second option is they get taken over (enter Paramount).

I guess the third option is to fold, go into administration. I don't know Matt at all, but I would expect his ego will not let that happen.

Sir Anthony arrives, so Marg gives him a summary of what we have been discussing, and we discuss the impact to Sentinel of the loan going bad, and again, I stress the reputational damage will be greater than the financial.

Time to head off and Sir Anthony confirms he has set up the meeting with Shane, 'on a slightly misleading basis,' as he has used the company name of one of his other directorships so the Paramount connection should come from left field. We head out to grab a cab over to the city. We enter Sentinel's office in an old building; not flash, and their office is rather small and shabby, could do with a freshen up. The receptionist shows us through to the boardroom asking if we would like anything to drink, and I take a water.

Shane comes bustling in, seemingly surprised to see three of us, greets us and shakes hands all round.

Sir Anthony then admits to a slight subterfuge and tells Shane outright we are here to discuss Futurcomm. He starts off by saying, 'I apologise for the slight subterfuge, but we are here to discuss Futurcomm.'

Shane looks from one to the other of us, clearly caught off guard.

As Sir Anthony seems reluctant to start the ball rolling, I dive straight in. 'Shane, we know you have lent Futurcomm $1.25 million for their move on Mypone. We know the data you are now seeing does not match what Matt had brought to you to get the loan. We know they will struggle to pay the interest on this loan, let alone repay it. We know Matt has been a naughty boy, obtaining information he was not entitled to. And he is going to pay a heavy price. You will too. Imagine the reputational damage you will incur if this loan goes bad.' I pause here, to build a little tension. 'But maybe we can be your white knight and alleviate some of your pain. Have I left anything out?'

To his credit, he smiles slightly (or is that a grimace?) and says, 'No, I think that is a rather concise summary, unfortunately.'

I leave Sir Anthony to take up the reins, and he starts the negotiation by suggesting, 'We are willing to buy the Futurcomm debt at sixty-five per cent of the face value. This will eliminate the risk of the whole loan going bad.'

Of course, Shane is shocked at this option, so I sit there and let them go to and fro. It's obvious Shane is a streetfighter and knows his way around a negotiation, so Sir Anthony is not getting too far.

As we had agreed, he changes tack and instead suggests they convert the loan from Futurcomm to Paramount for, say, a twelve-month term but at a more commercial rate of six per cent, with Paramount retaining full recovery rights against Futurcomm. This silences Shane for a while as he considers it. This would enable him to avoid having to declare the loan has gone bad and has been converted to a long-term loan. His problem I guess will be in getting his investors to accept a four to five per cent return when they are used to fifteen to sixteen per cent.

I chip in, 'If you absorb the interest shortfall yourself, this will be far cheaper than the damage to your reputation.'

This gets me an appraising look from both Shane and the chairman.

I see in Shane's eyes he has made a decision, but being who he is, he comes back arguing six per cent is way too low; it needs to be 10 per cent for it to work for him. So, I leave it to Sir Anthony to counter, and they to and fro again, finally agreeing on eight per cent.

They agree to the terms of a Term Sheet, where Paramount take over the Futurcomm debt, and this is rewritten to a term of twelve months with an interest rate of eight per cent, with Paramount having full recovery rights against Futurcomm. They also agree that Shane will not discuss this transaction with Matt or anyone at Futurcomm, so that Sir Anthony can have the pleasure of telling him in person. As a sweetener, Sir Anthony asks if Shane wants to add the undrawn $1.25 million in at the same terms, but Shane smiles and declines, saying, 'Long-term loans are not our thing.'

Ah, well, no harm in asking. Paramount have their own resources to fund the purchase of Futurcomm and, I hope, Mypone as well.

Once the term sheet is signed by both parties we head out, taking our copy with us, and Sir Anthony turns to us both, smiling and saying, 'That went well. Do you have time for lunch, Mort?'

'Sure,' I say, 'my flight doesn't leave until 3:30 p.m.'

Over lunch, they confirm they have all their ducks in a row and are now planning on seeking a meeting with Matt over at Futurcomm. In fact, Sir Anthony has decided they aren't going to make an appointment, but rather arrive unannounced.

'Good move,' I tell him, thinking I will take the credit – I'm rubbing off on him!

They plan on doing this tomorrow morning hitting their office around nine, and I ask for them to let me know how that goes.

'Certainly will,' says Marg, who is obviously enjoying this episode in their business.

48

'Rutherford.'

'Do you recognise my voice, General?'

A pause, then Major General Rutherford responds, 'Yes I do.'

I reply, 'Sir, I have an issue I wish to discuss with you.'

Again the pause, and whilst I have clearly caught MGC off guard, there's no doubt he is catching up with himself quickly.

'Let me see what I can clear—'

I interrupt him, 'I'm in the street outside, Sir.'

Another pause, as I'm sure this would have shocked him: *How did you get my number?* and further, *How do you know where I am?* would be rattling around his head.

'Very well, come on in; I will meet you at reception.' He hangs up.

I walk across the car park and enter the non-descript office building where MGC has a suite of offices. Sure enough, he is already standing at the reception desk waiting, still that straight backed army posture, one individual who suited the old-style baton under his arm whilst on parade.

I almost salute but stop myself.

He smiles, puts out his hand, and says, 'Ireland, good to see you.' He looks me up and down, saying, 'Keeping yourself trim, I see.'

'Yes, Sir, too many years of practice to let them go to waste.

Likewise, Sir, you still look the part,' I say, which garners a smile in response.

'Let's go in here, shall we?' He opens a door, before pausing and saying to the young woman behind the reception desk, 'Two straight black coffees, my dear, please.'

We move into a large meeting room, and I remove my satchel bag from my shoulder, placing it on the table, and extracting two files from it, placing them one on top of the other in front of me.

After the coffee is served, MGC looks at me and says, 'Well, that is certainly a first; no one is meant to know my phone number, let alone where I am, so we must have taught you well, Mort. How is Pig, by the way?'

'Pig's fine and sends his regards, Sir; we're working together in the private sector these days.'

'Yes, you did some good work for Tony Harrison, I hear. So, tell me first – before we get into the purpose of this mystery visit – how did you get my phone number and where I am.'

No sense trying to avoid the questions, so I answer straight up, 'Well, when Sir Anthony mentioned you the other day, I realised you might be the only person I could trust with a critical problem Pig and I have uncovered, so I skimmed his phone to capture your phone contact details, and then once I landed here, it was easy to track where your phone was; a fair assumption you wouldn't be far away.'

'Not hard at all if you know what you are doing, then,' he replies, and I nod to the affirmative.

He sits there, at the top of the table, and nods to me.

'Sir this is a long story, so you are going to have to bear with me, but once I have finished, you will appreciate this is a critical problem for our country.'

His eyebrows arch up at this, but he says nothing.

I pull the folders apart, but keep them in front of me, take a sip of coffee and start the story. 'You might recall, Sir, my wife was killed in an accident whilst I was deployed on assignment. I didn't even get back for the funeral. When I cashed out, one of the first things I did was to investigate my wife's accident; it was just something I had to do – partly from guilt, I guess, at having missed her funeral. I quickly found out the other driver was, is, a serving policeman, a detective sergeant, in fact. When I read the coroner's report, I found this wasn't mentioned, nor had blood or alcohol tests been done.

'Both these points seemed strange. When I looked at the damaged police car, I found it had a round green sticker on the registration plates and learnt this was for a special group within Queensland Police. As far as we can tell, a cadre of six, headlined by a Detective Inspector Joe Lancaster. I set up surveillance camera and mics at their favourite pub and quickly learnt of "it" going down. It turns out, "it" was a local Brothers Mob bikie member who was gunned down two days later. They knew about it and did nothing; in fact, we have recently learnt Lancaster in his alias of Joe Lowry paid for the hit.'

A little later I concluded: 'Sir, in summary – and this is detailed in the Executive Summary here'—I tap the folder—'we have this cadre of six Queensland police officers, clearly corrupt and, in fact, running illegal businesses, providing protection and facilitating murder. What we can prove is: Lancaster and Lowry are one and the same. He paid US$300,000 for Carlos Santana to take down Bevan Hogan, the Brothers Mob bikie. We have proof Santana was here in Australia at the time. He has recently paid Santana a further US$200,000 which we believe is a deposit for a hit on Noel Dyson in the next couple of weeks. He runs eight businesses and is being paid "bookkeeping fees" by another eight, mainly nightclubs, bars, and a massage parlour. He is also being paid $5,000 per month each by two heavyweight unions, so not sure what service he is providing them, no doubt prior warning for raids, or going slow on responding to complaints.

'He has proven contacts within the Queensland Department of the Premier and Cabinet, who were fully involved in the recent attempt to discredit Noel Dyson the state opposition leader. He has proven connections at assistant commissioner level at Federal Police and Victorian Police. He is blackmailing the Queensland Police commissioner and has incriminating evidence against another Queensland Police assistant commissioner, so has effective free reign in what he does.

'You must ask if he has influence over someone within Border Force, as Santana is on the INTERPOL watch list, so his photo coming in and out of the country should have raised a flag. He may even have connections within the Department of Defence, for we have him on tape saying when talking about me: "Not even I can get access to his record, so we can't assume his is just an Army grunt." So where to turn? That is why I am sitting in front of you now, Sir.'

General Rutherford pulls the folder over and slowly looks through the documents, images and photos, supporting everything we have on the group. Then the questions start. 'Why do you think he is lining up a hit on Dyson?'

'We have him on tape discussing that possibility, and the proof of the payment to Santana.'

'How the hell can you access international bank account details?' he asks, looking directly at me.

'As you know, Sir, we were both seconded to the Yanks for a while, and did some good work for them. Some of them are happy to return favours.'

He just looks at me, and I return the direct stare, not being intimidated. 'So, I am gathering this unofficial data sharing is far quicker than anything official?'

'Yes, Sir, often within hours. They recognise we have a live situation here, with a world-class assassin likely to appear on the scene any day now.' Then I add, 'We should know within a few hours if or when Santana arrives in country.'

'But not through official channels?'

'No, Sir, we don't have those connections locally, and far too risky too, in my view now.'

More questions follow, but it's clear the General accepts the detail of what I have presented. And once he has completed quizzing me, the critical question to me is, what can he do about it?

It's taken nearly two hours, but the General finally says, 'Shit, Mort, you certainly have uncovered a nasty situation. And perhaps more to the point, it is ideal you have brought it to me. I have a semi-official function within government, reporting direct to the Prime Minister, and that is where this must go. If you would like to go out to the café in the lobby and wait for me, I need to make a couple of calls. I will come and find you when I am ready. The coffee and food is good, by the way.'

I nod and say, 'Thank you, Sir,' gather up my copy of my report, and we exit the meeting room. I head over to the café whilst MGC heads further into the offices. I order a coffee (long black, as always), a BLT and a blueberry muffin. Whilst waiting for my meal, I call Pig and bring him up to speed, and of course, pass on MGC's regards.

Pig replies, 'He's a good old stick, and it sounds like we struck it lucky reaching out to him. How did he take it, being so easily tracked?'

'Not sure that'll be the end of that discussion judging by the annoyed tone he used,' I reply.

My BLT arrives, so I tell Pig I'll keep him posted and hang up. I'm just finishing my muffin when I notice the receptionist heading towards me.

She smiles and says, 'Sir, General Rutherford asks if you can join him again?'

I nod and get up to follow her, and as she lets me back into the same meeting room, she asks if I would like another coffee, so of course I say, 'Thank you, that would be nice!'

My coffee arrives before the General, but he then bustles in, saying 'I have set the cat amongst the pigeons, Mort, and we are meeting the Prime Minister at 4:30 p.m. That's the earliest they can squeeze us in.'

I shrug, as I'm not going anywhere, and ask, 'Who else will be there, General?'

He nods as if saying, 'fair point', and replies, 'I have suggested no other agency involvement as yet, so I would expect it will be the two of us, the PM, and his chief of staff Karen Jones.'

That's fine by me. Karen Jones is notorious for being a ball-breaker, so it'll be interesting to see for myself.

The General continues, 'No disrespect, Mort, but I would like you to stay here, so we can go over to Parliament House together. I have my staff preparing you a pass as we speak; they will come in shortly to get your signature and provide a high-level pass for you.'

I nod, thinking, *Wow, he is taking this seriously.*

He continues, 'They will also sort out some accommodation for you, as you will not be going home tonight.'

Again, I nod. I had hoped – expected – I wouldn't be.

He excuses himself, saying he must 'get back to it', so I make myself comfortable and pull out my laptop and use my phone to access the internet. There's a light knock on the door, and a middle-aged guy comes in with a bundle of papers needing to be signed; I look through them and see I'm being granted a temporary level two security pass. Not sure if level one is the top or the bottom!

I text Pig, telling him I will be meeting the PM at 4:30 p.m.

and am not allowed to leave the office in the meantime. I also text Suzie, saying all is going well so far and that I will not be home tonight. She replies with a smiley face (what did people do before these things?).

Just after 4:00 p.m., the General comes in carrying a pass on a lanyard, matching the one around his neck. He hands this to me and suggests I leave my laptop in the car to avoid security delays. An official car with a driver is waiting out the front when we exit, and clearly it's the General's usual service, as he says to the driver, 'Parliament House, Frank – to see the PM, so the side entrance.'

The driver smiles and nods and, after giving me the once over, gives me a nod also.

We're whisked through security upon arrival at Parliament House through an underground car park entrance and then up to the executive level, where we go through a second round of security; then, with the General leading the way, we head over to an impressive suite of offices. The gatekeeper (receptionist, no doubt, by her official title) is a frosty older lady, who wouldn't tolerate fools lightly by the look of her, and by the look of her two security off-siders you wouldn't come back twice if not invited. The General at least gets a quick smile, whilst I'm assessed very quickly while the General introduces me to her, and I nod. She simply gets back to her work – minion ignored.

We sit where told and wait patiently. Yes, I'm good at it.

A smartly dressed lady comes bustling out of the office, smiling, and saying, 'Hello, General, hadn't expected to see you today!' as they shake hands.

He then turns and says, 'Karen, Mort Ireland, former Group111 Sergeant.'

'Honour to meet you, Mort,' she says as we shake.

I smile and nod, thinking, *Well, that's a nice start.*

Karen leads the way into the inner sanctum, and there is our Prime Minister John Carson standing and coming around from behind his desk to greet us. He, of course, greets the General first and then comes over to me and introduces himself by saying, 'Mort, having read your file this afternoon, let me say, thank you for your service and outstanding efforts along the way. I am John Carson, and I am honoured to meet you.'

I am, of course, a little nonplussed by this greeting, not having expected anything like that – in fact, I had expected to be treated more as a nuisance, so good, it looks like I can start on the front foot.

I reply, 'Thank you, Sir, I appreciate your words.' And we all sit down at a small side meeting table. Karen has her phone out and I think, *Geez, that seems rude, playing with her phone whilst in a meeting with the PM.*

The PM starts off saying, 'Well, General, you were rather vague on the phone earlier, but if you say something is rather urgent, I tend to take notice. So, Mort, let us hear what this is all about.'

I take a deep breath – no one has offered coffee, so I have to go without – and head straight into a similar recital to what I had given the General earlier. A little way in and I realise Karen is, in fact, taking notes on her phone, not playing, as she asks a couple of pertinent questions.

Once again, I detail what we know. 'So, Sir, in summary, and this is detailed in the Executive Summary here'—I tap the folder—'we have this cadre of six Queensland Police officers, clearly corrupt and in fact running illegal businesses, and facilitating murder. What we can prove is:

1. Lancaster and Lowry are one and the same.
2. He paid US$300,000 for Carlos Santana to take down Bevan Hogan, the Brothers Mob bikie.
3. We have proof Santana was here in Australia at the time.

4. Lowry/Lancaster has recently paid Santana a further US$200,000 which we believe is a deposit for a hit on Noel Dyson in the next couple of weeks.
5. He runs eight businesses and is being paid "bookkeeping fees" by another eight, mainly nightclubs, bars and a massage parlour, which we suspect is protection money. He is also being paid $5,000 per month each by two heavyweight unions, so not sure what service he is providing them – no doubt warning for raids, or going slow on responding to complaints.
6. He was behind the recent attempt to discredit Noel Dyson, the state opposition leader.
7. He has proven contacts within the Department of the Premier and Cabinet of Queensland, who were fully involved in the recent attempt to discredit Noel Dyson.
8. He has proven connections at assistant commissioner level at both the Australian Federal Police and Victoria Police.
9. He is blackmailing the Queensland Police commissioner and has incriminating evidence against another Queensland Police assistant commissioner, so has effective free reign in what he does.
10. You must ask if he also has influence over someone within Border Force as Santana is on the INTERPOL watch list, so his photo coming in and out of the country should have raised a flag.
11. He may even have connections within the Department of Defence for we have him on tape saying when talking about me, 'Not even I can get access to his record, so we can't assume this is just an Army grunt.'

'That's why I tracked the General down, Sir.'

The PM is silent for some time as he takes this all in and then says, 'Mort, you have gathered all of this proof on your own, with no official assistance?' in a clearly questioning tone.

I reply, 'Yes, Sir, with the assistance of my long-term Army colleague, Pig.'

This gets a snort (get it?) from Karen, who says, 'I can't use that as a name in my minutes.'

I smile at her and say, 'Julien', and she nods thanks.

'To get back to your question, Prime Minister, yes, I am well trained in this field, as maybe the General has already attested, but I also use top-grade technology, likely better than any police service or agency here. I also don't follow the rules, making me more flexible than any official function; flying below the radar is the only way we would have uncovered this whole plot, as he appears to have so many contacts and trip wires set up, so he would have warning if anyone was sniffing around officially. He's a suspicious bastard,' I add.

Karen asks, 'How did all this fall into place? I understand how it started trying to dig into your wife's accident, but it seems such a complex web.'

I nod and say, 'Pure coincidence. I'm also working a commercial case – industrial espionage – and one of the investors was a Joe Lowry. He used the same email address I knew Lancaster used. Which, considering how sophisticated some of his dealings are, it is just plain dumb. But once we made that discovery – and this was only seven days ago – it has all unravelled for us.'

'Are you saying he put those two girls up to lie about a night with Dyson?'

'Yes, we have much of it on tape.'

The PM chips in, 'Dyson was lucky they picked the wrong date, wasn't he?'

I smile and say, 'No luck about it, Sir. We changed the date in their story.' This gets a look of shock from all three, as the General hadn't picked up on this part of the story.

'How?' comes from Karen.

'Well, we have this cadre under audio surveillance in their cars, and at their weekly catch up at the pub every Thursday, and one of them mentioned they had the draft on his laptop, so when we got a chance, we accessed his laptop and changed that date, after checking to see when he had been out of the country.'

'So, you hacked his laptop?' Again, from Karen.

'Well, that's not an expression we use; hacking implies the bad guys, whereas we are definitely the good guys,' I say, smiling at her. This gets a twitch of a smile from her.

The PM pipes up, saying, 'Noel said he got a message from someone telling him to check his passport; that was you?'

I nod, affirmative.

'So where are these girls now?' Karen asks.

'They're being taken care of; they're having a good time, but this week they're moving on with their lives and have moved interstate to start afresh.'

Karen seems to be very interested in the girls, which, I'm thinking, is side-tracking the purpose of the meeting, but I add, 'to Melbourne.'

She nods, flips over a card, and writes a name and phone no on it. She passes it to me and tells me, 'Get them to give Carol a call; she'll help them get sorted – and I don't mean back on the game.'

I nod and say, 'Thanks!'

'Who is paying you for all this time and cost then?' Karen asks.

'No one, it's all coming from my pocket.'

Karen and the PM share a glance, and he nods, so Karen continues, 'Send me a bill when it's finished, and I'll sort it.'

'Thank you,' I reply, looking at both of them. I'm truly impressed;

I hadn't expected that sort of help, although the costs are starting to mount up, so I'm not going to say no!

Silence falls as everyone digests the full facts of the situation, but I decide to make sure everyone understands the urgency by saying, 'Right now, we know Carlos Santana has been paid to do another hit. This payment was made ten days ago, and judging by the previous timeline, the hit should take place sometime in the next one to two weeks. We believe the target to be Noel Dyson.

'Santana is renown as an assassin, favouring long shots, like a sniper. As my record shows, I am a good sniper, and Pig and I'—I glance over at Karen, and she nods—'who was my spotter throughout my Army sniper career, have reviewed Dyson's known upcoming events, and he is planning public rallies on the steps of Brisbane City Hall in King George Square for the next four Saturday evenings. Any of these would be an ideal event for a sniper attack.

'We've even walked the street and the area checking for best likely points of attack. We've also accessed the street CCTV coverage, so we can keep an eye out for Santana, but in truth, we hope he has one of the bent coppers with him, as he has many different disguises.'

The PM turns to MGC and says, 'General, what are our options. considering we can't trust any of our police services, and can't send the army blundering in?'

The General nods in my direction and says, 'We couldn't do better than Mort and Pig; in the likely timeframe we don't have the operational skill sets available, we can certainly give them any support they will need, but to ensure the assassination fails and we are out to put a stop to this cadre once and for all, we are talking to our best option.'

All three turn and look at me, and I'm sitting there thinking, *Shit, me and my big mouth!*

I take the lead, saying, 'Well, if that's the case, we'll need to be appointed to some form of official capacity with full authority to act as required, including terminating anyone trying to destroy the fabric of our society as we know it – not as many of these bleeding hearts out there see it. Our identities would always have to remain confidential. We'll also need to be tooled up, and I can give MGC – sorry – the General, a list of armaments we would need, but we're talking hours, not days, to get this mobilised.'

Not only Karen has been taking notes this time, but the General as well, who then looks at the PM and says, 'Sir, I suggest we reinstate them both into the Army – they're both still reservists, after all – and then second them to your security division, as they have far more autonomous authority than the police or anyone else. We can then use Harris as the facilitator and liaison between us.'

The PM nods, as he thinks this through, then picks up the phone and says, 'Ann, can you have Major Harris join us please?' And he hangs up the phone.

A minute later there's a knock on the door, and Jerry Harris – sorry, Major Harris – strides in, sees me, and slides me a smile as he addresses the PM and General.

The PM leads by saying, 'Major, we have a critical crisis about to hit up in Brisbane that Mort here has just brought to our attention. We are reinstating him and "Pig" back into the army and then seconding them immediately to your command, with full authority and full force of the special powers your division has. You will act as liaison between them and the General, and provide every and all support and resources they require.'

Harris replies, 'Certainly, Sir. And the timing of this?'

'Effective immediately, Mort needs to be back in Brisbane tomorrow, so please ensure everything is in place before he goes.'

'Certainly, Sir, I don't see a problem.' Looking at me, he says,

'What sort of weaponry you looking for, Mort?'

I pull out a slip of paper from my satchel and pass it over; the General also learns over so he can read it with Major Harris, who whistles and says, 'Shit, Mort, you going back to war?'

'I hope not, but democracy is at stake,' is my reply.

The General asks, 'What about Dyson? Is he aware of any of this?'

'No, Sir,' I reply, 'right now, we can only tell him a theory, and frankly, I don't want to make him aware too early as he is likely to react and possibly scare them off, or more critically, make them change tactics, which we won't be able to cover. I have his phone number and will not put him at risk, but it's likely to be a last-minute call.'

The PM then suggests the three of us reconvene to work the logistics and support structure; standing up, he reaches out his hand to shake, saying, 'Mort, I am sorry to put all this on you and your colleague'—clearly not comfortable calling someone Pig—'but it looks like you are our best chance to break this up and bring about a speedy and hopefully safe conclusion.'

I stand up also and say, 'Thank you, Sir, I appreciate your support and confidence.'

As the meeting breaks up, Karen asks me quietly, 'Why did you call General Rutherford "MGC"?'

'Major General Charlie,' I reply. 'Besides, he's mad keen on his cricket, so it sort of has a double meaning.'

Major Harris is also waiting and now reaches out to shake hands, saying, 'Geez, Mort, it's been a while. I thought that looked like you coming in with the General, and here you go into another battle.'

'Yes, and I thought I'd put this all behind me.'

The General, who was watching us, says, 'So you two know each other?'

'Yes,' I reply, 'besides him captaining the NSW Cockroaches in our footy games, he was my CO in Group111 when I first went over. Ask him how many games he won,' I add with a smile.

Harris quickly comes back, 'Yeah, well, we should have won that last one; you didn't score that try.'

Of course I'm smiling when I clap him on the shoulder and say, 'What's the scoreboard say, Jerry?'

They all laugh, knowing the intense rivalry there is between NSW and Queensland – and not only on the football field!

As we're about to leave his office, the PM asks quietly, 'Mort, what did you find about your wife's accident?'

I think, *how thoughtful*, and I say, 'Sir, nothing conclusive, but every Thursday evening, this group meet for a few drinks – normally four or five schooners. Then they drive home. And yes, Liz was killed on a Thursday, and no blood or alcohol tests were done.' I'm met with a sombre silence, so I nod and head out of the PM's office; Jerry takes the lead, and the General and I follow him to his office.

Jerry sits down at his desk, saying, 'Okay, armaments you have covered; communication?'

I tell him Pig and I usually use our phones which are encrypted, so we can add him to our team so he can hear and be heard, but questioned whether reception down here in Canberra would still be okay.

Jerry comes back, saying, 'All of Canberra is covered by 5G, unlike you blokes out in the sticks, so reception should be fine.'

I respond, 'You're just wanting to make sure you can stay in your warm and comfy office, and not have to come out to the sticks!' said with a smile, of course, and even the General smiles slightly.

The General comments, 'It's hard to come to grips with the fact that corruption is so rampant up there in Queensland.'

I reply, 'The combination of a weak premier with loyalties divided between her union masters and the voters, and a ruthless upper-level policeman – it's history repeating its self, except this time, it's the Labour mob who vowed to always ensure open and transparent government and then more and more govern almost by deceit. Tony Fitzgerald will be turning in his grave.'

The General and Jerry nod, and our discussion moves back to logistics and support.

Then, I point out, 'When we bring this to a head, we need to arrest the Premier, and likely some of her cabinet, as she is not a decision-maker, thus, it's highly likely other senior politicians are involved. We know her Chief of Staff and his assistant are in deep, and not only the cadre of police, but also the police commissioner, and at least one assistant commissioner. So, with this huge layer of top leadership removed, who will run the state until elections can be held? Further, ideally, the arrests need to be made if not simultaneously, at least fairly quickly after each other.'

This has the General grimly taking notes and commenting, 'Mort, I will need to take all this up with the PM; you are not to worry about the aftermath, but to focus on a clean outcome.'

'That's fine, General, but you'—I indicate them both—'will need to ensure there is support – Army or whoever – when this goes down. If I take down a serving police officer I'll have the whole Queensland Police Service on my tail, and I certainly don't intend to take them all on, only the dirty ones.'

The General looks even glummer as the full ramifications of this pending action grow. It turns into a late night by the time we've made some sensible plans, and the General drops me back at the War Museum to pick up my rental before I head to a local Best Western Motel for the night.

Once checked in, and with room service ordered, I dial Pig, knowing that he won't pick up if George is home, but he does and

I'm a little surprised. He tells me he's taken over my spare bedroom, that he and George need a little space right now. Of course, he knows he is always welcome, so no issue, but I am concerned for him, nonetheless. I bring him up to speed and tell him I'm booked on the first flight back tomorrow, and he says that all is cool, and nothing has changed whilst I've been away.

I text Suzie to say all is sorted and that I'll be home tomorrow, but no, I'm not getting away with a text, and even though it's a little late, my phone rings immediately, and she's asking for the full story. No way am I giving her the full rundown over the phone, so I give her the basics; then room service is knocking on my door with my steak, so it's time to say nighty night.

49

It's now Thursday morning. I flew back into Brisbane, and on the spur of the moment decided to call in and take Suzie for a quick early lunch before heading back to the office. I enter their offices and the young receptionists asks me if she can help.

I say, 'I am here to see Suzie.'

'And can I tell who is calling?'

'Mort.'

Immediately, I can sense others in the open plan office stopping to look at me, as did the receptionist, before recovering and picking up the phone and whispering into it. I look around the office, causing a couple of the ladies to duck their heads down; then I hear a door open and a smartly dressed middle aged lady comes striding over towards me.

'Mort?' she asks.

I nod.

'I am Jenny, Suzie's paralegal.'

We shake hands, and I smile and nod.

She goes on, 'Suzie is on the phone with a client, but I'm sure she will be out as soon as she's finished. I left a note on her desk, but just wanted to come and check you out myself, see if what she has said was true.'

I smile and ask, 'So is it?'

Before she can answer, Suzie is heading our way, already with her handbag, and seemingly in a hurry, so I say goodbye to Jenny, and smile.

Suzie says, 'Hi,' grabs my hand and we head outside.

'So, what's the rush?' I ask once we are safely outside.

She smiles and says, 'I don't want them filling your head with things about me.'

Hmm, I think, *not a truthful answer* (if you know what I mean!), but I let it go as she leads me into a little café where we order a couple of wraps and coffee to go as she says there's a lovely little park around the corner where we can eat. Sure enough, there is, and we're lucky enough to get an empty table.

Once seated, she leans over and gives me a kiss and says, 'Hi' again with a smile.

I reply, 'That's better. So why no kiss in the office?'

She blushes a little and says, 'They tease me enough, so I don't need to add to it! And by the way, Jenny just texted me to say you're more hunk than I had told her!'

'You tell Jenny I like her already,' I reply, which she does, her fingers flying over the keys.

'So how did you go in Canberra?' she asks around a mouthful of wrap.

'Pretty good. Had a meeting with the PM—'

Her mouth falls open at this statement, making me laugh.

I nod and say, 'Yes, the General has some semi-official role reporting direct for the PM, so it was very lucky I reached out to him. Pig and I are back on the books and have been seconded to the PM's personal security division, which apparently has wide-ranging authority and powers, so I'm fully protected should anything go down. But we're on our own – they decided they had no better resources than us to handle the situation.'

Whilst I'm talking, my phone rings, and when I answer, Pig says, 'He's here. Santana arrived early Tuesday morning. Midge apologises, but he's using another identity and he slipped through the first pass. He's using the name Eddie Wallace – that's why we hadn't noticed the flight booking if it was made by Lancaster's travel agency.'

'Okay,' I reply, 'we'll put a call into Jerry when I get to the office, as we have to expect it's going down on Saturday, weather permitting. I'm just having a quick lunch with Suzie, so should be there in half an hour or so.'

'Say hi to Suzie for me; see you then,' and he hangs up.

Shit.

Suzie, of course, is now looking at me, clearly concerned, so I reach over and put my hand on hers, saying, 'As you have guessed, Santana arrived on Tuesday, so it looks like it's going to be a pretty explosive weekend.' I squeeze her hand gently. 'Suzie, I really need you to go home Friday night and not leave your apartment until things settle down, likely Sunday or Monday – if anything happens at all. Don't open the door to anyone unless it's Pig or me. Text me if you want to talk, as I am likely going to be very busy and preoccupied.'

'You're scaring me, Mort,' she says.

I nod. 'I don't mean to, but then maybe I do if you stay home, you'll be in the safest place. Then, when it's all over, I will come and get you.'

'I am not worried about me, you goose; I am worried about you getting injured, or worse.'

Gee, I think, *that's nice – someone caring about me – I like it!* 'I'll be fine; they're sending up all the armoury we asked for, and we have full bulletproof suits, and I have done this for a living for the last fifteen years, so we do know what we're doing. Also, Pig has taken over my spare bedroom; he says he and George need some space.'

Her concern shows on her face; then she pulls a face and says, 'Poor Julien, I will give him a call tonight.'

'Yeah, I've been a little worried about him for a couple of weeks; doesn't seem to be himself, so I'm not sure what is going on.'

I've finished my wrap, but Suzie seems to have lost her appetite, so I finish hers as well and lean over the table and give her a kiss, which lingers. When it breaks off, she says to me in a tight voice, 'I don't want that to be our last kiss, Ireland; I have plans for you, so don't you forget it!'

I throw her a mock salute and we get up; she heads back to the office and the myriad of questions from her work colleagues, and I head back to the car park and back to the office.

50

I get back to the office after my quick lunch, and Pig and I sit to discuss the arrival of Santana in the guise of Eddie Wallace. We agree this elevates the likelihood that the hit is planned for Saturday night, Dyson's first planned public rally on the steps of Brisbane Town Hall in King George Square. We put in a call to Jerry Harris, former Major of Group111 and now head of the Prime Minister's security division. A good man to have in our corner. We brief Jerry, and he agrees this increases the probability of Saturday night being D-Day. He confirms our armaments have shipped overnight, so these should turn up this afternoon, and Pig pipes up saying they arrived about an hour ago; they're all locked up safe and sound. We discuss with Jerry our plans for the next twenty-four to forty-eight hours, needing to try and identify where Santana is staying, but what happens if like last time, there is no trace.

After hanging up, I tell Pig I need to zero in Betsy, the long gun I used as a sniper. I had requested the same gun, and Jerry had mentioned it had been retired after I finished with it. It should be in the garage with the other armaments. Of course, to fire a long gun with a range of anywhere between 400 and 1,000 metres, you need a bit of room, and I tell Pig I had a family friend with a few hundred acres in Numinbah Valley, so I was going to give her a call.

She knows I had been in the military for a few years, so hopefully she'll buy my excuse of 'just wanting to keep my eye in'. He agrees he doesn't have a better idea, so I give Diane a call and after a chat (there is no quick chat with Diane!), she's happy for me to pop down. I set it for 9:00 a.m. the next morning, just to make sure the kids are all at school, as Betsy is not a quiet girl – she makes quite a BANG when she fires.

I decide to go and get Betsy out of her case and check her condition. She has clearly been well looked after by the armaments crew, well-oiled and with a protective coating of oil, which I start wiping off. Of course, out of habit, I disassemble her and give her a thorough clean, and then re-assemble her again, so I know everything is fitted correctly. I dig out a dozen .308 Winchester bullets, not that I expect to need that many unless someone fiddled with her settings, which is highly unlikely.

Pig and I then sit down, and he says, 'Shit we have forty-eight hours till this goes down!'

I nod, then get up to get coffees. As I make these, I say to Pig, 'So, what's with you and George?'

He pulls a face and says, 'It's been a little tense the last few weeks, to the extent that I'm wondering if there is someone else; you know, I go home for the weekend and then he *has* to go into the office on Sunday. So over the weekend, and on impulse really, I hid a transmitter app on his phone, partly as it might help us with this, and also partly to see if there is someone else. I feel bloody guilty about doing it because I feel I've broken a line of trust by installing it, but nevertheless, it's on there, and is working well. He does seem to be very friendly with that dick Jack Herbert – you know, the one that attended the press conference and is clearly in the thick of this thing. It looks like George leaves his phone on his desk at work, as the clarity of the audio is very good. Not surprising really, as that's what he does at home too.

'So, as I said, I was feeling pretty guilty about doing that and then, on Monday night, he had let's say a personal – make that, VERY personal – chat with Jack, so I thought, stuff it, I need some fresh air, so I left him a note and packed my duffel and here I am.

'He's tried to call me a couple of times, leaving messages, asking for me to call him, but I'm going to get this shit behind us before facing him again.'

I get up and go over to him and give him a hug and a tight squeeze, letting him know I am here for him and he's welcome upstairs as long as he needs it. I tell him Suzie knows and is likely to give him a call tonight.

Pig adds, 'If he's tied up in any of this, even if only on the periphery, he might be heading to the big house for a few years anyway!'

I nod and say, 'Well, house and board come with obligations, you know; we take turns cooking and cleaning, so you're up for dinner tonight and I'll have kitchen duties.'

I then recount how I missed a call yesterday afternoon from Marg at Paramount and had rung her back this morning whilst waiting for my flight in Canberra. She was a little excited, almost breathless, and I must say eager to tell me how their visit to Futurcomm had gone, explaining:

'Sir Anthony and I arrived a little after lunch on Tuesday, prepared with a formal lawyer's letter of demand for the $1.25 million loan plus interest. When we presented this to Matt, he got really shitty and pissed off, but Sir Anthony played it straight down the line, telling him he has fourteen days to settle the loan in full. Of course, we knew they didn't have the resources, so that's when Sir Anthony changed tack and offered to buy his personal shares – at a discount of course!

'Their shares are trading around $0.65 against an issue price of $1.00 each, so Sir Anthony offered to buy sufficient of his shares at $0.50 to settle the loan. Matt just got shittier, started getting loud and abusive; it wasn't until Sir Anthony asked if we needed to call security, that he settled down a bit. They haggled a little, but Sir Anthony wouldn't budge from $0.55 each, so he'll have to sell us over two million of his shares. Of course, we knew that meant he would then drop below fifty per cent ownership and effective control. Which I'm sure was a big part of why he was so pissed off. What he didn't know was we had already purchased a further two million shares on market, have been accumulating these since we agreed on this course of action, in fact,' she adds, and I could sense the smile in her voice, thinking they had put one over me.

'That meant we had control of just under twenty per cent of the shares. Once he had agreed to sell his shares, we tabled a further letter advising him we had 19.8 per cent of his shares and were seeking a data room to proceed with due diligence.

'In a fit of rage, Matt offered the rest of his shares, so Sir Anthony offered him $0.50 for these, and wouldn't budge! He finally accepted this, so we walked out owning over sixty per cent of Futurcomm!

'We then went directly over to Mypone and introduced ourselves to Jess, their CEO, and let her know that Futurcomm was now owned by Paramount, and she was to deal with me from here on. Jess seemed pleased about this and couldn't have been more helpful. We let her know that we were still intending to complete the due diligence and intended to continue with the acquisition if it made sense, although we were clear the price would be somewhat lower than Matt had offered. Jess seemed to know he had grossly overvalued her business and seemed keen to work with us.

'So, wow, it's been an exciting few days,' she finishes, 'and I just have time to congratulate them on making a big positive out of what could have been a significant problem and say goodbye as my flight is boarding.'

*

A little later in the evening over dinner, to which Suzie seemed to invite herself after chatting with Pig earlier, we talk about how best to inspect around the City Hall, and Suzie remembers she had been up to a meeting on the twenty-fifth floor of an office building in George Street, which has an awesome view over the top of the City Hall. Pig and I agree we will go and have a look tomorrow as well as walk around the area, trying to get a feel for a good sniper's nest.

Friday morning, up and off for a run, Pig coming with me as he hasn't sorted his own route out yet, but we run easily both with our own thoughts of the next twenty-four to forty-eight hours. Quick breakfast – yes, still those Weet-Bix! – and we hit the road in the Prado, heading down to Numinbah Valley in the Gold Coast hinterland. Fortunately, we're heading against the worst of the traffic that's heading into Brisbane for work. We stop at the little café in the valley to restore our caffeine levels, and then I give Diane a call as agreed. She tells me she has been called away but has left the gate unlocked, so head right on in.

I had chosen the Prado with good reason as we are now on a farm, so there are only farm tracks, and I head up the western side of the valley, getting my bearings as it has been a good number of years since I was here, but my memory is pretty good and the little clump of trees I had thought of as a good shooting position was exactly where I remembered. We get out and checking out the side of the hill, looking for at least 600 to 800 metres of clear sight, and with some form of hill or embankment behind for the bullets to bury into. Yes, to the right we have clear sight of 842 metres according to our range finder, so Pig heads off with six coke cans, and I give him a yell at 400, 600 and last two at 800 metres; then he comes back. Meanwhile, I have assumed the position, flat on the ground, making myself comfortable after digging a little hollow for my hip, and start sighting in on the first can. Pig arrives back donning his earphones and head piece so we can talk without yelling. He sits behind and to my left with the range finder so he can see the target. I let him know I'm ready and then focus on slowing my breathing down, which is as essential as getting a good read on the wind direction and strength, as over these distances, every little thing matters.

BOOM—

Round one is gone, and I see the first can at 400 metres spin sideways. Pig tells me I only clipped it, thus a slight change to the sights, and I refocus on the second can.

BOOM—

This time, the can disintegrates and pig confirms in my ear, so I move up to the first 600-metre can, refocus, and—

BOOM—

It too disappears in a puff. So, I disregard the second can at 600, readjust the sights for 800, and focus on the can on the right this time. Refocus, control breathing—

BOOM—

Yep, that one is turned to dust as well, so I'm happy with that as a sighting session. Pig comes over and we fist bump.

He says, 'Good shooting.'

'Yeah,' I agree, 'not bad after nearly two years since I last fired the old girl!'

We head back to the office to put Betsy back in the gun safe, which is a little overloaded with all the firepower delivered yesterday. But still locked tight, so safe. Our bulletproof suits and clothing sets are hanging up beside the gun safe, like old times.

We head off into the city to scout the area around City Hall, making 275 George Street our first stop so we can get a good overview at least. But first, coffee!

As Suzie had told us, this office tower gave commanding views of the city, and directly overlooked City Hall. Whilst standing in a lawyer's lobby, we just admire the view.

When approached by the receptionist, Pig just smiles and says, 'No, we don't have an appointment; we're just admiring the view!' and she leaves us alone.

With a good idea of the lay of the land, we now walked down Ann Street towards City Hall, walking straight past King George Square which faces City Hall, and where the crowd will be both sitting and standing for Dyson's address tomorrow. We head on down, looking at the various office towers, tagging those we think would be ideal, but it's going to be like a needle in a haystack, as all of these office towers overlook City Hall, and so could be used as a sniper nest. Not going to be easy.

Now we head back down Ann Street looking for a spot where we can set up, hoping to spot the sniper and eliminate him before he gets his shot away. This at least is a little easier, as we both agree the Sarina Russo building is the best from our perspective. Being slightly past City Hall with good clear vision back along Ann Street at all the tower blocks we have tagged. We walk into the lobby to see what sort of security is visible. It's an international language school, with many people coming and going. We expect accessing it discreetly tomorrow afternoon, Saturday, shouldn't be a problem. Pig notes a CCTV camera on the outside, so we'll access that, which will give us a better idea of how many people are around at five tonight. There is also an underground car park and we agree this would be by far our best access point, as we can get the van in, unload Betsy and our other weaponry, not having to carry it in in broad daylight. Of course, they are all stored in cases, so not like we are walking around openly with our submachine guns!

We go over to the other side of City Hall to Adelaide Street, and quickly decide it's a no-go. No clear line of sight to the stage already set up on City Hall steps, so if Santana is as good as Midge reckons, he'll not be over this side. This is a huge relief, because there is still only two of us, so I'm not sure how we could have covered two streets.

By now it's mid-afternoon, and as we head back to the office I call Jerry to bring him up to date, saying we have identified the best sniper points, and where we will set up as a counter surveillance point. Jerry goes on to tell us he has moved up to Brisbane and is setting up a control point in a room at the Sofitel Hotel, just along from City Hall. He adds he has reached out to a long-term friend from university, current Queensland Assistant Commissioner Melinda Black, and she is now in isolation with him at the hotel. He told her to pack a bag for the weekend and tell her husband, kids and staff she was heading away for a weekend retreat.

'I have her phone, and all phones in the hotel suite are disconnected, to ensure you are not put at risk, but let me tell you, Mel – who is sitting next to me listening – is ropable about being treated like a suspect.'

I reply, 'Well, Mel, whilst I can sympathise, it's not your body on the line.'

We turn around and go meet them both at the Sofitel, as it's easier to run through plans face-to-face, particularly with someone you don't know. We park in the Sofitel valet and hand over the keys, telling them we'll only be an hour or two, and head inside and up to room 665 – via the café for four long blacks and muffins – and knock on the door. Jerry opens it, and we see a smartly dressed woman, early fifties at a guess (easy to guess when you know Jerry is early fifties) along with a couple of others bent over their laptops.

Melinda comes forward, introducing herself before Jerry has a chance, saying, 'Nice to meet you both, but I would prefer it be on a more pleasant occasion. So, you two have brought bloody Lancaster down, finally, have you?'

'No, we have the evidence, but he's still out there, no doubt orchestrating tomorrow's main event,' I reply.

'So why not bring him in? That should shut down the whole operation,' she continues.

I glance at Jerry, who gives me a quick nod, I respond, 'This goes way higher than Lancaster. Sure, he's the one who has put this together, but it's the political connection that needs to be wiped out, and that decision has been taken way above your paygrade as well as mine.'

I add just to be clear that I'm not going to be going back over the whys and wherefores. She seems to sense this and desists.

We then talk through how to handle the aftermath, and when we start talking about having to arrest the Premier, her deputy, the attorney general and numerous senior bureaucrats, as well as the police commissioner, she clearly hadn't been briefed to that level yet and so suddenly understood the enormity of why she had been brought in, and why she couldn't speak to anyone.

'Holy shit' she responds as she seeks somewhere to sit down.

After a few moments to gather her thoughts, we then ask her to prepare a list of police she knew she could depend on to keep their mouths shut and get the job done as we needed these teams in place for tomorrow night in case the hit goes down. And if I'm successful in eliminating the risk, then they will need to quickly deploy these trusted police to arrest Lancaster and his crew. She would need a second group led by trusted senior police to manage the arrests of the known politicians and bureaucrats. It had been decided that some army squads were also being secretly deployed to Brisbane, and it was expected some of these squads would assist with the senior arrests and also to secure Parliament House, City Hall and other significant properties as a show of force.

By this time, it is dinner time and as they had ordered pizzas and burgers from room service, Pig and I decide to stay and enjoy this, saving the need to cook (or order in) when we get home. A little later, on the way home, I ask Pig how he's feeling with the collapse, at least temporarily, of his relationship with George – they had been together a long time, after all.

He replies, 'Well, I still feel guilty about putting that app on his phone, but if what he was saying to that arsehole Jack the other night is true, then we are done and dusted anyway. I'm not going to tell you what he said, but it was very hurtful and shows he or they seem to think they are some elite group born to rule us mere mortals.'

I reach out and put my hand on his arm, and say, 'Mate, I'm here whenever you need me – understand?'

'Yes, Mort, I do. Thank you. Suzie has been really good too; it's good having a female to talk to – they are so much more empathic and understanding.'

I nod. Suzie and Pig had had quite a chat last night before and after tea. In fact, I hardly spent any time with her. Not that I'm the jealous type! 'You're okay and able to focus over the next few days?' a question I didn't need to ask, but equally, it had to be asked.

The response is a twisted smile as he turns to me, knowing instinctively I had to ask the question, but that I knew the answer anyway. I get a nod and, 'Too right, we've got this.'

When we get back to the office, we check the audio from all the cadres' cars, but again, no mention of coming events, which is concerning as Thursday night's drinks didn't tell us much, although Lancaster didn't appear, and the only comment of note was Fleming saying, 'Okay, you all know your roles for Saturday?' nods all round, so Fleming adds, 'Okay, just don't fuck this up, or all our heads will be on the block.'

51

Saturday dawns clear and mild, another day in 'Queensland, beautiful one day, perfect the next.' *Yeah, but maybe not perfect today*, I think. I've allowed myself to sleep in, not bothering with a run either, when I rise I note Pig hasn't risen either, so he is of like mind. The public rally is not scheduled to start until 7:00 p.m., with Dyson due to appear for his speech around 7:30 p.m., so we have a few hours.

After turning the coffee machine on and sorting my breakfast, adding bananas to my usual Weet-Bix, I log in to check the audio from overnight. Surprisingly, there's a call from Lancaster, clearly sitting in his car and talking to an unknown person, but an American, so I am guessing Santana, running through a few details, but nothing helpful to us except that they were collecting him at 5:00 p.m. to install him by 6:15 p.m., so a full hour prior to the likely hit time.

Well, that takes the uncertainty out of the day. We now know it's a definite goer. I flick the audio to Jerry for his review, suggesting that Melinda could put someone undercover along Ann Street, near the buildings we tagged, and we might get lucky and spot them going in, as one of the coppers is likely to be with him. I send the audio to Midge asking for confirmation of the voice as Santana.

Pig wanders in around then, so we chat as he helps himself to breakfast as my phone rings and I see its Suzie, so I wander out of the kitchen to have a little privacy. She's ringing to say hi basically and to see how I slept, all alone on a Friday night!

'Like a lamb,' I tell her, which was not quite the truth; there is a bit on my mind at the moment.

She responds, 'Not the right answer, Ireland!' and I can hear the smile behind her words.

'What about you then?'

'Oh, like a lamb,' she responds, and we both laugh.

She asks what's the plan and, without wanting to be paranoid – I do know how many conversations are recorded – I don't say too much other than it seems to be today and we will likely head out around 3:00 p.m. to get ourselves set up, and have to check our gear shortly, make sure we don't overlook anything, all vague enough to mean nothing to anyone eavesdropping, but also clear enough for Suzie.

I finish the call by saying, *'Do not leave home.* Clear?'

'Yes, Master,' is the response, so I say, 'Now that's the right answer, Dunn!' and she blows me a raspberry as we both hang up laughing.

I head back to the kitchen to grab another coffee, and off down the stairs we go to the office to start checking and packing our equipment.

We have both kept our full Kevlar bulletproof suits. These were given to us by the Americans previously and are full-body suits, covering full torso, arms, legs, have neck guards, and come also with bullet proof helmets and face visors – far superior to those offered to us in Canberra. We know these work, having worn them in firefights previously. Whilst you know when you take a hit, it is only a bump that will come out as a bruise later – far better than the alternative!

We have them stored in standard suit bags, so they don't look out of place being carried around.

I open the gun safe, and firstly I take out Betsy, put the case on the table, and pull her out. Pig comes over and has another look – the three of us have spent many hours together in some pretty isolated and desolate places and had a few hairy moments after all.

Pig comments, 'Any more notches?'

'No,' I reply, 'still only my fourteen; the armament sergeant told me it was being retired when I handed it in, most new blokes no doubt preferring the newer Blaser model over the older SR98 like Betsy.'

Even though I cleaned her after the sighting in, with so much riding on the shot this afternoon, I disassemble her again, giving her a thorough cleaning before putting her back together again, adding a full box of ammo to the case as well.

Pig and I have agreed we'll also take our favoured EF88 assault rifle capable of both automatic fire and single shot, along with our personal H and K USP handguns. These were our service pistols, and we bought them like most army types when we retired. We'll be 'loaded for bear' as the words go in the old favourite song 'Convoy'.

Pig's phone starts up; this time its AC/DC belting out 'Black Ice' as a ring tone, and we smile and shake our heads almost in unison, and when Pig answers, Midge says, 'Thought I should give you some home grown music this time, boys!'

'Spot on, Midge,' is Pig's reply.

'Yes, that's Santana you have on that tape, and that's Lancaster/Lowry he's talking to, is it not?' he checks.

'Yep,' Pig replies.

Midge continues, 'So you guys have got some action today, then?'

'Yes, we think we know the who and where, but need to find him before he fires a shot, and of course, we can't involve the police at any level, so it's not going to be easy,' Pig replies.

'Well, boys, I'll monitor what I can, but best of luck and make sure you let me know the outcome.'

'Certainly will, but likely to be all over the news, win or lose,' Pig finishes.

Midge responds, 'I hear you. Good luck, boys,' and he's gone.

Having the armaments sorted, we move onto our clothing, which is a bit of a challenge as we can't wear our old camo suits for obvious reasons with their handy pockets for bits of everything. Pig has found some overalls that have enough pockets for ammo, smoke bombs, etc., and will fit over our Kevlar suits comfortably. We also kept our day packs and these have first aid, water, snacks, a couple of stun grenades and other knickknacks. Pig bought the snacks, so I know these will be better than typical army rations – in fact, I sampled one whilst packing and had to compliment him on his selection. Pig packs a drone into the van as well, as he'll be monitoring the roof tops of all adjacent buildings. By now, we're both getting keyed up, ready for action, but it's still a little early to head into town.

Then MGC calls, just touching base to see if there are any changes, and whilst I'm sure he's in constant contact with Jerry who is his designated liaison, he obviously wants to understand how we are feeling. I assure him we're good and on schedule. He mentions he and the PM will be on live feed for the duration.

Pig and I decide to wander down the road to our favourite café for a late lunch. BLT and coffee for me, whilst Pig goes for a burger with the works.

It's 3:30 p.m.: time to make tracks.

52

We're in the city and can see what looks like a pretty reasonable crowd building for the rally later this afternoon; we crawl down Ann Street through the traffic, then access the underground carpark of the Sarina Russo building, having no problems using our special key card. We find a park and reverse the van in, ready for a quick exit if required. We rang the security number earlier and as there was no answer; we're reasonably confident the building will be empty, and that's the way we find it.

Taking the lift to the sixth floor, we walk towards the Ann Street side of the building, checking a few offices as we go, to ensure we get the best view back down the street. We get to the corner office and like in most buildings the corner office is a larger one – someone relatively senior, we assume. We check the view and discuss before deciding we will go up to the seventh floor to see if this gives us a better line of sight. We prefer to be looking down on our target rather than up. We agree this is the better option, so I start unpacking Betsy while Pig moves furniture out of the way to give me direct access to the window at the best angle. Mind you, we still don't know where our target is going to be.

The windows are pretty grubby, so we don't get a good clear view, but that's okay for now, as I plan on cutting the pane out when the time comes anyway.

Once we have the furniture out of the way, Pig grabs his drone and heads up to the roof to launch it and start his aerial patrol. We're mic'd up, with Jerry in the loop as well. Jerry confirms they have four plain patrol cars with four armed police in each positioned around a perimeter of King George Square, with a plan to shut down all escape routes once 'it' happens. Clearly, this won't be enough if they run off on foot, but better than letting them get suspicious by too heavy a presence.

Whilst sitting there patiently (it's a virtue, remember!), Pig comes over the mic, saying, 'Shit, listen to this.'

I hear Lancaster's voice saying, 'Yeah, I know you have told me he has cleared it, but I want to hear him say it.'

Then muted swearing and then another voice I suspect is Jack saying, 'Sir, Joe Lancaster wants a word,' followed by, 'What? What does he want with me? You handle it.'

'He wants you to give him the go ahead personally,' Jack answers.

There is more muffled talking before the Premier's voice can be heard, 'Hello, Joe?'

'Yes,' he replies.

'We're all ready to strike, but I need you to give me the final go ahead and confirm you will honour your side of the deal afterwards.'

'Jack has already conveyed my instruction,' Premier Aldred responds.

'I need to hear it from you,' Lancaster growls, now showing signs of irritation.

'Very well,' he says. 'Queensland needs me. Proceed,' and hangs up.

'Shit,' says Pig, 'he just signed his own prison sentence.'

'He certainly did,' I reply. 'Make sure Jerry has it as well.'

'Will do. Out,' Pig responds.

As 6:30pm comes around, I get up and cut the whole windowpane out, cutting right up against the edge, so it won't look suspicious to anyone checking the buildings out. There are no blinds or curtains in the office, so they can't give me away by fluttering in the light breeze. Using suction cups to hold it, I place the pane flat on the floor in the opposite corner of the office. I resettle down using both my range finder and view finder on the scope to sweep all the likely buildings looking for any sign of movement. Pig has another rangefinder up on the roof which he is using, as it's good to have two different angles.

Come seven o'clock, and we still haven't seen any sign of movement or activity, and I can tell from the mic others are getting anxious. I mute out the outside world, switching to another channel so it's only Pig and me. They can hear us, but we can't hear them.

The rally has started below us, we can hear the MC warming the crowd up, then a local band take the stage for a couple of lively tunes, the crowd singing along with them, plenty of blue ribbons and banners fluttering in the wind. We're used to blocking out distractions, although a loud band is not one we have experienced previously.

'Got him,' I say. '145 Ann Street, fifth floor, far right corner. I don't have clear vision, only part of his lower body and legs; he's quite a way back from the window. I can also see the legs of someone else standing further back. Not a clear shot at present.'

Shit.

We're lucky: Santana had only cut the bottom half of the windowpane out, and this anomaly is what drew my attention to them.

Pig comes back, 'Confirmed.'

I tell Pig to send the text to Dyson, 'DO NOT GO OUT', from the prepaid phone that I told him about his passports, so I'm banking on him recognising the number. But no, I suddenly hear the announcer saying, 'And here is who you are waiting for, Noel Dyson!'

The crowd burst into applause, and chant 'Dyson, Dyson, Dyson', whilst I focus solely on my target. I see him start to move, to reposition for a clearer shot, thinking, *Keep moving, buddy, a bit more,* as I adjust my aim slightly to account for his new position.

My target, Santana, has now settled into his firing position; I can sense he is close to pulling the trigger—

BOOM—

Betsy lets off her usual loud bang and I see my target take the bullet, left shoulder where I aimed. Not wanting to kill the bloke, I quickly work the bolt, chambering a new round, and see someone learn over him to check on him.

Left kneecap, I think.

BOOM—Betsy does her thing again and I see this bloke collapse as well.

I report, 'Two down, no others visible, one shoulder shot, the other kneecapped.' I always did think the IRA knew what they were doing, kneecapping traitors, marked for life.

The noise of the shots has not gone unnoticed and there is pandemonium with the crowd screaming, all trying to go in different directions at once to get away from the sound of gun fire. This is Brisbane, after all; this is unheard of.

Pig tells me he's on his way down, so I quickly dismantle Betsy and replace her in her case. I pick up the two shells but don't bother repositioning the furniture. After all, with the window removed, it is obvious what went on here. Jerry updates us, telling us that he has dispatched both police and paramedics to 145 Ann Street, and told all police to come out into the open and identify Lancaster and his crew.

Pig and I meet up as arranged back at the van; we fist bump, jump in the van and exit onto Ann Street, heading out of the CBD across the river to await the next steps.

We're both back on the live channel and I get a message from

MGC to switch to channel 27, so we do, and the General comes on saying, 'Well done, boys, hopefully a clean shoot.'

I reply, 'It was, Sir. It won't be fatal as long as the paramedics do their job, but he won't be shooting anyone for a long time, if at all.'

He adds, 'The PM is listening and wants a word.'

Pig and I look at each other, eyebrows raised; we then hear the Prime Minister's distinct voice come on.

He says, 'Mort and Julien, thank you for bringing this to a happy conclusion; well done.'

'Thank you, Sir,' I reply, 'but it's not over yet; we need to capture Lancaster and his crew and of course arrest all who knew and planned this.'

We say our goodbyes and Pig and I head over to South Brisbane to a little café along Stanley Street, not far from the Mater Hospital. We had agreed with Jerry yesterday we would stay clear of the CBD and be ready for quick action once the location of any of the police cadre became clear.

We had used this café before, run by a Jordanian couple, easy parking out the back, good food and, of course, good coffee. We take a booth at the back with a nod to Yazeed the owner to give us privacy, and we settle down to watch and listen as events unfold. You might think I would have a reaction to having just shot a fellow human, but as always, my targets are bad people, intent on doing bad things, so I have no qualms about it. I'm comfortable, as is Pig, as we have discussed how we feel a few times now in the aftermath of shootings and action.

We tune into the channel and listen to Jerry and Mel (mainly Mel now running the police action around King George Square), and she has put out an APB on Lancaster and his crew – setting a few police tongues wagging, no doubt. They've all gone off air, but Pig is monitoring all their cars, hoping to catch anything. But silence.

53

I'm talking to Jerry by phone nearly an hour later as they get the situation under control around the square, when Pig grabs my shoulder and says in an agitated tone – very unlike Pig – 'Listen to this.'

I put Jerry on hold and wake my laptop up; Pig reaches across and deftly brings up what he wants me to listen too whilst I slip my headphones on and I hear Lancaster saying, 'Josh, what was the name of that lawyer you tried to chat up? I just saw that big Army bloke, you know, the man whose wife Benson hit, leaving a building in a van straight after the shooting.'

Armitage answers, 'Ah, Suzie something,' he pauses, obviously trying to remember, then continues, 'Suzie Dunn.'

Lancaster continues, 'Well, go and get her and take her to the safe house.'

Armitage responds, 'You mean now?'

Lancaster's response is immediate, 'Yes, now, you idiot; we saw the two of them together that night, so they're clearly an item, and we might need her as leverage.'

'Okay, I'm on it. I remember looking up where she lives over at New Farm, so it won't take me long.'

'Good, get on it and don't stuff it up,' Lancaster concludes.

Pig is watching me, and when he sees I have finished listening, he says, 'Sorry mate, that was over an hour ago. I've been listening live, and only just started going back over the stored audio.'

I nod, already calling Suzie's mobile and getting the engaged tone. I say to Pig, 'Check the tracker on Armitage's car, see where it's showing up, and I'll check the coordinates from Suzie's phone.'

Jerry is squawking from my phone, so I tell him, 'It looks like they've identified Suzie, my partner, and have or are trying to kidnap her.'

'Shit,' is the reply. Helpful.

Pig dryly comments, 'Suzie will be pleased she has been elevated to partner!'

I give him a quick smile; then as the coordinates from Suzie's phone come in, I see it is moving east along Wynnum Road, so clearly she is not at home where she is meant to be. I tell Pig and we prepare to leave.

Pig comes back saying, 'I have two of their cars stationary at Heath Place Canon Hill, and a third –Armitage – travelling east along Wynnum Road.'

'That matches Suzie's signal, so I'm guessing they're also headed to Heath Place,' I reply.

We quickly pack up, wave goodbye to Yazeed and hustle to the van. Pig drives. Fortunately, from Stanley Street it's a fairly direct route east onto Wynnum Road and we have an ETA of only fifteen minutes. Bringing Jerry up to date, he asks if we need back up and we say no, we'll need to suss it out when we get there, but we don't want to spook them, that they're going to be pretty edgy anyway with their little empire crumbling around them.

'Might need to put paramedics on alert before we go in,' I add.

I'm watching the coordinates from Suzie's phone, which is still engaged, and they're now also stationary in Heath Place. I say to

Pig, 'Looks like Suzie called someone and left the phone on to make sure we could track her – pretty cool thinking,' and I give a little fist pump, thinking, *That's my girl!*

Pig nods and says, 'She's switched on, there's no doubt; except in her choice in men of course,' and we share a smile.

From Google Maps, we can see Heath Place is a little cul-de-sac, so we slowly go past the entrance to it on Winton Crescent, but of course it's now after 9:00 p.m., dark and for a change cloudy, so we head to the village common – a park only a few blocks away – and Pig sets up a drone, fitting it with an infrared lens so we will be able to see in the dark. Up it goes, and he quickly gets it oriented and whizzes over the rooftops until we can see the three cop cars parked in Heath Place; two are parked side by side in the driveway, the other on the street.

He brings it up over the house, checking if there are signs of anyone monitoring the surrounds, but it seems everyone is inside. He then has it do a full 360 so we can get the layout of the house, a single story, built almost to the boundary fence line, so barely enough room for someone to walk down either side, which is a bit limiting. However, there is green space behind the house with no immediate neighbours, so that will be good access, although the whole back wall is sliding glass doors, so any movement in the back yard would be obvious to anyone in what appeared to be the large living space. The 360 has showed us nearly every light is on in the house with the curtains pulled so we can't see which room Suzie is being kept in, but Pig has another trick up his sleeve, and he activates a heat sensor on the drone and does another 360. This shows we have three people (showing as heat sources) in the back-left hand room, sitting in a cluster, possibly around a table, and another two in the front bedroom, which is probably the master bedroom.

With that settled, he brings the drone down and hovers just above the roof to see if we can get any audio. Whilst we can hear muffled voices, we can't hear what is being said. He then brings it down on the left side at the back hoping the rear glass sliders are open, and sure enough we can identify Fleming, Armitage and Johnstone's voices. No sound from Benson or Suzie, so it's a fair bet she is bound and gagged in the front room with Benson on watch. From what we can hear, they seem to be waiting to hear from Lancaster as to what to do next. The tension in their voices is obvious with Johnstone and Armitage in particular commenting that they are 'Fucked now.'

'You betcha,' Pig agrees.

Pig leaves the drone hovering there, hoping we will hear something useful, and we make our plans, sitting on a park bench in the dark. Flexible and practical; that's us! There's a crackle of thunder above and we look up.

I grumble, 'A good old Queensland summer storm, just what we need!'

As it starts to rain, we head back to the van to finish our preparations, leaving the drone hovering and capturing what is being said, which we will hear through our earplugs. We check in with Jerry and tell him we'll be going in shortly, having previously agreed (make that demanded) no police presence so there would be no slip ups. Apparently, Mel had acquiesced and has not put up a fight. We now agree a platoon of soldiers to deploy ASAP and hotfoot it to Heath Place as backup and to handle the prisoners. He has also requested paramedics be positioned at the nearby Kmart on the corner of Creek and Wynnum Roads, so they can quickly be on site if need be.

We didn't expect to need our Kevlar bullet proof suits for the sniper attack, but we had put them on before leaving home, not knowing when we might need them, hoping of course, we wouldn't. But now we know we will. Whilst we are in the van tooling up, the rain gets heavier, with lightning and thunder booming. Suddenly the whole suburb is pitched into darkness after an almighty lightning flash, obviously hitting a power line somewhere nearby. We look at each other and nod. Darkness is the perfect cover, so we quickly decide to leave the van where it is and jog back to Heath Place, through the heavy rain. We wait some ten minutes to give any households time to check their meter box to check if the meter has tripped, but then again, one look outside and they will see the whole street and suburb is in darkness.

We slip away from the van having donned our old army waterproof jackets, and under these our shoulder slings which help hide our assault rifles. We have our pistols in shoulder holsters as well, well hidden from the any passing public. Don't ask what else we have in the backpacks – that's a surprise!

We trot off back up the road as Jerry comes through the earpieces to advise the platoon are ten minutes out and will quietly cordon off Heath Place when they get there and await further instructions.

It doesn't take us long to make it back to Heath Place and we slow to a walk and, having already agreed on a plan, silently split up. We approach the house from separate angles. The drone hasn't caught any conversation of concern; they're all stumbling around in the dark with only cigarette lighters as lights. Pig and I squeeze over as far as we can to the edge of properties to make it harder to be seen. We are both conscious that street and house lights might come on at any second, making us as visible as in daylight. Let's hope not!

As planned, Pig works his way down the left side of the house towards the back, whilst I wait at the front door. I hear him grunt, knowing that he'll whip into action on the count of three.

Smash—

Boom—

Smash—

Boom—

The first noise is Pig putting his elbow through the side window of the lounge room, the second is him dropping a smoke bomb into the room. The next noise is me booting down the front door – yes, my size twelves can do that, even when the door is locked. But only after extensive training and knowing exactly where to kick!

I'm in the small front hall, pivot at the door to the front bedroom in time to see Benson holding Suzie around the throat and a pistol to her head. I can only see half his face, but I do see the smirk on his face as he thinks he has the upper hand.

Without hesitation and looking him in the eye, I shoot. No ifs, no buts—

Bang!—

He drops to the floor, blood and gore disgorging from his head wound where his eye used to be. Dead before he hits the floor.

I say, 'You killed my wife.'

Suzie has also dropped to the floor with a scream, and I use my boot to push her farther away from the spreading blood and ooze before she gets any more on her. She crawls farther away, sobbing.

I reach down, put my hand on her shoulder and say, 'You're safe now.'

She replies through her sobs, 'You could have shot me!'

I reply, 'I don't miss.'

I re-enter the hall and head towards the back, but Pig has everything under control. We bump fists, and he calls in the army; I head back to Suzie. She's still sobbing, but now she's sitting up with her back to the wall, clearly traumatised by seeing Benson dead in front of her. I bend down and pick her up, carry her into another bedroom and put her down on the bed. I gently cut the zip ties tying her wrists together.

She reaches up and puts her arms around me, sobbing and saying, 'I am so sorry, Mort. He told me you sent him, and I guess I wanted to believe it; I didn't think. When I saw who it was, I knew I was in trouble.'

'Shh, shh,' I say, 'you are safe now; I will never let anyone hurt you. You did good leaving your phone on, proud of you,' which gets a semblance of a smile.

She sits up and we have a long hug.

Pig goes past the bedroom door, saying, 'Hurry up, you two, we're about to have company.'

Two soldiers appear in the door, picture perfect routine for approaching an unidentifiable entrance, so Pig and I identify ourselves, guns nowhere in sight, and then go outside whilst the Lieutenant leading the platoon enters confirms one dead, and three incapacitated and secure. Pig had rendered them unconscious whilst they were affected by the gas, and then using zip ties, secured their hands behind their backs. No more than a headache between them.

The paramedics are next through the door, and I tell them nothing here for them. They look at Pig and I, then at the soldiers all in full battle dress, and must have been thinking, *Wow, what's going on here?*

Pig steps into the bedroom with me, and we quietly confer. I tell him I'm going to get Suzie away somewhere safe before the place turns into a circus, and suggest he wake Fleming and see what he can get out of him. We need to find Lancaster and put an end to this. Whilst we're talking, I hear a phone ringing somewhere, so stick my head out into the hall room and see a soldier coming towards me with a phone vibrating. I see it has Lancaster's name on the glowing face. So I answer it, but don't say anything.

'Flem, that you?' growls Lancaster.

Silence.

Again, 'Flem, everything all right?'

This time, I say, 'No. Not for Flem or any of your crew, Lancaster, or for you.'

Silence for a beat. Then, 'Fuck you!' Original, isn't he!

'I'm coming for you, Lancaster – or do you prefer Lowry? I don't care either way, you are going *down*.' I hear the sharp intake of breath when I called him Lowry, so clearly he was shocked we knew his second identity.

He forces a laugh and says, 'You. You won't even find me.'

I reply, 'Keep talking, we nearly have your location all ready.'

He hangs up. Not true, of course, but I just need him rattled.

I throw the phone to Pig and say, 'See if you can get that call triangulated. I'm taking Suzie somewhere safe. Let me know what you get out of Fleming. Good luck.'

With the lieutenant telling me I need to stay and with the other soldiers all looking on, I pick Suzie up and march out the door and walk up the road, putting her down so she could walk after exiting the house; she was not impressed being carried!

After ignoring the gathering crowd on the street even in the heavy rain and passing through the army checkpoint at the end of the road, we get back to the van. I help Suzie in, secure her seatbelt, once again being told she wasn't an invalid and I start the van and move off. We quickly get onto Creek Road heading south, and I look over at Suzie and see she is crying quietly. I gently put my hand on her arm and give it a little squeeze. She doesn't recoil at my touch, which I had half expected, so I leave it there for a few minutes. Then I grab my phone and call Maria.

She answers saying, 'Hiya, boss.'

I reply, 'Code six.'

Silence, then, 'Shit, shit, okay.'

I reply, 'Check for an incoming text in two,' and hang up.

Suzie asks, 'What's code six mean?' seemingly quickly recovering from her kidnapping.

I reply, 'Code six is an unofficial army "soldier in distress" call, and the unwritten code is you stop what you are doing and respond. Now.' One-handed, I start typing in an address.

Suzie grabs the phone and says, 'Tell me.'

I relay the address and she types it in and presses send.

'Thanks,' I say. 'Send another: "ETA twelve-thirty. You?".'

She does this without question, then asks, 'Why are we going to Ormeau?'

'I'm taking you to my uncle Albert's place. He's away overseas so it's locked up; it's isolated, and with Maria riding shotgun, you'll be safe. I'm not taking any more chances with you.'

A text comes in from Maria: 'Twelve thirty-five.'

'Ormeau is a pleasant acreage area halfway between Brisbane and the Gold Coast. My uncle Albert's wife died a few years ago, and he travels a lot, but has this lovely big home on two acres. Aunty Steph used to love her horses, so the property is always immaculate with its white rail fences. We can use it for the next couple of days till we know it's safe.'

We arrive at the house, and I punch in the security code and drive up the driveway. I park outside the large garage and we exit the van. The rain has eased up here, only a light drizzle, so we run around to the back door, and I pull a key off a nail in a nearby tree and open the door. It's a large two-storey home, plenty of room for a big family, so Suzie and Maria will rattle around in here.

Suzie has a wander around, saying, 'Wow, this is lovely.'

I say, 'You better find a shower, and we need to find you some clothes,' so I guide her to the guest bedroom with its ensuite and start to help her undress, but get slapped away.

She says, 'I can undress myself,' rather indignantly, so I pinch a kiss and leave her to it.

Knowing other cousins and family also use the house when Uncle Albert is away, I rummage through the drawers and wardrobe and find some ladies' underwear – goodness knows if they are the right size – and an old fashioned towelling robe, which I take and put just outside the ensuite door, telling Suzie that a choice of clothing awaits.

I head back to the back door, having heard another car coming down the drive, and sure enough, it's Maria in her trusty Ford Territory. She jumps out of the car, armed with a handgun, asking if everything is okay.

I say, 'Yes,' and give her a brief run down on events so far, and as soon as I say Suzie had been kidnapped, she takes off inside to find her, so I leave them to it. I could hear them both having a cry but showed my patience by not going and disturbing them even though I'm eager to get away and hunt down Lancaster.

Not too long later, they come out together, and before I can complement Suzie on her clothes choice, I get a mouthful from Maria for having put Suzie at risk. Even Suzie is telling her it's okay, but I take it, as there is absolutely only one reason she had been abducted, and that was because of me. When Maria finally stops to catch her breath, I tell her I agree with her. Sort of takes the wind out of her sails.

'Look, girls, there is a lot more shit going to go down tonight, so I need to get back and get into it. Suzie, make sure you do whatever Maria tells you. Maria, I trust you to look after Suzie, because you know what will happen to you if you don't.'

I get the death stare from her. Not a happy girly.

I reach over and give Suzie a quick kiss, telling her I'll let her know when things are done, and hit the road as she tells me, 'Be careful.'

54

Once back on the road back to Brisbane, I call Pig on the phone, preferring the privacy of the phone over the radio where numerous others will be listening. I ask him how he got on with Fleming and he replies, 'Didn't get much, claimed he didn't know where he would be, and what he might do. The cops have checked his home, but he isn't there, and as far as we know he doesn't have any other property where he could be hiding.'

'He'll be at the Jackals' Clubhouse,' I say.

'Why do you reckon that?' comes back Pig.

'Well, makes sense. He knows there is a big showdown coming; they are well prepared to defend it. Remember we were impressed by what we could see on that drive by, and they will help him down to the last man,' I conclude.

'So meet me at the BP truck stop along Logan Motorway, and we can then go in together; I have an ETA of 2:00 a.m.,' I tell Pig.

'Okay,' he replies. 'I'll have to borrow some wheels and get my skates on.'

'Once you're in transit, call, and we'll update Jerry.'

'Roger,' he responds.

A short time later, Pig comes over the radio, and we call up Jerry and I brief him, 'I believe Lancaster will be holed up at the Jackals

Bikies' Clubhouse, which is really a compound, ten-foot-high staked fence surrounding four or five homes inside. Only two entrances, so considering how close he is to them, I am sure he will get plenty of support trying to take down some police.'

'Shit,' says Jerry.

Assistant Commissioner Black chimes in, 'You can't go in there alone; they'll be armed to the teeth, just fixing for a fight.'

'Yes, and whose fault is that? The police have largely left them alone, allowing them to build their resources up even in contravention of the law, so now we have an alternative force on our hands. We know how to do this, we aren't constrained by your police protocols, and we are fully equipped to end this.'

I'm met by silence, which I take as tacit agreement. We then discuss our plans, which haven't been fully formulated yet; we'll know more once we get there and have used a drone to take a look see, but one thing's for sure: us coming won't be a surprise, but the force we will hit with sure will be.

I order them (me, a mere former sergeant!) to ensure there are no police or army anywhere within ten kilometres of their clubhouse in Cardiff Street, Darra. A short time later, my phone rings and it's MGC calling after Jerry has brought him up to date. I'm a bit surprised he doesn't order me to stand down; in fact, he doesn't even try to dissuade me. Rather, he wants to discuss our plans. Once again, I say we haven't formulated any yet and won't until we've had a quick aerial look-see once we arrive.

He suggests sending backup, but I urge him not to (don't mind 'ordering' a major around but wasn't going to try it on a major general!). I say, 'These are ruthless people, General; they've been building their resources up for months, years even, unimpeded by the police, and I'm sure they have trip wires or lookouts on surrounding access roads. So as soon as any official-type vehicle, especially more than one, is seen, you can guarantee they will know.'

'Very well then, Mort. I will have Jerry hold the full force we can free up ready to go as soon as you start your attack. Good luck.'

'Thank you, Sir,' I reply, and we hang up.

I make the truck stop a little early – not much traffic on the roads at this hour. I go inside and order two coffees and BLTs. We need sustenance, after all. Having taken the opportunity to clean some of the blood (Benson's, not mine) off my overalls whilst at Ormeau, I don't stand out, just another tradie on the road. Pig arrives just before the food is delivered, and he is looking as calm as always. We don't say too much as we eat, but he does confirm an Army team have given him a lift. They're sitting outside in their rental and will only come inside once we leave so there is no connection. They will be part of the backup force once they're given the word. Pig assures me these boys seem to know what they are doing – not 'green newbies.'

We hit the road, and I continue to drive. We head onto the Centenary Highway, take the Sumner Road exit, turn right back over the highway then pull up outside the nursery, just off the roundabout. This is a dead-end road, and once we're over the crest of the rise, we're out of sight of anyone on the road. We watch the area for any movement for a few minutes, then get out. Pig grabs the drone through the side door and launches it. Initially, he keeps it hovering over our location in ever increasing circles, with the infrared and heat sensors on, checking for any human activity, but none to be seen. With a nod, he sends it on a direct route to the compound – these little beauties have GPS these days, so input the address and off it goes.

He initially keeps higher than usual, as we aren't sure how sophisticated their defences will be, but whilst there is movement on the ground within the compound, there's no sign of a drone monitoring their compound. He lowers the drone, which enables us to better identify the heat sources moving around the compound, and we see two armed guards patrolling and a couple of large dogs also on the loose. By the size of them, we suspect Alsatians. We also note they have parked a car across both access points, and Pig notes the one parked across the main entrance is Lancaster's police Falcon, and I reply, 'Well, that's an open taunt, isn't it? The arsehole.'

We discuss access points, likely ambush points once the perimeter is breached, and agree on a plan and the timing of our action. The main entrance is in Russford Street with the police Falcon as the first barrier, then the large ten-foot-high steel gate. We know we have these covered. We decide Pig won't breach the second access point, but breach the boundary fence a bit further down Cardiff Street, so we're working our way more directly towards the main house but on a slight angle to each other from opposite sides of the property and won't be in each other's direct line of fire.

We watch the guards' routine for a little while, but we're both keen to get this done, and frankly, it doesn't matter where the guards are going to be – we know they will be firing at us, so this will easily identify their locations. And we have a shock in store for them plus any other opposition we find. Judging by the lights on in the house in the middle of the compound, we suspect this will be their stronghold, and where we will get both the most resistance and also likely find Lancaster, once we have dispensed with the resistance.

Plans made, we bump fists and, leaving the drone in place so Pig can monitor during our approach, we get back into the van. Having decided we can't afford to drive too close at the risk of alerting them, we cut into the nearby industrial suburb and park in an industrial complex car park on Bluestone Court. A delivery van certainly is not out of place around here. This leaves us a 400 metre cross country walk, so no biggie.

Before we leave the van, I radio in to Jerry and Mel, advising them we're about ten minutes from a go, and asking them to ensure some of the first to arrive set up a perimeter along Monier Road either side of Cardiff Street, as it is all open ground so a likely exit point, and also a possible helicopter landing point for rescuing Lancaster and other senior mob members. They explain their plans for setting up a perimeter once the action starts, and I view their plans on Google Maps, and I can't fault it.

'Looks good,' I tell them. I sign off, telling them I'll press the transmit button when we're ready to go.

Pig and I go to the side door of the van and get our equipment sorted. Most is in exactly the same place we put them before leaving the office, how many hours ago? First our back packs, guns and equipment. We blacken our faces, so we look the real deal.

The cross country is a little harder than it looked with an eight-foot-high barrier wall at the back of the industrial complex, then a small creek running through the paddock, so our boots get a little wet. Once across Monier Road, we work our way across more open paddocks to Cardiff Street. Leaving Pig there, I slip across Cardiff Street into more trees to work my way up towards my target – the main entrance – but taking the long way to avoid coming out into the open too soon.

In no time at all, we're both in position. A big breath, and I press transmit as promised and step into the open.

BOOM—

This boom is far louder than Betsy; it is a hand-held rocket launcher, after all. My boom is followed by a second as Pig joins the party. I reload and wait for the dust and smoke to clear, and whilst doing that, Pig shoots out the power line, plunging the compound into darkness. We expect they'll have a backup power generator, but this will not be the same thing, so in the meantime, I pull down my night vision goggles. Sure enough, there's not too much left of Lancaster's Falcon; it has been picked up and smashed through the steel gates as if they were matchsticks. This, as expected, gives me a clear sight of the main house in the compound, so—

BOOM—

I launch a second rocket direct at the main wall of the house, and—

BOOM—

Pig does the same from his side, targeting what we expect to be the secondary house. I walk directly down through the entrance and immediately come under sustained fire from the house on the left. Again, this is what we expected, but with each shot, I easily identify the shooters' positions and reveal our secret weapon – heat seeking bullets. Yes, these aren't yet official in any army anywhere, but we used them for trials whilst on some deployments, and they worked so well we kept a few samples. We know they work. Every time there is a blast of gunfire, I respond with one or two single shots, and these are always answered by screams of agony. Not me, though. Whilst I have taken a few hits, even one to the visor, I am good, as some of these will result in bruises tomorrow, so the armoured suit is doing its job well. Pig is doing exactly the same on the other side of the compound. In a lull in the firing, I give him a chirp – our secret sign to say all is good, and he responds the same.

Then within a minute or two, he says, 'One,' which tells me he is already in position at the back door of the main house. In the brief silence, it's reassuring to hear sirens coming from everywhere.

I reach what remains of the main entrance to the main house. Knowing Pig is already in position, I turn the gun onto auto and prepare to enter. I throw a small rock against the wall in front of the door, and this generates a short burst of fire from my left, so down on my knees and I move quietly in the door at half the height expected. I already have the gunman in my sights before he realises

I'm there. Almost a waste of ammo, but a two-shot burst and he's down. I stay there kneeling, and sure enough, another bikie bursts from the doorway on the right, having seen his mate topple and another short burst and he too is done with. These boys are typical bikies, tough as when dressed in their colours, but totally out of their depth in a firefight.

I hear Pig going through a similar process, so I regain my feet, and as agreed, I start moving to my left to clear the rest of the house, whilst Pig also goes left, so we have the whole house covered. All of a sudden, there's a barrage of gunfire raking the side of the house that I'm walking through, and due to the rocket damage I did earlier, I'm in clear sight of someone. I switch to single shot and let our intelligent bullets do their work. More grunts and moans ensue (for some reason, these heat seeking bullets work far better on single shot than auto. Fine by me.)

Finally, I hear Pig say, 'Lancaster's here, back right corner. I've got him covered.'

'Wait whilst I clear the house,' I reply, and quickly resume clearing the house room by room.

Suddenly, I hear a burst of rapid fire coming from Pig's location, and I hear a grunt from him. Grunts aren't part of our code, so I know he's taken a round, and promptly head in his direction. I enter what must have been to the main lounge, seeing Pig lying on the floor to my right as two others disappear through a second entrance into the kitchen.

Before I can get to Pig, he says, 'Go get him. I've taken one in the hand, so go.'

I immediately change direction to follow the fleeing tough boys, and as they exit the house, heading to the third house on the compound, I take down the bikie who is trailing Lancaster and set off across the open space in pursuit. Lancaster makes it to the doorway and turns and fires a pistol at me; I just keep coming, and he keeps firing, hitting me only occasionally. I'm even grinning as I reach him and whip him with the butt of my machine pistol. He collapses to the floor. I disarm him, quickly checking to see if he has further weapons on him, removing a knife from his calf. I give him another tap to the head to keep him unconscious whilst I clear the rest of the house. Finding no one, I head back to find Lancaster sitting up, grinning, aiming a pistol at me.

I smile and say, 'You'll have to do better than that, arsehole. You know how many shots I've taken already; go on take your best shot. But you're going down. Just think of the fun you are going to have in prison, a bent copper – you will be everyone's best mate. Bent over one way all day and bent over the other way every night. What a life you have before you.'

Quite a speech after all the rapid action of the last few minutes.

With a 'Fuck you,' he turns the gun on himself. He pulls the trigger.

I don't try to stop him. Simpler and easier that way. He dies instantly, blowing his own brains out.

Silence.

In the distance, I can still hear sirens and at least one helicopter, but I call up Pig to check on him. Knowing Jerry is listening too, I say, 'Lancaster is down, main house clear, third house clear, not sure about houses two and four on left.'

Jerry replies, 'We are approaching two and four now. Stay where you both are.'

I reply, 'I'm heading back to the main house to check on Pig; do not engage.'

'Clear,' is the response from Jerry.

I trot back across the compound and enter the back door only after Pig calls out 'clear.' I take my helmet off; this too is new-age technology, bulletproof like the rest of our body armour. I approach him; now that it's over, he too has removed his helmet.

We fist bump and I ask him, 'Where you hit?' and he raises his right hand, his lead and shooting hand, which is bleeding through a bandage he has already placed on the wound.

'What, you wimp, you call that a wound?' and we both smile, and I lean down and give him a hug, a man hug, that is.

I sit down on the floor next to him, lean back against the wall, shoulder to shoulder. Job done. Bloody good job done.

55

FOUR HOURS LATER

I pull up at Uncle Albert's in Ormeau. The new day has dawned, and both Suzie and Maria have come out to greet me. I get a big hug and kiss from Suzie, and I give her a big squeeze, so she knows how pleased I am to see her. Maria is not a hugger, so we bump fists, but bugger it, I give her a hug anyway. I grab a couple of bags out of the Camry; I left the van in the garage and swapped into the car for comfort.

I hand one to Suzie and say, 'Here, I grabbed you some clothes from my place.'

'Why? Don't you like my attire?' she asks, doing a little thing showing off a daggy pair of trackies and the hoodie she is wearing. She gets a smile in reply.

We get inside and I immediately sit down in a lounge chair, and Suzie goes to the kitchen returning with straight black coffee, hands it to me and then gives me a long, lingering kiss.

Maria clears her throat, saying, 'Hey, remember you're not alone here!' which prompts Suzie to stop and sit on the arm of my chair.

'So what happened?' she asks.

I give them a nearly full recount of the evening, finishing by saying Pig only needed treatment from the paramedics, just a couple of stitches, so he's fine.

Suzie asks, 'So where is he?'

'At my place; I told him he's welcome to come down here if he wants, but he said he wanted to be alone today at least.'

Suzie replies, 'He shouldn't be alone; we will have to go and get him or stay with him.'

Maria asks, 'How many shots did you take?' a typical soldier's question.

'I counted ten on the body and two on the helmet,' I reply.

Suzie gasps and immediately gets up and gives me another hug. I'm beginning to like this.

I tell them the PM is making a public address at 8:00 a.m. from Queensland Parliament, which is coming up, so Maria gets up and switches on the TV, pulling up Channel Seven just as they cross live for a breaking news story.

We sit and listen to the PM speak; he is flanked by a couple of junior members of the state government, one now acting premier, and also Melissa Black, who has been appointed acting police commissioner.

Naturally, so early in the story, he is a bit vague about the details, only saying that the Premier, his deputy and a number of his senior staff and some influential members of the police service had all been charged with corruption and, in some instances, attempted murder.

And of course, the question is asked, 'Is the storming of the Jackals Bikie Gang's clubhouse associated with his announcement?'

He replies, 'Yes, a small law enforcement team had stormed the barricaded clubhouse, sustaining automatic weapon fire, but had won the day by capturing a number of the Jackals outlaws. The kingpin of the whole corrupt cadre took his own life whilst hiding in the clubhouse. We have recovered a significant cache of automatic weapons, a large quantity of methamphetamine and cannabis, and they are still counting the money they have found hidden in an underground safe.'

I yawn and say, 'I need some sleep; I need to be back at police headquarters at noon for a full debrief.' I grab Suzie's hand, saying, 'They need to talk to you as well, get your side of the story.'

She nods.

I head off to the bedroom and Suzie comes in, tucks me in with a long and lingering kiss, and I am sound asleep. A deserved sleep.

56

FOUR DAYS LATER

We are back home now; most of the debriefing is done. Pig's hand is healing nicely, so we're kicking back, taking it easy for a few days.

The Paramount deal and our little crusade have kept us on our toes. Whilst the political ramifications are a long way from over, these don't bother me too much; the PM has facilitated a consensus across all political parties that they will push through an urgent Act of Parliament to force a general election for the state. With so many senior officials and politicians facing serious criminal charges, this seems to be the only safe way forward.

George, Pig's former partner, is one of many facing serious charges and has so far been refused bail. Pig went and saw him, but the meeting didn't go well. George had already guessed that Pig and I were instrumental in bringing down the premier, so he was very indignant that we didn't understand the big picture.

'How many despots around the world make the same claim?' Pig asked me that evening.

An image of me, rocket launcher on my shoulder, has emerged on the internet; apparently, a news helicopter was flying back to its base when we fired the first rockets at the bikie fort and had captured footage of my actions. The authorities moved quickly and suppressed the video, but were too late to stop this one image from appearing. It has gone viral. I'm not recognisable with the smoke and dust swirling around me. In fact, I look thoroughly menacing, even if I do say so myself. Big man, fully armed, night vision googles over a full-face helmet – what's not to be scared of?

When I say not recognisable, Liz's mother Sandy left a message for me asking if I was okay, saying she had seen me on 'tellie'.

Dad too has realised it was me, and I got a text, 'You okay?'

'Yes, Dad, all good!' I replied.

Of course, they're the exceptions, both having known me most of my life. I gave Sandy a call to assure her I was okay and asked her not to mention to anyone it was me. A bit late for that, I know, but no harm asking. Sandy has always been like a second mother to me. After all, Liz and I went through high school together, and our year twelve formal was our first date.

Maria had, after persistent demands from Stacey, passed Pig's phone number on to her, and Stacey had rung Pig, suspecting we had been in the middle of the action, and they had chatted a few times since. I pointed out to him she didn't seem concerned about me, only him, which got me a grunt (get it?).

Midge gave us a call; this time it's Amy Shark singing 'Everybody Rise' coming from Pig's phone as a ring tone. After we bring him up to date on the action, I compliment him, telling him Amy lived just down the road at the Gold Coast and is a true Aussie.

I receive three text messages and one phone call from Colleen Hill, the *Courier Mail* journalist, saying, 'you owe me an exclusive', obviously putting two and two together.

I send a reply, 'OSA (Official Secrets Act)'. But this doesn't dissuade her. Knowing her morning routine from when Pig was checking her out before we approached her, I invite Suzie along so when Colleen arrives at her usual coffee pick-up joint, I invite her to join us. She instantly recognises my voice, and we have a good chat.

Having briefed Suzie in what I planned on doing, I then used her to ensure I didn't breach any obligations I had under the OSA, but still giving Colleen sufficient background information for her to dig up much of the full story. She's pretty pumped when we leave.

Before we left, Colleen looked at me, saying, 'You're the bloke in the video, aren't you?' I smiled as we departed.

57

FOUR WEEKS LATER

Suzie and I are sitting on the beach at dusk on Fraser Island. Pig is back in our beach house firing up the BBQ. It has been a whirlwind four weeks since the Dyson assassination attempt, Suzie's abduction, and the takedown of the Jackals bikie headquarters. We deserve the break we have given ourselves up here on Fraser Island.

Fraser Island is the world's largest sand island. No roads, no bitumen – the entire island is a national park. The ocean beach is the main road. But only when the tide permits. It's four-wheel-drive-only country. A short ferry ride dumps you on the beach at the southern tip (unless you're going to the one true resort on the island, Kingfisher Bay – then you can get a ferry to there direct) but the bulk of tourists come on at the southern tip and drive the 90-mile beach to their camp or accommodation spot. We aren't camping. We have the luxury of an ocean front beach house at Eurong, the largest settlement on the island.

The great thing about Fraser is it has very limited modern-day facilities. Yes, you have phone and Wi-Fi, but no TV coverage. Every building or complex needs its own power generation; no power is provided. Clearly then, this limits who is going to visit. The beach at dusk. A beautiful time on Fraser. So peaceful. No sound other than that of the rolling breakers pounding in on the beach.

The tranquillity rolls over you. Just what we need.

We came up a couple of days ago after being in Canberra for an official thank-you dinner by the Prime Minister, where we all had dinner at The Lodge, his official residence. This included his family, so Pig, Suzie and I were made very welcome. With Major General Rutherford, his wife, Jerry Harris and the PM's chief of staff Karen Jones as the only other guests, we felt like the guests of honour!

After the semi-official thank-you session, the PM had invited Pig and me to a side office along with MGC. He then explained that MGC would be heading up a new covert division under the umbrella of the Department of Defence that would be tasked with identifying and eliminating foreign powers' efforts to infiltrate and possibly damage Australia's interests through cyber or hacking attacks. He explained that this division, named Section V, would work in conjunction with the Australian Cyber Security Centre (ACSC) and would be responsible for protecting our nation's digital interests across both commercial and public domains.

He continued, 'You two have proven you are the perfect team members we need to battle this new style of war. You will have no doubt read or heard in the media how some foreign powers, and I'm not naming anyone specifically, as I'm not sure you can trust your so-called friends in this day and age either, appear to be targeting not just Australia's secrets, but clearly other nations and even some industries globally have been targeted as a whole. We need to get on the front foot in this environment, and we need you on board to assist.'

Wow, this is a surprise to Pig and me. I hadn't understood the seriousness of these hacking attacks we had heard about on the news. We looked at each other and nodded together.

He continued, 'It was obvious when you presented the crisis in Brisbane, how underprepared we were. This type of situation is now a modern reality. In fact, digital warfare, if you want to call it that, is a higher probability than conventional war these days. Your digital communication skills, combined with your combat capabilities, are resources we need to have on board.'

I replied, 'We would be happy to, Sir, but the one thing that stands out from the Brisbane crisis was we have to be working under the radar, and without protocol constraints; otherwise we're wasting everyone's time.'

Both the PM and General nodded in agreement, so I asked the General, 'Sir, are you in favour of us joining your team?'

'Absolutely I am; I even warned the Prime Minister I wouldn't know where to start if you two turned him down, and he told me he "will win you over, even if I have to hog tie you both down"!'

This, of course, made us all laugh, and we shook hands all round. We agreed to meet with MGC and go into more detail in the morning before flying home. We walked back into the session where drinks and hors d'oeuvres were being served, and I noticed Karen showing Suzie something on her phone and a look of horror on Suzie's face. I wondered what it was.

A little later, Suzie came over quietly, grabbed my hand and held on tight, making me wonder once again what Karen had shown her. But in truth, I'm guessing what it could be.

Yes, once we are alone in our hotel room later, Suzie tells me she had watched the news video that didn't make it to air, showing me under attack from the bikies. The video, which I had seen the day after the assault, clearly shows me taking hits, twelve in all. Most would have been fatal without the Kevlar suit and visor helmet. Suzie doesn't say too much but hugs me tightly.

Next morning, Suzie joins us for our meeting with MGC, having explained to her last night about the invitation. She's a little concerned about it being risky, but I assure her there are far bigger things to worry about here.

And besides, I think, *Pig and I have proven even to her we are quite capable!*

Our meeting turns out to be rather lengthy, our flight having to be rebooked onto a later flight, but we agree on terms for our services, on an as-needed contractor basis. Suzie proves her worth in ensuring our services contract is watertight, and I think she is quite pleased she has also contributed to our success.

I also had a lengthy email from Marg a week or so back, giving all the details of their success in acquiring both Futurcomm and Mypone, and they would be announcing the merger, as they were calling it, to the press in a few days' time. She also tells me that Cameron had resigned, as he and Sofia had decided to stay in Nepal and work for a children's charity there, helping house, feed and school kids. Quite a surprise to me, as I hadn't seen any good in Cameron. I reply to her, saying, 'That's good, so you'll be needing to buy my shares in both target companies!'

This prompts a phone call from her, asking, 'Did you buy shares in both companies?'

I answer, 'Yes and in Paramount as well.'

Marg replies, sounding a little disappointed, 'Oh, we thought it was our idea to buy Mypone, as it wasn't part of the plan you proposed.'

I agree with her and then add, 'Yes, but I was confident you would follow the lead and take the shot, a three-way play was always my expectation,' hoping my smile comes through in my voice.

I guess it must have as Marg laughs and says, 'Well, Sir Anthony might be a little miffed when I tell him you had led us to the water, expecting us to drink! But I'm sure he won't mind paying you the extra you'll make on your shares!' and we have a further laugh.

I also ask who is the new CEO with Cameron not returning, and Marg again surprises me, saying that Jess, the CEO of Mypone, had accepted the role, having impressed Sir Anthony and Marg with her attitude and ideas for the future, with Marg adding, 'And I'm excited to work alongside her. Merging the three businesses in this manner changes the whole market scenario for us and we can't wait to explore it.'

We say goodbye, and Marg warns me to expect an invitation to a celebratory dinner in the coming weeks, once all the merger details are finalised.

Premier Aldred (former Premier Aldred, that is), the darling of the media, was loudly complaining of a conspiracy, and the media had taken up the call. When the clamour got too loud, the Prime Minister called a press conference up in Brisbane, and played the recording of the conversation between Lancaster, Herbert and the Premier, introducing it by saying, 'Let me play you a recording, one of two the authorities have of this same conversation'—Pig's app on George's phone had also recorded the conversation, placing him in the Premier's office during the call—'The first voice you will hear is Detective Inspector Lancaster, then Jack Herbert, Deputy Chief of Staff, and the third voice you will recognise.'

He played the tape to deathly silence. Upon completion, he advised the media the tape was date and time stamped and took place at 6:15 p.m. on the day of the assassination attempt. He also went on to advise the investigation and prosecution had been handed over to Australian Federal Police to ensure there was no contamination of evidence.

Colleen the journalist had done herself proud writing a good in-depth article not only about the actual recent events, but also highlighting the reasons the corruption was able to flourish, weak politicians and police hierarchy and a generally soft policing approach, seemingly endorsed by both, i.e., coming down hard on soft targets, but not putting any effort into bringing any group who stood up to them as the Bikies had for a number of years. She was already being talked about as a Walkley Award winner.

Suzie and I continue to enjoy the solitude sitting on the sand, now being watched by a couple of dingoes. These wild dogs are true-blooded native wild dogs, as no domestic dogs are allowed on Fraser Island. They're renowned for stealing unguarded food, and even occasionally small children. They are true hunters and certainly not to be trusted. So, I'm keeping a wary eye on them.

Pig wanders down, bringing us both a refill and joins us, telling us dinner will be ready in a few minutes. So, a short time later, I stand up, and bend down and give my hand to Suzie to help her up, and we walk back up through the sand dunes arm-in-arm to the beach house and our dinner.

THE END

WHO IS MORT?

Morton Chris Ireland

Morton Chris (not Christopher!) Ireland was born at Ipswich General Hospital on 8 May 1986 to parents Edith & Chris. He was a big baby at 4.2 kilograms with a swath of black hair. The black hair and dark complexion stood out because both parents had fair complexions and light, sandy coloured hair.

Edith's older brother, Albert, quickly and regularly suggested she had had a fling with a 'tall, dark and handsome stranger'. Edith, as was her want, simply ignored this until Mort's second birthday, with all the family gathered when once again he brought it up. Edith countered by saying, 'Albert, give it up. We all know Mum's mother, YaYa, was Greek, and she had five brothers, all big blokes. Besides, you're the one with the Greek nose!'

This brought plenty of laughter from the extended family gathered, as Albert fingered his nose as if to say, 'what's wrong with my nose?'

Edith and Chris had long agreed that if their baby was a girl, Edith would name her. If a boy, Chris had the honours. They chose not to know beforehand whether it was to be a boy or girl, and neither of them shared the names they were favouring.

Of course, when Chris announced Mort's name in the recovery ward, Edith was not happy.

'What sort of name is Morton?' she complained.

'Well, better than Bribie,' Chris countered. 'You've been saying for months, when the baby arrives, I won't be able to go fishing anywhere near as much, so I think Morton is a good choice, as it reminds me of what I'm missing! Besides, there's nothing wrong with Mort as a boy's name. My second choice was Bribie'—his second favourite fishing beach—'so I'm sure that would have gone down a treat!'

Edith and Chris had all but given up on having a family. They had been trying for years to no avail, so when Edith suddenly missed her period, she chose not to say anything immediately to Chris until she had taken a pregnancy test. Of course, this was way before IVF offered parents more options. Their scientific options were limited to taking Edith's temperature and the timing of her menstrual cycle.

Still, they were both genuinely excited that they now had a baby on the way. Chris was tasked with painting the third bedroom, and they reviewed their baby shopping list for when a baby might be on its way. Being a little superstitious, they had not bought any of these items. And, with money always tight, there was no sense spending money before you knew you would definitely need it.

The day Chris went to the hospital to bring his wife and son home was a very exciting event for him. Unbeknownst to Edith, he had decorated the inside of the house with 'Welcome Home' banners and had, whilst she was in hospital, repainted the baby's room in a light blue.

As first-time parents they were both nervous and a little unsure what to do each time Mort cried, but with both grandmothers literally just around the corner, there was no shortage of advice!

They settled into their new routine, Chris not even grousing (too much, anyway!) about being home every weekend, when he would regularly go away to Moreton or Bribie islands camping and fishing with his little tinnie (small aluminium fishing boat powered by a small outboard motor).

Chris worked as a linie or linesman for Telecom (as Telstra was then known), so he was outside most of the day in the sun, rain and occasional hail! But as everyone knows, they aren't over-worked and even back then he wrangled his hours to get an early break on most Fridays. Now with another mouth to feed, and not going away fishing, he chose to work the extra hours for the overtime. This is way before maternity leave, and Edith had always been anxious about how the money would work out with only one pay packet coming in. So, the extra overtime did come in handy.

She had worked at the Booval Post Office for many years, and they had promised her a job when she was ready to return to work. But apart from the money, she loved the idea of being a fulltime mum for her baby boy!

They lived in a traditional Queenslander in Hibiscus Avenue Flinders View, an older, well-established suburb of Ipswich.

Ipswich was in fact the first capital of Queensland. It is a long-established city and whilst these days it is more a satellite suburb of the ever-growing Brisbane, it has a long and proud history of its blue-collar roots. Its growth based as it was on the multiple coal mines surrounding Ipswich plus its heavy engineering based around the long-established Queensland Rail workshops there in the city.

It also has a proud history as a birthplace of many famous sportspeople, of which the latest is Ash Barty.

Chris had his shed out the back (his 'man cave', long before the term was coined), that housed his tinnie and camping equipment and numerous other tools and machinery so he could tinker around.

Being quite handy, he was always repairing neighbours' mowers and equipment for a bit of extra cash.

Through Mort's infant years life was pretty good. After he turned two, Edith was able to get a part-time job at the North Ipswich Post Office, a bit of a drive compared to Booval, but it was a small operation with only one or two staff needed. She worked there three days a week plus Saturday morning with both grandmothers having Mort a day and a half each, and Chris given the responsibility every Saturday morning, when they would spend most of the time out in the shed, Chris tinkering, Mort playing with his favourite toys. Usually getting quite grubby, much to Edith's annoyance. Chris's typical answer was, 'He's a boy – what do you expect?'

Mort continued to be a hunk of a lad, always bigger than everyone his own age. When he started school at Raceview State, he was the biggest kid in the year. He, like most boys of the era, always had a footy in his hand, kicking it, passing it, and in the interval and lunch time, games of touch were always quickly organised. Mort was one of the first to be picked when the sides were picked.

As a student, he didn't excel, but always got through with rarely a bad or negative response.

He was keen not only on footy (Ipswich is rugby league heartland!), but also cricket – or any sport if it got him out of the classroom. When he joined up to play under sevens rugby league at the nearby Brothers Juniors, both proud parents went along every week to watch.

Due to his size he always dominated, and when he went up to the under twelves, he was also being taught how to use his size to better advantage by one of the coaches, a former Bronco NRL player. Naturally the whole team of little under twelves was in awe of this 'real Bronco' (the Broncos are the foundation NRL team in nearby Brisbane) so everything he said was followed very seriously.

However, when it came to him wanting to play cricket on a Saturday, Edith drew the line declaring 'That's fine, Mort. Your dad will be taking you. Besides, I have to work Saturdays.'

Chris had no such excuse so got to sit and watch Mort and his team mates every Saturday morning running around and not doing much. Still, Mort seemed to enjoy it. Although maybe it was nothing more than filling in time until footy started again.

Through these early years family holidays usually entailed camping somewhere along the coast. As Mort got a bit older, Edith often chose to stay home, declaring, 'it is more of a holiday for me to stay home alone instead of having to look after two kids'. Although every couple of years they would splurge out and rent a holiday unit at Burleigh Heads on the Gold Coast (a favourite haunt for holidaying Ipswich people).

As he entered his teen years (there were no pre-teens in those days!) being selected in representative football teams became the norm, and whilst exciting for him, it also created a bit of a challenge, as some of the rep teams depended on the parents to get the kids to the various venues. And as everyone knows, Queensland and Australia are big places.

Comps in Queensland could be as far away as Cairns (some 1500 kilometres away); a lengthy drive in those days, as air fares were way outside the budget. Chris would often have to take a few days off to get him there and back, and, unbeknownst to Mort, often slept in the car, an aging Toyota Land Cruiser 60S, to save the cost of a motel. Mort of course would be billeted out and Chris would sneak a shower in the changerooms during training or one of the other teams' games.

Mort's on-field success also came with a bit of notoriety, as other teams started targeting him, some with cheap shots, others with putting two or three players marking him. Mort showed his footy nous pretty quickly by then sharing the ball more, so he wasn't the only player trucking it up. This impressed the coaches, as apparently no one had suggested this to him.

His 'fame', so to speak, also brought him to the attention of Ipswich Boys' Grammar, a local Rugby Union focused GPS school. He was offered a scholarship to Ipswich Boys' based on his ability to play Rugby Union. So, through his high school years, he played Rugby Union at school and League for his club, Brothers, at the weekend. The increased discipline required by Ipswich Grammar improved not only his footy, but his grades as well.

There was also no doubting his commitment to both sports either, as at least five days a week he pounded the pavement on an eight-kilometre early morning run and Chris had bought him a used set of weights and heavy punching bag and numerous other fitness equipment, all installed in Chris's shed. This meant they often spent hours together in the shed of an evening, neither having much time or interest in watching much TV. Unless it was sport of course.

Even though Chris and Mort were close, sharing as they did many evenings together in the shed, Edith was Mort's real confidant. She got to know all his dreams, insecurities and whatever worried him. Mort seemed comfortable talking about his dream of being a professional footballer, but at the same time recognising to make it to the top and represent Australia (which child keen on sport doesn't have this dream?) would require a lot of hard work, discipline, and a good dose of luck to avoiding serious injuries.

Through his early teenage years he had not shown any interest in girls. Until he did. This happened very suddenly.

As was a 'rite of passage' for all fifteen-years-olds back then, as soon as he turned fifteen, Mort had applied to Woolworths (Australian supermarket chain), sat through their tests and was offered a job as a checkout operator at nearby Booval Fair. He and

Chris had agreed he could buy Chris's old Nissan Navara for $2500, so he was dead keen to start earning a wage. An outsider would question who was getting the better deal here, as the Navara was a well-used ute!

A few weeks on the job, on a Thursday night shift, a new young girl came onto the checkout next to him and smiled at him. That was it! He was smitten.

Her name was Liz Jacobson. She too had just turned fifteen and went to Ipswich Girls' Grammar. Of course, going to an all-boys school, his social skills were not the best and in the first couple of weeks he was tongue-tied trying to talk to her.

Then five weeks later a massive summer storm, for which Queensland is renowned, smashed through Ipswich on the Thursday evening, with all of Ipswich and much of Southeast Queensland losing power. No power which means no lights, no cash registers, and no EFTPOS; nothing worked. The staff were all sent home early. But this was before everyone had mobile phones and of course public phones were also down, so neither Liz nor Mort could contact their parents to come and collect them. Mort would normally run home after shift, so was not expecting anyone to pick him up.

He offered to stay with Liz whilst she waited for her mum, sheltering at the entrance to the shopping centre. They had to wait two hours, as Liz's mum, Sandy, did not realise all power was out, assuming it was only their suburb. And they talked. And talked. This was a new experience for Mort, usually a man of few words, but here he was chatting openly to this girl, Liz.

Eventually Sandy turned up, aghast they had been waiting outside through the torrential rain, and Liz, perhaps without thinking, asked her mum if they could drop Mort home on their way. This was way out of the blue for Sandy too – never had there been any mention of Mort, or any other boys previously. Of course, she graciously agreed, but it was a silent trip to Mort's place. Except for Sandys inquisition of this big lad, suddenly friends with her daughter. Liz surprisingly chose to sit in the back with Mort, rather than her usual seat in the front! A point not lost on her mother.

Unbeknown to Mum, Liz had also held Mort's hand for a short time, giving Mort a real jolt, and thrill! Of course, Mort then faced another inquisition when he got inside with both Mum and Dad appearing to ask who had just dropped him off. A sudden change in the family landscape.

From then on, Liz and Mort would see each other at work most weeks and occasionally at weekends and holidays. She started also being a regular at his footy games. As both parents often reiterated, they were barely fifteen. That did not stop them spending time on the phone of course. But, being before mobile phones, they had to use their home phones, so both parents were easily able to listen in.

As their friendship developed, they both were welcomed into each other's home, so Mort became almost like a son to the Jacobsons, and Liz a daughter to Edith and Chris. Liz even joining Mort and his family on a holiday at Burleigh Heads, but happily declined to join Mort and Chris on any of their camping trips.

Early on, Bill, Liz's father, had sat Mort down and laid down the law about sex, pointing out the age of consent was sixteen and, 'if you have sex with my daughter a day before, I will cut your balls off'. Liz was aghast and embarrassed by her father, but when Mort confided this later to Chris, he looked at his son and said, 'And I will hold you down whilst he does it'. There was no doubt Mort knew where he stood.

Liz was also a keen sportsperson, not at a champion level but a good club swimmer and keen netballer. Mort's footy skills continued to grow and with that, his reputation. He was being selected in both Queensland Rugby League and rugby squads, with both codes encouraging him to drop the other and focus only on one.

Mort made the Ipswich Boys' Grammar 1st XV in grade eleven, and then to the surprise of many was appointed captain of the 1st XV in year twelve, his final year. This was a prestigious appointment as it carried a lot of responsibility at the school. Again, to the surprise of many, Mort took this responsibility in his stride and Chris and Edith (and no doubt Liz) were extremely proud of how he had grown up.

In his final year Mort was also selected as a non-travelling reserve for the Australian schoolboys Rugby Union team. Any member of this team, in any year, is on the fast track to football success. Alas he was kept out of the actual team by a couple of others who both went on to have distinguished Wallaby [an Australian Rugby team] careers.

Even with his success with Rugby Union, League was his first love. He had long dreamed of playing NRL and becoming a Bronco. Mort and his parents had agreed he could remain at home, rent free for two years after he finished school, whilst he tried to make it into the big league in footy. He still had to work part time, now at Red Rooster, a fast-food chain. He had bought Chris's old ute before he left school, so he was independent, not being reliant on Chris or Edith for transport.

On the other hand, Liz, who had grown into a serious, studious young lady, had been accepted into Griffith University on the Gold Coast to study Bachelor of Education, so she could fulfil her long held dream of being a primary school teacher. With Mort still living in Ipswich and Liz broadening her horizons as a student on the Gold Coast, their relationship entered a new phase. But one they both adapted to. When training and work commitments permitted, Mort would head down the Gold Coast for a night or two. Likewise, Liz took the opportunity when it came up to head home.

Mort had signed on at the Ipswich Jets, a natural progression from his Brothers junior club, and was still based in Ipswich. It was also a feeder club for the Brisbane Broncos, Mort's ultimate goal. The Jets have a long and proud history of Broncos and even Australian football greats, so it was a proud and historic club. His wasn't on a big contract, but he was pleased to be paid to play the game he loved.

Unfortunately, life after school did not go well for Mort. His first year out, he sustained a serious knee injury. His first serious injury. This meant he was side-lined for the rest of the season and would not be fit until mid-way through the second years pre-season training. Whilst he diligently followed the instructions and advice from the medical support team at the Ipswich Jets, they dropped him from their contracted players group. This hit Mort pretty hard, and he lost a lot of confidence in where he was heading.

At about the same time he started developing a friendship with a new boy at the club, Archie Brown. Archie, a ginger headed prop from neighbouring Inala had a vastly different upbringing, coming from a single parent family (he didn't know his father), and his mum had two other younger mouths to feed beside him. He was a good player though, and tough as nails.

Mort all through school, never developed any close friendships, other than Liz. Plenty of friends, but no close mates. So, Archie coming on the scene was, in the first instance at least, thought to be a good thing. But then they started hanging out late at night, Mort receiving a couple of warnings from the police after being evicted with Archie from hotels and night clubs. His deteriorating behaviour was not lost on Chris, Edith, or Liz. And whilst he had always been open with his mum, and a lesser extent with Liz and Chris, now he just clammed up.

As his two years of free living was coming to a close, and whilst he was still in the Jets playing squad, he wasn't getting much game time. His parents wanted him to make a decision. But as he admitted to them, he knew he needed a trade, but none of the traditional trades, such as plumber, electrician, carpenter, mechanic, etc., held any interest to him. Therein lay his quandary.

One Saturday evening, not long before his twenty-first birthday, Mort was delivered home in a police car. As it was summer, it was still light, so this occasion was clear to see by all the neighbours. Sergeant 'Bronco' Rogers, well known to both Mort and Chris from his association with Brothers Leagues Club, delivered a clearly drunk Mort to his parents.

He gave Mort a very blunt message, in front of his parents. 'Mort, this is your last chance. Being caught in a stolen vehicle and being drunk in public, if I had charged you, you may well have gone to prison. I know you are a good lad, you have good family around you, so I am giving you this one last chance. Stuff up again, and you will be locked up. Am I getting through to you kid?' Policing the old-fashioned way!

Mort stood sullenly through the lecture, and nodded his head in agreement.

Sergeant Rogers went on, 'Keep away from young Archie, too, he is heading for jail time.'

Through this whole lecture, Edith was crying her eyes out, inconsolable. Mort couldn't keep his eyes off his mum whilst Chris tried his best to comfort her, looking daggers at his son. As soon as the sergeant left, Mort bolted to his room and shut the door. He refused to answer Chris when he went knocking, wanting to talk.

He didn't surface the next day for breakfast or lunch. Then mid-afternoon Liz knocked on the front door, her mum sitting in her car in the driveway and unlike normal, Liz waited to be let in. When Edith knocked on Mort's door telling him Liz was here to see him, he sullenly opened the door and went to meet Liz.

With Liz in tears, she handed Mort back the friendship ring he had bought and given her on her eighteenth birthday, saying through her tears, 'Mort whilst I love you, I do not and cannot like the person you are becoming. I have been so proud of you these last few years, growing into a great person, not only on the footy field, but now, I just don't know you. Nor do I want to know you.'

With this and with a silent, pleading look to Edith, she bolted back out the front door, with Mort, Chris and Edith following her silently.

She got in her mum's car, and they drove away, Liz watching Mort as long as she could, but not offering a smile or wave. Edith was once again in tears. Mort headed back to his room, slamming the door.

Next day, a Monday, both Chris and Edith left for work as normal, leaving Mort alone and undisturbed in his room. However, when Edith got home from work that day, Mort was sitting in the kitchen drinking coffee. He had cleaned himself up, and was smartly dressed, much to her relief.

After he had made her a coffee as well, he started, 'Mum I know I've hurt you with my recent behaviour. I can't fully explain it. It was simply too easy to follow Archie's lead and go with the flow.'

Here he leans over, and they hug, with Edith having a cry as he says, 'I'm so sorry, Mum.'

He then continued, 'I'm not getting anywhere with my footy, I'm not even enjoying it at present, and Sergeant Rogers has given me the wakeup call I needed. As you know I want to do a trade but don't know which one. So today I went into Brisbane. To the Army recruitment office. I'm going to join the army.'

This gets another burst of tears from Edith, as she realises her son has found his way, but she will be losing him at the same time. After she settles down, she asks the inevitable question, 'what about Liz?'

Mort looks at her and says, 'I have told Liz I will win her back. She doesn't know about the Army yet, although I don't think she will be surprised as I have talked about it off and on over the years.'

They hug again and Mort disappears up to his room, having confirmed he will be down for dinner as normal at six.

The family dinner that night entailed an open and frank discussion between the three of them, both Chris and Edith ensuring Mort understood how close he came to throwing everything he had worked so hard for away. They naturally quizzed him on what he hoped to gain from joining the Army, when he admitted he wasn't sure although he was quite keen to have a go at their 'communications' traineeship.

In discussing his breakup with Liz, he also admitted she had caught him kissing Diane, one of her friends.

'Why?' was Edith's question.

Mort shrugged before admitting, 'There was nothing in it. I was drunk at the time.'

Edith then reinforced to him, 'Well, just remember, you have broken her trust now, so you will have to work hard to prove you are worthy of it again.'

Mort hung his head as her point rammed home.

Mort and Liz had agreed he would head down the Gold Coast the next morning and meet for lunch. She chose the Coffee Club at Robina Town Centre to meet. Here he detailed his plans, of joining the Army, signing on for an initial five years, and how he hoped to come out with a trade in communications, which appealed to him far more than any of the traditional trades.

With a few tears thrown in, they agreed to remain a couple until he passed his march out parade after some eighty days of training and was a fully-fledged soldier. To show his commitment, he promised Liz she could trust him and assured her he had always been, and would remain, faithful to her.

It took a couple of months for the process to work out, with formal signing on, initial fitness test and medicals, but Mort eventually headed off to Kapooka, near Wagga Wagga, to commence his soldier training. In the Army he started playing both league and union for his battalion and then for Army in their annual grudge matches against both the Air Force and Navy. And he found his love for footy again. Whilst his time on the Australian Army remains classified, after passing this soldier training, he was allocated to 1RAR based in Townsville. He was accepted as a trainee communications technician. Additionally, early on, Mort had shown great aptitude as a marksman, being offered a position in the sniper training school, and this is where Mort and Pig met.

Mort and Liz continued their long-distance relationship, Liz had accepted back the friendship ring when Mort offered it to her on his first break after his passing out parade, which Chris, Edith, and Liz had proudly attended.

When Liz graduated, she was appointed to a teaching role at Annandale State School in Townsville, and they moved into a unit together there. A short time later Mort proposed, Liz accepted, and the wedding date was set. However, Mort's army duties got in the way of their plans, as he was to be deployed again (he had a short deployment to East Timor previously) to Iraq. With a rumoured longer-term deployment to Afghanistan also imminent, Liz and Mort decided to bring their wedding forward. So, with only three weeks' notice, they were married at the delightful and historic Woodlands in Marburg, outside Ipswich. Mort of course teased Liz that everyone would assume she was pregnant.

By this time Mort and Pig had met and had become fast friends. Pig was honoured to be asked to be best man at the wedding. The honeymoon had to be postponed to sometime in the future, as the war in Afghanistan grew and Mort, with his growing expertise in both communication and now a skilled sniper, had been warned he would likely be spending considerable time on deployment there.

At the end of Mort's initial five-year term, he signed up for another five years. This caused a little friction between the two of them, as Liz, essentially alone in Townsville, was restless, perhaps wanting to get on with life.

Shortly after he had signed on for his second five-year term, his mum, Edith was diagnosed with ovarian cancer. It was well advanced when diagnosed and was essentially untreatable. Chris decided to retire so they could spend as much time together and he would always been on hand to assist her. The news hit Mort very hard. He took leave immediately to fly home and spent some time with his mum. Liz also flew down from Townsville to be there for her as well. Edith deteriorated very quickly and, three months later, Mort was home again, this time for her funeral. A sad time for him and his family.

During this period, Mort and Pig had teamed up as a lethal two-man team. Both being excellent marksmen and having complimentary communications skills, they did many secret missions behind enemy lines. With Mort being the better marksman, Pig would act as his spotter and on the digital communications side, where Pig had the superior skills, the roles were reversed, with Pig being the leader. Both had been promoted to the rank of sergeant early on and remained there for the duration of their army careers.

Perhaps the only plus from Mort's constant deployments (apart from earning tax-free wages!) was that he and Liz were able to travel internationally more easily and cheaply. They would plan their annual holiday and fly separately to their chosen destination, and in Mort's words 'have another honeymoon'. They visited the

Canadian Rockies, Maldives, Central Europe, and England during these holidays.

As the end of his second five-year term approached Mort again was keen to re-sign. But Liz was most unhappy with this. When he did sign up again, she made the decision to sell their unit in Townsville and move back to Brisbane, renting a unit in Stafford near her new school, Mt Maria college, as she moved across into the catholic education system.

Not long after Mort (and, coincidentally, Pig) had re-signed for a third term, whilst on patrol in their Bushmaster [an Australian-made armoured vehicle], they hit an IED, then came under attack. Pig's left leg was crushed under the overturned Bushie and he could not be quickly removed due to the ongoing firefight. He was eventually extracted by helicopter and, after having his left leg amputated below the knee, evacuated to a US Army hospital in Germany, for further treatment and rehabilitation. Eventually he had returned to Australia where he received a medical discharge, and moved into civilian life.

Then, one Thursday night, Liz was killed in a traffic accident, when another car drove through a red light and T-boned Liz's car, killing her instantly. At the time, Mort was on a secret mission, deep behind enemy lines, and the army hierarchy decided to not convey the sad news until he was extracted ten days later. On being told of Liz's death on his return to base, he had some very choice words to say to his CO and jumped on the first plane home.

Sadly, he was too late for the funeral, with Liz's parents both very unhappy he had missed the funeral and failed to respond to any of the numerous messages they had left for him. Even once the situation was explained to them, whilst being slightly mollified, it did not change their disappointment in Mort. He tidied up her affairs and headed back to Afghanistan a couple of weeks later.

As the end of his third five-year term approached, he knew he had had enough and planned his retirement. Like many long-term soldiers, he was a little apprehensive on what civvy life would be like after living the structured life within the army for such a long time. However, over the years, he had learned many excellent skills, had proven his worth time and again, not only as a soldier, but in the area of digital communications, having been sent across to the USA for some very specific and unique skills training. He also worked closely with the army's LEWTs (Light Electronic Warfare Team) as part of his special forces work behind enemy lines.

As he contemplated life after the army, he was keen to commercialise these skills and so developed a plan to start his own business, specialising in this area. Thus, Digital Data Solutions was born. But his first priority was to investigate Liz's accident. He had read everything he could find (including some things he should not have been able to read) and this convinced him there was something fishy about the accident. He was on a mission. One of his own choosing for a change.

Shawline Publishing Group Pty Ltd
www.shawlinepublishing.com.au

SHAWLINE
PUBLISHING
GROUP

More great Shawline titles can be found by scanning the QR code below.
New titles also available through Books@Home Pty Ltd.
Subscribe today at www.booksathome.com.au or scan the QR code below.